The hair on the back of her neck prickled, and she'd learned over the years to trust that feeling.

Barefoot, she opened the door a crack and peered into the main cabin. Empty. Where was everyone? She crossed the floor and about halfway her foot slid in something sticky. The coppery scent hit her nostrils as she squatted to investigate.

Blood.

Her instincts kicked into full alert—she crouched lower, her eyes darting left and right. A trap! They'd been lured here to die. Drawn in by scheming vampires—she knew they weren't to be trusted. She had to reach the cockpit and force the plane down. Somehow. She had to get back on the ground. There she had more of a chance—more control.

For the first time she noticed a dripping noise coming from up ahead. Antoinette tilted her head, trying to locate the source, and inched forward. The galley. She whipped aside the concertina door to find Mary slumped against the wall, lifeless eyes staring at the ceiling, her throat ripped open. The blood formed vivid crimson rivulets against her pallid skin. The eyes were the worst, terror frozen in their vacant gaze.

But something gnawed at Antoinette's thoughts.

Why would Christian murder his own staff?

Night's Cold Kiss

A DARK BRETHREN NOVEL

TRACEY O'HARA

An Imprint of HarperCollins*Publishers*

This is a work of fiction. Names, characters, places, and incidents are drawn from the author's imagination or are used fictitiously and are not to be construed as real. Any resemblance to actual events, locales, organizations, or persons, living or dead, is entirely coincidental.

EOS
An Imprint of HarperCollins*Publishers*
10 East 53rd Street
New York, New York 10022-5299

Copyright © 2009 by Tracey O'Hara
Cover art by Larry Rostant
ISBN 978-0-06-178313-5
www.eosbooks.com

First Eos paperback printing: September 2009
First Avon Books special printing: April 2009

HarperCollins® and Eos® are registered trademarks of HarperCollins Publishers.

Printed in the U.S.A.

10 9 8 7 6 5 4 3 2 1

For my boys
David, Corey and Seamus

acknowledgments

I've dreamed of writing the acknowledgments for my first book, but now that it is here I find the task rather difficult and daunting. First, I want to thank my fabulous agent, Jennifer Schober—from holding my hand at an awards ceremony to your endless belief in me, your support has meant more than I can say. I'd also like to thank Karen Solem for your sage advice and guidance. To my editor, Diana Gill, and assistant editor, Emily Krump, I have thoroughly enjoyed working with you both on this book.

To all those people who've helped shape me as a writer, I thank you. It's impossible to name you all, but you know who you are—from early on with the Claytons Critters to the published authors who've offered me advice. Thanks to all who've judged my work in contests—especially Serena, whose belief that this book would be published kept me going in dark days.

Thanks to my local writing group, and to Margaret of Intrigue Bookstore for the endless source of inspiration and for letting us meet in your fabulous store. A special thanks to the Go-Gos—AJ, Erica, Kirsty and Jo—and to Melissa, who've all commiserated, congratulated, critiqued and crapped on with me. You girls rock. Cathy— you hold a very special place in my heart. I thank you for the "Damn good story" speech when the doubt demons came to play, and for your endless support in reading and re-reading this story.

Lastly, but most importantly, I would like to thank my extended family, including my parents Betty and Tim, Bob and Donna, and my mother-in-law, Joan, for encouraging me to follow my dream. And I'd especially like to thank my mother, my aunt Jean and my cousin Deb for being my personal cheering squad. Finally, to my boys, Corey and Seamus, and my husband, David—the love of my life, my rock and my hero—without you, I could not have done this.

Night's Cold Kiss

1

Hunter and Hunted

Antoinette crept along the alley, unknown shadows pressing in on her from the darkness. Perspiration beaded on her upper lip, and she swiped a hand across her face before the salty moisture slipped unwelcome to the corners of her mouth.

Sweat trickled down her back. She tugged the damp T-shirt away from her sticky skin. Sucking the humid air into her lungs was like trying to breathe through a warm wet blanket.

Damn this heat. Why couldn't he have picked someplace a little cooler?

But she knew why. Miami was the perfect hunting ground with its transient population.

Over the last two weeks she'd tracked the vampiric Necrodreniac across three states with her brother, Nici. The killer's trail of bodies had led them here and now they were so close she could almost taste it.

A scream pierced the still darkness. She dropped, her hand wrapping around the pistol grip. A second cry ripped through the night and she relaxed. Only a couple of tomcats fighting.

Other sounds began to filter through: water dripped somewhere to her right, distant police sirens wailed, and animals shrieked—both the two-legged and the four-legged varieties—but not a hint of her target.

As she turned her head, she caught a glint on the ground and looked up to her right at the broken window on the side of the old warehouse. Glass crunched beneath her boots as she gripped the windowsill to haul herself up.

She remained balanced on the sill until her eyes adjusted to the gloom. The stench from inside hit her with an almost physical force; the foul aroma was made up of musty wet paper, stale urine, and animal feces. But underlying it all lurked something more subtle—and much more disturbing. The smell of pain, the smell of evil, the smell of death itself. The reek of a Necrodreniac lair.

Christian waited, silent and patient. He heard her long before he saw her from his vantage point in the rafters thirty feet above the warehouse floor.

She entered through the same window he'd used earlier and he breathed her in, holding the scent, tasting it, savoring it. Human.

She perched on the windowsill, her nose wrinkled in disgust and her eyes narrowed as she peered into the far corners of the abandoned building. Even if she'd looked up, he'd have been safe from discovery, his position secured by shadow. After a few moments she dropped to land quietly, sinking into a low crouch with hands braced on the floor and head tilted to listen.

Her outfit—from her SWAT tactical vest down to solid black army boots—looked perfect for a covert mission and enhanced her slim, athletic, but unmistakably feminine figure. She wore no perfume or synthetic scent, only her own natural fragrance. A thick braid of pale blond hair fell over one shoulder, the end brushing the floor as she hunkered down. Definitely a Venator and judging from her actions, a well-seasoned one, although he guessed she could be no more than twenty-five.

A pistol was secured in the front holster of the SWAT

vest just under her left breast and a sheathed katana sword was strapped to her back, the handle within easy reach over her right shoulder. His interest piqued, she was either very stupid or an extremely skilled old-school hunter. Christian predicted the latter.

Rising to her feet, she continued to move along the wall. From the corner of his eye, Christian caught a blur of movement as a stray cat landed softly on the windowsill. The scruffy feline took one look at her then leapt inside to race behind some boxes piled near the wall.

The sound of her heart pounded, as clear and heavy as distant thunder. If he were closer, he'd be able to taste the fear on the air she exhaled, yet her first instinct had put the blade in her hand. Impressive. Watching her in action might provide a pleasing distraction. He breathed her in again and licked his lips, his appetite roused.

Wonder if she tasted as good as she smelled.

Antoinette closed her eyes and forced her breathing to slow as she slid the sword back into the sheath.

Bloody cat.

Inhaling deeply, she pulled herself together and glanced around. An involuntary shiver ran up her spine and she shook it out. It wasn't like her to be so jumpy; something here was off, but she couldn't put a finger on it. While she didn't sense any immediate danger, the hair on the back of her neck prickled.

On the far side of the building was a door, the very thing she looked for. Antoinette ripped open a Velcro pocket on her vest. A drop of moisture slid down the bridge of her nose and dropped from the end onto the back of her hand. She flicked it away and cursed under her breath. Nici got to sit in the van's air-conditioned comfort while she scrabbled around dark alleys and stinky abandoned warehouses.

She smiled and shook her head. *I wouldn't have it any other way.* Waiting in the van would've driven her crazy. It was just as well she'd passed the Venator exams and not

Nici—he was much better at computers and all that technical shit.

Licking her dry lips, she pulled out her flashlight, crossed the room and placed an ear against the door. *Metal, not wood.* The unexpected coolness under her cheek offered a brief, but blessed, relief.

Nothing came from beyond, not a single sound. The handle turned easily under her hand—a sign of recent habitation—and with a gentle push, the door swung open.

The dreniac's scent wafted from the basement, fresher than the lingering trace out here, but still not recent. If he was hunting, he'd return soon enough. She hoped. Swallowing hard, she stepped into the open doorway. Just because he wasn't home didn't mean there weren't other nasty surprises waiting down there.

Antoinette looked down the narrow stairs leading into the inky blackness below and pulled the gun from its holster. Though her heart did beat a little faster, her palms were dry and hands steady.

Antoinette released the clip to check the ammo—the special hollow point bullets were filled with silver nitrate, the only poison effective on dreniacs. She'd checked it a dozen times before the mission, but better to be safe than sorry. Carefully she slid the clip back into place with her palm, flicked off the safety, and started down the stairs.

Each step took her deeper into the dark basement and each step a little more cautious. She flicked on the flashlight and braced it over her gun, pointing the beam straight ahead. The door at the top of the stairs shut with a bang. Her heart leapt to her throat and she twisted to check the staircase behind. *Empty.*

Sweat cooled on her skin with dropping temperature as she descended. Cocking her head from side to side, she listened for signs of ambush. Seconds grew into minutes without even a rustle and she continued on.

The sour tang of spilled whiskey and stale sex grew stronger as she continued down the stairs. She brought the back of her gun hand against her nose to ward off the stench of other more disturbing odors, to little avail.

At the bottom of the staircase her footfalls echoed across the concrete floor, loud in the eerie silence. Her foot sent an empty wine bottle skittering across the newspaper-littered floor and she followed it with the beam of the flashlight. It rolled to a stop a few feet away . . . right by a high-heeled red leather boot. *Shit.*

Antoinette swung the flashlight beam along the boot to reach a pale leg then a lingerie-clad torso, and, finally, a tousled head of blond hair. Her stomach churned as she moved to squat beside the body. *Damn.* She really hated this part of her job, especially if they'd been dead awhile. Tucking the flashlight awkwardly between her shoulder and chin, she reached over and pulled the fine hair away from the face to uncover glassy blue eyes staring into space.

A relieved chuckle burst free before she could stop it. A dummy—lifelike—but definitely just a dummy.

A wider arc with the flashlight exposed more dummies and blow-up sex dolls scattered among the debris.

Filth. This dreniac's MO was sexual deviancy with a penchant for necrophilia. He must use the sex dolls between kills. Little wonder the bounty had doubled in the last week. But was he still here or had he skipped on to his next hunting ground?

Antoinette searched the litter with the flashlight beam. Lacking the scent of heavily decaying flesh, he obviously didn't keep the bodies with him like some did. Probably tortured them here, judging from the smell of old blood and feces, then dumped them elsewhere.

Suddenly, the beam hit upon a backpack, half hidden in the garbage. Inside she found clothes and other bits and pieces, but nothing of any real interest . . . until her fingers brushed against something more solid. She pulled out a smaller bag and opened it to find a large wad of cash, some coins, and several items matching the descriptions of personal objects belonging to the target's past victims. His souvenirs.

He'd return; there was no way he'd leave these behind. She put it back where she'd found it and wiped her palms on her jeans, her skin prickling with disgust.

There was nothing to do now except settle in and wait. But not down here, not in the dark, where he belonged and held the advantage.

The staircase didn't seem nearly as long going up as it had coming down. When she reached the door, she stopped to listen. Still nothing, but then again, he could be out there . . . waiting. She stepped into the outer room and glanced around, aiming her weapon into the corners, at the window, toward the cartons. All clear.

Darkness concealed the corners and the high rafters. She sniffed the foul air, searching for fresh dreniac scent. The newspapers had reported a body found early this morning, tortured, throat ripped open, and raped after death—a trademark kill for this sick bastard. His stench would be ripe with the recent death.

As she turned away the hairs on the back of her neck prickled and she spun back around. There was something watching from those rafters. Something . . . or someone. She could feel eyes on her and stepped closer, squinting up into the darkness. She couldn't make anything out, but—

A tinkle of glass came from outside and she ducked behind the cartons for cover. At the sound of something heavy landing on the floor, Antoinette tensed. Here he was. Finally. Adrenaline pumped through her veins; she felt the path it traveled through her bloodstream and welcomed the sharp focus it brought.

She circled around behind the dreniac, using the cartons for cover. He was much bigger than she'd anticipated. And he presented her with another complication—he wasn't alone.

Christian relaxed a little. The scuffle along the alley outside had announced the target's arrival long before the woman heard it. The dreniac had saved him from discovery as the Venator had been looking right at Christian—as if somehow sensing his presence even in the darkness. Then she'd disappeared as the dreniac made his clumsy entrance.

Now the unmistakable reek of death marked the target for what he was—a Necrodreniac—the very worst of his Aeternus kind. Christian fought down loathing.

This one liked inflicting pain and fear. Heightening the emotions of a victim changed the flavor of their blood, and made the intoxication more potent for the dreniac when they killed. Each emotion offered a different experience. Sweet blood of passion gave a euphoric high, whereas tangy fear had a sharp, focused rush, not dissimilar to cocaine use in humans, or so he'd been told.

The dreniac wasn't alone either. A young girl hung limply over his shoulder, and Christian knew from the rhythmic beat of her heart that she was still alive.

He decided not to interfere between the human Venator and the dreniac, not yet anyway. Venators were generally very territorial over their kills and it was against CHaPR directions for an agent such as himself to interfere with a trained Venator's target. At the very least it should prove to be an interesting—if not downright entertaining—fight to watch.

Her cardboard hiding place must have hindered her line of fire, for she crept out with the handgun aimed at the dreniac. The pistol was steady in her hand, her heart rate only slightly elevated, a steely determination etched on her face.

"Clever girl." Christian's voice, no more than a whisper—like silk across glass—was far too soft for those below to hear.

The huge dreniac was more than a match for a human, even one as capable as she appeared to be. But her movements were smooth, confident and perfect, each step deliberate and careful as she moved in for the shot.

A squeal cut through the still air and the woman froze, her expression startled, her heart hammering. Two feet away from her the stray cat sat with its jaws clamped around the throat of a large twitching rat.

The dreniac glanced toward the feline and turned back to the basement door, taking another step before stopping and sniffing the air. A low growl hummed, building to a roar as he dropped the semiconscious victim and leapt toward the Venator with the lightning speed of his kind, reaching her within half a blink of a human eye. The dreniac's huge paw-like hand swept sideways and she tried to duck. But the blow connected, snapping her head back and sending her flying into the pile of cartons.

If she'd been a few seconds slower in reacting, the backhand would've taken her head right off. She was on her feet in an instant, raising her hand to the side of her head and shaking it for a second. The blow had sent her firearm flying and she reached back to unsheathe the sword.

Christian leaned forward, eager to see what she'd do next but ready to intervene if things got ugly. Well, uglier. He could do it now, but that would invalidate any bounty she was due.

"Stupid girl." The dreniac voice oozed contempt. "Do you really think you can take me with that puny blade?"

Again he leapt. This time she planted her feet and waited. With perfect timing, she moved left and sliced downward with the razor sharp katana. She spun back to face the dreniac, who gaped in horrified disbelief at his right arm, which now ended at the wrist. The hand lay twitching at his feet, severed with surgical precision. Dark blood spattered across her face as she brought the sword around.

The dreniac's shock was short-lived and his face twisted with rage. "You bitch." He launched himself toward her for a third time.

She twisted out of his grasp, but not fast enough. His remaining hand raked just beneath the SWAT vest, opening a set of parallel wounds above her hip with his clawlike nails. A whiff of fresh human blood hit Christian, hot and heady. Nothing like the foul ooze spilling from the veins of the dreniac. Christian's fangs nudged his gums and he tensed, ready to jump between them.

Before Christian could act, she spun and swung the blade in a wide powerful arc, using the dreniac's speed against him. He ran right into the blade—stopping him dead in his tracks. His mouth formed a silent O as dark red, almost black, beads wept from the diagonal slash across his neck. As the body dropped to its knees the head tilted to the right, fell with a wet thud, and rolled toward her. The incredulous expression on the severed head looked almost comical as it stopped at her feet.

2

over and out

Antoinette's vision swam and she leaned forward, arm braced against her knee for support, gasping for breath. Slowly, the agony in the side of her face dulled to a throbbing ache, and she breathed through the dizziness. It helped, but not much. When she finally managed to get enough air in her lungs to speak, she took the cell phone from her pocket and turned it on. A Venator never took an active cell to a hunt; dreniacs could sense the electronic hum.

"Nici, it's done," she said into the cell when it picked up.

"Are you okay?" he asked.

"Just a few cuts and bruises, nothing much."

"Liar."

Her brother knew her too well.

"There's a girl in here, unconscious. Get the van closer and bring the first aid kit. I'll guide you in."

"Okay, I'll be there in a minute."

Antoinette pushed a crate to the window, grabbed a folding mirror from her left utility pocket, and climbed up to wait for Nici. Nausea washed over her from the exertion and she leaned against the ledge for support as a wave of dizziness made her head spin.

Headlights entered the narrow alley and flashed on and off. She held the mirror out of the window at an angle to catch the light. A few minutes later Nici jumped through the window and landed heavily on the floor with a grunt, then turned to help her.

"Don't worry about me, check on the girl." She slapped his arm away and his brow creased in that familiar you're-so-stubborn expression of his.

While he busied himself with the girl, Antoinette climbed down, taking care not to move too quickly in case the throbbing in her head intensified. At the moment it had dulled from the level of being run over by a sixteen wheeler to merely a jackhammer drilling her brain.

"She'll live," Nici said after giving the girl a quick once-over. "Although she'll have one hell of a headache."

Her and me both. "Can we move her?" For the first time Antoinette realized the victim couldn't be more than fifteen. *So young.*

Nici held open the girl's eyelids and flashed the light across her pupils. "Don't think there's anything broken, but she has a pretty mean concussion." He looked up at Antoinette. "And she needs to be cleaned up."

The girl stank of fresh urine. She must have been scared half to death to piss herself like that.

He stood and wiped his hands on the back of his pants. "Okay, now let's take a look at you." He turned her face toward him and shone his flashlight into her eyes. "Hmm . . . You're gonna have one hell of a shiner, and we'd better get you to a clinic to make sure you haven't cracked your skull. What else?"

She lifted the bottom of the partially shredded vest and Nici lowered the flashlight beam to reveal the blood soaking her pants.

He sucked his breath through his teeth. "Nasty!" He took some gauze from the medical kit and taped it in place. "That'll do for now. They're pretty shallow and shouldn't

need stitches but we'd better get some antibiotics into you."
Nici threw a glance at the headless body. "That dreniac
doesn't exactly look the Martha Stewart type."

"You should see downstairs." Her nose wrinkled with
disgust.

"Then you'd better photograph the evidence up here while
I do down there."

"You're on." She carried a small digital in her vest pocket.
"His pack is down there with his souvenirs—make sure you
grab them for evidence."

"The Department can arrange for them to be returned
to the victims' families." He started toward the door then
turned and pulled a drink bottle from his kit. "Here, catch."

She snatched it out of the air and inhaled sharply through
her teeth as pain slammed through her head.

"Sorry, sis," he said with a shrug. "You're getting a bit
slow, but your reflexes are still pretty good."

"Little brother," she said, rolling her right shoulder, "you
owe me a shoulder massage for that. I think you might've
jarred something."

"Sure I did." He winked and strode to the basement door.
His gait was marred by a slight limp, legacy of an accident
a couple of years back. He must be cramped from sitting in
the van, because she usually didn't notice it anymore.

At the basement door, Nici dialed his cell. "I want to report
a Necrodreniac excision carried out on target one-seven-
nine-six-two-one-zero-six-alpha-charlie. We need NCB
cleanup and verification at a warehouse in the Liberty City
Area . . ." Nici's voice faded as he descended the stairs while
reporting the hit to Necrodreniac Control Branch, part of the
Department of Parahuman Security—or the Department as
it was more commonly known—a semi-governmental body
responsible for parahuman law enforcement.

Once Nici had disappeared, Antoinette collapsed against
the nearest crate and licked her dry lips. The liquid in the
bottle sloshed invitingly as she popped the top and brought it

to her mouth. The warm sports drink flowed salty-sweet over her thirst-thick tongue and slid down her parched throat.

Antoinette picked up the katana to wipe the soiled blade with the bottom of her shirt. It would have to do until she could clean it with the proper care and attention it deserved.

After resheathing the blade, she snapped a few photos of the scene for the paperwork. They would get a good bounty on this one—he'd killed over fifteen girls they knew of, probably more.

Nici returned as she took the last picture with a nod to indicate he was done downstairs. They picked up the unconscious girl's body and maneuvered her out the window and into the van.

Something still niggled at her, the same hair-raising feeling as before. She glanced at the dreniac's headless body, lying where it fell, already fouling the air further with its stinking decay. Dreniac bodies went bad fast. She felt no sorrow—no remorse—only the usual rage burning deep in her heart. How many dreniac deaths would avenge her mother's murder? How much blood would wash away the images of Mama's pale corpse lying in a pool of crimson? She sighed and shook her head, taking one last look at the dark-cloaked rafters on the far side of the warehouse, and then followed her brother through the window.

The following night, Christian entered the hotel lobby. Bright light reflected off every available surface—from the marbled floors to the gilded mirrors. He slid his dark sunglasses into place to cut the glare.

A multitude of perfumes hammered him from all directions, overloading his senses. It was always harder to control his heightened abilities when tired and hungry. Christian crossed the foyer to the busy reception desk, ignoring the lustful glances across the lobby.

After the long night waiting for the dreniac in the warehouse, he'd spent an exhausting day with the local NCB boys filling out reports and answering questions. He did learn one useful thing, the brother-and-sister Venator team was none other than Nicolae and Antoinette Petrescu. Now, there was a real blast from the past.

What he needed now was a hot shower and a bite to eat—literally. It'd been more than two days since his last meal and his hunger grew stronger and more insistent with every passing second.

A young couple stood at the desk, the boy-man in a wedding tux and the girl-woman in a bridal gown. Their faces glowed and eyes remained locked together like most young lovers. She turned her head at Christian's approach and twirled a lock of hair around her finger, smiling as she swept an appreciative glance in his direction

The boy scowled and pulled her back to face him. "Hey."

"Sorry, baby," she said, throwing her arms over the boy's shoulders and pressing herself against him, but her eyes stayed locked with Christian's for a second longer.

While they waited, the couple continued to fondle each other with the eagerness of newlyweds. Their excitement intensified Christian's already acute hunger, but he kept his ill temper in check—it wasn't their fault he felt like he'd spent the day in a Dumpster.

He ran his tongue over the tips of his descending fangs, finding the couple's sexual intoxication extremely appetizing.

"Mr. Laroque. May I help you, sir?" a male clerk asked.

Christian turned his attention from the honeymoon couple to the desk clerk. "Any messages?"

"Yes, sir," he said, handing him a pile of slips.

He thanked the clerk and made his way to the elevator where the young couple was already waiting. If he didn't feel so grimy from a day spent in the filthy warehouse, he would've waited for the next lift. But right now he needed a shower, some fresh clothes, and to feed. He put the last thought out of his mind as he entered and hit his floor number.

The couple continued their necking in the corner. The bride giggled and whispered, "Stop it, he'll see."

"So what? He won't pay us no mind. You're my wife now," the boy whispered back and she giggled again. Neither was aware or cared that he heard every word of their whispered exchange.

The scent of their arousal filled him, driving his hunger to the edge of endurance. Their rising passion grew stronger; it would be so easy to have them both—right here, right now—a bit of seduction and they'd be his.

But he wouldn't. It was no longer his way to take what was not offered of free will. Besides, the girl was pregnant—very early, but he detected the tiny fluttering beat under the girl's passion-accelerated heart rate.

To distract himself, Christian glanced at the messages. His brow creased at the name on the last slip. The elevator door opened and Christian cleared his throat when they made no move to leave.

"Oh. It's our floor, Ronnie," the bride said, the shade of her already flushed cheeks deepening. "Thanks, mister."

"No problem." Christian stared ahead, not looking at them. "By the way, congratulations on your wedding and good luck with the baby," he said as they left the elevator, knowing it would perplex them. A bit of petty payback for the havoc they played with his appetite.

The couple exchanged a surprised glance, and the girl cocked her head to the side, her forehead creased. "Um . . . thanks, sir," she muttered before they hurried away, whispering in confusion.

With his hunger deepened by the couple's passion, he entered his room, headed straight for the bar fridge, and took out a bottle. The blood lay cold in his hand and he stared at it before placing it back on the shelf. Tonight he needed more than a snack. Tonight he needed a meal. He crossed to the phone and dialed.

A businesslike voice answered on the second ring. "Crimson Angels."

"This is Christian Laroque."

"Yes, Mr. Laroque. What can we do for you this evening?"

"I want a girl, young, but not too young." An image of the blond Venator entered his head unbidden, spiking his hunger.

"I have the perfect girl. Her name is Giselle."

"Good, send her to the Fontainebleau Hilton. I'll arrange it with the front desk."

"She'll be there within the hour, Mr. Laroque."

He hung up the phone, took the slips from his pocket, and found the number on the last message.

"Viktor?" he asked when it connected.

"Christian, my old friend. It's been a while," said the familiar voice at the other end of the line. "What are you doing?"

"Came down on a job and got sidetracked with a little dreniac problem. What about you? Have you been in hiding from someone?"

"Only your mother." Viktor chuckled at the old joke before his voice took on a more serious note. "It looks like it's starting again."

Christian ran his hand through his hair. They hadn't spoken in years, not since the end of The Troubles. Christian knew exactly what it meant. "As bad as last time?"

"Worse, but I don't want to get into it over the phone. When can we meet?"

"I'm finishing up here and will be flying back to New York early tomorrow night."

"Good—I'll meet you at the airport." Urgency colored Viktor's voice.

"All right, I'll see you then . . . Oh, and Viktor—"

"Yes?"

"It's good to hear your voice again."

"Yours too, old friend, yours too."

Christian contacted the front desk to make arrangements for his visitor, then he took a hot shower. A knock at the door interrupted his dressing. He slid his arms into a clean silk shirt and left it unbuttoned as he answered the door.

A beautiful young woman with creamy, coffee-colored skin and dark eyes focused on his naked chest and arched an eyebrow. "Mr. Laroque?"

"Yes. But please—call me Christian."

A seductive smile graced her deep red lips as she crossed into the suite. "Good evening, Christian. My name's Giselle."

He took her hand and raised her long, slender fingers to his lips. Her pulse hammered through her wrist under his fingertips, sharpening his hunger.

She turned her back, encouraging him to take her coat. Beneath it she wore a strappy red mini dress that left her shoulders and neck bare. Her hair was pinned up and he bent forward to inhale her womanly fragrance. Like a connoisseur testing the bouquet of a fine wine, he breathed her in. He wanted to take her here in the doorway, but the predator in him yearned for the chase.

After closing the door and hanging her coat over the back of a chair, he guided her into the living room with a hand on the small of her back.

"Why don't you wait on the balcony and I'll join you there in a minute," he said, pouring her some champagne. She tilted her head, raised the glass, and left him. Christian poured another for himself, which he downed in one swallow as he watched her for a moment through the billowing curtains. His predator stirred. He stepped out and ran his hand over her shoulder.

She gave a start at his touch and spun to look at him. "Oh . . . I didn't hear you," she said, a slight quaver in her voice.

You weren't meant to, my sweet. He smiled, and her pupils dilated as he held her gaze.

He licked his lips as his eyes drifted to the delicate curve of her throat, but he wanted to draw out the anticipation, let his hunger build to even greater intensity.

She tilted back her head, taking a sip from her glass. Mesmerized, he watched her throat work as she swallowed. A small drop escaped the corner of her mouth and ran down her neck to the hollow at the base. He bent forward and licked it away. She sucked in and held her breath for a few heartbeats.

He let his gaze drop to the swell of her breasts. They rose and fell with each enticing breath, the outline of her nipples straining against the thin fabric. Taking her glass, he placed it on a nearby table and moved closer to run his hands along her silky bare arms. Her crimson lips begged to be kissed and he complied, crushing her against him to meld his mouth with hers.

A moan escaped her as he ran his hand down the curve of her back until he was able to reach under the fabric of her dress to touch her naked skin beneath.

"Let's go inside," she murmured against his lips.

"Let's not." He broke away and stepped back a few feet. "And let down your hair," he demanded.

For a moment longer she just looked at him, which only heightened his anticipation. Then slowly, one by one, she removed the pins and allowed her hair to tumble down around her shoulders. Rolling her head, she fanned it through the night air like liquid black silk catching the moonlight.

She moved in a silent provocative dance, closing the distance between them, and stopped when her shins met the edge of the chair between his thighs. She ran her hands inside his shirt, across the bare flesh of his chest. Her heartbeat thundering, and he felt her pulse pounding through her hot, questing palms as she ran them over his torso. In turn, he ran his slowly down her back and under the hem of her short dress—her smooth skin was supple under his fingertips. He continued to move his hands over her hips until the soft fabric bunched around her waist. Underneath she wore a lacy thong.

He reached behind her and with agonizing slowness, undid the zipper. His eyes locked with hers—they begged him to hurry—he smiled, slow and deliberate, as he ran his hands along her sides, raising the dress higher and higher. Giselle lifted her arms above her head so he could slip it off completely, allowing her hair to tumble down over her bare back in a dark waterfall.

Pulling her toward him, he bent her back and ran his tongue along the hollow between her breasts. Sighing, she tossed back her head as he took one rosy nipple into his mouth. A flick of his tongue and it hardened in response—she whimpered when he did the same to the other. Wrapping his arms around her, Christian pulled her closer, sliding up to her soft inviting throat.

Her blood pumped strong, pulsing through her jugular just beneath his lips. His fangs strained to their full length and the hunger growled through his body like an instinctive beast. But instead of giving in to it, he set about arousing her more, making her blood sing.

Touching, tasting.

Her breath came quicker—her heart beat faster—her blood pumped sweeter. He could smell it, almost taste it.

So sweet, but it could be so much sweeter still.

The skimpy underwear came apart easily in his hands and he casually discarded it over the railing, the lacy fabric disappearing into the night.

Gasping in delight, she moved to undo his trousers but he grabbed her wrists.

"Please, please," she begged. "I want to feel you."

"Not yet." He stood and carried her to the balcony rail.

She gripped his shoulders, fear replacing the excitement in her eyes.

"I won't let you fall," he whispered in her ear.

Her passion's blood was sweet and spicy, but her fear would give it a sharp tang.

Balancing her with one hand, he opened his trousers. His need to feed was almost unbearable as he entered her with one hard thrust. *Not yet . . . wait . . . wait for the right moment.* His anticipation grew.

At first they moved together slowly. She soon forgot her precarious position and wrapped her legs around his hips, matching his strokes, her body moving against his with delicious sensations.

Gradually their rhythm quickened and the excitement grew. She leaned back and a cry escaped her as he thrust deeply, again, and again, the tension building in his groin.

At the moment of her climax he pulled her toward him and pierced the soft skin of her neck with his fangs. Hot, sweet, spicy nectar filled his mouth and slid down his throat in a revitalizing rush, triggering his own release. He pulled back and watched her face as a second orgasm took her, then sank his teeth in again.

3

whɑt goes ɑround

Her warm blood pumped through his veins, dispelling his fatigue and invigorating tired muscles. He ran his tongue gently over the puncture marks on her neck, so the enzymes in his saliva would seal the wound, leaving no trace of his feeding.

She still panted with the heat of what they had shared and sighed as he withdrew. He helped her down from her precarious perch and she bent to pick up her discarded dress and slipped it on.

Leaning against the balcony railing, he listened to the waves washing up on the beach just beyond the hotel's vast lagoon pool as he rebuttoned his trousers.

"How long have you been with the agency?" he asked, making small talk. It felt cheap to rush a donor out the door after he was finished.

"About three months now. I'm putting myself through law school." She picked up her discarded glass and leaned beside him, the sheen on her skin glistening in the moonlight.

"Why did you become a donor?"

"The agency pays well, though some think it's degrading to let the Aeternus feed from them. An ex-friend of mine said I was no better than a proverbial cow. But . . ." She turned and looked him in the eye, then dropped her gaze from his. "There's another reason."

"HIV." He'd tasted it in her blood.

Color rose in her cheeks as she met his eyes. "Courtesy of my first boyfriend."

He nodded, knowing quite a few donors with HIV. Since the Aeternus were immune to human disease, it was a safe way for infected humans to have casual sex without the worry of passing on their affliction.

She studied her hands. "A friend of mine was dying of cancer and she talked an Aeternus into *embracing* her." A single tear slipped from her eye, tracing a silver path down her cheek.

"I assume it didn't end well," he said.

Her face was pale in the moonlight as she shook her head. "She died two weeks ago." She sucked back a tearful breath, catching her lower lip between her teeth—then gave him a shaky smile. "She said that she'd rather die trying than lose her hair to chemo."

Christian shook his head. Most of those embraced died a very painful death as their body tore itself apart trying to adjust to the DNA changes.

Humans—when would they learn?

"This guy she was seeing said if she could raise ten thousand dollars, he would do it. I tried to talk her out of it, but she refused to listen."

That got his attention. It wasn't against the law to embrace someone if they truly wanted it, but it was against the law to take payment for it.

"Who was this man?" He tried to keep his voice calm so he didn't frighten her.

"I don't know, she wouldn't tell me." The girl looked at him. "It was wrong what he did to her, wasn't it? And to leave her like that . . ." She wrapped her arms around herself, and despite the heat, shivered.

The third this month—maybe Viktor's right, it is starting

again. "I can get someone to look into it if you give me the details."

"Would you? I really didn't know who to report it to." Her face lit up and her eyes glistened with unshed tears. "You know, I have no other plans for the night, I could stay if you like." She lowered her eyes and looked at him through downcast lashes.

He was tempted, but shook his head. "Thanks for the offer, but I have too much work to do tonight."

Her face fell. He guided her back inside and helped her into her coat.

"Here's something extra for you." He held out a couple of folded hundred dollar bills.

She looked at the money, but didn't take it. "You don't need to do that, I had a nice time."

"It's a gift, for you."

Her face darkened. "I'm not a prostitute. I thought we had a good time. The agency pays me well to donate, it's a job. If I like the client I sometimes offer more, but I never take money for sex. That would make it feel . . . dirty."

"I'm sorry." He bent forward and brushed her cheek with his lips. "I had a nice time too."

She gave him a stiff half-smile and nodded as she buttoned her coat, then left without another word. He closed the door after her. Humans. He would never understand them.

In the dining area he set up his laptop and logged into the Department of Parahuman Security system. The Department mission statement blazed across the top of the Web page: "To protect and enforce the laws to the benefit of parahumans and humans alike."

An instant message flashed up within seconds. *"Where have you been?"*

Christian smiled at Doc's lack of platitudes. Intel's administrator was business as usual. He typed his response. "Hello to you too, Doc."

"I've been trying to contact you for two days now—what have you been up to?"

"Working, what else? I've been with the local boys all day. By the way, it looks like I've got a lead on another embracing scam death."

"We've had reports of a half dozen more deaths in the past few days, and from all over the country. That's why I've been trying to reach you."

"So it's more than one guy then?"

"Worse—dreniacs."

Christian's heart sank. To be embraced by a dreniac meant that, if the human survived, they would be infected with Necrodrenia—a full-blown addiction to death-highs and chaos. An all-too-familiar scenario.

"Then it's no coincidence Viktor has contacted me."

"He's resurfaced? When?" Doc's response flashed on the screen.

"I spoke to him just over an hour ago. He wants to talk when I get back to New York. Can you dig up some old files for me on the case he was working on? Send them in an encrypted e-mail."

"Okay."

"Thanks, Doc. And I'd appreciate it if you made it top priority."

"I'm on it. I'll get back to you ASAP."

First Antoinette then Viktor. Both disappearing from his life around the same time and now appearing again. It had to be more than a coincidence.

He typed Antoinette's name into the Department's search engine and it came back with numerous hits. Busy girl. He opened her profile and a picture appeared on the screen of a Venator in martial arts gear and standing in front of a low wooden structure next to a large man leaning on a cane. The caption read, "Antoinette and Sergei Petrescu of the Petrescu School of Training." One of the best private schools in the country for preparing to become a Venator.

It's her—I knew it.

Reading on, he wasn't surprised to find she'd been trained by her uncle, Sergei, since it was to his care that Christian had delivered a very young Antoinette and her brother sixteen years ago.

Antoinette the warrior, even back then. She'd protected her little brother ferociously, trying to keep him away from Christian with fire burning in her eyes and determination fierce on her face. She'd seen him as the big, bad Aeternus boogie man; he should've known she'd grow up to be a Venator.

And she'd been busy. Already one hundred and forty-two confirmed Necrodreniac excisions were credited to her name—one hundred and forty-three, he corrected, remembering the one from the night before.

Christian hadn't thought of Sergei in years either. When Sergei was younger, an accident had prevented him from becoming a Venator himself. But that hadn't stopped him from training some of the best since Antoinette's father, Grigore. Sergei had started the school shortly after coming to America sixteen years ago.

The computer chimed incoming mail, breaking his train of thought.

"You're a legend, Doc," he said out loud to the empty room when he opened the e-mail to find the documents he'd requested.

After decrypting them, he opened the first file and read through the summary notes on The Troubles, as they had been called, over a decade and a half ago.

At last he came to what he was looking for—the crime scene report of a murder committed toward the end of that period.

The first attached photograph was of a little girl with blond ringlets and large emerald eyes in her tiny haunted face—a six-year-old Antoinette Petrescu. She sat on a stone floor beside her grief-stricken father as she held tightly to the free hand of a small thumb-sucking boy. The next picture was of a woman with long fair hair lying facedown in a pool of blood on the stone floor. Marianna—Antoinette's murdered mother.

* * *

Antoinette put away her equipment when Sensei Takimura entered the training room followed by the orderly double line of first-grade students. She bowed respectfully to her former teacher as the six-year-olds grabbed their wooden swords in readiness for their *kenjitsu* lesson.

She watched the Japanese elder take the kids through their training *katas*, hardly able to remember when she was that young. The school taught many forms of martial arts, not only training the body but disciplining the mind as well. Anything to give human Venators the slightest advantage against their physically superior foes.

She ran the end of the towel hanging around her neck across her damp brow and she left the room. It'd only been a week since she and Nici had returned home from the Miami mission, and already she was itching to take on a new job, but her injuries had slowed her down—and she hated it. She was starting to get a bit edgy but even after a fairly light workout, perspiration bathed her skin and her side ached like a bastard.

"Sis!" Nici jogged up the hall to meet her. "Uncle wants to speak to you in the office—immediately."

She headed back the way Nici had come, but after a few steps she realized he wasn't following. "You coming?"

He shrugged and shook his head. "But I do need to talk to you about something important later. Come find me when you're done." His expression gave nothing away, but he had a tightness around his eyes, which usually meant he was keeping something from her.

Antoinette frowned. What could that mean? Nici had failed the dreniac Venator exams a few years ago, though he'd always preferred the hi-tech stuff anyway. But they were partners and they'd always done everything together.

She walked the short distance to her uncle's office and knocked on the door before entering. Sergei sat behind his desk, dark circles under red eyes. He looked like he hadn't slept—something was up.

She sat in the seat opposite him. "What's wrong?"

"Nic has been killed." His Romanian accent was heavy with grief.

"Of course he hasn't. I just saw him."

He shook his head and waved his hand. "Not Nici. Your Uncle Nic—my brother." He slapped his open palm on his chest.

Antoinette froze. She hadn't known Uncle Nic very well and hadn't seen him since she was a child—before Sergei had brought them to America.

"A dreniac—"

Sergei held up his hand, cutting her off. "No. He was murdered, shot in the head." His shoulders slumped. "And there have been others—like before."

She sat stunned, implications dawning on her. Uncle Nicolae headed the Guild in his sector. With dreniac incidents on the rise and now the assassination of Nicolae and other officials . . .

She leaned forward. "The Troubles?"

"You're right, Sergei. She is extremely quick," a velvety voice spoke from behind. Antoinette turned and fell into the most brilliant blue eyes she'd ever seen. Her stomach jumped, knocking the breath from her lungs.

His lean frame rested casually against the wall, hands in the pockets of his stylish dark Armani suit. Midnight hair brushed the collar of his red silk shirt, which lay open at the throat and his pale skin shone beneath in shocking contrast. It suited him.

Her gaze ran over the rest of him, sensing the power coiled beneath his casual demeanor. Like a cobra ready to strike. She raised her eyes to his and they stared back with a twinkle of amusement.

Those eyes . . . recognition dawned. *What's an Aeternus doing here? And not just any Aeternus but . . .*

"Antoinette, this is—"

She cut her uncle off with a dark glare. "I know who he is." She dropped her voice to a deadly level. "Since when do we invite the likes of the Crimson Executioner into our training school?"

Christian kept his expression casual—no one had called him by the old title to his face in over a century. Surprise, confusion, and then fury danced across her fine features. Tendrils of damp blond hair stuck to her cheeks flushed from fresh exercise, highlighting the deep purplish bruise from the dreniac encounter in Miami. Her eyes burned with an emerald fire, almost searing him where he stood.

He straightened and took his right hand out of his pocket, extending it to her as he moved forward. She glanced at it then whipped around so hard her braid slammed against her shoulder as she turned her back on him, leaving him hanging.

"Why is he here?" The edge to her voice cut deeper than any blade.

Her skin glowed with a fine sheen of perspiration and damp patches marked her workout sweats. Antoinette's deliciously hot scent brought an image of her naked beneath him, moaning in pleasure as he bent to take her throat. He quickly scrubbed it from his mind. It wasn't what he came here for and he had no time for such distractions. "Miss Petrescu, if I may—"

"I was not addressing you, vampire." She spat out the last as she would a foul-tasting morsel.

"Antoinette," her uncle roared.

She flashed a contrite expression, but only for a second. When her eyes met his her blood sang with bitterness and hatred. He could smell it on her breath, taste it in the air around her. So full of anger. Such deep and powerful fury.

Christian refused to let his irritation show. "We prefer the term Aeternus to that parasitic name you humans have coined."

"I think it's best if I talk to my niece alone, Christian. I'll call you with my answer," Sergei said.

Christian nodded. "I'm sorry we're meeting under such

tragic circumstances, yet again. Your brother was a good man, just like Grigore."

That got her attention. Her head snapped around at the mention of her father's name. When he smiled, her eyes narrowed into slits.

"It's been a long time." Sergei reached over to clasp Christian's outstretched hand. "And we are in your debt again. Thank you for bringing this to us."

Christian offered his hand to Antoinette, only to have it ignored a second time. He shrugged and returned it to his pocket before leaving the room.

Christian approached the waiting limousine.

"Mr. Laroque, sir," the chauffeur said, tipping his cap as he held open the rear door.

"Take me to the hotel, Mike." Christian glanced back one last time, shook his head, and climbed into the seat. "I think I need a stiff drink," he murmured to himself.

Having met Antoinette face-to-face, he began to doubt whether they'd be able to remain in the same room for more than five minutes, let alone work together. He needed to think.

As the chauffeur closed the door behind him, Christian sank back into the luxurious leather seat and frowned. She'd seemed intriguing and clever when she'd dealt with the dreniac in Miami, but the meeting tonight hadn't quite gone to plan. He hadn't anticipated how extreme her resentment would be. Maybe this wasn't such a good idea after all.

There must be some other way. *Dammit!*

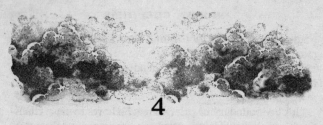

4
A Dark Past

Antoinette watched the Aeternus leave. He didn't just move, he flowed. Like a river that ran deep—calm on the surface but with power and danger hidden beneath. Her mouth dried.

The moment he was gone she turned on her uncle. "How could you let that creature in here?" Her whole body trembled, bitterness rising in the back of her throat.

"He came to me with important information." Sergei shook his head sadly, his disappointment creasing the corners of his eyes. "Please sit. We have a lot to discuss."

But the anger wouldn't let her. She paced back and forth, frustrated and afraid. What was her uncle thinking? Sergei waited, silent and stony until she sank into her seat.

"You know of the CHaPR Treaty and what it means for the continued safety for all races," Sergei said. "And you know your great-great-great-grandfather, Nicolae, was an instrumental part in its creation. That is why the first-born Petrescu son bears his name."

The first thing any Venator learned was the laws of the CHaPR Treaty and the history surrounding its conception.

"For centuries, the Aeternus hunted humans and dreniacs went unchecked. In turn we hunted them and the war was bloody with huge losses on both sides."

"I don't need a history lesson, Uncle." Her side hurt and a headache pounded behind her eyes. The last thing she wanted was a fight with her uncle, but her temper was growing short.

Sergei closed his eyes for a brief second, a sure sign she'd pushed the boundary of his tolerance. He removed a chain with a small key from around his neck and unlocked a drawer in his desk. He placed a velvet-wrapped bundle on the desk before peeling back the layers of deep burgundy cloth to reveal an ancient leather-bound book.

"It's the journal of the first Nicolae Petrescu, our ancestor. The Guild would have it locked away in a huge vault if they knew it existed, but it's our family legacy, passed from generation to generation."

Her uncle ran his hand reverently over the embossed cover. "This is the family crest. In these pages, Nicolae tells of secret meetings between himself and Ignatius, Christian's father, one of the most powerful Aeternus Elders. Nicolae was also an influential man among his people, but he mourned the loss of three sons and didn't want to lose any more. Ignatius had losses of his own—his first wife and daughter were murdered in an attack on his estates in Bulgaria. Both men were tired of the bloodshed and devastation the war had yielded, and wanted to live in peace.

"They continued to meet secretly for some time and jointly formed a plan to bring the two sides together for peace talks. The very first meeting was arranged for the night of the full moon in July 1887. Three Aeternus emissaries arrived at a designated meeting place in Budapest, including Ignatius, who acted as their spokesman. When the talks were well under way, Emil, Nicolae's brother, attacked with a group of men. They murdered Christian's father and wife when they killed the Aeternus emissaries." Sergei paused, pinching the bridge of his nose.

Antoinette knew the rest of the story. Christian, enraged with grief over his father and wife's murder, began hunting down and slaughtering all those responsible. He killed so many rebels while tracking down the traitors, that he earned his title the Crimson Executioner.

Talk of peace seemed impossible until Christian, the one they'd all expected to lead the attack against the humans, approached Nicolae instead. Christian's grief had not been sated by the carnage he'd wrought; in fact his remorse was so great, Nicolae took pity on him. But the Aeternus Council of Elders would never agree to peace while the one man responsible for the attack was still free. Nicolae had to make the most difficult decision of his life. Face more war and more death or give up his only brother, Emil.

Nicolae chose the latter, with the assurance that in return for his support with the Aeternus Elders no repercussions from the humans would be taken against Christian for the deaths he'd dealt. If the Crimson Executioner could be made to see reason, then there was hope for them all. From that single act of cooperation and mutual trust, peace talks became possible again.

Emil was tried by the Aeternus Council of Elders and sentenced to death by public beheading, only this time Christian looked on instead of playing the executioner.

"What does this have to do with the present and the Aeternus's visit?" Antoinette looked up, trying to maintain a calm appearance.

Sergei stood up and limped around the desk, his cane thumping on the floor until he came to a stop beside her. "Christian is not our enemy. You have to let go of the past."

"But Uncle—" All that history happened over a hundred years ago, but she couldn't get past the fact Christian had slaughtered so many humans in cold blood.

Sergei straightened. "I've decided that we should attend the annual CHaPR conference this year. I need to talk to some old friends."

"But, Uncle, they've been trying to get you to go for years and you always steered away from the politics of the Guild and CHaPR. What's different now?"

"You need to have more exposure to parahumans; you've

isolated yourself from contact for far too long. It's time to live in the real world, Antoinette."

Antoinette glanced at Sergei, the sting of his words cut deep.

His expression softened. "Look, if half of what Christian tells me is true, we may be in for some very rough times. I need to look into these incidents myself, and what better place to start than at the conference all my colleagues will be attending? The evidence Christian brought points to the involvement of someone within the Guild itself. I need to be sure before I turn my back on the Guild once and for all."

Antoinette narrowed her eyes. "That's impossible. Why would the Guild be involved? Its purpose is to protect us from *his* kind—why should we trust the word of a filthy bloodsucker?"

Antoinette's head rocked back, the side of her face stinging. She looked up at her uncle's thunderous face and raised her hand to her cheek. Sergei had never laid a hand on her before but then she'd never spoken with such disrespect either.

"Firstly, we owe Christian a personal debt." Sergei's voice took on a harsh yet controlled tone. "Christian saved your lives when he brought you and Nici to us. And . . ." Sergei leaned forward on his cane, his face grim. "Let's not forget what else occurred when The Troubles plagued us last time—you lost both your parents."

It didn't really matter what hotel Christian was in, they were all the same. He headed straight for the bar and ordered a double scotch straight up. He downed it in one mouthful and signaled for another.

"Went that well, did it?" a familiar voice asked.

"Join me for a drink, Viktor?" Christian turned to catch the amused glint in his friend's amber eyes.

"Sure, if you're buying." The handsome blond man's laughter attracted the attention of a nearby stunner who fluffed her bleached blond hair and smiled in their direction.

Viktor chuckled again, slapping Christian's shoulder. "But let's go somewhere more . . . private."

They walked to an alley a few blocks away and arrived just in time to see the large, bald doorman turning away a curious human couple.

"Evening, Keith," Christian said to the giant ursian bouncer who resembled an African god carved from polished obsidian. "More curious tourists I see."

"Mr. Laroque, Mr. Dushic." Keith greeted each of them with a nod of his large scarred head and turned to watch the drunken couple stumble back the way they'd come. "The Princess has stopped all unescorted humans from entering."

Christian had seen it before, dozens of times. Human males try to impress their girlfriends by taking them to an exotically dangerous club and end up with more than they bargained for when some horny or thirsty Aeternus starts fanging on their date.

"Is your mistress in tonight?" Christian asked.

"Yes, sir." Keith's voice rumbled as he reached out a colossal arm to hold the door for them. "The Princess is within."

Before entering, Viktor stopped. "Is there anything special on the menu?"

"I'm sure *she* has something to your taste, Mr. Dushic," Keith replied.

The club's gloom was welcome after the bright streetlights and they walked down a hall lined with gauzy curtained privacy cubicles. Sighs and moans emanated as they passed. This club was different from the one Christian usually frequented in New York, but he enjoyed the change of scene.

Christian and Viktor stopped at the entrance to the club's inner sanctum where a DJ played for an undulating crowd on the dance floor.

The Princess stood on the other side of the room talking to a group of people but immediately turned in their direction as if sensing their presence.

The tall dark-skinned woman smiled as she came toward

them. Her white lace dress left very little to the imagination: high rounded breasts nearly spilled out of the thin strips of cloth that passed for a top, and the high splits of her skirt left her long, shapely legs bare to the hip. She moved like the royalty she was, and the crowded dance floor parted before her.

Christian placed her outstretched hand to his lips. "Akentia—you're looking as lovely as ever."

The regal Aeternus Elder accepted his compliment with a graceful tilt of her head. "And you, Christian, are as charming as ever." Then she turned her smile on his companion. "Viktor, it's been a long time. I was sorry to hear I'd missed you last night."

"I only came with Christian on this trip to bask in your beauty, highness." Viktor flashed his extended fangs and kissed her offered hand.

The lushness of her full lips meant she'd recently fed and her white teeth glowed in stark contrast to her ebony skin as she returned his smile. "Liar! I am sure my presence is not what brings two of the Department's finest to my little club. You'll need a private room, yes?" She turned and clicked her fingers. "And I'll have my children attend you."

Immediately two of Akentia's "children," as she referred to her donors, appeared at her side; one a raven-haired girl dressed in a skintight black leather mini dress and the other a stunning blond man in a white see-through body shirt and matching snug leather pants.

"They're fresh," Akentia said, smoothing the hair on the girl's head. "This one hasn't known the fang." She reached out and slid a cool palm down Christian's cheek. "You could be her first—we could both be her first."

Akentia offered him a compliment and he was tempted. To awaken a fang-virgin to the delights of feeding was a beautiful experience for both participants, and with Akentia involved it was sure to be explosive.

Viktor licked his lips and ran his hand across the young man's chest. He didn't discriminate between the sexes when it came to feeding or pleasures of the flesh. Man or woman, he enjoyed both equally.

But, much to his own disappointment, Christian bent over Akentia's long slim fingers and brushed them with his lips again. "We'll take the room, Princess, but we have much to discuss and can't afford the distraction. Perhaps another time?"

Disappointment flashed across Viktor's face, but then he nodded. "Sorry, Princess, but he's right I'm afraid."

"Anything you wish, my dear boy." Akentia's hand slid across Christian's chest, her own eyes reflecting the glimmer of regret. "Marcus, show these gentlemen to the Peacock Room, and bring them a couple of bottles from my private stock."

"Yes, Mistress," the boy said, bowing low and then leading the way.

He pressed a panel to open a hidden door behind a velvet curtain, holding it aside so the two men could pass. They entered the tastefully decorated room. A one-way mirror filled the length of the wall and looked out onto the dance floor. Plush leather lounges were scattered around for comfort and pleasure. Viktor closed the curtains on the dancers and then sat opposite Christian. "So did he believe you?"

Before Christian could answer, the boy reappeared carrying a tray and placed it on the low table. He exchanged a quick heated glance with Viktor before withdrawing. Viktor watched him until the door closed.

"Sergei couldn't ignore the evidence," Christian said when he was sure they were alone again. "But it was better that you didn't come with me in the end. Good call."

"She's definitely Grigore's daughter." Viktor pulled the cork stopper from the bottle and poured a splash of crimson into the glass. After a sip, he smiled approvingly. "Akentia's taste is impeccable, as usual." He filled a fresh glass and passed it to Christian before refilling his own. The freshly drawn blood warmed the glass in Christian's hand. Viktor sat back and draped an arm along the back of the lounge.

"What did he say?" Viktor asked, growing serious.

"I think he'll agree to his niece's involvement." Christian drained the crimson nectar and placed his empty glass back on the table.

"Excellent. Just what I'd hoped but we still have to be careful who we trust." Viktor said, pouring himself some more, then offered the bottle to Christian.

He shook his head. "How do you know you can trust me?"

"Who says I do?" Viktor's stoic expression held no hint of humor, then it dissolved into a grin.

For a moment Christian had the impression his friend wasn't entirely joking. Viktor's grin faded, but the warmth didn't leave his eyes.

"Christian, my old friend, you could never lie to me. Take Dominique, for example. I knew you were in love with her long before you'd even admitted it to yourself. Every time you denied it, I could hear the truth in your voice and see it in your eyes when you looked at her."

Pain pierced Christian's heart at the mention of his late wife's name. She'd been kindness and love personified. The war tore at her heart with each loss of life. "All that useless death and destruction," she used to say. So when his father had approached them about a truce with the humans, Dominique had jumped at the chance, even though Christian had thought it was insane. She'd quickly joined Ignatius's cause, agreeing to be an emissary, but when they'd been murdered Christian had wanted to wipe humanity from the face of the earth.

Viktor had saved him then; he'd opened Christian's eyes to the fact it wasn't humans he was angry with—it was himself for not being there to protect them.

"Christian . . ."

He looked up at his friend to find his pain and loss mirrored in Viktor's face. He'd also suffered. The third assassinated emissary had been Viktor's father, Mikhail.

"I'm sorry." Viktor dropped his gaze. "I shouldn't have brought that up."

"Don't apologize. It was a difficult time for both of us. The act of a few misguided men happened long ago and I've stopped blaming anyone. Including myself."

Time to change the subject. "So if the Guild won't cooperate why isn't CHaPR stepping in?"

"The Guild is autonomous and hasn't broken any laws. They've repeatedly denied any leaks from within their number. Sir Roger Wilberforce-Smythe, the human CHaPR ambassador, repeatedly blocks any attempts by the Department to become involved. He refuses to see the patterns similar to The Troubles when the Council almost split into two factions. If that happens then all we've achieved will be . . ." Viktor trailed off and his eyes went blank.

"Viktor?" Christian prompted.

His friend shook his head. "We have to gather more evidence, force them to open their eyes."

"So how—will we use the girl?"

"We'll use her—somehow get her to draw out the one we're after. You must convince her that you're genuine. It's essential to gain her trust."

"I know, but that's easier said than done. With Sergei's fall from grace with the Guild, I see no other way to get near them," Christian said.

"What does she know about it?"

"I don't know. Sergei didn't seem willing to go into it, but I'm pretty certain she's not aware of the tension between Sergei and Sir Roger."

"Excellent. Let's keep it that way for now." Leather creaked as Viktor shifted in his seat. "What about Grigore? What does she think happened to him?"

Christian stared down at his hands. "Sergei never told her the truth; she still thinks he's dead."

Viktor sighed heavily. "He could be for all I know. It's been weeks now since he disappeared. It's just not like him to stay out of contact this long."

Christian sank back into the soft seat. "Did he give you any other clues?"

"No more than what I've already told you."

It was something cryptic about a contact within the Guild and a distant Petrescu family member being involved. Christian stood, frustration pounding at his temples. "But that doesn't tell us much."

"Which is why we must use Grigore's daughter as bait." Viktor crossed his legs and smoothed out an imaginary wrinkle on his pants before fixing Christian with a stern gaze. "There's no other way."

At that moment Viktor's cell phone went off with a funky techno beat and he held up a finger to Christian as he answered it. "Talk to me."

"Right," Viktor said after a minute and flipped his phone shut before looking at Christian, his face all business. "We have to get back to New York ASAP. Looks like the human ambassador to CHaPR is the next target. But we still don't know who the leak in the Guild is and if we can't get Antoinette to draw them out, our plan could fall apart."

5
Goodbyes

Nici was waiting outside for her as she left the training room.

"Sorry—but can we leave this until tomorrow?" Antoinette asked. She was bone tired, the weight of the day suddenly pressing down on her.

Nici reached up and tugged his left ear, a sure sign he was nervous. But then he dropped his hand and straightened. "No. I need to talk to you now—it's really important."

Antoinette's stomach clenched in premonition. "What is it?"

"Let's go to the eating hall, it's usually empty this time of night." Nici avoided her eyes.

As predicted, no one was around. All the students were in bed long ago, training started before sunup. She'd been one of those students once and while life had seemed hard at the time, it had really been much simpler. Now she and Nici only used the family's school as a home base in between missions, not knowing where they'd be from one day to the next.

They sat at the end of a long communal dining table but now that he had her attention, Nici seemed reluctant to speak.

She reached across the table for his hand. "Nici, what is it?"

"I've been offered a place with the Guild," he said, so softly she barely heard him.

Antoinette withdrew her hand and sat back. A foreboding shadow darkened her heart. "You're leaving me?"

He looked up suddenly, his jaw jutting. "It's not like that."

"No?" she whispered. "You're my brother, we're supposed to stick together."

She instantly regretted her words. By the guilt and anguish on his face, he'd not made this decision lightly and didn't need her making it even harder. "When do you leave?"

"In a few days." His face filled with pride, she'd never seen him so sure of himself, so confident. "They're really impressed with my designs and want me to start as soon as possible. It's London—the best lab facilities in the world—and I'll finally have a chance to fight in my own way."

"But you do—"

"No, Antoinette," he softened his tone, "you do. I sit in the van waiting to find out if you've killed or have been killed, sick with worry and hoping it isn't the latter. This way I get to work on equipment to help save the lives of Venators like you."

Nici had always tinkered on things in the workshop and Antoinette had to admit his designs were good. In London, he'd really be able to achieve his full potential.

She caught movement out of the corner of her eye. A young woman stood half hidden in the doorway of the kitchen, watching them. Tatiana, Nici's girlfriend, and another tech-head. Tatiana dropped her gaze to the ground and backed away from the door—she was always timid around Antoinette.

"I see," Antoinette said. "You're not accepting this R&D position just for yourself, are you?"

Nici followed her gaze and the girl reappeared in the doorway, her lips trembled as she tried a shaky smile.

"She's pregnant." Nici's eyes softened before he steeled

himself again. "Look—you're the Venator, not me, that's the way it's always been. And to be honest, I don't really have the stomach for it anymore."

"What about our parents' deaths?" Antoinette snatched at his hand, the fear of losing him overwhelming. "Doesn't that mean anything to you?"

"Of course it does." He pulled his hand out of hers and ran it over his face. "But it's not going to bring them back, is it?"

He was right, and if she was truthful with herself, she'd sensed his unhappiness for a while now. "How long have you known about the job?"

"They contacted me two days ago, but I sent in the application a month before that." Nici looked at his hands.

"Why didn't you tell me?" Antoinette asked.

"I tried. But every time I saw your face I knew—"

"That I wouldn't like it." And he was right.

He nodded. "I felt like I was abandoning you," he said. "But I'm not like you Antoinette, I don't have your . . ."

"Obsession?" she finished for him, placing her elbows on the table and leaning in.

"I was going to say passion, but yes, obsession is a good word." He searched her face. "Look, I have a wife and I'm about to become a father—"

She sat up straight. "Wait a minute, you're already married?"

He held out his left hand, showing her the wedding ring she'd been too preoccupied to notice before. "We did it this afternoon."

"You should have told me," Antoinette said, the hurt creeping into her tone. "I could have been there for you."

"We didn't want any fuss." Meaning they hadn't wanted to give her a chance to stop it.

Antoinette sighed. Her little brother had become a man and she'd missed it. It was time to let him go. "I'm really happy for you and Tatiana."

Antoinette came around the table and Nici stood. As she

threw her arms about his neck, the tears slipped down her cheeks. "And I'm so proud of you. But who's going to take care of me now?"

"You'll do that yourself, same as always." He squeezed her tightly. "You've never really needed me."

She choked back a sob as she caught Tatiana's relieved expression over his shoulder.

Antoinette wiped away the dampness under her eyes. "You'd better go to your . . . wife. She looks like she needs you." Then she grabbed both of his hands in hers. "My blessings to you both." She spoke the family's traditional words, those their mother would have said if she were alive.

His smile widened, and she could swear she caught a slight glisten in his eyes. "Thank you, sis."

Nici leaned forward and planted a soft kiss on her forehead. Sergei had told her they'd be leaving with Christian tomorrow for New York City, so she wouldn't have much time with her brother before then. This was goodbye.

Tatiana rushed across the room and threw her arms around his neck. Antoinette noticed the slight swell of the girl's stomach as she returned the girl's tentative smile.

"Congratulations!" She stepped forward and gave the girl a somewhat awkward hug. "Welcome to the family."

"Thank you," Tatiana whispered.

Nici gave her hand a quick squeeze before the couple, arm in arm, left the room. And so did a part of her heart. Because no matter what happened now, things would never be quite the same between her and Nici again.

"So he told you, then?" Sergei came out of the shadows.

"How long have you been there?"

"Long enough," he said, limping forward.

"You've known for some time too, haven't you?"

Sergei nodded. "He came to me just after they found out about Tatiana's pregnancy. I told him he had to tell you tonight before we leave."

"That's the reason you're taking me with you to the CHaPR conference, isn't it? You thought it would be better for Nici and Tatiana if I wasn't around, just in case I didn't approve."

Sergei's face split into a grin. "You know me well, niece, but that's only part of the reason you're coming."

"It's okay Uncle. Nici deserves to be happy," Antoinette said.

"Will you give up hunting now?" Sergei tilted his head and looked at her with a strange unreadable expression.

"You know I can't."

With a sad little smile, he nodded then turned and left her in the large empty hall.

She suddenly felt truly alone for the first time in her life.

Christian drummed his fingers on his thigh and looked out of the stationary aircraft's window.

"When are they due to arrive?" Viktor asked, sitting across from Christian, sipping red wine while he caressed the head of the large Siberian Malamute at his side.

"Any minute now." Christian frowned, checking his watch for the third time in ten minutes. "Actually I would've expected them half an hour ago."

"Well, you know what women are like, always keeping us waiting." Viktor said.

"Antoinette is not like other women," Christian said, remembering the way she dispatched the dreniac with such efficient precision.

Viktor raised an eyebrow and Christian turned to stare out of the window again. A vehicle approached, and from the sound of the engine it had to be the limousine he'd sent to pick up the humans.

Mary, the flight attendant, stuck her head in through the door. "Your guests have arrived, sir. Captain Rogers will conduct the preflight checks while they board."

"Excellent—have him get under way as soon as possible." Christian prepared to greet his guests.

Sergei was first through, followed closely by Antoinette carrying a rucksack over her shoulder and a long wooden

case. Both glanced around the interior of the refurbished
Boeing 747 with wide-eyed awe.

"Intel sure knows how to fly its agents in style," Sergei
said.

"Actually, this is my own personal jet," Christian said. "It
was a commercial aircraft I had refitted. The accommodations are down here and up the stairs are the comms center
and my office.

He felt Antoinette's gaze on him, but when he looked at
her, she turned away.

"Viktor, you remember Sergei Petrescu and this is his
niece. Antoinette, this is Viktor Dushic, a fellow Intel agent
and a friend."

She threw Viktor a cool, tight smile that didn't reach her
eyes.

"Sorry we're late," Sergei said as he sank into the large
leather seat beside Viktor and propped his walking stick
against his knee.

"That's all right. We know what it's like traveling with
a woman. I was just discussing that very topic with Christian."

Viktor had that look in his eye—the one that meant trouble. Christian cringed inwardly. Sure enough, Antoinette
didn't disappoint. The glare she gave Viktor would've frozen
the fires of Hades.

"Actually, it's my fault," Sergei said, throwing his niece a
stern look. "Well, my wife's really. She hates it when I leave
home and spends ages making sure I've forgotten nothing."

"Aunt Katerina's just worried about you." She may have
been talking to her uncle but she stared directly at Viktor,
who arched his eyebrow. He was definitely enjoying baiting
her. Christian tried to silence him with a warning glare, but
he knew it wouldn't work. Viktor was having far too much
fun and seemed determined to push her buttons.

"Well then, once we get the rest of your luggage on board,
we'll be able to take off."

"I do believe you are trying to get a rise out of me." She

laid the wooden case on a nearby chair and placed her hands
on her hips. "Only vain or stupid people carry more than
they need and I have everything in these two cases." She
paused, looking Viktor up and down. "Besides, I doubt
there'd be any room left once your bags had been loaded—
even on a plane this size."

"Ouch." Viktor theatrically slapped his hand over his heart
and winked. "And what is it you have in the case? A flute?
Perhaps an oboe? No, no, I got it—you're a pool hustler."

The corners of Antoinette's mouth twitched. Christian
hated his friend at that moment. He knew damned well it
was her weapons. Antoinette undid the clips of the wooden
case and opened the lid. She took out the beautiful black and
red katana Christian had seen her use in Miami.

Viktor whistled though his teeth. "Careful, little girl—
you might cut yourself with that thing." The twinkle in his
eye grew brighter.

Antoinette returned a tight, deadly smile and flicked out
the blade then slid it down the front of Viktor's shirt and
resheathed it again almost before he'd known what'd hit him.

Viktor took a sip of his wine, the epitome of calmness as
he looked down at his now open, buttonless shirt. "If you
wanted me to undress, all you had to do was ask."

"Stop teasing our guest, Viktor." Christian tried to keep
his voice even, and failed. She may have meant it as intimi-
dation but it had been far too intimate for his liking.

Viktor gazed pointedly at Christian over the top of his
glass as Antoinette laid the blade back in its bed of blue
velvet and clipped the case shut.

"Mary will help you with your bags before we get under
way." Christian signaled to get the flight attendant.

Antoinette gave her pack to the woman but kept the
wooden case.

"It's all right—I'll make sure it's stowed safely," Mary
said as she bent to take the case from her.

Antoinette shook her head and pulled it out of the flight
attendant's reach.

"It has to be secured for takeoff," Mary explained.

Christian moved forward. Antoinette's shoulders dropped defensively and her eyes narrowed as she hugged the case against her chest.

Antoinette gripped the case tighter, her eyes darting left and right, seeking escape. She wasn't about to trust her weapons to an Aeternus or his hired bimbo.

Christian stopped and held up his hands. "It's okay. Mary, just show her where to stow them herself."

"Yes, sir."

The flight attendant took a few steps to the left and with a delicate sweep of her hand she brought Antoinette's attention to the straps against the wall and the briefcases already secured there. He could probably have used his Aeternus emotion-control mojo on her if he'd wanted, but he hadn't.

"Sorry." Her face heated up. "It's just hard to . . ." Her words trailed off.

"Trust?" Christian asked.

It was a good word, but still difficult to do. She threw back her shoulders, handed the case to Mary, and gave her a tight smile of apology.

She noticed a large dog for the first time lying on the far side of Viktor. It tilted its head and sat up. She squatted to eye level, patting her knees to entice him closer. "Aren't you a beautiful boy?"

"Cerberus doesn't like strangers," Viktor warned.

The dog placed his head on her thigh, saying hello with his large intelligent eyes as much as his wagging tail.

"Good boy." She scratched behind his ear and ruffled the both sides of his head, and looked up to catch the flash of surprise across Viktor's face.

"My niece has special way with animals," Sergei said, smiling at her. "Since she was a little girl."

"So I see." Viktor's eyes narrowed as if really seeing her for the first time. "He likes you, trusts you. I can sense it so clearly."

So could she, but not in the same way Viktor meant. The Aeternus had the ability to sense and project emotions, and animals were more susceptible. She'd once seen a dreniac start a large and deadly dog fight just for the fun it. But obviously this Aeternus used his ability with his pet in a more caring way.

She looked at Viktor, really looked. He was as different to Christian as night to day. While Christian wasn't overly tall, neither was he short.

Viktor on the other hand would be well over six foot, judging from his sitting position. Where Christian was well built, though not overly muscular, Viktor was lean to the point of skinny with high cheekbones, full lips, and waist-length bleached blond hair making him appear rather effeminate.

Even their style of clothing was at odds. Christian wore a casual knit top over faded denim jeans; Viktor wore black rock-and-roll pants with buckles down the leg, snakeskin Cuban heeled boots, a black shirt now open to the waist, and a knee-length white coat. The hair and clothing gave him an almost androgynous appearance—a Japanese manga hero made living flesh.

Christian was all male—powerful and intense. Viktor on the other hand was . . . *beautiful* and there was something else about him she couldn't help but like.

Viktor smiled. "If I put my head in your lap like that . . ." he teased.

She glared and bent forward to plant a kiss on Cerberus's muzzle. The dog rolled over onto his back, tale whipping back and forth in delight.

"You're far too beautiful to be named after the hound of hell," she said, giving the dog's stomach a good scratch.

"She has quite an effect on the male sex," Viktor said with a gleam in his eye. "Even I feel like rolling over for a tummy rub."

"Beasts have always been a specialty of mine," she said dryly.

Viktor leaned forward in his seat. "A wit as sharp as her

beauty, I see. I like her, Sergei," he said, raising his glass with long feminine fingers. "I like her a lot." He drained the remaining wine and handed the empty glass to Mary.

Antoinette hid her smile in the dog's coat as she gave him another hug. Cerberus sat up and leaned his weight against her, lapping up the attention, his tongue lolling from the side of his mouth.

"Mr. Laroque, the pilot has clearance. We're ready to depart," the flight attendant announced.

"Good," Christian said. "Then we should still make New York before dawn."

The engines whined and the aircraft moved slowly out of the hangar and toward the runway. Antoinette took her seat and fought the unsettling churn of her stomach. She closed her eyes, silently reciting a calming mantra. It didn't help. She gripped the arms of her seat, and then sensing someone watching her, opened her eyes. *Christian.*

Her cheeks flamed. "I hate flying."

For a moment he looked at her with disbelief, then nodded.

"Mary," he said. "Bring a double brandy for Ms Petrescu before we take off."

"There's no need—" Antoinette started to say.

Sergei cut her off. "Nonsense, Christian is right; it's just what you need." He shrugged sheepishly. "We're land people, we don't fly much."

"Mary, make it brandies all round." Christian smiled.

Antoinette reluctantly took a glass from the tray when it came. Usually she avoided spirits, but she needed something to fortify her nerves. Flying—her one great fear. Sergei was right—they were land people. On land, she had control and in the air she had none.

It wasn't just the thought of flying that had her in a spin. The extravagance of the plane overwhelmed her—fitted out with plush leather lounges and expensive furnishings, it was more lavish than any hotel she'd ever stayed in. And it all belonged to Christian. With this kind of money came power. But what kind of power?

Viktor led Cerberus to a sky kennel fixed for safety during takeoff. Then he took a brandy from the tray and gave Mary a peck on the cheek before returning to his seat.

Just the smell of the strong spirit stole her breath. As she downed a large gulp, tears sprang to her eyes and the liquor scorched a fiery trail down her throat, sucking the rest of the air from her lungs. She choked back a coughing fit, at the same time trying to drag oxygen back into her burning chest.

Viktor chuckled. "Good to see a woman who can hold her liquor."

She glared at the smug piece of shit and he winked as she brought the glass to her lips for a second go. The next mouthful went down much more smoothly. The buzz soon made it worthwhile and by the time the plane reached the runway she'd finished the rest and felt lightheaded, the biting sting in her throat subsiding to a warming glow.

Surreptitiously she glanced at the two Aeternus. The only vampires she'd ever really dealt with before were dreniacs—half insane, vicious killers addicted to death-highs. With them, it was easy—destroy them quickly before they destroyed you or anyone else. But this was something new. Two living, breathing Aeternus, and PID agents to boot. She should feel safe with guys. So why did her gut roll over every time Christian's deep blue eyes turned her way?

6

night sweats

The engine whine grew louder. Antoinette tightened the belt and clutched the arms of the seat as the plane began to pick up speed. She hated this part even more than landing. There was no turning back now.

The plane hurtled down the runway, committed to taking off, the front lifted and the movement smoothed out as the wheels left the tarmac, climbing steadily. She had a moment of near panic as the retracting landing gear thumped loudly beneath the plane.

"I expect there will be quite a stir at the conference this year," Viktor said a little more loudly than necessary.

Was he trying to distract her?

"Really?" Sergei said. "Do tell."

The conference was an annual event attended by representatives of the human and parahuman people. Her uncle had refused to participate since . . . since she couldn't remember when. To be going now was completely contradictory to his usual reluctance. And that didn't bode well for the seriousness of the situation.

Viktor turned to her uncle, mock surprise written all over his face. "The Mer-people have agreed to officially attend for the first time, it should be very interesting."

Antoinette frowned and sat back in her seat, suddenly tired. Sergei and Viktor continued to talk about parahuman politics while Christian approached the flight attendant. He glanced in Antoinette's direction and said something to the woman. A moment later, the elegant flight attendant came over.

"Ms Petrescu." She bowed her head gracefully. "Mr. Laroque has asked me to show you where you can freshen up."

Do I look that bad? Still it would be nice to wash her face; the brandy had made her flushed and warm. She followed Mary toward a door at the tail end of the cabin.

"Everything you need is in here, Miss Petrescu." Mary opened the door for her. Antoinette looked into the room, her breath catching. Although Mary didn't exactly smile, Antoinette detected a twinkle of amusement. She must look like some country bumpkin coming to the city for the first time.

"You can freshen up through there." Mary indicated to a door past the opulent full-size bed with gold brocade quilt and pillows. Antoinette removed her shoes to cross the rich burgundy carpet. The bathroom had marble bench tops, a full-size shower and spa. The tiles felt cool beneath her bare feet.

Catching her disheveled reflection in the mirror above the basin, she leaned in closer. No wonder they'd suggested she come in here—she looked like hell.

Her eyes, emphasized by dark circles, were sunken in her head and a feverish flush covered her cheeks. She massaged the temples of her pounding head and turned on the faucet, splashing her face. The water, like ice over hot coals, dashed the heat on her cheeks. She reached for one of the fluffy white towels hanging from the brass rail beside the counter.

Feeling a little better, she found some painkillers under the counter and took a second look at the bed. Maybe if she just lay down for a bit . . .

* * *

Antoinette crawled from the bed, running a hand over her face to wipe away the sleep. She glanced at her watch. Shit. It'd been an hour. She'd only wanted to close her eyes for a minute. What would her uncle think?

Wait . . . something's wrong. Nothing she could put a finger on, but the hair on the back of her neck prickled, and she'd learned over the years to trust that feeling.

Barefoot, she opened the door a crack and peered into the main cabin. Empty. Where was everyone? The dim lights formed dark shadows around the edges of the cabin, making it difficult to see. She let the door close behind her. Only the faint, constant drone of the engines echoed through the room and she frowned.

Halfway across the floor, her foot slid in something sticky. The coppery scent hit her nostrils as she squatted to investigate. Blood. Her instincts kicked into full alert—she crouched lower, her eyes darting left and right.

A trap! They'd been lured here to die. Drawn in by scheming vampires—she knew they weren't to be trusted.

Well, they wouldn't get her without a fight. Oh God, Sergei. She went for her weapons case only to find it gone.

Shit! The bastards had taken it. She had to reach the cockpit and force the plane down. Somehow. She had to get back on the ground. There she had more of a chance—more control.

For the first time she noticed a dripping noise coming from up ahead. Antoinette tilted her head, trying to locate the source and inched forward. The galley.

She whipped aside the concertina door to find Mary slumped against the wall, lifeless eyes staring at the ceiling, her throat ripped open. The blood formed vivid crimson rivulets against her pallid skin. But the eyes were the worst, terror frozen in their vacant gaze.

An overturned coffeepot lay on the counter. A large fat drop fell slowly with a splat into a pool of mingled blood and coffee on the floor beside Mary. Something gnawed at Antoinette's thoughts. Why would Christian murder his staff?

Maybe it was the other one.

The cockpit door to her right banged shut as the plane dipped with a pocket of turbulence. Antoinette's heart lodged into her throat and her stomach sank; already knowing what she'd find. She steeled herself and carefully pushed open the door.

The breath left her lungs in a whoosh and she felt as if she'd been sucker-punched in the gut. Blood was splattered across the inside of the windshield in the telltale sign of arterial spray. The captain lolled sideways in the chair, his hand wrapped around a gun as the controls moved on their own. Thank God for autopilot.

Antoinette turned the copilot's chair, hoping against hope he may still be alive, yet knowing he wouldn't. The man had a gaping hole where his throat had once been, just like the captain.

So brutal. This wasn't the frenzied attack to satisfy a death-high. This has been done slowly out of pleasure— pure, simple, and perverted pleasure. Besides, there was no trace of the telltale scent in the recycled air.

She tried to push down the bitter taste of panic rising up the back of her throat as her heart beat wildly in her chest. She must not give in to fear—it would get her killed more quickly than anything else.

A strange warmth bloomed in her mind and spread throughout her body, clouding her thoughts and soothing away the feelings of horror at the scene in front of her.

She turned. Her breath quickening. Christian stood a few feet away—shirtless. Her body betrayed her at the sight of his bare chest; his lean, well-defined frame glowed in the dim light. Her fingers itched to rake through his hair and trace the ridges across his stomach.

She grew hot and ran her hands over her hips, lifting her dress high as she rubbed her thighs together.

No, came a voice from within. She shook her head,

trying to clear the creeping fog. What had she come here looking for?

Focus, take back control. There was something she had to do. Something important, only she couldn't remember what it was.

He held out a beckoning hand and her feet moved on their own.

Stop—he's doing this to you.

But she couldn't stop. His eyes drew her in, brilliant blue like the Aegean Sea. She wanted to dive into their cool depths and lose herself forever.

She reached him and he pulled her against his chest. His hot scent overpowered her senses, making her weak and turning her legs to jelly.

He forced her back against the wall, pinning her wrists above her head, claiming her mouth with his, devouring her. And she let him. His hardness pressed against her and she knew she wanted him, right here, right now. If he'd let go of her wrists, she'd rip off those trousers and show him just how much.

This time the voice inside screamed. *You have to stop. Snap out of it before it's too late. This is wrong.*

But how could it be wrong to be in his arms? How could it be wrong to have his lips on hers? This was right.

"Oh so right," she whispered, and sighed as he moved his kisses to her throat.

A groan escaped her and her skin burned with feverish pleasure. He unbuttoned her dress, reached inside, cupped a lace-covered breast, and brushed her erect nipple with the pad of his thumb.

She swayed with heady pleasure, her knees almost buckling and she cried out. He traced kisses across her naked skin. When he moved back to her throat, she thought she would burst if he didn't take her soon.

His lips brushed her ear. "Hush little baby, don't say a word," he whispered.

She froze. That rhyme—why that rhyme? The one *he* had sung.

As if plunged into icy water, her passion died. She wrenched her wrists from his grasp then pushed him away to find that instead of Christian's stirring blue eyes, a cold pale gaze stared back. Lank brown hair had replaced thick dark locks.

She knew his face so well. It'd visited every childhood nightmare. That same cold smile chilled her now, just as it had back then.

"Mama's gonna buy you a mockingbird." The killer continued to sing the same haunting lullaby he'd sung all those years ago as he slit her mother's throat before her six-year-old eyes.

She felt warmth pooling around her feet and she looked down expecting to see she'd wet herself with fright, just as she had back then. But it was blood. Her blood.

The scream tore from her throat. "Nooooooo!"

7

mother, oh mother

Sitting bolt upright, chest heaving, Antoinette shook herself out of the nightmare. Perspiration ran down her face and the dress clung to her damp skin. Gulping back air, she looked at her watch. Only about fifteen minutes had passed.

It'd been several years since he'd visited her sleep. Dream demons and memories haunted her as she stumbled into the bathroom. The reflection of her flushed face blurred as tears filled her eyes and her brain hammered against the inside of her skull.

The night Dante Rubins slit her mother's throat Antoinette had been six years old and just as helpless as she was in her dream. The image of Mama's blue eyes dimming as death took her had haunted Antoinette ever since. Dante had maintained a total hold over Antoinette's mind and body, making her watch the lifeblood seep from her mother's jugular to soak the front her dress.

Maybe the dream was an omen, warning her against becoming too complacent, reminding her of who and what Christian and his friend were. Things were never as they appeared on the surface and she sensed they were hiding something. The Aeternus were not to be trusted. *Ever.*

She'd never turn her back on a dreniac, nor should she on
an Aeternus.

After Antoinette tidied herself up, she found her shoes
and slipped them on. When she reached the door, her shaking hand stopped inches from the handle. Her heart pounded
as the nightmare aftershocks haunted her.

Déjà vu.

Get a hold of yourself—it was just a dream.

Still, she had to crack the door slightly to be able to hear
anything in this soundproofed room. Through the gap she
heard familiar voices, speaking in low tones and relaxed her
forehead against the wall to gather herself.

"Are you certain she doesn't know?" that Viktor-guy said.

She pressed her ear closer to the crack.

"Yes," her uncle's voice answered. "If she did she would
have . . ." His voice trailed off as he moved away and she
could no longer make out what he was saying.

Would have what? Who were they talking about?

"Still, she'll have to be told eventually," Christian's voice
said with a sting in his tone.

"Da. But not yet." Sergei only reverted to his native
tongue when he was drunk, very tired, or stressed, and he
didn't sound all that drunk or tired.

"It'll have to be soon if she is going to help with the investigation," Christian said.

"Let me find out what I can from my Guild contacts first.
It's a matter requiring . . . delicacy. Not Antoinette's greatest
forte."

She stiffened in stunned silence, her hand now resting on
the handle. Why would Uncle Sergei keep things from her?
There was only one way to find out.

The suite door flew open and crashed against the wall.
Christian turned as Antoinette exploded into the room, eyes
firing and face flushed.

"What's going on here?" she demanded, her fists clenching and unclenching.

Sergei leaned forward against his cane. "Antoinette, I—"

She turned on him. "Even you . . ." Her voice rose a hysterical octave. "Sneaking around behind my back, keeping secrets from me. I would never have expected it of you, Uncle."

Sergei looked away, his shoulders slumping.

"That's enough." Christian's voice was controlled, belying the anger that seethed within—she'd pushed too far.

Turning on him, she met his gaze squarely. "You mind your own business, vampire," she spat.

"I've told you not to call us that, and this is my business. You're a guest on my plane and you'll respect all of my guests."

"I'll not be spoken to like a child."

"Then stop behaving like one," Sergei barked.

Her eyes widened in shock and then they narrowed dangerously on Christian before she crossed the distance between them. "What'll you do? Throw me off the plane?"

"Don't tempt me."

"You could try, bloodsucker." She pulled back her arm and punched him right in the face.

He did nothing to block it and after his head rocked back he looked her in the eye as he licked the drop of blood that trickled from the corner of his mouth.

"Antoinette," Sergei roared, coming to his feet.

Christian caught her next swing by the wrist mere inches from his face. "Is it any wonder you've not been told anything when you go off half-cocked—attacking first and questions later?" he said through gritted teeth.

Tears welled and she stopped struggling against him. Then he noticed her flushed face, the beads of sweat on her brow and upper lip, and the way she flinched when he held her arm. Christian pulled her closer, placing his hand on her forehead. Heat radiated from her in waves. She struggled, trying to push him away but he held her tighter.

"You're unwell," he said.

Her eyes widened.

"Is that true?" Sergei asked, his brows knitting in worry.

She slowly nodded and turned to Sergei. "I thought it was just a headache."

"Your wound," Sergei said. "It's infected, isn't it?"

Christian guessed the same thing.

Antoinette shrugged her shoulders. "You know how quickly these things can turn."

"Damn it—why didn't you say something earlier?" Christian demanded.

"Because I thought it was just a headache," she repeated, her eyes glittering feverishly highlighting her black eye.

"Well, we'd better get this infection under control—now," Christian said. "Come on."

"I'll see a doctor when we reach New York." She backed away a step.

"NO—We'll take care of it now." He took her by the wrist.

She stubbornly raised her chin.

Stupid, proud little fool. But he didn't have time for this crap.

Grabbing her by the elbow, he pulled her closer—her eyes widened and she turned from a deep pink to a flaming flush. She stamped hard on his foot. An Aeternus he may be, but he still felt pain.

The last of his patience evaporated. With one smooth movement he scooped her up and carried her into the room she'd erupted from so dramatically minutes earlier.

When he reached the crumpled bed, he dumped her unceremoniously on it. Her face screwed up as she grunted and scowled at him; he felt a momentary stab of guilt for his rough handling.

"How dare you?" she spat.

"I dare as I please," he said coolly.

Sergei stood in the open door. "Let Christian tend to it, niece."

"I want to see a human doctor. What would an Aeternus know about humans?"

"Sorry, but I'm the closest thing you've got." Christian

crossed his arms. "I've practice medicine on humans before, now—take off that dress and let me have a look."

Her stubborn chin rose higher as she glared at him.

"If you don't take it off I'll be forced to do it myself," he warned. "And with the mood I'm in, it won't be gentle."

From the corner of his eye he saw Sergei back out of the room, shutting the door behind him. When she didn't move he took a step toward her.

"Okay." She held up a restraining hand. "Okay—I'll do it." She climbed off the bed and reached for the zipper on the side of the dress before looking at him over her shoulder. "Do you mind?"

"Not at all." He leaned his shoulder casually against the wall. "I've seen a naked body or two in my time."

"Not mine, you haven't," she said, then swore under her breath before turning her back to him to slip the dress over her head.

His stomach knotted as he ran his gaze over her semi-naked curves covered only by tiny lace panties and a matching bra. The ivory lingerie against her creamy skin was more than he'd been prepared for. Her body was honed to Venator perfection by hours of martial arts training, yet soft in all the right places.

A red and black dragon tattoo sat in the small of her perfect back, the tip of the tail disappearing into the crevice between her buttocks just beneath her panties. His pants suddenly seemed tighter and fangs nudged his gums on either side of his front teeth.

He hadn't lied when he said he'd seen a female or two. He'd seen literally hundreds, maybe even thousands, of women in varying stages of dress and undress in his life time. But he'd rarely seen anything of such beauty. Antoinette was put together perfectly. Her muscles danced beneath her skin enlivening the tattoo dragon—he swore the beast watched him. What would it be like to run his lips across this skin art? Would it feel as alive as it looked? And how he'd love to trace that tail to its conclusion . . .

"Well, now what?" she asked, her back still to him.

Thank goodness his loose top covered the bulge in his jeans. "Um . . . lie down on the bed while I wash my hands," he said, swallowing hard.

He closed the bathroom door and leaned his hands against the counter, trying to regain a hold of himself. "She's just another human—there's nothing special about her." But he could hear the lie in his own voice.

"Did you say something?" she called from the other room.

"No." He glanced at his reflection before retrieving some medical supplies from the cabinet under the counter.

He hadn't lied about practicing medicine—although he purposely hadn't mentioned that it was mostly during the American Civil War, and not on many women patients. Now that had definitely been a baptism by fire—or, should he say *blood*.

Antoinette felt embarrassingly naked, something she'd never felt before. She'd grown up in a unisex Venator preparatory school where there was little room for modesty with communal showers, locker rooms, and absolutely no privacy. Now she had her own room back at the school dorms, but she still shared the rest.

He didn't say she couldn't cover herself. As Christian rattled around in the bathroom she grabbed the bedspread from the end of the bed and drew it up to her chest. Unfortunately, the movement set off a wave of nausea and the pain flared again. She lay back against the pillows, breathing through the throbbing ache. It wasn't nearly as bad as before, though, when he'd picked her up—she'd had to bite her lip to stop from crying out.

She could endure pain; it was part of being a Venator. What she had trouble with was his hands on her skin. His cool touch felt too good against her fevered flesh, like a welcome breeze on a hot summer's day.

She clenched the blanket in her fists. Damn, she must be really sick to get all girly and poetic. Her stomach roiled. She wasn't sure if this was nausea or the memory of the way he'd unceremoniously dumped her onto the bed. *Bastard.*

Then again she had asked for it by punching him. And in a perverse kind of way, she'd liked it. Normally she had better control over her tongue and temper, but Christian seemed to bring out the worst in her for some reason.

The bathroom door opened. Christian carried a tray into the room and pulled a nearby stool closer. As he sat down, he reached out and ripped away her covering and the old dressing in quick succession before she had a chance to prepare herself or argue.

"Ow!"

"Keep still," he growled.

She tried to sit up and see what he was doing, but he pushed her back against the pillows.

"I said, keep still." Christian's stony face had a slight frown creasing his brow.

"I just want to see."

He silenced her with a glare and she decided not to push it any further as he poked and prodded around the wound. Antoinette became suddenly aware of how close his fingertips were to the sensitive underside of her breast and swallowed hard. Every burning brush of his touch spread heat across her already feverish skin.

"We need to put a poultice on the wound to draw out the infection." He rose and returned to the bathroom.

The sound of movement from the other room piqued her curiosity and she propped onto her elbows to look at the angry flesh around the parallel gashes just above her right hip bone. She had never allowed a wound to get this bad before. Christian was right, though, if it remained untreated, she'd be very sick indeed. The fever made her body feel on fire.

"Can't you behave yourself for five seconds?" he said from the bathroom doorway. "I told you to stay still."

"I just wanted to see," she said for a second time. "It was healing really well."

"Dreniacs can carry some nasty shit," he said.

"Yeah, this one was especially . . ." She frowned, rising higher onto her elbows. "I never told you it was a dreniac wound."

"I assumed, given your profession." He looked away quickly and she got the sense he was hiding something, then his unyielding eyes met hers. "Now, lie down and let me finish."

When she did as she was told, he raised a questioning eyebrow. "What, no arguments?"

Tiredness washed over her. "No," she said, closing her eyes.

Antoinette opened them in time to see him pick up a scalpel from the tray on the bedside table and nick the tip of his finger. A few drops of dark blood fell onto the salve smeared on the dressing.

"What are you doing?" she asked in horror.

"This will heal you faster than any human medicine can."

"No." She tried to climb off the bed. "Get it away from me."

He grabbed her by the wrist and pulled her back. "I don't have time for this crap," he growled, the menace in his voice raising goose bumps on her skin. She struggled but he held her helpless and then his voice softened. "This may burn a little." And he placed the dressing to her wound with gentle fingers.

A fiery intense pain lit up all the nerve endings in her side and she sucked back her breath, grimacing. "I thought this was supposed to make me feel better."

"Give it time," he murmured, fixing the dressing in place with some tape.

Fire exploded in her side, and her vision grayed from the pain, then slowly the searing dulled to a burning and finally to a slight tingling warmth.

"I'm also giving you a shot of painkiller." He picked up a needle and drew in clear liquid from an ampoule.

She quashed an instinctive flash of distrust and held out her arm.

He shook his head with a malicious smirk. "Roll over."

"You have got to be kidding."

"Nope."

"Surely the arm is just as good." She held it out again—hopeful.

He shook his head. *Shit.* She huffed and rolled gingerly onto her side, holding her breath. His pulled down the top of her panties and she swallowed nervously, his touch setting off a tingle in her lower back. She heard the flick of the syringe, smelled the sharp scent of an alcohol swab before its cold touch and then the sting of the needle.

"I didn't need it," she lied—her headache still pounded heavily behind her eyes even if her side was no longer on fire.

"You can get dressed now." Christian's voice held an odd, gravelly timbre.

Antoinette turned to see ill-concealed hunger as his gaze slid down her scantily clad body, triggering her own heat. He wanted her—that much was clear. The woman in her felt a bolt of satisfaction; the Venator saw something she might be able to manipulate in future. Antoinette swung her legs off the bed and stood up way too fast, sending her head into a spin. She staggered forward and her feet entangled in the discarded dress on the floor. Pinwheeling her arms, she tried desperately to stay upright, but fell—right into his lap. Just as she started to get her bearings a thunderclap of red-hot desire hit with a force that would've knocked her on her ass if she hadn't already been sitting. And then she did something she would never have dreamt of in a million years. She kissed him.

At first he remained rigid—she'd caught him by complete surprise, but no more than she'd caught herself. His lips were surprisingly soft and yet firm under hers. Then he responded and—*whoa, baby*—nerve endings lit up like Christmas trees and the fourth of July combined.

It'd been nearly a year since she'd been with a man, but sex had never been big on her agenda. This was different. Her body responded like dry land after drought-breaking rains, soaking up his heat, demanding more. He murmured something in her ear her lust-imbued mind couldn't comprehend.

"What?" she asked, in a daze.

"My blood . . . an aphrodisiac," he said between kisses.

Her foggy brain couldn't or wouldn't grasp his meaning and she pulled his head down to hers again so he could no longer talk. Antoinette was beyond caring. He was male—she was one horny woman—what could be the harm in a bit of a good time? She turned in his arms and swung her legs over his lap, straddling him.

He held her away by the shoulders. "Antoinette, I won't be able to stop if you keep on like this. I won't be able to control myself when the blood-thrall takes over." His breath brushed her skin with the same burning heat as his body.

In answer, she leaned forward and pinched the skin above his jugular between her teeth. A low throaty purr with an undertone of menace rumbled under her hand on his chest.

It heightened her excitement and she nipped his throat again. This time Christian growled and slid the straps of her bra down over her shoulders, reaching behind to unfasten the clasp with practiced single-handed ease. She sighed loudly as the lacy constraints fell away and the cool air hit her hot, heavy breasts. Her nipples tightened under his intense gaze, spreading a warm tingle along the invisible strands joined to the apex between her thighs.

"Oh God," Christian whispered and he leaned forward, taking a hardened nub between his lips.

Antoinette threw back her head and moaned, fireworks exploding behind her eyes. This had never happened to her before. Whatever he was doing to her she didn't want him to stop. She started to rock in his lap, keeping with the rhythm of his powerful draws on her sensitive swollen flesh. When he released her nipple, a loud sob escaped her and he pinned her arms behind, effectively immobilizing her as he took the other nipple in between his lips. Nothing had ever felt this good. The orgasm seemed to start at her toes and rocket through her body. Nothing had ever come close . . .

"OH MY G . . . ahhhhhhhhh."

8

вloodlusт

Christian continued to suckle as she shuddered against him. Her hooded glassy eyes and the unexpected surprise on her face almost made him come too, but thanks to the tight constraint of his jeans she was able to hold back. One orgasm was only the start for someone in the heavy throes of bloodthrall. The blood he'd used to heal her had hit her bloodstream through the wound and brought it on.

He should have been more prepared for her reaction but he hadn't expected this much intensity. If he didn't know she was a Petrescu—the royalty of Venators—he'd swear she had Latent blood in her veins. Latents were acutely more susceptible to the effects of Aeternus blood than normal humans.

His lust rose, demanding to be quenched, going past the point of no return. She shoved him so his back hit the wall behind the stool and ripped his shirt over his head, but when she reached for the fly on his jeans he grabbed her wrists. She let out a tiny frustrated moan, and as he covered the sound with his lips she threw her arms around his neck. Christian stood with her still clinging to him and after unwrapping her arms, he threw her back on the bed where she spun, baring her teeth and glaring. Obviously she felt better;

the bruise had faded quite a bit. Now from the look in her eye, this wasn't going to be gentle, not by a long shot.

Antoinette leapt off the other side of the bed. Her breasts heaved with each short panting breath as she glared at him, begging him and daring him in the same sultry expression. She snagged her bottom lip with her teeth and a tiny crimson drop swelled at the corner of her mouth. He zoned in on the growing bead of blood, quivering with the need to taste it.

Christian growled and his fangs extended to their full delicious length. There were two ways to feed the hungry beast within—blood and sex. And right now it demanded the latter. He dropped into a crouch then leapt, clearing the bed. The force bore them both into the bathroom. His blood-thrall overruled any sliver of control he had left and the only way to stop it now was complete and utter satiation. His . . . and hers.

Antoinette was so caught up in the grips of the blood-thrall she didn't show any signs of fear. Instead she dug her nails hard into his shoulder. He welcomed the pain. Christian snared the crimson droplet at the corner of her mouth and her lips parted, expecting his kiss. Instead, he turned her to face the mirror. He reached around to cup her breasts in both hands, pressing his erection against her ass and watching her expression in the mirror as he squeezed the pert peaks. She sighed and her lashes brushed her cheeks as her lids closed and her head fell back against his shoulder.

"Open your eyes, Antoinette," he whispered in her ear. "I want you to see everything I do to you."

Her eyes flung open, smoky green with arousal as he ran his hand across her stomach heading downward.

Oh God! Antoinette's body screamed with the need for more. He held her eyes in the mirror, his face floating over her left shoulder. There was something in his expression, something animal. One of his hands rested, fingers splayed just under her navel, while his other traveled frustratingly close to her breasts.

Suddenly he yanked away the bandage over her wound. The tape ripped her skin, an instant of pain, so erotically exciting her legs trembled. She waited for the pain but the wound had already healed to two pink puckered scars. And when he ran the tip of his index finger across them, goose bumps rippled on her flesh.

Christian's breath brushed her ear, even hotter than the heat she felt inside. He traced the underside of her breast then moved his fingers in concentric circles coming so close, but never quite touching tip of her nipple. Just when she thought she would go crazy he squeezed her hard nub. The sensation was so intense she almost came again, her hips jerked and her knees buckled. But Christian caught her around the waist and held her upright.

Slowly, when her legs stopped quivering, both his hands traveled south toward the edge of her lace panties. Her breathing froze as he teased the waist elastic and his erection leapt in its confines against her lower back. She spread her legs further apart and Christian's fingers disappeared behind the lace and slid inside. Antoinette fell forward to lean her hands on the vanity counter, her hair falling over her shoulders and obscuring her view. Each maddening flick had her thighs twitching and trembling in time. He gathered her hair into the fist of his free hand as if to see her face while he drove her to the point of insanity . . . and beyond?

Christian removed his hand from between her thighs and ran it over her ass, his body quivering behind her. His eyes were closed when she looked up at his reflection in the mirror; he breathed roughly through his mouth, showing the long gleaming fangs. His eyelids were hooded slits, heat and menace radiating from the deep blue depths.

An animal-like growl rumbled in his chest when she tried to stand upright, and he pushed her forward until her elbows lay on the counter. He held her there while he yanked the fly on his jeans.

"Please . . ." she croaked, the need for him to be inside her almost unbearable. "Hurry!"

In one smooth movement he slid her panties down over the curve of her hips and she kicked them away. She planted her feet wider to give him access but he didn't move. With a frustrated groan she arched her back, pushing her back against his hard warm length. He growled again, and with a hand to steady her he plunged in, all the way. She threw back her head, a cry escaping her throat as he filled her with absolute exquisiteness.

She was helpless. He held her hair in one hand and the other caressed the sensitive flesh at the base of her spine. He withdrew his full length then plunged all the way in again with as much delicious force as the first thrust. She cried out again. They locked eyes in the mirror as he began to thrust with more purpose, slowing building the rhythm. Christian let go of her hair and grabbed her hips with both hands. On each inward thrust, he pulled her toward him—for the first time in her life she didn't care that she had no control.

Pressure started to build as his cock rammed home, hitting the sweet spot high in front, sending explosive sensations slamming into her cervix. He took her so hard and so fast, she rode the waves of pleasure. All of a sudden she reached the crest and fell headlong into incredible crashing waves of ecstasy. Shortly after, Christian shuddered behind her and his weight fell forward onto her back.

The moment he came, Antoinette shook herself out of the dreamlike state she'd been under. The spell was broken— the blood-thrall complete. Through the whole episode she'd had no thought beyond the sex they were having, nothing else had mattered—including why. Her reflection had passion painting a wild flush to her cheeks and across her chest, while her hair was a tumbled mess matching the turmoil of her mind.

Christian pulled up his jeans, the animalistic sheen in his eyes receding to be replaced by his natural blue. As he rebuttoned his fly she ran her gaze over the hairless six-pack stomach, and the natural V curve of his hip that arrowed down to his . . .

Antoinette shook off the last of the thrall and shoved him out of the bathroom, slamming and locking the door on his bewilderment. Then she turned to the mirror, though she could barely stand the sight of herself. How could she have slept with . . . with . . . the enemy? No, not slept with—fucked. He'd put that poison in her blood. It was his fault.

Sex was a form of release, nothing more. She was careful to pick partners who wouldn't come looking for her afterward. Their faceless bodies were nothing more than a means to an end. She didn't need the head-trips that went with relationships. Sometimes after a hunt she craved the release of pent-up tension, but she was always in total control—of both her orgasm and his.

However, this time it was different. She'd felt more than the usual superficial attraction. Even if the blood-thrall had fanned her desire she knew if there had been any other males in the room, even human, she still would have jumped Christian.

Alarm bells clanged in Christian's head. What had happened had been way too intense. He usually had much more control even in the midst of blood-thrall. And he knew better than to get involved with a human—it brought nothing but pain. The last woman he'd formed a more than casual relationship with had betrayed him and left him a hollow, broken shell for decades.

Shaking the bad memories from his head, he knocked quietly on the bathroom door.

"Yes?" she answered from the other side.

"Just checking that you're all right," he said.

"I'm fine." Her tone was crisp and sharp.

"Are you sure? I just want to . . ."

"I said I'm fine." Her don't-fuck-with-me tone rose slightly.

"Fine," he hissed, thinking of no better retort.

Then he crossed to the other door and almost ripped it from the frame as he pulled it open then slammed it behind him.

He could feel Viktor and Sergei's eyes on him as he moved to the bar. Thank God for soundproofing. He poured a large measure of scotch, and downed it in one mouthful. Alcohol was the one thing from his pre-awakened days he could still enjoy, although he needed significantly more to get any effect.

"Your niece is one of the most infuriating females I've ever met," he said to Sergei as he poured a second.

"She can be a handful." Sergei shook his head and chuckled, and then his face grew stony. "But she's also the best I've ever trained, even better than her father. She has a strong will, but in many ways she's rather innocent."

Not if you'd seen what just went on in the next room.

Did they know? It was hard to read Sergei, so he turned his attention to Viktor, who raised a questioning eyebrow. The scotch glass suddenly exploded in his hand.

"Shit!" he said as a large piece wedged itself in his palm, the sharp pain almost a relief.

He pulled it out with a gush of dark blood. Mary rushed forward with a couple of hand towels from the galley and began cleaning up. He took one and wiped his palm. The cuts immediately started to knit—within a few moments there wouldn't even be a scar left to tell the tale.

"Antoinette has never worked with the Aeternus before. It will take some time," Sergei said.

He tried to ignore the strange glances Viktor gave him as he poured a fresh glass of scotch.

"What?" he finally growled when he could take no more.

"Nothing," Viktor said, "nothing at all." But his eyes said differently as they darted to the door then back to Christian.

He knew. *Dammit.* Christian's temper kicked up a notch as he downed the rest of the scotch and poured another. Could this day get any worse? He could smell her scent all over him and his groin twitched in response. Viktor would've smelt it too. Christian could still feel Antoinette in his arms, the texture of her soft skin under his palm, the silky caress of her hair as it'd slipped through his fingers.

He started to get hard all over again and drowned the thoughts with a scotch chaser just as the door opened. Antoinette made a more subdued entrance, a sharp contrast to her last one. Her cheeks were flushed, but she refused to look at him, or anyone else for that matter.

"Are you feeling better?" Sergei asked.

She nodded slowly and shuffled past him to sit at the far end of the sofa by the window before turning to stare out into the inky blackness.

Cerberus jumped up onto the lounge and lay down beside her, placing his head in her lap. Christian threw an accusatory glance in Viktor's direction, but from the expression on his friend's face, he was just as surprised.

"Are you okay?" Christian asked.

No response.

"Antoinette?"

Still no answer, she just continued to stare out the window. When he touched her lightly on shoulder to get her attention, she jolted and Cerberus, picking up her surprise, lifted his head and growled softly.

Antoinette smiled and stroked the dog's fur as she looked at Christian and she whispered, "Good boy—good boy."

The fire in her eyes flared again.

Blue tinged the inky sky, signaling the approach of dawn as the limousine pulled up outside Christian's Manhattan brownstone. His ever-efficient butler, Kavindish, stood waiting at the open front door. Christian still could never work out if the butler had a sixth sense or just impeccable timing.

Christian stepped from the car and looked up at his house. It was good to be home.

"Good morning, sir." Kavindish stepped forward to take Christian's coat. "I trust you had a pleasant trip?"

"Interesting, Kavindish, very interesting." Christian peeled off his gloves and passed them to the butler. "Viktor will be staying with us for a while."

"I anticipated your request, sir. Mr. Dushic's room has already been prepared." Kavindish bowed his head.

"Thank you, Kavindish," Christian said.

"You also have another guest, sir."

Christian frowned—apart from Viktor there was only one other person Kavindish would allow to access his home. Christian sighed and rubbed the back of his head. All he'd wanted was a shower and some rest. "Where is she?"

"In the drawing room, sir." Kavindish snapped his fingers and Susan, the maid, appeared.

As she bent down to pick up his bag, Susan looked up at Christian. "Welcome home, boss."

"Susan," Kavindish said, his tone tinged with disapproval.

She straightened, "Sorry, welcome home, sir." As she turned, she gave Christian an impudent wink and he covered his smile by moving to the drawing room. Female laughter tinkled from behind its closed doors.

Shit! What did she want now? He closed his eyes as his hand hovered over the handle. With a heavy sigh he flung open the door to find the beautiful raven-haired woman on his sofa sandwiched between two semi-naked, blond musclemen.

"Lilijana," he said.

She smiled sweetly from among the heap of arms and legs. "Christian, darling," she said, disentangling herself from the three-way embrace.

He brushed her offered cheek dutifully. "What do you want?" he asked, not in the mood for her usual games.

"Don't look so annoyed, darling. Does a mother need a reason to visit her son?" she asked, her bottom lip sticking out.

"Why are you here, Lilijana?" he asked, keeping his temper in check.

"I've come to town to attend the ball, of course."

"What's wrong with your penthouse?"

"It's being redecorated, darling." She batted her long lashes over her blue eyes. "You wouldn't toss your own mother out on the street this close to dawn, would you?"

"Of course not," Christian ran his hand through his hair.

"Very nice, Lili." Viktor had positioned himself on the sofa between Lilijana's companions. "Where did you find these gorgeous specimens?"

"Viktor, it's been a while." Her eyes narrowed and she turned back to Christian. "What have you boys been up to?"

"We've been in catching up, gambling, and partaking of the nightlife. You know—the usual," Viktor said with a flick of his wrist, his eyes never leaving the male human to his right.

Christian noticed for the first time the two men were identical twins. "Mother, you'd better see to your pets. Viktor looks hungry."

"You only call me Mother when you're really annoyed with me." This time she crossed her arms under her breasts to go with the petulant pout.

He ran his hand through his hair again and dropped his hand when his mother smiled at catching his telltale sign of frustration. Damn, why did she do this to him? "Look— it's been a long trip and daylight is near. I just want to get to bed."

"Fine—you do that, darling. I'll catch up with Viktor." She glanced toward the sofa where he sat running a forefinger across the left twin's lips while the right twin caressed Victor's thigh.

Christian threw him a warning glance, knowing Lilijana all too well. Viktor grinned back and winked. He was no fool.

"Oh, one other thing," Lilijana said, "Your sister is here too Viktor."

Christian had started for the door, but stopped, his heart sinking.

"I'll catch up with Leri later," Viktor said, his fangs gleaming white and ready. "Can I have one? Please?"

Christian shook his head. Better and better, his mother *and* his former lover had descended upon him, and they couldn't have picked a worse time.

He made his way to the second floor and his bedroom, and her perfume warned him before he opened the door—to find Viktor's naked sister draped across his bed.

She smiled and stretched languorously. "Hello, Christian. I'd expected you sooner."

"This is not a good time, Valerica."

"Oh come on, Christian." Her tongue snaked around her forefinger before she ran it across her lower lip.

He'd had more than enough of women and their bloody games for one night. "I mean it. All I want is a shower and sleep," he growled, getting close to the limit of his patience.

"I can wash your back for you." Valerica sat up and smiled.

He walked to the side of the bed and bent so close their noses almost touched. Triumph flooded Valerica's features and she leaned in for his kiss. Christian snagged her discarded lace robe from the floor and took a step back before throwing it at her. Her eyes widened.

"I told you, I'm not in the mood."

Her amber eyes—the same as Viktor's—narrowed. "Very well." She donned the negligee and crawled from the bed, closing the distance between them. "But if you change your mind, you know where to find me."

He dropped his gaze to her willowy figure under the open lacy robe. In the past he would've taken her up on the invitation, but tonight he wanted more of that firm athletic roundness, breasts that overflowed his hands, long platinum hair . . .

His hardness swelled in his jeans. Valerica smiled as she took a step closer and a silken curtain of brown hair slipped across his arm as she rubbed her hand against his crotch.

He grabbed her wrist roughly. "Go and borrow one of Lilijana's toys, Valerica. I'm sure she can spare one if your brother hasn't already worn them out." He stepped away and turned his back to her. The walls shook with the force of the door she slammed behind her.

He unbuttoned his trousers and crossed to the bathroom. *Now for that shower.*

Christian was drying off when Kavindish's familiar knock sounded at his door.

"Come in."

The butler entered carrying a crimson-filled glass on a silver tray.

"Thought you could use a meal before you retire, sir. You looked a bit pale."

"Thank you, Kavindish." Christian took the glass and drank deeply. "Have my other guests retired?"

"Yes, sir."

"Good. Raise me at the usual time—I'll be going out early this evening." Anything to avoid his guests.

9

ᴀʀᴇɴᴀ ᴏ𝖿 ʜᴇʀᴏᴇꜱ ᴀɴᴅ ꜰᴏᴏʟꜱ

It'd been ten years since Antoinette had set foot inside the hallowed halls of the Academy of Parahuman Studies New York campus. Being a child prodigy Antoinette had had offers from several of the specialist training colleges both here and abroad, but she'd chosen New York because it had the best Venator training facilities, which she'd heard were now even better.

Sergei's cane tapped across the marble floor, echoing off the high ornate ceilings of the empty hall. A clanging bell drowned out the sounds of their progress and soon the corridors filled with the buzz of noisy young people of all ages, races, shapes, and colors.

"Sergei—" an ancient voice called above the din.

"Rudolf—so you aren't dead yet?" Sergei answered Antoinette's former instructor.

Rudolf had been ancient when she'd met him as a child and in all this time he hadn't changed one bit. Sergei had told her the old man had looked exactly the same when he and Grigore were boys training under him—before the accident had left Sergei with a severe limp.

"Instructor," she said, bowing formally.

The wizened little man smiled and held out his arms.

"Enough of that—you never did it when you were a student, why start now? Give me a hug."

She smiled back and wrapped her arms around him. He felt fragile, like tissue paper stretched over bone, but she knew from experience how quick and strong he really was. He had been one of her few friends during her time here and the only reason she'd made it through.

He held her at arm's length. "You're looking fit and doing well from all reports."

"You look . . ." she stepped back a little.

"Older," he said, chuckling.

"No," Antoinette said, "just the same actually. Are you sure you're not part parahuman?"

"Not that I'm aware, but I was an orphan." He tapped her arm lightly with his walking stick.

"Well now . . . Sergei Petrescu. What a great pleasure to see you here." A deep soft voice came from behind.

Sergei turned to meet the approaching tall man. He appeared to be in his late thirties, early forties she guessed, and rather attractive with light brown hair and a strong features.

"Lucian," Sergei said in a booming voice. "Lucian Moretti."

The man's face split into a friendly grin. Dark intelligent eyes danced in his chiseled face, and the corners of his generous mouth titled under his almost too-big nose.

"Lucian," Rudolf said, "this is Antoinette, Sergei's niece and a former student here at the Academy."

"The pleasure is all mine." He raised her hand to his lips and brushed her skin with a featherlight touch, the barest of contact. It was an old-fashioned gesture she'd usually find annoying but from him it was flattering.

He clasped Sergei's hand in both of his. "Sergei—it's so good to see you again."

"And you too, Lucian."

"How's the school?"

"Thriving, thanks. We have over three hundred students

in seven grades now and quite a few even look good enough to come here in a few years." Sergei grinned and turned to Antoinette. "Lucian worked for a while under your Uncle Nic in Paris."

Lucian's smile slipped. "I was truly sorry to hear about Nic's passing. He was a good man and taught me so much."

"Thank you." Grief tightened around Sergei's eyes.

"So, are you teaching here?" Antoinette asked, changing to a less painful subject.

"Not really, I'm here on a research grant. But I'm also on the Academy board."

Sergei grinned and gripped Lucian's shoulder. "You were always much better with books than you were with physical training."

"Lucian, would you please show Antoinette the changes we've made since she was here while Sergei and I catch up?" Rudolf said. "I'm sure she'd rather have the company of someone more her own age than two cantankerous old men."

"Speak for yourself," Sergei said as he wrapped an arm around the Rudolf's shoulder. "I'm not old."

"That sounds like a marvelous idea." Lucian grinned. "It'd be my honor."

She accepted his offered arm without hesitation, feeling instantly comfortable. Sergei and Rudolf shuffled off in the opposite direction, their heads already bent together in discussion.

"They'll be at it for hours," she said, watching them walk away, each leaning on his walking stick. She turned to look up at her guide. "Thanks for babysitting."

Lucian chuckled. "Are you kidding? I get to escort the famous Antoinette Petrescu."

"I'm not famous." She waved off his compliment and glanced away to cover the small pleased grin.

"You're the youngest Venator to graduate the Academy at the tender age of sixteen. Half the trophies in cabinet have your name on it. And every kid that graduates Venator train-

ing has tried to beat the record score you set in the Trials."
He leaned closer and whispered. "You're famous, and I'm
using you to improve my image."

She blushed, something she was unaccustomed to doing.
However, his image didn't seem in need of improvement—
students greeted him warmly by name as they passed in the
halls and he waved to them in return.

"So where shall we start?" he asked.

"How about the new training arena? I've heard it's the
most advanced in the world—I'd love to take a look," she
said.

"Well, you're in luck—they're running an exercise today.
Would you like to observe?"

"That'd be great."

"This way then." He took her left elbow and led her out of
the main hall.

Students, books, the warren of classrooms and training
rooms, the familiarity of it all brought back memories and
not all good. She hadn't exactly been popular here with her
single-minded focus.

Lucian led her through the halls of the Academy until
they reached an area that hadn't existed when Antoinette
had been a student. They passed through a large set of doors
and the scent of a dreniac hit her. In a barred room paced a
small hunched, twitchy figure in a worn dark-gray hoodie
with faded lettering that looked something like BIATCH on
the back. She turned and hissed at them, fangs showing, but
the bars were plated in silver and the creature wouldn't come
any nearer. As she turned away, she could have sworn the
dreniac winked at her, but it must've just been a twitch.

"It's a little early in the year for holding any Trials isn't
it?" Antoinette asked.

Lucian shrugged noncommittally as they made their way
up the stairs at the far end of the corridor.

They only used real dreniacs in the Trial; it was the final
rite of passage for a Venator. The initiates had two chances

to make their first kill, or they failed forever. Maybe the dreniac was for someone's second-chance test.

The arena was huge, roughly the size of a national ice hockey rink and glassed in like an observation area above an operating theater. Half a dozen rows of red flip-up seats circled a well-lit pit in the center. Halfway down the length of the arena a group of teenagers sat around, joking and laughing among themselves. The kids didn't even notice as Lucian led her to the front row.

Antoinette got her first look at the arena floor twenty feet below. It looked like a movie set of an abandoned warehouse, reminding her of her last dreniac encounter. Her hand automatically covered the area where she'd been wounded. She could hardly believe the infected gashes of only a few days ago were now all healed as was her black eye. However, that train of thought led her to somewhere she wasn't prepared to go yet. She would eventually have to deal with what happened between her and Christian, just not now.

"Impressed?" Lucian asked, bringing her back to the present with a start.

"Yes, very."

Lucian pointed to a small glassed-in area on the other side of the arena where a small humanoid shape moved. "It has state-of-the-art lighting and with the atmospheric effects controlled from the booth up there we can do any setting from a foggy night to rain, or set it up like this for an indoor hunt." He sounded like a kid at his first baseball game. "They also control the video and audio feeds into the observation gallery."

Antoinette noticed speakers and large flat video displays placed around the stadium. Suddenly the screen filled with the image of a sandy-haired youth with movie-star good-looks. He swaggered through the opening gate at the far end of the field, whistling to himself and looked familiar.

Antoinette could almost taste the excitement in the air.

"It's about to start, let's take our seats," Lucian suggested.

A cheer went up from his classmates, but he couldn't seem to hear them. The observation windows must be sound-proofed, which made perfect sense. The boy shielded his eyes and searched the upper area, grinning when he finally saw his fellow students gesturing madly at him. He gave them a cocky half-wave salute.

"Mark is this year's top student in the Necrodreniac Venator class, trained at your uncle's school," Lucian said.

Of course—that's where she'd seen him—two years ago. He's been a cocky little shit back then too.

"This is the first exercise of this class." Lucian winked.

Antoinette smiled, knowing what he meant; the young hotshot was about to find himself on his ass.

A buzz came from the speakers above them and a dis-embodied voice announced. "The exercise begins in three minutes. Would the participant please make his way to the designated starting point?"

A hush fell over the audience as the boy swaggered to his position in the center of the pit and blew a cheeky kiss to someone in the gallery. A blond girl with large hoop ear-rings leaned forward to return it.

From up here the setup below looked much like a maze of wooden crates and cardboard cartons. Visibility would be difficult for the exercise participant, but those above had a clear view thanks to the height and the large screens.

The image changed from the close-up on the student's face to a shot from behind and further away. Antoinette no-ticed the cameras set up around the pit at differing levels allowing the action to be shown from many angles. Very high-tech.

The lights dimmed further as the boy stopped. He wore jeans and a leather Academy bomber jacket over a white T-shirt. Odd choice. He seemed to prefer looking good than wearing something more practical. The boy began rotating his head, hopping up and down and shaking out his arms and legs to loosen them.

Antoinette had a little chuckle to herself. He may think

he was ready but he was in for a rude shock. The student who showed the most potential in the class was always the first through an exercise to teach the rest that talent was not always a guarantee of success. The Academy tradition of making an example of the best and brightest was well-kept from the new students.

Antoinette had been top in her class too. Already unpopular with the other students because of her aloofness, the fall she suffered in front of them had been the most humiliating experience she'd ever had. But it taught her to never get too overconfident and never take anything for granted.

Some of the screens showed two different views—including an infrared shot. A door on the other side of the pit opened and a dark figure slipped inside. She couldn't tell if it was male or female as it wore a jacket with the hood pulled down low, but from the speed and the way it moved it definitely wasn't human. Then she realized that it was the same hoodie with faded lettering she saw the dreniac in the cage wearing.

She sat forward in her chair. Surely they wouldn't put an unseasoned boy in with a real dreniac—that would be insanity—that would be murder. She tried to stand but Lucian put a hand on her forearm.

"I thought you said this was his first time," she whispered.

"He'll be fine." Lucian leaned his face closer to hers. "Trust me."

Trust. She'd never trusted anyone except her family, and he was a perfect stranger. Yet— Something in his tone and his expression made her relax. She felt she'd known him longer than the little time they'd spent together. And surely they wouldn't let the boy come to any harm this early in the term. She sat back in her seat, her stomach still churning with nerves.

The boy's face loomed larger than life on the screen above the arena, his smug half-smile firmly in place as he indifferently twisted his wooden bokken. Wooden—it wasn't even a real weapon and he was facing a dreniac. Lucian leaned forward as the dark shape stepped from the shadows a few feet from the boy. Antoinette held her breath.

It was female with the typical twitchiness of an addict dying for a death-fix. The boy's smile hadn't slipped—in fact it grew even cockier as he casually fell into position.

The dreniac hissed, showing her long white fangs and before the boy, or anyone else, was ready, she attacked. Antoinette tensed and shocked gasps rose from the other students as the female slammed the boy on his back. Sitting on his chest, she opened a shallow cut on his cheek with one of her long talonlike fingernails and, with a purr of pure pleasure, licked the blood.

The boy's smug grin disappeared, replaced by a mix of horror and revulsion. The dreniac laughed and leapt away, disappearing behind the cartons again. She obviously wanted to play with her prey before she finally killed him.

The boy rose to his feet and picked up his wooden training sword. The tip shook ever so slightly in his white-knuckled grip. He touched his fingers to his cheek and brought them away, his face growing pale as he gazed at the smear of blood. Then his expression steeled, out of fear or anger, Antoinette couldn't be sure.

The boy shook off the jacket, the first smart thing she'd seen him do, but it snagged on his wrist ruining the effect. He flapped his arm impatiently. Antoinette sighed. Fear would've been so much better for focusing his instincts— anger would only cloud his mind and make him prone to stupid mistakes.

This time the boy went much more carefully, cocking his head from side to side, listening to locate his elusive attacker. His grip on the wooden bokken was rigid and stiff, his lips were drawn into a tight thin line. He was too tense.

The dark figure circled behind him. Antoinette wanted to shout out and warn the boy as the dreniac climbed the crates to his right. He turned, from the screen close-up Antoinette noticed his nostrils flair and he lifted his head. He had the scent. Good.

He took a step toward the crates but the dreniac threw an empty soda can over to the far side of the room. It clattered loudly and the boy turned his head toward the noise. He seemed torn—Antoinette knew from experience his instincts were telling him to follow the scent. He ignored them and turned toward the sound. The dreniac launched from above, landing on his back. She drove her head forward and sunk her fangs into his shoulder. The boy screamed—a damp patch had formed in his jeans near the groin and a crimson stain spread across his white T-shirt.

The watching class gasped in unison. Antoinette searched the arena for the guardians to intercede before the dreniac killed him, but there didn't seem to be any—the boy was alone. She gripped the arms of the seat and started to rise but Lucian's hand stilled her.

Again the dreniac released him and disappeared. Now the boy was really afraid, the bokken shook visibly in his hand, but his fear had passed straight to terror.

His eyes darted left and right and after every step he'd turn and check behind. Sweat beaded on his upper lip and his forehead, blood seeped into his shirt and Antoinette knew he was lost. Next time the dreniac attacked, the boy would be dead. She had to stop it.

Before she could move the dreniac appeared to his right, disarmed him and bent his head to expose his throat. He was so frozen in his fear he didn't even try to fight back. Antoinette wrenched her arm away, looking for a way to get into the arena. Then the lights came up. The dreniac leaned forward—Antoinette placed both hands on the observation glass, helpless.

10

Lessons Learned

The female dreniac pushed back the hood, the typical Necrodrenia twitchiness gone, and she smoothed her short blond hair as she glanced up at the students above and waved. Instead of opening the boy's throat, she ripped away his shirt and licked his wounds, sealing them. A cheer went up among the students.

The two figures left the arena below and a minute later only the female joined the rest of the class in the gallery area.

"Is he okay?" asked the girl with the hoop earrings.

"He'll be fine, his wounds have already healed." The female turned to the rest of the class. "But it could've been much worse if this was more than an exercise. What did we learn from today?" she asked the class. "Can you tell me what Mark did wrong?"

Hands went up quickly and students started calling out their answers to their teacher.

"He was overconfident," one student said.

"Very good," replied the teacher, "but what else?"

A heated discussion started among the students, and the teacher moderated where required.

"I thought she was a real dreniac," Antoinette whispered to Lucian.

He leaned closer. "She's good isn't she?"

"Yes—but—the dreniac scent?" Antoinette eyed the woman. "Even now, she still smells like one."

"Some of my finest work." He smiled and looked at the teacher. "Try again and tell me what you really smell."

She closed her eyes and drew in the heavy scent of Necrodrenia. "It has a slight metallic undertone, almost . . . like ozone."

"Most humans don't pick that up but it becomes more apparent with time. You've got a really good nose," Lucian said. "I manufactured the false scent by accident in the lab, as a byproduct of an experiment I was doing with Aeternus blood. The odor was so close that she," he nodded his head in the direction of the pretend-dreniac-come-teacher, "asked if she could use it to make her training exercises more realistic. I agreed. She's one of the best teachers we've had here since—well, a very long time."

"He let his temper get the better of him," one of the students yelled out above the rest, drawing Antoinette's attention back to the discussion going on. "Excellent," the teacher said. "But what else should he have done? What is a Venator's most valuable defense mechanism?"

The students muttered and mumbled, blank looks on their faces.

"His instincts," Antoinette whispered under her breath, willing one of the kids to say it.

The teacher's head swiveled in Antoinette's direction. "That's right—could you repeat that for the class?"

Antoinette sank into her seat until Lucian nudged her with his elbow.

She leaned forward and clasped her hands together as eager faces stared in her direction. "The boy should've listened more carefully to his instincts and not let his head overrule what his gut was telling him."

"Correct." The teacher's face broke into a wide smile and she turned to the rest of the class. "Always trust your instincts! They're your natural defense against danger, so use them. In today's society, most humans are taught to ignore their instincts—you must unlearn this now."

Antoinette sat back and the Aeternus teacher pierced her with a sharp, probing gaze. "And let's all thank our mystery guest for her insightful answer."

As the polite clapping started, Lucian stood with flourish. "Ladies and Gentlemen—Ms. Antoinette Petrescu."

An excited buzz rose from the students.

"This is a special treat," the teacher said, turning a smile on Antoinette. "Maybe we can get Miss Petrescu to give us the benefit of her experience."

The class clapped and cheered enthusiastically. Antoinette held out her hands and shook her head, trying to beg off.

Lucian grinned and leaned forward. "Go on—they'll learn so much from you, even if it's nothing more than how difficult a journey it can be."

"I have a feeling I've just been set up," she said.

"I'm sorry." His brow creased with worry. "I didn't think you'd mind—we can leave."

The students seemed so excited, and Lucian so contrite, how could she possibly say no?

She sighed. "Okay."

Cheers and whistles erupted from the students as Antoinette rose to join the group. She shook hands with the teacher. "Sorry for taking over your class."

The teacher smiled. "It's my pleasure, it's not often my kids get a chance to learn from someone of your caliber."

"What would you like to know?" Antoinette asked the fresh, beaming faces. She was used to teaching a class or two, but she usually took the younger ones.

The teacher opened the discussion. "What was the most important lesson you learned after you left the Academy?"

"That I was nowhere near as prepared as I thought I was when it came to the reality of hunting."

"But you were the highest-scoring graduating student in the last century," a dark-eyed girl in the front row said.

"Yes, but in the real world you must rely on only yourself. There are no teachers to keep you safe, no guardians to step in when a dreniac gets difficult. The best way to go in is armed with as much knowledge about your target as you can possibly get. Look for their weaknesses and exploit them to your advantage. Always remember they are stronger, faster, and more ready to kill than you are, so any advantage you have can tilt the balance in your favor."

A kid in front leaned forward, bright glittery eyes zoning with intensity on her face. Something about the kid was off. "How many dreniac excisions have you performed in your career?"

"Over a hundred and forty."

His gaze wandered down to her chest and then back to her face, his sly grin putting her on guard. He was definitely trouble.

"Do you get to choose your own missions now?" a girl at the back asked.

"Yes. But during my probation period I was assigned to missions that suited my experience and I often had an observer along. Still there's little leeway for error—one mistake and you're dead. You all know the statistics—over one-third of you will not pass training. For those of you that do, over half of you will either quit or die within the first probationary year. This is a dangerous business. Only the best become career Venators."

"Have you ever thought of taking on another Venator as a hunting partner?" the love-struck girl with the hoop earrings asked. "Wouldn't two be better than one?"

"Unfortunately, not always. My brother is . . . was my tech, but I hunted alone. Besides the fact I don't play well with others, it's easy to get a partner or yourself killed in a double attack. Don't get me wrong, there are some very successful hunting teams out there. It's just not for me."

"I heard your probation was much shorter than normal?" the next kid asked.

"Yes—nine months. By that time I had proven my skills enough for them to start letting me choose my own missions, but I had to work really hard for it."

A collective murmur rippled through the kids. They seemed impressed.

The teacher stepped forward raising her hands. "The usual probation period is two years—only under exceptional circumstances is it any shorter."

"How many did you kill during your probation?" the creepy kid asked.

She could feel him mentally undressing her and swallowed a rather snarky response. No use dropping to his level.

"As many as I was assigned," she replied.

He knew he was getting to her. His tongue darted over his lips and his grin deepened. "I hear some Venators like to fuck after a kill, do you?"

She kept her expression neutral, but her fingernails bit into her palms. Antoinette tried not to react to his obvious goading, partly because it was true. Sometimes, she needed to reaffirm her humanity with sex after a hunt was done, but always with some random bar pickup she wouldn't have to explain things to. As she tried to formulate an answer Lucian appeared at her side, taking her elbow.

"I think that's enough for today." Then he leaned toward the creepy kid and his tone lowered. "And that was your last chance—you're out."

"You can't kick me out, you're not even a teacher," the boy sneered.

"No—but I'm on the board. I know you're already on probation and you've been warned several times. The board will back me on this."

The boy jumped to his feet and came nose to nose with Lucian, neither one backing down. Finally, the student broke off, snorting his contempt as he made his way to the exit.

"Please thank Ms. Petrescu for her time." The teacher's voice was just as tightly controlled as Lucian's had been.

The rest of the students rose and made their way to the

exit after him, talking in hushed tones, throwing glances over their shoulders at Lucian as they left.

"I appreciate you giving the class your time," the teacher said. "But I'm so sorry about that." She squeezed Antoinette's hand in both of hers then she followed her students.

Antoinette sucked air back into her lungs and let out a shaky breath. "There's something really wrong with that boy—he'll never have the discipline to be a Venator."

"I know. We've known for a while now but needed just one more demerit to get rid of him." Lucian sounded a little sorry, but then he brightened. "Let me make it up to you. Are you staying nearby?"

She nodded.

"Good, I'll buy you dinner."

Eventually it always came to this, men. She waved him off. "You don't have to do that, I've dealt with worse before."

"Please! It's the least I can do. Besides, I know a really wonderful little Italian restaurant."

"I don't think it's a good idea." Just when she was really starting to enjoy his company.

Lucian straightened. "Oh—hang on. I don't mean that kind of dinner. All innocent, I promise. I just don't often get to have dinner with someone famous. Please. I promise to be the perfect gentleman."

Her hands relaxed and she gave him what she hoped looked like a smile. "All right then, that'd be nice."

After a few red wines and some incredible pasta Lucian walked Antoinette along the almost empty streets back to her hotel. She felt relaxed for the first time in days. Thanks to Lucian. He'd been true to his word, no passes, not even flirting.

He was smart, funny, and had a way of instantly putting her at ease. She didn't feel like a fish out of water around him and he seemed to genuinely enjoy her company instead of just looking for a way into her pants.

"So—did you like Gino's?" he asked.

"Yes, very m—" A rough hand closed over her mouth from behind and a cold sharpness pressed against the side of her throat.

"Don't scream or your boyfriend gets a bullet in the ribs," a harsh voice growled in her ear.

Antoinette chanced a sideways glance. Lucian was flanked by two hooded figures, both wearing sunglasses. One held a gun to Lucian's side. She sensed more behind them and inwardly cursed. She'd been so lulled by the dinner and her companion she'd let her guard down. But she needed to assess the situation before acting or she may get Lucian hurt . . . or worse.

"Back this way," said the one squeezing tight on her upper arm. There was something familiar about him but she couldn't quite put her finger on it.

They were led back to a darkened alley. Obviously the men had been waiting there for potential victims.

The last thing she needed to do now was panic or lose her temper. This situation called for a cool head and clear thinking.

The alley hooked around to the right so they couldn't be seen from the main street. Lights hung on the walls of the flanking buildings, but most were either broken or flickering dangerously close to blowing. Debris littered the alley and it stank of stale booze and urine, a home away from home for a Venator.

The men whispered among themselves, but Antoinette couldn't make out what they were saying.

"My wallet is in my coat pocket," Lucian said. "You can take it all, just let us go."

Antoinette glanced his way, his voice had a slight tremor but he showed no outward signs of fear. The hooded figure to his right laughed, pressing the gun harder against Lucian's ribs. However the gunman had a slipshod grip on the weapon and she'd easily be able to disarm him if their positions were reversed.

There were five of them, their faces obscured by either sunglasses or ski masks under hooded jackets.

"Come on dude, show us what she's got. Let's see her tits," one of the other attackers said.

The masked mugger pinned her against a dirty wall and ripped open her jacket with one hand. Underneath she wore a silk shirt over a loose skirt. He grabbed her left breast roughly with his knife hand, the handle bit into her flesh and she tried not to flinch away.

"Hey!" Lucian yelled as he lurched forward and was rewarded with a punch to the mouth then another to the gut. He doubled over, spitting out blood, which was dark in the dim light.

"C'mon, dude, are we gonna do this or what?" the gunman said.

One of the men became twitchy, moving rapidly from one foot to the other, giggling almost hysterically. She tried to move but was spun around and shoved harder against the wall face-first. The brickwork bit into her cheek as her jacket was yanked roughly off her back.

A scuffle broke out behind her and was silenced by two loud meaty thumps. Her attacker turned her back around to face him and she took the opportunity to glance at Lucian. He hung slumped between two men; one of them lifted his head by a fist full of hair at the crown. A dark trickle ran from Lucian's right brow down his cheek. They let go and his head lolled forward again.

A sneering masked face blocked Lucian from her view and she raised her eyes to meet his. There was something familiar about those eyes. He lowered the knife, bringing it level with her belly, then began to cut the buttons from her shirt one at a time.

"Be nice or we'll slit your throat before that stuck-up professor," his low voice growled in her ear. "Alive or dead—you choose. Makes no difference to me what you are when I fuck you."

11

Bᴌacᴋ Tιᴇꜱ αnd Aᴛᴛιᴛuᴅᴇ

Antoinette stilled. The way he said "fuck." She took a closer look at his eyes and his grin widened in the same snide way. It was the rude little prick from this afternoon. And he was even more stupid than she'd first thought—taking on a fully trained Venator with just one gun and a knife. Well, this was all to her advantage.

"Ooh, yeah," she purred, relaxing her body against him. "All that death is such a turn-on, isn't it?"

She and Lucian weren't random victims—these men had been waiting for them. The boy froze, her response confusing him, and then he chuckled.

"I'm going to make you watch while I fuck your little friend, Professor," the boy said. "Lift his head so he can see."

The man without the gun yanked Lucian's head back by his hair again. Lucian's eyes narrowed on her attacker, burning with helpless fury.

"Do I get to do all of you?" she asked.

"Yeah, baby," the nervous giggler said and let out another hyena-like laugh.

"Oh, wow," she breathed and her eyes dropped to the gun held loosely at Lucian's side then back up to his face. He glanced at it quickly, then nodded slightly. When the time was right Lucian would make a move for it.

"Sure, baby. If that's what you want." The creep leered. "But me first."

He unzipped his fly and dropped his pants then braced himself against the wall with his free hand.

"I'm so hot." Antoinette's shirt lay open to her waist—buttonless. She shucked it off and lifted her skirt high around her waist. "Touch me."

His eyes dropped between her thighs and ran his tongue over his thin lips. "I'm gonna need both hands for this."

He passed the knife to the giggler who was almost bursting with excitement.

Antoinette took his hand and ran it up her inner thigh to her panties. She swallowed the burning bile creeping up her throat as his fingers kneaded her flesh while she grasped his straining erection and lowered her hand to encircle his heavy balls.

"Yeah, that's it, baby," he moaned and dropped his head to her shoulder.

Just before his fingers reached her underwear, she clasped her thighs together. He jerked his head up and she smiled sweetly. He looked down and tried to tug his hand free of thigh muscles trained to hold her weight while hanging upside down on a rope. She had him right where she wanted him. If he tried to move his other hand away from the wall he'd overbalance. He was hers now and she watched the realization dawn in his eyes.

His stiff flesh shrunk quickly under her hand as she squeezed. His eyes widened, the nervous smile slipping fully from his lips. She increased the pressure and he let out a heavy groan and his buddies cheered still thinking he was enjoying himself.

He tried to pull away from her but she held him tight and gripped harder. Large eyes bugged out of his head, tears streamed down his cheek, and a strangled cry rattled in his throat. She gave one final crushing clench. Something popped and his screams pierced the alley as he dropped to his knees with his hand still trapped in the viselike grip of her thighs.

The other men froze, unsure of what was happening, just as she'd hoped. Lucian took advantage of their surprise by heaving backward, pulling the two holding him off balance and crashing them into the one behind. The armed attacker dropped the gun and Lucian sent it skittering down a nearby drain with a sideways sweep of his foot.

Now that the gun was out of the picture, Antoinette held all the aces. She twisted her lower body sharply to the left and chopped down with her right hand, snapping his wrists. She relaxed and he flopped to his side and pulled his knees to his chest. Tears and snot smeared across his face, mingling with the filth on the ground.

The skirt fell to cover her legs again, but she yanked it off—it would only encumber her movement. Lucian backed away from the others to stand by her side. Loose and ready for attack he picked up her discarded silk shirt. At first she thought he was going to give it to her, but he began to wind one end around his fist.

With student-boy out of action the other four stood uncertain until the giggler took off back down the alley, no longer giggling. His desertion seemed to spur the others into action. The three of them looked at each other and, as one, ran toward Antoinette and Lucian.

With all of her might she kicked the side of the knee of the first, busting his leg with an audible crunch. He dropped to the ground, instantly out of action. The one to the far right lunged at Lucian, who dodged away from the blade in his attacker's hand. He wrapped her silk shirt around the wrist of his opponent's knife arm and pinned it behind his back. Lucian then smashed him face-first into the brick wall, opening the thug's cheek and nose.

Antoinette pulled back her arm and punched the last one full in the face. His lips burst open like ripe plums spraying blood across Antoinette's chest. He fell to his knees at her feet and she brought her knee up to connect with his chin. The audible crunch of breaking teeth preceded the sound of his skull slamming into the pavement behind him. He lay sprawled and unconscious among old newspaper and discarded burger wrappers, his ruined face gurgling with each breath.

"Duck!" Lucian picked up a dustbin lid and threw it like a Frisbee. She lowered and metal whizzed overhead and hit something behind her. Antoinette turned to see a knife skittering away from the man with the busted knee who was now dazed on the ground. He'd been close enough to jam that blade into her back. Lucian had saved her life.

He took off his jacket and wrapped it around her blood spattered semi-nakedness.

"Thank you," she said pulling the jacket tighter. Now that the danger was over the adrenaline ebbed and cold seeped into her bones instead. She suppressed a shiver.

Lucian wrapped his arm around her shoulders and glanced at the groaning attackers. His face split into a cheeky grin. "So—want to be my date for the CHaPR party?"

The Hilton Grand Ballroom swarmed with representatives of the parahuman races, all in attendance for the formal conclusion of the CHaPR conference.

Valerica clung to Christian's arm as they entered the packed room while Viktor patted the hand Lilijana rested in the crook of his elbow. The ballroom held a sea of black and white—with the males in tuxedos and most of the women wearing either black or white gowns.

Christian leaned in to his friend. "There's Sir Roger."

Viktor followed his direction and nodded at the real reason Viktor and Christian had rushed back to New York. Intel had received a tip that an assassination attempt could be made tonight on the human CHaPR ambassador. Christian and Viktor were there to keep an eye on the ambassador and represent the Department.

"I see we aren't the only ones playing nursemaid tonight," Viktor said, his eyes fixed off to the left.

"Hmmm," Christian said. "Oberon, the head of Personal Security."

"I heard he got bumped from the Violent Crimes Unit down to this babysitting gig."

"Yeah, poor bastard, such a waste. Apparently it wasn't pretty either."

As if sensing they were discussing him, the large man turned his head and met Christian's eyes, his heavy brow knitting.

"Uh-oh, we've been made," Viktor said.

The large bear of a man lumbered across the room.

"Laroque," Oberon's deep voice rumbled. "I trust we aren't going to have a problem."

"Not if you keep out from under foot," Christian returned.

Oberon's frown deepened. "I'm here to do a job, just like you."

Viktor stepped between the two of them. "We're all here representing the Department. Let's not make any of us look stupid. Okay?"

"Humph," Oberon muttered, and with one last scowl turned on his heel and marched away in ground-eating strides. Everyone seemed to sense him coming and opened a path before him.

"I can see Oberon hasn't graduated charm school since I saw him last," Viktor said.

Christian snuffed. "If anything, he's worse. We've butted heads over cases before, he's beyond stubborn."

Lilijana turned to Valerica. "Sounds like someone else I know."

Christian scowled when Valerica giggled. He'd almost forgotten about the women.

A ripple of movement parted the crowded room as Akentia, dressed in signature white, made her way toward them with full entourage in tow. Christian bowed in the formal greeting of royalty as did the others in his group. This was an official event and all deference would be shown to the closest thing they had to the head of their society since the Treaty prohibited any ruling monarch.

"It's good to see you all here," she said. "Lilijana, it has been too long."

"Yes it has, majesty." Lilijana kissed the royal ring on the princess's outstretched hand.

She turned her attention to Viktor. "I see you've reunited with your sister."

The twins each kissed the ring in turn, though Viktor couldn't help giving her a cheeky wink. Akentia's lips twitched.

"Christian." The princess held her hand out to him. "A word."

"Yes, majesty." He took it and kissed the ring as the others had and she led him away a few steps.

Akentia put her full lips to his ear. "There is death in the air tonight, be on your guard."

The princess was a known clairvoyant, though her power was greatly diminished from the ancient royalty of old.

"Thank you, majesty," he said. "We are taking precautions."

"Good to know," she said, and with a flick of her wrist she dismissed him and summoned her entourage. With one last nod at Christian she moved off into the crowd.

"What was that about," Viktor whispered.

"She's sensed something and wants us to be on our guard," Christian answered.

"Lilijana!" Sir Roger's booming voice cut off any further conversation as they turned toward him. His round fleshy face split into a wide grin as he shuffled his bulky frame in their direction. "You look more beautiful every time I see you." His breath wheezed heavily. "I missed you at the conference sessions this year." He pressed his liverlike lips to the back of her hand.

Her mouth tilted, but only Christian saw the revulsion behind her forced smile. "You know how they just bore me to tears. I've got much better things to do than sit around listening to a bunch of stuffy old men and women arguing about things beyond my silly little head." She waved her hand in the air.

"Ah—how easy it is to forget that you're more than just a slip of a girl." The ambassador patted her hand.

"Oh, Sir Roger Wilberforce-Smythe—are you flirting with me?" She tittered, playfully tapping his chest with the tips of her manicured nails.

"You can't blame an old man for trying," Sir Roger said and turned to grasp Christian's hand. "And it's good to see you again, Laroque." His gazed flicked to Valerica and his fleshy smile deepened. "I see you have brought the best-looking ladies with you to the ball."

"Thank you, Ambassador." Valerica's smile widened and she clutched Christian's arm.

Sir Roger hardly seemed to hear her as he stared over their shoulder. "Hmm . . . looks like you might have some competition, ladies."

Christian followed the ambassador's gaze and his breath caught low in his throat. Antoinette stood at the entrance, a vision in a sleeveless royal blue and silver Chinese gown. Her blond locks were piled on top of her head with silken ringlets curling around her face and kissing the back of her neck, all held in place with what looked like a pair of ornate silver chopsticks.

She turned around to pass her coat over the check-in counter and Christian's collar tightened around his throat. The dress left very little to the imagination, clinging to her body in all the right places. A split in the filmy material ran up the length of her right leg and Christian caught a flash of black lace high on her thigh as she moved. He'd bet his next warm meal she had a weapon strapped high on that thigh and the split was to give her easy access.

Everyone in the room turned to stare as Lucian Moretti took her arm and guided her into the room, a flash of color disappearing into a black sea.

12

A Tango with Danger

Antoinette lacked any moisture to lick her lips, which was just as well—this lipstick had cost a fortune. So many people gaping at her: her stomach went round and round like a washer and her heart hammered double time in her chest. Crowds had never been her favorite thing.

Lucian patted the hand she'd hooked through the crook of his arm and she managed a shaky smile.

"They aren't going to eat you," Lucian whispered in her ear.

"I shouldn't have listened to that stupid salesgirl and bought this dress," she whispered out of the side of her mouth. "Everyone else is wearing black and white."

"Nonsense, you look beautiful."

She looked up at him, screwing her nose. "I stick out like a sore thumb."

"And I'm the envy of the entire room." Lucian's infectious chuckle chased away some of the knots in her stomach. "Every man here wants to be where I am right now and every woman wishes she were you."

She gave him her best attempt at a smile. He snagged a couple of glasses from a passing drinks waiter and handed one to her.

She shook her head.

"Go on—it'll make you feel better."

What the hell. She smiled and took a large swallow—the bubbles tickled all the way down to calm the last of her butterflies.

"That's my girl," Lucian said. "Come, I want to introduce you to the ambassador."

He took her arm and led her further into the room. Antoinette missed a step when she looked up and saw Christian standing among a group of people. Lucian caught her elbow and steadied her before guiding her toward them.

Christian was striking in a black tuxedo jacket over a black shirt and bloodred bow tie. Classically dressed and yet not. The tall woman on his arm in a stunning black dress flicked strangely familiar amber eyes over Antoinette as they approached. Warmth tickled her face as she met his eyes for the first time since their heated encounter on his plane.

"You're looking very lovely tonight, Antoinette," Viktor said, bending over her hand. His long silken blond hair fell over his shoulders. He wore a black, thigh-length, Asian-influenced jacket—still the image of a manga hero.

"Blue suits you," Christian said softly as he followed Viktor's lead—his lips burning the back of her hand. Her face heated even more and her gaze dropped to his feet. She was so out of her element here.

"Ah—this must be Sergei's niece. I was talking about you with my assistant Andrew this afternoon." The ambassador's voice was as large as the man himself. Sir Roger scanned the room. "Where is that fool? Anyway—no matter. Knew your father, you know. And your mother."

The familiar hollow pang stung at the mention of her parents, but Viktor distracted her by introducing the woman possessively clutching Christian's arm.

"Antoinette, this is my sister, Valerica."

No wonder those eyes looked so familiar.

Valerica greeted her with a condescending arch of a perfect eyebrow. In fact, everything about her was perfect—

with her full mouth, almond-shaped amber eyes and honey brown straight hair sweeping her lean supermodel shoulders, she could have stepped straight out of *Vogue* or *Elle*. Apart from Viktor's dyed blond hair, the siblings were the spitting image of each other.

"How do you do?" Antoinette held out her hand.

Valerica regarded her coolly and then turned away on the pretense of greeting someone else.

Viktor patted the hand of the woman at his side. "And this is Lilijana—Christian's mother."

Antoinette was taken aback; her gaze flicked to the silent Christian, the resemblance was amazing. Lilijana had the same jet black hair and sharp blue eyes, which narrowed as she ran them over Antoinette from head to toe. Antoinette had the feeling she'd just failed some important test. Christian stepped back a little. Antoinette felt his piercing stare still on her but she refused to even look in his direction.

Why wouldn't he speak?

Viktor caught her eye and winked, she couldn't stop the corners of her mouth from twitching.

"Is your uncle coming tonight?" Sir Roger asked.

"I'm afraid not, sir," she said. "He isn't comfortable at these type of events."

"Disappointing, I would've liked to have caught up with him." But Sir Roger seemed more relieved than disappointed.

A dark-haired, bearded man came up from behind the ambassador and placed a hand on the large man's red-sashed shoulder.

"There you are." Sir Roger slapped the newcomer on the back with enough force to send the man forward a step. "This is my assistant, Andrew Williams."

The man gave the group a tight agitated smile and leaned forward to whisper in Sir Roger's ear.

The ambassador nodded. "Well—must go and circulate—do my duty. Enjoy yourselves."

The hefty man moved off through the growing crowd,

stopping to greet various people as he went and there seemed to be a huge mental sigh of relief from those around her.

Antoinette caught movement out of the corner of her eye. Someone gestured frantically in their direction and Lucian groaned.

"Please excuse me; I have something I must attend to." He took Antoinette's hand and whispered, "I'll only be a moment."

Antoinette felt the heat of Christian's stare from where she stood, and she wasn't the only one to notice.

"Shouldn't we mingle too?" Valerica said, piercing Antoinette with a challenging glare.

Christian's brow creased. "Viktor?"

"You go ahead. I'll wait here with the lovely Ms. Petrescu." Viktor took her hand and brought it to his lips. "We can't leave her standing here all alone. That would be rude." The last comment he addressed to his sister who tossed her head.

Christian said nothing but his face darkened as Valerica clutched tighter on his arm.

Antoinette gave Viktor's hand a gentle squeeze of thanks. Lilijana took Christian's other arm and the three of them moved off together.

"You're looking much better than the last time we saw each other," Viktor said, releasing her fingers when they were alone.

"Yes. My wound has healed completely thanks to Christian's blood poultice. Even my black eye is gone." Her eyes gravitated to where Christian greeted some dignitaries. Valerica stared back at her and ran her hand over his shoulder then whispered to Lilijana.

Antoinette took another sip from her champagne glass and turned to Viktor. "Your sister doesn't like me much."

"My sister is in love with Christian, always has been. And she sees you as a threat."

"Why?"

"You have Christian's attention, therefore you're a threat."

"He hardly even acknowledged me. I don't see what she has to worry about."

"Ah, you see that's why she's worried. If he had made a fuss over you or was openly flattering, she'd be fine. My sister has been pining after Christian for centuries, and can read him like a book." He leaned closer. "And she is ever hopeful he'll finally see her as more than an occasional lover."

"Aren't you worried she might get hurt?" If it had been Nici she would've done anything to protect him from an inconsiderate lover.

"I vowed long ago never to fight with Christian over a woman again—not even my sister. Anyway, she's old enough to take care of herself."

"Again?"

"Long story." He shrugged, a smile tugging at his lips. "And far too boring for an auspicious event such as this."

"You don't want to be here any more than I do," she said. "And, I have time to kill."

Viktor's eyes twinkled, his sigh full of theatrics. "Well, if I must. Okay—I'll tell you all about the lovely Carolina."

"Carolina? I thought you meant his wife."

"I do—his second one, who we knew around the turn of the century when we were living in New Orleans." He took her hand and put it in the crook of his elbow. "Carolina's father wanted a husband for his little girl and Carolina wanted a rich one. Christian and I were the richest, most eligible husband material around. But he was still feeling the loss of his father and his first wife." Viktor's smile saddened.

She reached out and placed a hand on his arm. "He loved her very much, didn't he?"

"Yes—with a love that almost killed him." His smile brightened a little, but remained tinged with sadness. "I don't know why he was so drawn to Carolina—she was nothing like Dominique—but she was ravishing. However, underneath all that beauty was an ugliness you wouldn't believe. I could see it. Christian couldn't and we argued—a lot."

"She came between you."

Viktor looked at Christian who still stood with his back to them. "Carolina loved no one but herself, she was a greedy, selfish person. When she found out what we were, she wanted to be embraced—to live young and beautiful forever. I told Christian she was no good, and he threw me out of the house."

"Then he did it, didn't he?" she asked. "He embraced her?"

Viktor nodded.

"What happened? Did she die in the transition?"

Viktor shook his head, his silken hair brushing her arm lightly.

"Oh no—she made it through all right but she succumbed to Necrodrenia. Then she tried to frame Christian for her kills."

"No wonder he doesn't trust women."

"He doesn't trust humans. They've been responsible for the loss of everything he's ever held dear. Unfortunately for him, your race is necessary for our survival, and he can't escape that fact."

"What happened to Carolina?" Antoinette drained the last of her champagne.

"He killed her; he felt it was his responsibility." Viktor dropped her hand from his arm and signaled a waiter. "And shortly after we joined the Department."

He replaced her empty glass with a fresh drink and took a sip of his own. Antoinette followed his gaze to a gigantic man on the other side of the room.

"Who's that?" she asked.

"Just an old friend." He grinned and raised his glass but the other man scowled back.

"Not very friendly."

Viktor chuckled. "You don't know the half of it."

"Antoinette." Lucian came up from behind and took her elbow. "Sorry to keep you waiting."

"Thanks for keeping me company, Viktor." Antoinette gave his hand another squeeze before Lucian led her away.

* * *

The evening flew by in a blur of names and faces. It seemed
everyone wanted to talk to her, check her out. She felt like a
prize horse for inspection. It was a wonder no one had asked
her to open her mouth so they could look at her teeth.

Antoinette's head spun and she put a cool palm to her
forehead—too much champagne. As soon as her glass was
empty someone seemed to press a fresh one into her hand.

She'd just finished being pawed on the dance floor by one
of the Mer representatives. He'd groped her incessantly. His
hand kept dropping to her ass and she'd had to keep returning it to her waist while his not-so-fresh fishy breath had
her trying hard to keep down her dinner and the copious
champagne.

Lucian had been busy most of the night. While his research at the Academy was his main focus, it was clear he
was being groomed for CHaPR and had been tied up most
of the time with diplomats and dignitaries, leaving her with
so much free time for dancing and being groped by all and
sundry. Lucky her.

Antoinette suppressed a groan and forced a smile as the
Guild secretary made his way toward her. Earlier he'd had
an in-depth discussion with her breasts, never once looking
at her face.

"Ms. Petrescu . . ." he said to her chest, licking his overwet
lips. "Can I—"

"I'm sorry, but Miss Petrescu has promised me this dance."
Christian's velvet tone cut in.

Antoinette swiveled to meet his blue eyes. Maybe she'd
be safer with the secretary after all. But she didn't have a
chance to refuse as Christian grabbed her hand and dragged
her out onto the floor.

"You looked in need of rescue," he said, holding her
against him, his cheek brushing hers as they started to move
to the music.

His musky scent invaded her senses, overpowering and
fantastic—she could hardly draw breath. Too much of her

touched him and she pushed back a little, trying to put some air between them.

"I am quite capable of taking care of myself, thank you." It came out harsher than she'd intended.

"Really?" he said with a hint of amusement. "I thought you looked rather green with your last dance partner."

"You saw that?"

He inclined his head.

"What are you doing here with that science geek?" Christian looked at Lucian who was talking animatedly to a group of official-looking men.

"I like him. And don't be so quick to judge a book by its cover," she said, remembering how Lucian had handled himself with the thugs in the alley.

"Hmph." Christian swirled her in a tight circle. "Not much of a cover."

She drew back a little and looked him in the eye. "Jealous much?"

If an Aeternus could blush, Antoinette was sure he would have.

"Don't be ridiculous," he growled and pressed his palm lower on her back.

The imprint of his hand burned into her bare back, doing strange things to her pulse. She turned her head away, only to lock eyes with a frosty amber glare.

"Besides, your girlfriend doesn't seem too happy either," she said.

Valerica stood just off the dance floor, her arms tightly crossed and a scowl creasing her perfect brow.

Christian glanced over his shoulder. "She's just an old friend."

"Really? That's not what Viktor told me."

He frowned. "What did he say?"

"That you two were lovers."

"Once upon a time—very long ago. Why? Jealous?" His mouth quirked at the corners.

Now it was her turn to blush. Her breath quickened at the

sensation of his body pressed against hers—his firm thigh moving between hers as he twirled her around the floor— shoulder muscles flexing under her fingers as he held her.

"Do you know what you're doing to me?" he asked, his breath brushing her lips.

She closed her eyes, hardly daring to breathe. The evidence was pressed against her stomach sending ripples of desire pooling low in her stomach. Oh God. She closed her eyes, swallowing the moan building low in her throat. This can't happen again.

She forced steel into her voice. "That's your problem, not mine."

"Since that night on the plane, I haven't been able to drive you from my mind." He slowly traced a fingertip down her backbone.

She couldn't suppress a shudder.

"Stop that," she hissed and laid a hand against his chest, trying to put a little distance between them.

Her eyes dropped to his mouth. Big mistake.

"You feel it too," he said. "Don't you?"

"No—last time was the blood-thrall. It won't happen again."

He suddenly dipped her, his gaze sweeping down to her breasts and back to her mouth. He licked his lips. "Liar."

She raised her knee and ran her inner thigh up to his waist as part of the dance move. Her breath hitched in her throat as he ran his hand down the back of her leg. His fingers trailed along the tender nerves, stopping briefly over the garter and the sheathed knife she had safely tucked out of view. Then he snapped her into a standing position and pressed her tightly against his chest.

Her mind searched for some safe subject as her heart beat in her throat. "You're a good dancer." She winced at how lame she sounded.

"I've had plenty of practice," he breathed in her ear. "At many things." He sucked her lobe between his teeth and gently nipped.

She almost came there and then. Her blood turned to molten lava in her veins, she wouldn't be able to resist him much longer, blood-thrall or no blood-thrall.

Someone cleared their throat behind him and Christian stopped moving but still held her close.

Antoinette was equally relieved and disappointed to see Lucian's hand on Christian's shoulder. "Sorry to interrupt, but I need to steal back my date."

"Of course." He released her and instantly stepped away inclining his head graciously. "Ms. Petrescu."

He held her gaze for a few seconds longer, then turned and walked away. While her legs threatened to collapse under her, his stride was sure and confident.

"Sir Roger wants to talk to you," Lucian said.

Antoinette nodded vaguely, watching Christian disappear into the throng. Valerica shot a vicious glare at her then followed hot on his heels.

"Lucian, thank goodness." A stylish elderly woman grabbed him by the arm. "My husband needs your help."

"Wait here Antoinette—I'll be back in a moment," Lucian said and went with the older woman.

Antoinette sat down at the nearest empty table, removing her shoe to massage her foot. Damn heels! A man had to be responsible for inventing such implements of torture. She continued to rub. The fire Christian had stoked in her blood began to cool. Thank God for the old woman; she'd given Antoinette a few more minutes to collect herself.

Someone brushed past her, humming something familiar and leaving her with a sense of—wrongness. She looked up but no one seemed near enough.

"Hush little baby . . ."

The words swept past her ear on a breath. She jumped up—looking around—heart pounding against the walls of her chest. Did she imagine it? Was she having a waking dream about Dante again? It couldn't be him, surely. He was dead. Her father had killed him years ago.

She scanned the crowd for the Aeternus who'd murdered her mother, knowing he couldn't be there.

"Don't say a word . . ."

Barely more than a whisper.

She spun back to the right, sensing someone close yet finding no one.

Suddenly, across the room, she connected with his familiar cold eyes for half a nightmarish heartbeat, then she blinked and he was gone. If he'd ever really been there at all. It was impossible.

Antoinette slowed her breathing and scanned the gathering again. It was just the champagne and her imagination. There was nothing—

A hand closed around her elbow. Her heart jolted into her throat as she involuntarily recoiled, her shoe dropping with a thud to the floor.

13

Date with an Ambassador

"Hey." Lucian pulled her closer and put his arms around her shoulders. "I didn't mean to scare you."

Antoinette felt foolish and relaxed against him for a moment, soaking up his comfort then drew back and gave him a smile.

"Are you okay?" He placed a finger under her chin, his features twisting in concern. "You look like you've seen a ghost."

She let the air escape her lungs, hoping it sounded like an offhanded laugh instead of the hysteria that bubbled just below the surface. Was she going insane?

"I think the evening and the champagne have gone to my head." She winced at her shaky voice.

"You do look awfully pale. How about we go see what the ambassador wants and then I'll take you back to your hotel?"

"That'd be good."

He bent down to pick up her shoe and gently slipped it back on her foot. No lingering touches, nothing untoward, just a simple helping hand.

"Lean on me," he said, holding out his elbow.

Antoinette didn't hesitate and slipped her arm through his.

"Is the old woman okay?" Antoinette asked, trying to keep her voice even.

"What?" Lucian frowned. "Oh. Yes. The evening and champagne have taken their toll on her husband too, although it's more likely the champagne in his case. I've arranged a room for them in the hotel."

"That was nice of you."

"I do what I can," he said. "Now let's go—Sir Roger's waiting."

Antoinette heard the ambassador long before she saw him. He stood near the entrance talking to the gigantic man Viktor had exchanged looks with earlier. With them was a beautiful pale woman.

"Ah, you've found her. Good," the ambassador boomed.

"Your Excellency, I really think you should keep your bodyguards with you at all times," Oberon said. "The Department assigned them to protect you."

"Nonsense!" The ambassador waved away Oberon's concern. "I told Christian Laroque and now I'm telling you. I don't need a security detail protecting me inside my room. They can stand outside my door and that's final. Besides, I have two Guild members with me." He reached out and took Antoinette's right hand in his. "And this lovely creature is one of our most talented. I think I'll be safe enough in her hands."

He plastered a sloppy kiss on her knuckles. Antoinette fought the urge to wipe the back of her hand on her gown.

Oberon turned his stern frown on her, his top lip lifted into a half-sneer. "You can't be too prepared, Excellency."

"I'm in a hotel that has been secured by numerous Department and CHaPR divisions including your own—I don't think the extra intrusion is necessary," Sir Roger said.

"Whatever you say, Excellency." Somehow the agent made it sound like an insult.

He turned on his heels and stalked off in the other direction, the pale woman almost running to keep up.

Antoinette watched them go. She'd hate to get on the wrong side of that man.

Lucian and Sir Roger waited for her at the elevator. The two bodyguards entered after them and stood near the doors with hands clasped together in front.

Once the elevator started to ascend, Sir Roger took her hand. "My dear, do you know how much you look like your mother?"

"I've been told, Excellency." She had a picture of her parents by her bed at home.

"Yes—the spitting image. She and I were close once, you know. I would've married her if your father hadn't come along." His face went all dreamy with past memories for a moment. Antoinette glanced at Lucian, who shrugged.

Then Sir Roger straightened and pierced her with a probing glare. "So—what do you think of all this nonsense your uncle has been spouting? It's all totally preposterous of course."

"I'm sorry?" The change in tact caught her by surprise.

"He seems intent on creating a panic over a few unfortunate mishaps. I mean really, a couple of fires and a few accidental deaths . . ." He puffed out his chest. "They hardly constitute a return to The Troubles."

"I think it's a little more serious than a few accidents, Excellency." She struggled to keep her tone even. "My uncle isn't one for paranoid panic, and my Uncle Nicolae was one of those murdered."

"True, but the French Intelligence division did a thorough investigation into the whole matter. They reported he'd made a few enemies of late. Apparently he was having an affair with a married woman and her husband has been detained as a suspect."

Antoinette chewed her lower lip. Did Sergei know this? She caught Lucian's sympathetic expression. *He thought the same.*

Sir Roger seemed oblivious to her distress. "Do you know where this information is coming from?"

Lucian tensed and looked at her.

"Uncle Sergei hasn't shared his confidences with me." It wasn't a lie—not exactly.

"So why did you come here?" Sir Roger asked.

"My brother took up an R&D position with the Guild, London office. Uncle Sergei thought the conference might be a good opportunity to have a look at the graduating class." She looked Sir Roger in the eye, squaring her shoulders, daring him to disagree. "I need a new tech."

After a few tense seconds, his face broke into a smile and he slapped Lucian on the back.

"Good. We need more young people with your dedication. Come have a nightcap with me before you return to the party."

Antoinette's feet hurt, her heavy head already swam in an alcoholic haze. The last thing she needed was another drink with this pompous asshole.

"Thank you, Excellency, we'll be happy to," Lucian said before she had a chance to beg off.

The elevator doors opened to an empty hall on Sir Roger's floor. Antoinette shivered—a cold knot formed in her stomach. She shook it off, putting it down to her earlier moment of panic and the effects of the champagne.

The two beefy bodyguards took up their posts either side of the door as Sir Roger let them into his luxurious suite. A bottle of champagne sat chilling on the sideboard in the living room area. The Ambassador walked around the ivory damask chaise lounge and straight to the ice bucket. He lifted the bottle and began peeling back the foil cap, then indicated that Antoinette should take a seat.

A chill swept goose bumps up her arms. She caught the slight movement of the balcony drapes out of the corner of her eye and reached for the knife she'd stashed in her garter. A large pop rang out as the ambassador pulled the cork and she spun toward the sound.

His eyes went wide and his head rocked back, the bottle

falling from his hands. A red dot appeared on his forehead before he collapsed to the floor, the wall behind him now painted red.

Lucian reached inside his jacket but another silencer-muffled pop fired from beyond the balcony drapes before he could withdraw his weapon. A scarlet bloom appeared on his white dress shirt under the right side of his jacket.

It all happened in less than a blink of an eye. Antoinette crouched and threw her knife at the shape emerging from the curtains and was rewarded with a meaty thud followed by a grunt.

The assailant looked down at the handle, a familiar grin forming at the corners of his mouth. The second their eyes locked, Antoinette was immediately reduced to a six-year-old child again.

He's here.

And this time she knew it wasn't a dream. Somehow—impossibly—her mother's murderer stood before her. She froze, the same cold dread chilling her veins, just as it had over sixteen years ago.

Dante's fingers wrapped around the protruding handle and he drew it out, slow and steady, his evil grin unwavering. Then he ran the blood-smeared blade across his tongue before tossing it out the balcony door.

Damn, the blade was steel, not silver. As Antoinette reached up to pull the twin stilettos from her hair, he slammed her against the wall. His face closed in, inches from hers and he pinned her wrists above her head with his left hand. The pistol fell to the floor with a thud and he ran his hand up her bare arm and across her breast.

"Well now, little-one—you're all grown up." His cold voice sent ripples of fear through her body. He ran the back of his finger up her cheek and twisted it in one of her curls. "What a fine trophy you'd make."

His gaze swept down to the swell of her breasts and up again to meet her eyes. Christian had done the same thing during their dance and had made her heart flutter, but Dante sent a liquid nitrogen chill through her blood.

A familiar iciness crept over her mind. He pressed his body even closer—she could feel his excitement hard against her hip.

"It can't be—" She finally found her voice, barely above a whisper. "You're dead."

His chuckle was as humorless as his dead eyes. "Luckily I know a good doctor."

He leaned closer. Antoinette twisted her face away from his breath against her lips—he drew his tongue, wet and slimy, up her cheek. She shuddered as the saliva dried like foul bugs crawling on her skin.

"You taste just as sweet as your mother did."

She stopped struggling. Pure hot rage exploded in her chest. Hate swelled like a tidal wave, crashing against her, drowning her fear and clearing her mind. She was no longer a child—no longer helpless. He'd tormented her memories and her nightmares long enough; it all stopped now.

She opened her mouth and screamed.

His eyes rounded then narrowed dangerously. But the guards began pounding against the locked door. He released her so suddenly she lurched into the empty space he'd occupied, and noticed the gun on the floor beside her. Dropping to a squat she grabbed it and fired a shot after him. The bullet slammed into the wall a hair's breadth from his head as he disappeared through the curtain. She followed at a run through to the balcony, and . . . nothing. Not one sign of him above or below. *Shit.*

The brightly lit street many floors below brimmed with people—he could be any one of them, or none. She'd lost him. *Shit, shit.*

She barely registered the splintering crash of the doorframe exploding. Someone touched her shoulder. She spun, pointing the gun, ready to kill.

"Antoinette, it's me!" Christian said, holding up his hands in front of her face.

* * *

At first Christian wasn't sure she'd heard him. She stood panting, gun in hand, eyes haunted, and she seemed unreachable. Then she blinked and focused. The gun shook and fell from her fingers.

"Are you hurt?" he asked. "Have you been shot?"

She shook her head and then her knees buckled. He caught her, sweeping her up against his chest. Instead of fighting him, she wrapped her arms around his neck and laid her cheek against his shoulder as he carried her back into the room.

Christian put her down on the sofa. Viktor appeared at the door, then went to consult one of the agents on bodyguard duty. Fine job they did.

"How're the ambassador and Lucian?" Christian asked over his shoulder.

"Lucian has taken a bullet in the shoulder, and lives," Viktor said. "Unfortunately, Sir Roger's not so lucky."

Christian noticed the other agent had grabbed a towel and now pressed it against Lucian's shoulder. Viktor moved to join Christian and Antoinette.

"What happened?" Christian asked her.

Tears traced a path down her cheeks and it was few more minutes before she was able to talk. Finally she shook herself and took a deep hitching breath as she swiped her tears.

"He shot them from the balcony but . . ." She leaned closer, her eyes searching his. "Christian, it was him—Dante—the one who killed my mother."

"Impossible," Viktor said. "He's dead. I watched Dante's burning body fall from the window of a burning building. The fire consumed everything except for a charred finger with the half-melted remains of his family crest ring."

Antoinette turned pale and placed a hand over her mouth. "I think I'm going to be sick."

Christian grabbed a nearby trash bin, holding it while she emptied the contents of her stomach. Viktor disappeared into the bathroom and returned with a towel and a glass of water, handing both to her when she'd finished.

The EMTs arrived and rushed straight over to Lucian. Antoinette gave Christian and Viktor an embarrassed, shaky smile. "I'm not used to drinking."

She wiped her face with the towel then took a sip of the water. Christian placed the soiled bin in the bathroom and closed the door.

"It's shock more than the champagne." He sat on the coffee table in front of her, his knees either side of hers. "Now—"

A woman appeared at the door, pale and ethereal. He recognized her immediately.

"I'll be back in a sec," Christian said, lowering his voice. With a quick glancing exchange, Viktor slid in beside Antoinette and put his arm around her shoulder.

Christian approached the newcomer. "Bianca."

Bianca arched a pale eyebrow. "I didn't expect you to be here already Christian. I've been called in to help retrieve her statement. The coroner's office is sending over someone to look at the body."

Speak of the devil. Kathryn Jordan, the forensic pathologist, appeared at the door carrying a large black bag.

"Christian," the doctor said. "It's been a while."

"Good to see you, Kitt," he replied, giving her a nod. "The body's over there."

The diminutive woman looked drawn. She nodded and moved past them to where the late ambassador lay.

Christian turned back to Bianca. "So, are you here to orb her?"

The white witch nodded.

"Go easy, okay. I think she's had a severe shock; she's not making much sense at the moment."

"I'd better go question her."

Christian touched her elbow. "Like I said—go easy. Please."

* * *

The woman sat beside Antoinette on the sofa. "My name is Bianca Sin and I'm the head of thaumaturgical studies at the Academy. Because of the delicacy of this case I've been called in to consult." She held up a small glass sphere. "This a reconstruction orb. It's going to capture your experience of the incident while you recount it to me. Because of the subjective nature of the process it's not admissible in court and is completely voluntary. But if you do submit to the procedure, it may give us invaluable insight into the crime, which you may not be able to consciously remember. Do you understand?"

Antoinette nodded.

"Good. Now, are you willing to undergo the procedure?" the witch asked.

Antoinette nodded again.

"Excellent, but first you have to sign a waiver." She produced a form out of her briefcase. "Christian can be your witness."

Antoinette stared blankly at the paper in her hand for a minute. The words seemed to dance around the page, just beyond her understanding. But anxious to get it over with, she signed.

After the paperwork was completed, the witch placed the cold glass orb into Antoinette's hands. "Have you had anything to drink tonight?"

The orb warmed slightly. "Yes."

The witch swore. "That may affect the results but we'll just have to see what we get. Okay—in your own words, tell me what happened here tonight."

As Antoinette talked the glass sphere grew milky and warmer, throbbing against her palms so by the time she'd finished it glowed and was almost too hot to hold.

"So—you fired the murder weapon?" Bianca asked, taking the globe and wrapping it in a black velvet cloth.

"Yes," Antoinette said.

"Where is the gun now?"

"Um . . ." Antoinette looked at her empty hands and

around the floor. Oh God, I don't know. Panic bubbled; this was all starting to get out of control. "I can't—"

"She dropped it out on the balcony," Christian said.

Antoinette stole a grateful glance at him. He put a hand on her shoulder and she actually found it comforting instead of disturbing.

"Excuse me for a minute." Bianca pulled a cell phone from her jacket pocket and walked out onto the balcony.

A few moments later Bianca joined them, her face drawn and businesslike.

"I'm afraid they want you taken into VCU headquarters. Someone will be here to escort you shortly."

Did they really think she did it? She was a victim here, and they were treating her like a suspect. She turned to look at Christian, but his expression said it all—there was nothing he could do.

14

The Aftermath

Antoinette had since skipped past scared and moved straight to pissed. For the hundredth time, she stood and paced the small interview room. It was rank with the scent of stale perspiration, aggression, and fear. None of it helped her mood. Her head throbbed and a foul post-drinking sourness coated her tongue; she'd kill for a toothbrush or a drink of water.

The image in the mirror screwed up its face; she barely recognized it as herself. Dark circles ringing her eyes and smudged makeup made her look like a panda in drag. The bright orange jumpsuit they'd given her to wear when they took her dress looked as unflattering as prison garb possibly could—and she hadn't even been formally arrested. Yet.

They had poked and prodded, scraped and swabbed. Questioned her endlessly and then left her alone in this tiny room for well over two hours. Antoinette sat down again on the hard metal chair and leaned on the table bolted to the concrete floor. Nothing was soft in this room, including the harsh fluorescent lighting.

Leaning back in the chair, she glared directly at the mirror. "Bring it on," she mouthed to whoever was behind it.

A few moments later the door opened and the huge agent

from the party downstairs stepped inside carrying a folder she assumed was about her. He'd traded in his tuxedo for leathers, making him look like a cross between a biker and a rock star. Tall, dark, and menacing. His almost seven-foot frame made the small room even smaller.

"Ms. Petrescu." His sarcastic tone immediately put her on the defensive.

She didn't like him, not one little bit.

"I'm Oberon DuPrie, Special-Agent-in-Charge of Personal Security," he said, dropping the file on the table across from her. An ursian, that accounted for his size.

He didn't look like a typical agent in a black heavy metal T-shirt that stopped just above his navel, revealing an expanse of rippling abs. A line of dark hair started from his navel and disappeared behind the large Harley Davidson belt buckle. White gold or platinum and turquoise adorned his fingers and wrists, and secured his dark dreadlocks at the nape of his neck.

The door opened again and she slumped with relief when Christian and Viktor walked in. She'd never been so pleased to see an Aeternus in her life.

"What are you doing here, Laroque?" Oberon growled.

"We have a vested interest in this case, Oberon." Christian pulled a folded document from inside his tuxedo jacket. "Here's our authorization."

Oberon scanned the pages, his expression growing darker. "I don't like this, but there's very little I can do about it. You're not to interfere with my interrogation." He locked eyes with Christian. "Understood?"

"Calm down, Oberon. We may work for different divisions but we're all on the same side here." Viktor tried to defuse the rapidly mounting tension between Oberon and Christian.

Antoinette watched the silent battle of wills as they stared each other down. Finally Oberon nodded but the scowl never left his face as he dropped his gaze to her.

"Let's get down to business then." He slid into the chair opposite and leaned his elbows on the table. Christian took the last remaining chair at the head of the table and Viktor leaned against the wall behind him near the door.

"Tell me what happened," Oberon rumbled.

How many times would she have to go over this? She leaned back and crossed her arms. "The ambassador and Lucian Moretti were shot."

He slammed his hand on the table and leaned in closer. "Don't play games with me."

"I have already gone over this several times with your colleagues."

Oberon's lips thinned above his goatee. "I want to hear it again—from you."

Antoinette sighed and recounted how the attacker fired from the balcony leaving out, as she had done every time, the fact she recognized him as Dante Rubins—her mother's murderer.

"Where were the men that were assigned to guard Sir Roger?" Oberon asked.

Antoinette humored him. "They were standing outside the door."

"Why weren't they in the room?" Oberon barked at her.

"You know damned well why. Sir Roger told you before we went upstairs he wouldn't allow them inside."

Oberon's opened the file on the table, his lips thinning. "Your hands and clothing tested positive for gunshot residue. Why should I believe you didn't shoot the two men yourself and just made up this mystery intruder?"

This bastard was after a confession. Antoinette raised her chin as she met his hostile expression, refusing to flinch.

"Oberon," Christian said in an even voice. "She's already admitted to firing the gun."

She glanced at Christian out of the corner of her eye. The ticking muscles along his jaw were the only outward sign of emotion.

"I asked Ms. Petrescu the question." Oberon pierced Christian with his intense coal black stare. "You're here to observe. Keep your mouth shut or I'll have you thrown out. Authorization or not, this is still my investigation." Oberon swung his coal black eyes to her. "Now—why should I believe you?"

"Why would I want to shoot Sir Roger or Lucian?" she asked, incredulous.

Oberon's eyes narrowed. "Were you sleeping with Moretti?"

Antoinette rocked back in her seat, the metal bit into her backbone. Christian's hand formed a fist on the table, his knuckles white.

"That's none of your business," she said, pulling her shoulders straight.

"Everything is my business," Oberon said. "Now—answer the question."

She leaned forward. "Is this how you get your kicks—intimidating women into telling you about their sex lives?" She wasn't going to let him rattle her.

Viktor coughed, his eyes crinkling at the corners.

"I am trying to establish why you were in the room," Oberon said.

She met and held his gaze. "Because—I—was—his—date," she hissed through gritted teeth.

"How fortunate for you," Oberon said.

"What are you implying?" she asked, getting seriously pissed off now.

"As Lucian's date you had access to the ambassador few other people had."

"What are you playing at, Oberon?" Christian asked.

The ursian gave him a dirty look. "Come on, Laroque. It's common knowledge that Sir Roger was grooming Lucian to be his replacement in CHaPR—making Lucian the perfect way to get close to His Excellency."

"What possible motive could she have?" Christian asked.

Oberon leaned back and raised his massive hands behind

his head, grinning like the cat that got the cream. "Ms. Petrescu, it's no secret that there's been bad blood between the ambassador and your uncle since Sir Roger classified your father as a renegade. I think that's more than enough of a motive for murder."

He may as well have slapped her upside her face.

"Now wait a minute!" Viktor came away from the wall.

"What are you talking about?" Her father a renegade? She'd never heard this before.

Oberon leaned forward, dark eyes intent and he glanced quickly at Christian.

"You didn't know?" Oberon straightened, his brows coming together. "This is . . . unexpected."

Antoinette shifted her gaze from Viktor to Christian. They knew.

"What's going on?" she asked.

Neither Viktor nor Christian would make eye contact, only Oberon's piercing gaze met hers.

"Some time ago," Oberon said, "Roger Wilberforce-Smythe was head of the Venator Registration for the European division. When your father murdered the Aeternus, Dante Rubins, it was the late ambassador who put out a warrant for Grigore's arrest. But rather than face trial for Rubins's murder, Grigore drove his car over a cliff."

"No." She leapt to her feet—her chest tightening and her ears ringing. "You lie—my father's death was an accident."

"Oberon, enough," Christian said. "She knows nothing of this."

"No," she said, shaking her head. It couldn't be true. Her father wouldn't commit suicide.

"You stay out of this, Laroque—I've told you before." Oberon stood, leaning on his hands across the table. Christian rose to match him—nose to nose.

Before they could all choke on the testosterone in the room, the door opened.

"Can I have a word?" a plainclothes detective said, looking at Oberon.

The ursian glared at Antoinette then reluctantly left the room.

She turned on Christian. "What is going on?"

"We'll explain later." Viktor came around the table to clasp both of her shoulders. "First let's get you out of here." He leaned forward and whispered, "The walls here have ears."

Antoinette clenched her fists, her anger rising. The opening door cut off any chance of a reply. Oberon and the detective reappeared.

"You're free to go," the cop said and left the room again.

Oberon didn't like it one bit, she could see that written on his face.

"Then, unless there's anything else, we're done," she said, and turned her back on him. After a few seconds, she looked at Oberon over her shoulder. "Is there anything else?"

His lips almost disappeared as they thinned and his dark eyes were deadly, but he spun on his heel and left—the door slamming behind him. She dropped the smile.

"You know it's not wise to piss off a ursian," Viktor said.

She turned on him, curling her fingers into fists. "And it's not wise to piss me off either." That wiped the grin from his face. "Enough of these games—are you going to tell me what the hell happened to my father?"

"Not here," Christian said.

Oberon knew two things about Antoinette Petrescu. First, even though the forensic evidence had substantiated her story and cleared her of the shooting, she wasn't telling him the full truth about Sir Roger's murder. And second, she was a dead ringer for the new serial killer's victims. He hated the name they'd assigned to the perp. You'd think that sack-of-shit Roberts, who now headed the VCU, could've come up with something more original than "The Fang-whore Slasher."

Oberon stood in front of the whiteboard covered with photos and details of the six victims they'd uncovered so far. The before-shots of the women stared back at him. None had the amazing emerald eyes of Ms. Petrescu, but they all had the same lush Nordic blond hair, creamy complexion, and general build. Oberon was struck with the sudden thought; did she match their physical appearance or did they match hers?

Oberon wished he had access to firsthand information, but since he'd been kicked off the Violent Crimes Unit six months ago he could only access what his contact in VCU could pass him. *Thank God for Tony Geraldi.* This new killer was vicious.

The first body had been found floating in the river near Brooklyn two weeks ago. Since then several more had been recovered from the water in the same vicinity as the first. So far they hadn't uncovered any of the heads. Oberon's partner, Dylan, who'd left the VCU with him, had theorized the river currents might have carried the bodies away from the dumping place. But Oberon was inclined to think the killer kept them.

The victims were all human. Serial killers usually belonged to the FBI but here at the VCU headquarters they were taking an interest due to the fact all but one of the victims were known fang-whores and spikers and were in constant contact with the parahuman community. It could be the work of a dreniac—but the killings were too controlled, too precise.

The sixth victim had been a runaway and probably new to the game, given no record. Oberon learned from a copy of the report Tony had managed to get him that they'd had to use the tattoo on her hip to identify her remains.

The victims had dozens of shallow slashes to the torso and limbs. The lab reports said the wounds were made while they were still alive, resulting in exsanguination. Hours of immersion in the river destroyed any trace evidence, if there was any to destroy in the first pace. This guy was smart.

Six victims in a fortnight and yet nothing in the last few days. He should be concentrating on this business with the

Ambassador's murder, not obsessing over a case he no longer had a right to. But that ass-wipe Roberts wouldn't know a serial killer from the piss in his pants.

Oberon turned to face Antoinette and her Aeternus pals as they came down the passage, and crossed his arms as he leaned against the table. He fixed his eyes on the woman.

She met his gaze, then flicked to the case whiteboard behind him.

"Are you all right?" Christian asked.

She seemed about to say something then took a step closer. "Is this the Fang-whore Slasher case I've been reading about in the papers?" she asked Oberon, her gaze remaining fastened on the case board. "Are you working it?"

"Do you see that?" Dushic whispered to Laroque, looking from the victim photos to Antoinette and back to the pictures pinned on the whiteboard.

The Aeternus nodded.

"And you think he's targeting them for their profession, hence the name the Fang-whore Slasher." Her frown deepened and she moved around the desk taking a closer look at the photographs. "But I think they're just easier to access—he'll start taking others soon."

I was thinking the same thing. "Why do you say that?" Oberon asked curious to her reasoning.

"The fang-whores will start to get wise. Look at the way he slices them—so deliberate, each cut precise and probably slowly over hours." She turned around and looked at him. "He's having way too much fun to stop, don't you think?"

"It doesn't really matter what he thinks as he no longer has any interest in VCU cases." Roberts came out of the office to stand in front of the case board and crossed his arms. *The ass-wipe.* "We gave you access to the witness to ask your questions, Oberon. I think you're finished here."

The roar rushed up from his toes and he gave it voice. Catching the edge of the table, he heaved it against the wall. Wood disintegrated into flying splinters and papers fluttered all around the room. He breathed in through his nose and out his mouth, trying to calm the bear side of himself. It was exactly what got him demoted in the first place. Roberts sure knew how to push his buttons. One day he would get back at that little prick for kicking him off the team. But today was not that day. With one final glance at Antoinette, he turned on his heels and marched toward the exit.

15

strangers in the Night

Antoinette burst out through the doors onto the wide stone stairs. The sun would be up within the hour, but for now the night's cold kiss chased away some of the temper burning her cheeks. She felt a little calmer as she breathed deep, but was still very pissed.

The two Aeternus followed her, and then a cell phone started to ring. Christian pulled it from his pocket and flipped it open, cutting off the strains of Frank Sinatra's "Strangers in the Night."

Viktor looked at her, his mouth clamped shut, his eyes glittering. Christian didn't notice as he put the phone to his ear, and then he straightened almost to attention.

"Yes, sir. I'll be right there . . ." He flipped the cell closed, a scowl crinkling his forehead. "The boss wants to see me. Drive her back to my place and bring her up to date on Grigore. Take my car."

He tossed the keys to Viktor, who snatched them out of the air. After Christian disappeared inside, Viktor turned to her.

"Sinatra," he said, shaking his head. "I thought he grew out of that phase."

The tension burst and she giggled, until she remembered her father and the laughter died in her throat.

"Come on, you'll need a drink for this," Viktor said, taking her arm.

He led her down to the underground parking garage and a new black Audi S5 coupe. He held open the door while she climbed in then came around to take the driver's seat. The engine roared into life with a throaty purr and within minutes they were making their way through the city, Viktor expertly handling the car at breakneck speed.

The velocity pumped adrenaline through her blood-stream—just what she needed right now. She sighed and sank back into the leather seat.

"Feeling better?" Viktor asked, double clutching and shifting gears.

"Yes, actually." She glanced over at his profile. Strange that this man, this Aeternus, knew exactly the right thing to say and do. "So tell me about my father."

"Not yet." He took the next left hard, cutting into the other lane and missing another car by mere inches.

Antoinette fought the urge to throw her hands in the air and whoop with excitement and nerves.

Viktor took a hard right roaring along a narrow side street then out into another road, the back end sliding before Viktor accelerated, gaining traction to bring the car straight again.

Weaving in and out of the slight traffic, they soon reached a brownstone. Viktor pulled into an underground garage and cut the engine. Antoinette regretted the ride was over.

He flowed out of the driver's seat in one graceful motion and came around to open her door before she had a chance to gather herself.

"Come on, I'll buy you that drink," he said, holding out his hand.

She allowed him to lead her into the house and to a large drawing room. A butler appeared at the door shortly after they arrived, carrying a silver ice bucket.

"Welcome home, Mr. Dushic. The master called ahead

and told me of your guest." He bowed to Antoinette before placing the bucket on the bar. "Please ring if you require anything else. The master said he will not be home until nightfall and asked me to make up a room for the young lady."

"Excellent, Kavindish, I'll ring when she's ready to retire," Viktor said, crossing to the bar.

While he busied himself with the drinks, Antoinette looked around. She guessed the "master" was Christian and the room, like his airplane, held the finest of furniture and books. Not that she knew one fine piece of furniture from the next, but it looked expensive and it was definitely a man's room full of wood and leather.

Viktor strode across the room and handed her a balloon glass of brandy.

"Please, come and sit over here," he said.

She sank down next to him on a leather two-seat sofa. "So did my father commit suicide?"

"No," Viktor replied.

Relief washed over her. As a Venator she could think of nothing more cowardly, and as a daughter she could think of nothing more selfish.

"So it was an accident," she said.

"No," Viktor said again.

"You mean he was murdered." She knew it, her father had been an expert driver.

Viktor took a sip of his drink. "No."

Now Antoinette was confused. "What do you mean—no?"

"We set it all up—your father and I—he didn't die in that car accident."

Antoinette's glass slipped from her fingers and hit the floor. Amber liquid spilled out onto the fine, expensive carpet but she didn't care. A numbness crept up from her stomach, through her chest and into her face.

"Here," Viktor put his own glass to her lips. "Take a big sip, you'll feel much better."

She covered his hands with hers and guided the brandy to

her mouth. The fiery liquor ran down her throat and stung her eyes. She fought back the urge to cough, instead taking another large, shaky sip. Viktor let go and picked up the fallen glass and placed it on the table. He reached over to pin an errant curl behind her ear. She frowned and batted his hand away. *How dare he?*

"You remind me of Grigore when you're angry. He's been my closest friend for over a decade. You are so alike it's scary—the same moods, the same look in your eye, and the same drive."

All this time . . . her father had been alive all this time and she never knew. "Why did he leave us?"

"He couldn't take you on the run with him, he was a wanted man. We could never prove Dante killed your mother, and the Guild weren't so sure. We only had your identification and the word of a six-year-old didn't hold much sway."

Antoinette remembered going through thousands of mug shots only to point him out from a newspaper article on a Paris society event.

"Where is my father now?" she asked.

"I don't know. About a month ago he called me and arranged a meeting between me, him, and a mysterious inside source from the Guild. This was just after the assassinations started. He contacted me saying he had news of a conspiracy involving the Guild and somehow it involved your family as well. I showed up, they didn't, and I haven't heard from him since. It was shortly after that I contacted Christian for his help."

Antoinette stood, throwing the brandy balloon across the room. It shattered into a thousand pieces against the wall, brandy staining the paintwork. She had to get away from Viktor or she'd kill him. "So Christian's in on this too. What is his part in this game you're playing?"

"Christian's job was to deliver you and your little brother safely to your aunt and uncle. He had no more idea Grigore was alive than you did, until recently."

"And, Sergei, did he know?"

"About your father being alive, yes—about his disappearance, no. Grigore contacted Sergei two years after his
supposed death. He needed to know how his children were
being looked after."

All the years she grieved for her parents—and all along
her father had been living half a tiny world away. She felt so
betrayed.

After trying to sleep the day away, Antoinette felt on edge as
she stood with her uncle outside Christian's house. He took
her hand in his, but she pulled away. It still hurt too much.

"*Lishka* . . ." he pleaded.

"I'm not a child anymore," she snapped and turned away
from his hurt expression. "You've lied to me my entire
life."

"It was for your own protection as much as his. If you'd
known your father was alive, you would've tried to find him.
We didn't know who was watching and it was too dangerous. Please come home with me."

In a matter of hours, Antoinette's whole world had been
turned upside down. And even though she knew Sergei had
done it to protect her, she still found it hard to forgive him.
Viktor she could understand—he didn't know her—but
she'd trusted her uncle. She turned to look at him and her
heart broke at his pain-etched expression.

"I can't go home, Uncle." She reached out and cupped his
cheek. "Not yet anyway."

"So, you're staying," Christian said, melting out of the
shadows.

Antoinette swore. She'd wanted this moment alone with
her uncle.

"Yes," she said.

"She can stay with Viktor and me here," Christian said to
Sergei. "You won't need to worry."

Damn him. She swallowed and held up her chin. "I can
look after myself, thank you."

"Why do you want to stay so much?" Sergei asked.

"To find Dante and kill him." If she hadn't imagined the whole thing like everyone seemed to think.

"Lishka, Dante is already dead," her uncle said in the tone he used on his students.

"I have to find out for sure, Uncle. His eyes were so cold, and the way he said 'You taste just as sweet as your mother'." She shivered at the memory of his slimy tongue against her flesh. *"It was him."*

Christian looked at her more closely, but said nothing.

"Then I would sleep better if I knew you were here." Sergei turned to Christian.

She did need somewhere to stay—so why not? It was a big house and she did want to hear more about her father from Viktor. She sighed. "Okay, Uncle, I'll stay."

Sergei beamed and nodded to Christian. "Thank you, Christian. She is such a hothead and her brother isn't here to keep her out of trouble."

At the mention of Nici she realized she hadn't thought of him once during this whole mess. A pang of guilt squeezed her heart.

"So you didn't find out anything more from your sources in the Guild?" Christian asked.

Sergei shook his head. "Now I remember why I distanced myself from them. There are fractures appearing that worry me, and Sir Roger's murder has caused great upheaval. People are accusing each other of involvement in his death. Factions are jockeying their candidates as his replacement, and I fear it may get worse than it did during The Troubles. Our best hope would be if Lucian accepts the position. But who knows with his injury."

Guilt slid cold tendrils into her heart. She'd been so worried over her predicament; she'd forgotten how much worse off Lucian was. "Any change in his condition?"

Christian slid his hands into his pockets. "He's in stable condition and under guard at the hospital for the moment."

"Well, I'd better go or I'll miss my flight," Sergei said.

"Don't worry." Christian stepped forward and shook her uncle's hand. "We'll make sure she stays safe."

Antoinette hugged her uncle close. She may be pissed with him, but he was still the man who'd been the closest thing to a father she had. As the limo pulled away from the curb, she continued to wave until the car turned the corner and disappeared.

Christian turned and walked toward the house. Viktor met her at the door and leaned close. "You don't have to be brave all the time, you know."

Christian scowled in their direction before he disappeared into the drawing room.

"Come on, let's go for a walk and get a cup of coffee," Viktor said and wrapped her arm through his and then looked at her, his face breaking into a grin. "Or maybe something a little stronger? And I know the perfect place. Come on."

Antoinette thought a cowboy bar was a strange choice, but Viktor seemed to fit right in with blue jeans, black western style shirt, cowboy hat, and snakeskin boots. He even had his hair pulled into a ponytail, giving him more country-boy appeal. A honky-tonk band played in the far corner and a few people were either line dancing or doing the two-step on the open floor. It could have been worse; he'd originally threatened to take her to a karaoke bar.

"Come on, little lady, I'll buy ya a drink," he said in a rather sexy southern drawl, as he took her hand and dragged her to a nearby table.

Despite herself, she smiled and almost giggled, especially at the hot young thang in a miniskirt and cowboy boots shaking ass past their table. Viktor pushed up his hat, leaned back in his chair, and winked at the universal come-on smile she gave him, then watched her wiggle all the way to the bar.

The waitress stopped by, chewing gum and pulling a pen from her hair. "What can I git ya, hon."

Antoinette didn't even think. "Lemonade," she ordered.

"Scrap that," Viktor said, still in full southern mode. "We're celebratin'. Can ya bring her one of them fancy drinks with a little umbrella in it? We just decided to get ourselves hitched. Ain't that right, darlin'?"

Antoinette nearly fell off her chair and looked at him. He gave her a cheeky wink and mouthed, *Play along.*

Okay. "Y'll know it is, sugar pie." She reached over and squeezed his mouth into a pucker. Antoinette didn't know if her accent was any good, but Viktor seemed pleased enough.

"I brung her up here to New York special and everything," Viktor said. "Popped the question right in top o' that big ol' buildin'."

"Well, ain't that sweet." The waitress's acting wasn't nearly as good as Viktor's. "I'll get the bartender to mix up something real special, like. And for you, hon?"

Viktor tossed the waitress another award-winning grin. "I think I'll have me a Kentucky bourbon straight up, sugar. Hell—make it a double."

"Sure thang, hon, comin' right up."

"Okay, what the hell are you doing?" Antoinette hissed at the grinning Aeternus.

He pushed back the brim of the hat with a finger and almost split his face in half with his self-satisfied grin. "Sometimes it's just fun to pretend to be someone else for a while and this is the perfect place for it."

Was he insane?

"Don't look at me like that. The guy who owns this place is a canian friend of mine from Alabama, and it's just for the tourists and city folk—no self-respecting southern boy would come to a place this tacky. Look around, it's cliché heaven." He grabbed her head in both hands and gave her a big smacking kiss right on the lips. "So enjoy yourself—you just became aff-fee-onsed to the handsomest devil alive."

It was true. A souvenir stand sold hats, boots, and all things cowboy; a mechanical bull whirled and twirled, sending some poor Japanese girl flying, much to the mouth-covering amusement of her friends; and a woman gave line dancing tips to a group of middle-aged people at the edge of the dance floor. People came here to be something else.

Why not? It might be fun. Antoinette sat back and relaxed. She didn't feel so strange in the cotton summer dress she borrowed from the maid.

The waitress made her way back with the drinks. As she passed the table behind, a jerk smacked the server hard on the ass. The poor woman jumped and the drinks sloshed onto the tray. She turned to give the guy a dirty look, but the idiot just laughed right along with his three friends.

Antoinette fumed and started to rise. *How dare they treat that her like that?* Viktor put his hand over hers and shook his head slightly.

The waitress put down some sort of fruity drink with a slice of pineapple on the side and an umbrella in it, just like Viktor ordered.

"There you go," the waitress said, her southern accent forgotten and her face flushed. "Sorry about the spillage."

"Are you okay?" Antoinette asked.

The poor thing smiled weakly. "Part of the job."

Viktor put a couple of one-hundred-dollar bills on a dry part of her tray. "Keep the change for your trouble."

"Thank you, sir," she said, a giant smile replacing the frown. "And if you need anything else—" She pointed to SHERRY on her name tag. "Just holla."

While Viktor's outward appearance remained calm, his eyes glowed in amber anger. He picked up his drink and was about to take a sip when a big beefy hand descended on his shoulder.

"You got a problem, mate?" he said with some sort of British accent.

"No." Viktor leaned back in his chair and hooked his thumbs into his belt, looking up at the man. "I just think that wasn't very nice."

"It's what you're supposed to do in a place like this," the guy said.

Viktor frowned. "There is no place for rudeness. You owe that poor girl an apology."

"You think so, cowboy?" the big man blustered. "How about I beat the living shit out of you instead?"

"Now, buddy, why would you want to go and spoil a great night on the town for you and your buds? There'd be broken bones, missing teeth, and lots of blood."

"Yeah, mate, and it'll be all yours."

Antoinette readied for a fight, but Viktor just stood—eye to eye, placing his hands on the man's shoulders, and smiling—a full teeth-gleaming smile. The man's eyes dropped to Viktor's fangs and grew a little nervous.

"How 'bout we forget all about it and have this next round on me," Viktor said, patting the guy's shoulder.

"Um . . . sure, that'd be real nice." The man's smile wobbled around the edges. He turned around to join the hushed collective at his table.

Viktor signaled the waitress. "Sherry—a round on me for these good, ol' boys." He patted the man's back. "Y'all have fun now, ya hear."

Antoinette relaxed back into her seat. She hadn't even realized she'd been sitting on the edge until then.

"Darlin', will you honor me with a dance?" Viktor held out his hand.

When they reached the dance floor, Viktor twirled her around into a fast-paced two-step. He was good, very good. Dancing required similar skills to martial arts, it was all about timing and footwork. She watched the other couples on the floor and soon fell into the rhythm. She couldn't help but smile.

Then the music changed. Viktor pulled her into a slower-paced waltz. She looked over to the table behind theirs and saw the men sharing a joke with the waitress.

"You handled that situation rather well," she said. "It would've gone much differently if it'd been me."

"Let me guess—you would've punched the guy out then

had his friends to contend with, they would've ended up hurt because I would've had to step in to keep you safe, and then you would've been pissed because I saved you. That about right?"

She nodded. "Pretty fair summation, with one minor point of difference." She smiled. "I would *not* have needed you to step in."

"My point exactly." Viktor chuckled and pulled her closer and spun her around the floor. "You know, Antoinette, you don't always have to attack first."

"It's the only way I know," she whispered. Nothing could hurt her if she hurt it first. She put her head against his chest. It felt nice to lean on someone for a change. She felt so safe with Viktor.

She raised her head and looked up at him. "You are so much nicer than your friend."

Viktor's eyes darkened. "No, I'm not."

"I'm sorry, Viktor, I didn't mean—"

"You don't know anything about Christian."

It was the first time she'd seen him angry. She dropped her eyes to her feet and stopped dancing.

Viktor sighed and closed his eyes, pulled her back against him and started moving again. "Look, he's saved my life so many times and I his. But that isn't the reason I love him. He is like my brother and my best friend. Be careful what you do to him."

Heat rose in Antoinette's cheeks. "I have no intentions of doing anything to him."

"I see the naked hunger in both of you when you look at each other."

"You are kidding. The only thing I feel for Christian is—"

"Turn against him and you turn against me. And I warn you—I make a powerful enemy."

Antoinette took a step away from the truth in his eyes. Viktor didn't seem like an Aeternus that would give his loyalty lightly.

"I'll be careful," she said.

"Good" He smiled again and his eyes returned to their normal color. "Now, let's dance."

The band had started another faster paced song. Viktor led her back into the dance pack and they were soon two-stepping around the floor at a giddy speed.

After three more tunes and lots of laughing, she and Viktor returned to their table. Her untouched drink sat there look-ing all fruity and cheerful and she was now thirsty enough to drink it.

"Hey—it's the happy couple," called the guy who had almost flattened Viktor. "Sherry tells us you two are cel-ebrating."

Celebrating? Antoinette was just about to shake her head when Viktor stopped her with a squeeze of her hand.

"We sure are," Viktor said. "We got ourselves engaged this very afternoon."

The table of men cheered and the waitress laughed. "This here is some real southern boys—all the way from Australia."

"Why don't you and your lady come and join us? And no hard feelin's, hey." The big man put out his hand. "Name's Davo."

Viktor took his hand and shook it. "Well, how do, Davo. I'm Sammy-Dean and this is my fiancée, Mandy-Sue."

Antoinette just stood there. *Mandy-Sue?* Twenty minutes ago they were looking to bust heads, and now Viktor and the big Australian were becoming fast friends. She shook her head. She picked up her cocktail and took a sip through the straw. *Whoa, Nellie.* Juice it wasn't—it tasted about four parts rum and one part fruit. Well—maybe it was time for Mandy-Sue to have some fun. She sat down on Sammy-Dean's knee and smacked a big ol' kiss on his cheek.

A heavy pounding dragged her from sleep. Who was making that racket? And why weren't they in the training room? She rolled over on her stomach and dragged the pillow over her head. But the banging continued.

She flipped on her back again and opened her eyes to a moment of dizzy confusion. This wasn't her room at the school. Then the events of the past few days flooded back with vivid clarity and she remembered she was in New York. Someone knocked at her door again.

"Come in," she said, putting a hand to her pounding head.

Susan, the maid, entered and placed a tray on the nearby table. "Evening, miss."

Antoinette sat up and stretched, the bedding falling to her waist. "What time is it?"

"Past sunset, around seven-thirty," the maid said as she laid out enough to feed half a dozen people. "Here's something that may help settle your stomach." She handed Antoinette a glass of fizzing liquid.

"Thank you." Antoinette gratefully downed it, in a couple of swallows, screwing her nose at the foul taste. "My head feels like it's going to explode."

The maid smiled as she took the empty glass back. "I'm not surprised."

Antoinette wasn't a drinker at the best of times and the rum-laced fruit cocktails had hit her pretty hard. Viktor and the Australians had a great time—those boys could sure put it away.

She vaguely remembered Christian's thunderous expression when Viktor dragged her back to the house a short time before dawn. When Christian stalked away, Viktor burst out laughing and helped her to her room where, being the perfect gentleman, he dumped her on the bed and left.

The smell of hot-buttered toast and fresh coffee made her mouth water and her stomach rumble. While her head pounded—she didn't seem affected by the usual hangover nausea. Only her brain appeared a little muddled—like trying to think through a fog.

"I think I'll have a shower first." Antoinette crawled out of bed.

The maid stared, then dropped her eyes to the serving tray again.

Antoinette realized she was naked and slipped into the robe slung over the back of a chair. "Sorry."

"That's okay—I see naked people here all the time. But those scars on your hip . . ." Susan said. "They looked nasty."

Antoinette shrugged. "A close encounter with a dreniac, that's all."

Susan straightened. "It must be exciting to be a Venator."

Antoinette shrugged. "I've been one so long it's hard to remember anything else. It's been my life since I was a child. I guess it can be exciting."

"You must be very brave," Susan said.

"My brother calls it reckless," Antoinette said before entering the bathroom.

The shower was good, just what she'd need. She turned off the faucet and slipped back into fluffy robe. Steam fogged the mirror; she ran her palm across it to see her reflection. The hot water had colored her cheeks and refreshed her head.

She wrapped her wet hair in a towel and piled it on her head. With one last look at the dark circles under her eyes, she left the bathroom.

"Susan, tell me—" The rest of the question died on her lips as her gaze settled upon Christian sitting at the table sipping coffee.

At least she hoped it was coffee and not blood. Her hands went to the front of the bathrobe she'd hastily wrapped around herself and secured it tighter. "Where's Susan?"

"She has other duties," he said.

Her eyes fell on the waiting meal and her stomach growled.

"Sit down and eat while we talk," Christian said. The look of hunger in his eyes had nothing to do with food.

She pulled out the chair opposite him. "There's enough here to feed a small army," she said, popping a grape into her mouth.

His gaze fell to her lips. "Kavindish wasn't sure what you'd like."

"Good—cause I'm ravenous." She picked another grape and this time brought it to her lips and sucked slowly, watching him through her lashes. He seemed transfixed by her mouth, his eyes darkened.

She reached for a piece of toast and her robe fell open slightly. His eyes dropped. She could have closed the robe— yet she didn't. What was she doing?

What happened on the plane came back with solid clarity, sucking the breath from her body. She couldn't let that happen again. No matter how much she wanted it.

16

Home Alone

Christian suddenly and inexplicably missed food. He'd long forgotten the taste but not the pleasure food could give. He caught a glimpse of roundness as she reached across the table.

Antoinette straightened, pulled the robe shut and bit into the toast again. To take his mind off her nakedness, he poured a cup of coffee and handed it to her.

It cut him to see her and Viktor returning from a night on the town together even though Viktor had assured him it'd been innocent enough. They never lied to one another about women, not after Carolina. He'd also warned Christian to rein in his feeling for the lovely Ms. Petrescu. He was right. What had happened had been nothing more than an itch that needed scratching.

"Thanks," she said around a mouthful and reached for the cup, avoiding looking directly at him. Their fingers brushed and electricity shot up his arm even at such brief contact. She stopped mid-chew, shock registering on her face. After a heartbeat she swallowed and pulled the coffee to her lips.

Christian found it so hard to concentrate and he was growing hard just watching her eat. She wrapped soft lips around a luscious red strawberry, her eyelids dropping as she bit into the fruit. He imagined it was his tongue she sucked instead and the thought sent a heat wave through him, stronger than anything he'd felt in centuries. It was almost like the grip of a blood-thrall and his body reacted before his mind could catch. Juice ran down her chin as she bit into a piece of mango and her tongue darted out to catch it.

He watched her tender lips suck, her pink tongue lick, and crossed his legs on his throbbing groin. Thank goodness for the table.

"I really wish you'd stop looking at me like that," she said, her brow creasing. "What did you want anyway?"

"Viktor and I are going out."

The Lodge was no place for Antoinette. A prestigious club of influential Aeternus members and a few select, but affluent, humans. He and Viktor wanted to catch any rumors that were circulating about Sir Roger's murder.

"Where we going?" Antoinette asked, slipping more fruit into her mouth.

"We're not going anywhere. You're staying right here. Viktor and I have business to attend to." He pushed back his chair and walked to the door. "There's plenty to keep you occupied until we return. I have a well-stocked library downstairs and a training room where you can work out if you get too bored. Susan can show you the way." He closed the door on her angry scowl and smiled. Payback was a bitch.

After Christian left, Antoinette paced the room with her arms crossed, her fingers tapping out frustration on her upper arms. What had she been thinking, trying to seduce an Aeternus? She hadn't meant to, but when she saw Christian's face, and the way he watched her eat, it was easy to be seduced by the power she seemed to have over him for a brief second. Luckily he hadn't succumbed to her moment of weakness.

She'd never been one for sitting around and twiddling her thumbs. Why had they left her behind? They'd probably gone out to feed. She suppressed a shudder at the thought and paced to the other side of the room again. She had a sudden need to see Lucian, see how badly he was hurt for herself. She dressed quickly and made her way downstairs.

Kavindish appeared as if out of thin air. "Going somewhere, miss?"

"Just off for a walk." She took a step toward the door.

"I'm afraid I can't let you do that, miss."

Antoinette placed her hand on her hips. "You can't let me?"

Kavindish didn't bat an eyelid. "The master left instructions that you were to stay in the house tonight."

"Am I a prisoner?"

He remained solid between her and the door. "No, miss, it's for your own protection."

"I don't need protection. Now, if you don't move, Kavindish, I'll be forced to move you myself."

"You can try, miss."

Without warning she swung a kick at his head. But he blocked it with ease. He may not have looked much, but there was strength hiding under that suit and not even a slicked-back hair was out of place on his head. Not to be put off, she changed tactics and leveled a punch to his face and then brought her knee up, aiming for his groin. Again he blocked both attacks while scarcely moving, his face remaining passive.

"Well—never judge a butler by his cover," she said, impressed. "You're not such a cliché on legs after all."

Whatever he was, it wasn't human. His mouth twitched in one corner, but he remained the picture of impenetrable aloofness. She had to see Lucian, make sure he was safe but she wasn't getting past this butler. Time to take a leaf out of Viktor's book.

Antoinette held up her hands in surrender. "Okay, you win. Maybe it's for the best after last night. I think I'll do a bit of reading."

His eyes narrowed.

"If it's not too much trouble, could you bring me up some hot chocolate?" She gave him a weary smile.

He bowed stiffly. "Will there be anything else, miss?"

"No, that's all." She turned and made her way up the stairs again, turning halfway to find him still there watching.

Fifteen minutes later she tightened the belt on the fluffy bathrobe and answered the knock at her door. Kavindish carried in a tray and she pretended not to notice his surreptitious inspection. He was no dummy either.

But she'd been careful to look the part, right down to her matching fluffy slippers and the book tucked under her arm.

"Thanks, Kavindish. You can put it on the table."

She held the door open for him and waited. He looked at her jacket hanging over the back of the chair and her discarded jeans heaped on the floor. Briefly surveying the rest of the room, he headed for the door.

"Enjoy your chocolate, miss," he said with a little half-bow. "Don't hesitate to ring should you require anything else."

"Thanks, I will." She kept her expression tired, which only made his eyes narrow again. "But I think I'll return to bed, I'm feeling a little more hung over than I thought." She yawned widely and stretched. Maybe she'd pushed it a bit too far? The butler didn't move and looked even more suspicious.

Finally he bowed again. "Good night, miss."

"Good night, Kavindish."

As soon as the door was closed, she pressed her ear against it. Nothing. Walking to the table, she picked up the teaspoon and stirred, clinking loudly against the china. Then she dragged out the chair before tiptoeing back to the door. She heard his footsteps retreating down the hall.

Quick as a flash, she shucked off her bathrobe, pulled her jeans and jacket back on and opened the window. She'd already disabled the alarm and three floors to the ground was no big deal for a practicing Venator.

Antoinette swung her legs out and lowered her body over the edge, her toes stretching out for purchase on the drainpipe. Once she had a grip, she made easy work of descending the rest of the way. When she reached the ground, she wiped her hands on the back of her jeans and looked up. It shouldn't be too hard to get back up the same way.

Something brushed against her leg and she looked down to find Cerberus, his large pale blue eyes regarding her closely. He sat on his haunches, wagged his tail, and his tongue lolled out of the side of his mouth.

"Where did you come from?" she asked, then noticed the stairs leading down to a door with a dog flap.

"Out for an evening walk, are we?" She dropped and took his head in her hands. "I have to go and see my friend. You stay."

Antoinette pulled a pair of slip-on shoes from her pocket and slid them on before standing to zip her jacket. Jamming her fists into her pockets, she took a step toward the street and the dog followed.

"Cerberus, stay!" she commanded.

He sat again and tilted his head to the left, giving a little whine. She felt the dog watching her all the way down the narrow alley between Christian's brownstone and the one next door.

Before stepping into the street, she glanced back to see him still in the same position. His tail flapped merrily. She shook her head, glanced in both directions, and then quickly walked a couple of blocks before hailing a cab.

When Antoinette arrived at St. Vincent's Hospital in Manhattan the reception desk gave her Lucian's floor, but told her it was past visiting hours and she couldn't see him until the next day.

Like hell.

A little thing like visiting hours wasn't going to stop her when she'd gone to all this trouble. She lifted a white coat from an empty doctor's lounge and slipped into the stairwell.

When she reached Lucian's floor she crept out into the deserted hall. A couple of nurses sat at the station talking quietly.

Nothing else smelled like a hospital—chemical sterility covering the scent of sickness and death. Antoinette had a plan to distract one of the nurses, but not both.

Then, as if by divine intervention, one of the nurses stood. "I could do with a coffee. Want one?"

"Oh yes, please," the other said. "I'd give my firstborn for a hit of caffeine right now."

"Honey, I've seen your firstborn and you'd need a lot more than a cup of coffee for me to take on that little hellcat," the first nurse said.

"Well, it was worth a try."

They both burst out laughing.

This was her chance. When the first nurse disappeared Antoinette crept around the corner into a room and hit the call button beside a sleeping patient before dashing behind the door in the opposite room. Once the second nurse answered the buzzer, Antoinette zipped out and scanned the station charts for Lucian's room number. She found it.

Outside his room sat an empty chair where a guard should've sat. Antoinette bit back her anger and peered through the small glass window. A pale figure lay in the only bed, his head bandaged. She slipped in just as the second nurse returned to the station mumbling something about budget cuts and faulty equipment.

A small fluorescent light on the wall above Lucian's head cast his face in shadows, his eyes sunken and dark. She moved closer. His breathing was deep and steady and a bandage was clearly visible across his naked chest.

With the guard missing, she was afraid to leave him alone and after smoothing the covers at his side, she sat on the visitor's chair in the corner to watch over him for a while. Every now and then, one of the nurses would come, take his obs and write them in his chart. And each time Antoinette managed to hide behind the privacy curtain. Lucian remained asleep throughout it all, heavily sedated.

The visitor's chair was lumpy and dug into her hip, but she wriggled around to get as comfortable as possible.

Forming a cushion with the white doctor's coat she tucked one foot underneath her bottom and crossed her arms. Lucian's constant deep breathing lulled her mind; her head grew heavy . . .

"Antoinette?" someone croaked, jolting her awake.

"What?" she answered, her heart beating rapidly. At first she wasn't sure where she was.

"You were whimpering," the same voice said.

The fog cleared, Antoinette sat forward and Lucian's large intelligent eyes regarded her kindly from his bed.

"I must've fallen asleep." She stretched the stiffness from her neck and yawned. "Sorry."

He struggled to sit forward. Antoinette jumped up to put a pillow behind his shoulders, making it easier for him.

"What are you doing here? Not that I'm sorry you are." He sank back gratefully into the pillows, pain whitening the area around his eyes. "What were you dreaming about? The shooting?"

It had been Dante again, but she avoided his gaze and shrugged. "Maybe—I can't remember."

"Neither can I." He reached up and touched the bandage around his head. "I've tried, but I just can't. Apparently the blow I received from the coffee table on the way down not only knocked me out but gave me some kind of amnesia."

"So you didn't see the shooter at all."

"I'm afraid not." He frowned, looking at her more closely. "Why, what happened?"

She waved away his concerns. "Nothing, just too many nightmares."

"Nightmares?"

She sighed. "Yes, I've been dreaming about my mother's murder lately. I even thought it was Dante who shot you— but now I'm not so sure."

"You witnessed her murder didn't you?" Lucian asked. "Maybe the trauma of Sir Roger's shooting brought on some post traumatic stress."

"Maybe—but what I remember the most is the absolute power he had over me. He made me watch as he slit my mother's throat."

For a split second the image of Dante ascending the stairs holding out the doll she'd dropped sent a chill through her and she wrapped her arms around herself.

"You know, I've only just remembered my dolly," she whispered.

Lucian tilted his head, frowning. "Your dolly?"

She felt a tear slip down her face. "I'd wet myself and dropped my doll in pure terror. Dante picked it up and tried to get me to take it when my father arrived home. I remember reaching for it and . . ."

"And?"

She focused on him. "Later, when everything had died down, I looked for my doll. Papa had had it made especially, to look like me, and it was my favorite toy. But I never found it. To this day I don't know what happened to it."

A chill shivered down her spine and the images of the headless bodies pinned to the VCU crime board popped into her head. When she first looked at those faces all pinned together, they reminded her so much of her mother. If Dante is alive, then he's the Fang-whore Slasher, she was sure of it.

Lucian reached out his hand to her, his face pale and concerned. She shouldn't be boring him with stories from her past. He needed rest.

She stood up beside his bed. "It was a long time ago, before Sergei and Katerina took us in."

He sat up a little straighter. "When are you going home?"

"I'm not, at least not yet."

"Why?"

"I want to stick around for a bit, check out some things myself."

"Where are you staying?"

"At Christian Laroque's house for the time being. Viktor and he—" She wasn't ready to share the information about her father with anyone else yet. "My uncle asked them to keep an eye on me, in case the killer came back. Not that I need looking after," she added hastily.

That's right goddammit; I'm not some fragile princess, who swoons at the mere hint of trouble. Anger at her uncle resurfaced but she bit it back. This was neither the time nor place to vent.

"What the hell do you think you're doing?" an angry voice interrupted them.

17

After Hours

Antoinette spun to find a woman's silhouette filling the doorway, hands on hips.

"I just wanted to make sure my friend was okay." Antoinette looked at her watch, three A.M. She'd been here for hours. "I was able to walk in here with no one to stop me. Shouldn't there be a guard or something?"

The nurse's stance softened. "He should be there but seems to have wandered off again. Anyway, that's beside the point. Visiting hours ended long ago, you have to leave immediately."

"Can't you give us five more minutes?" Antoinette asked.

"I'm sorry I can't." The nurse's shoulders sank as she stepped closer to the bed to check on Lucian's pulse. "It's against regulations."

"Then I'll come back tomorrow, I mean later today," Antoinette said to Lucian.

"I won't be here. I'm being transferred to my house upstate. I have my own security and medical team on staff."

At least he'd be safe and she wouldn't have to worry.

"I'm sorry, but you have to leave now," the nurse said.

"Okay, okay." On impulse she leaned forward and kissed Lucian's forehead. "Be careful."

"You too." He gave her hand a final squeeze. "And if you need anything, let me know. The Academy will know how to contact me."

As she left the room a fat security guard sauntered up the hall with a magazine tucked under his arm, hitching his belt.

He saw her and puffed his out his chest. "Hey, you can't go in there."

"I've been in there for several hours. I think it's more important to know why you abandoned your post at least twice tonight. That man in there has been shot—someone tried to kill him. You're supposed to protect him. Where were you?" She pulled the magazine from under his arm.

Playboy. Disgusted, she tossed it back. It bounced off his chest and dropped to the floor.

His face flushed deep red, his mouth opening and shutting like a suffocating fish. "I had to take a leak."

"Well, while you were taking a leak, I was able to walk into Mr. Moretti's room completely unchallenged. If I'd been the killer, your charge would be long dead and you'd be in some deep shit." Antoinette felt the heat rising up her face, burning her ears. *Not totally true, but this fat fuck doesn't have a clue.*

The rent-a-cop shuffled his feet and looked everywhere but at her, then straightened his shoulders. "Who do you think you are? You can't give me orders."

"Look pal, I have connections with two of Intel's top agents and I know Oberon DuPrie personally." The guard paled at her slight stretch of the truth. "Lift your game and I won't mention I made this little impromptu evaluation. But next time I'll report you to your superiors and if anything happens to Mr. Moretti, I'm holding you responsible. Not her . . ." Antoinette pointed at the stunned nurse, "not the hospital, but *you*." She punctuated the last word with a poke to his jellyroll stomach.

Antoinette spun on her heel and strode toward the lift. The elevator chimed its arrival and as Antoinette hit the down button the nurse looked sourly at the pathetic excuse for a guard then grinned at Antoinette, giving her a double thumbs-up.

She left the hospital and hailed a cab, asking the driver to drop her several blocks from Christian's house. She needed time to think.

She was less than two blocks away when the hair on the back of her neck prickled. Then she noticed footsteps echoing off the pavement behind her. She stopped. So did the footsteps. Just one set. She didn't fear ordinary muggers and hoodlums, but something in her gut told her that wasn't what followed her.

She jammed her hands deeper into her jacket pockets and started off again, quickening her pace. So did her pursuer. When she reached the next street she ducked around the corner and pressed herself against the wall, holding her breath, listening to the footsteps growing closer. All of a sudden they stopped.

She waited. But no one came. Then the footsteps started again. This time from her left and down the street she'd turned into. It was the same rhythm to the steps, the same tempo echoing off the deserted street wet with the dew of the early morning.

Whoever it was had gotten ahead of her. The fine hair along her arms rose in solidarity with the ones on the back of her neck. A chill crept over her. She knew it was him. *Dante!*

Antoinette crossed the street quickly and continued in her original direction. So did the footsteps of her pursuer.

Enough of these games. She slowed down her steps. The footsteps grew louder behind her; the skin between her shoulders itched and prickled with expectation. After another minute she spun, hoping to catch him off guard. But again there was no one there. He was toying with her.

Then she heard the faint whistling on the wind. Coming from above—first to the right then to the left, as if he jumped from one building to another. Soon the strains of the Mocking Bird lullaby came closer and louder. It was the same tune she'd heard at the conference party, the same one he'd hummed as he murdered her mother, and this time she knew she wasn't imagining things.

"Dante . . ." she croaked, her voice deserting her. She swallowed and called into the early morning darkness. "Dante, I know you're there. Stop these games. Come out and face me."

"Well now, little one." He mocked from the shadows to her right. "Aren't you brave?" Now he was behind her.

"They tell me you're dead," she said.

His icy voice rumbled with what could have been a chuckle. "I know. Delicious isn't it?" The direction changed constantly as if he circled her. "And your father was my murderer. I couldn't have planned it better myself."

Terror froze her heartbeat. Her feet wouldn't move. He moved, quick and silent. She felt his breath in her hair for an instant then it was gone, leaving her to wonder if she'd imagined it. A chill crept up her legs.

"How did you escape the warehouse fire?" she asked.

His laughter crackled all around, surrounding her. Suddenly he was there, standing before her, wrapped in a dark gray cloak that hid everything except his face. When he smiled she saw his fangs extended and ready.

"Now, that would be telling, wouldn't it?" he said. "But let's just say that I was fortunate the warehouse was over water and I had a friend willing to help me out with a little push. I did give him a hand, or should I say finger?"

"So whose body did fall from the window?"

"Some poor unfortunate newly turned Aeternus in the right place at the wrong time."

"Now you're here, tormenting me," she whispered. "Why?"

"We have unfinished business, you and I. Your mother may have been the sweetest thing I'd ever tasted," he said, his tone dripping with honeyed sarcasm. "But you were even sweeter standing there in your nightgown, your dolly under your arm, your eyes big and round. I just wanted to eat you up. And now you are here, looking so much like your mother. The others are just pale imitations."

"The fang-whores." Her hands shook, a chill crept up her backbone. She'd been right.

"Ah yes." His face softened to a misty expression. "Their screams are songs to my ears. I wanted to make your mother scream. I want to make *you* scream." He focused on her. "Oh yes, I will make you sing for me." His eyes grew bright and piercing, burning her with their heat.

"No, I won't," she said, clenching her fists to stem the fear pumping through her. "I'm going to stop you."

"How, little one? How will you do that?" He smiled that same deadly smile he had on the night he drew the blade across her mother's creamy skin.

"I don't know yet, but I will." Try as she might, she couldn't keep the quiver from her voice.

"And what if I stop you first?" he asked.

She opened her mouth to answer him, but nothing came out.

"How can you stop me? You're just a human girl. Can you stop me from doing this?" Suddenly he was pinning her arms behind her back. She hadn't even seen him move. "Tell me, has Christian tasted your delights?" he whispered in her ear.

How did he do it? He'd turned her into a helpless child again as he leaned closer, his breath crawling over her skin as he sniffed at her neck. "What a woman you are. You make me so hot. Can you feel it?"

She could, pressed against her ass. Her stomach heaved.

"You're mine, little-one, all mine. And I will devour you." He drew closer to her throat—her skin feeling soiled where he touched. "But not tonight, not yet."

It wasn't until she'd fallen back a step that she realized he'd released her. She ran.

"Stop." His voice commanded before she took more than a few steps.

She did, her feet rooted to the ground as if glued.

"Turn."

And she did.

"Look at me."

Try as she might she couldn't stop her eyes from gravitating toward him.

A loud snarl came from her left. Cerberus stood in the street; hackles raised, teeth bared, and menace rumbling in his chest.

"Well now," Dante chuckled. "This has to be one of Viktor's pups."

The dog crept forward a step, his head low to the ground. The lips of his muzzle peeled back to reveal long, sharp canines and his gaze fixed firmly on Dante.

Dante waved his hand and Cerberus was lifted off his feet and thrown through the air, landing several feet away. The impact pushed the air from the dog's lungs in a loud whoosh.

Antoinette froze. She'd never seen anything like it before. No Aeternus or dreniac she'd ever heard of possessed telekinetic powers. This was something new.

The injured animal whimpered and she ran to his side as he struggled to his feet, wrapping her arm around his neck. Dante would tear him to pieces in the blink of an eye if Cerberus tried to attack again.

Cerberus's growl deepened and he snapped, saliva dripping from his lower jaw. Antoinette felt his tension thrumming against her chest as his body shook with rage.

"Well." Dante made a flourishing bow. "Another time, little-one." With an overdramatic swirl of his cape he was gone.

Antoinette would've laughed if the fear hadn't stolen her humor. She rubbed Cerberus's thick fur, burying her face in it as she caught her breath.

"Thank you, my guardian angel." She scratched behind his ears and hugged him close once more. "Come on, let's go home."

Cerberus followed close behind, occasionally stopping

to look back and growl. She reached the alley between the houses and moved to the drainpipe. After one final rub and a kiss to the top of his head, Cerberus stood in silent sentry as Antoinette climbed back up the drainpipe. When she reached the window he descended the side stairs and entered through the pet door as she pulled herself onto the windowsill. She should've left a lamp on—the room was too dark to see.

Suddenly she was yanked into the room and a rough hand snapped over her mouth. She was shoved onto the bed, pinned with the weight of a body on top of her. Only an Aeternus had that kind of strength. Her heart hammered against her chest. Dante had come to take her after all. He'd fooled her, and when she thought she was safe, he'd come. She tried to scream but the hand muffled the sound and a breath brushed her ear. She tensed, closed her eyes, and waited for the teeth against her throat.

18

caught in the act

"Where have you been?" Christian's voice tight was with suppressed anger as she lay beneath him. "I told you to stay here. Don't you know how dangerous it is out there right now?"

Her eyes flung open, relief blooming in their depths. Not the emotion he'd expected. Then he smelled the fear soaked into her pores. Her reaction had been a little too violent. Something had happened out there.

"What's wrong?" he asked.

His hand muffled her words and she struggled beneath him again but with nowhere near the violence as before. A frown creased her brow as she tried to move her head. With her human eyes she wouldn't be able to see him in the darkened room, though he could see every detail, every grimace, and every frown.

He removed his hand but her body still trembled beneath his.

"Do you mind getting off me now?" she asked impatiently.

"Apparently I do," he sighed against her ear, breathing in the scent of her hair.

Her fear was intoxicating and the touch of her breath

against his cheek did little to alleviate his excited state. His fangs descended, long and sharp.

No, not now. He pushed away, the cold air rushed between them.

"Where did you go tonight?" he demanded.

Antoinette reached for the bedside lamp and turned it on. Christian turned away from the brilliance.

"To see Lucian."

"Are you insane? Why didn't you wait for me or . . . or Viktor to go with you?" He turned around to see her thunderous face.

"You had no right telling your butler to keep me locked in the house like a prisoner. I've been a fully licensed Venator for several years now. I don't need you, Viktor, or your servant to look after me."

She was right of course—under normal circumstances. But these were far from normal circumstances. Why couldn't she see that? And why should he care?

"Look, we don't know what is going on or why Sir Roger was murdered. Until we can make some sense of this I don't think it's safe—"

"I don't care, I do not need a babysitter, and I won't tolerate being kept prisoner."

"We just need to know where you are in case—" Christian stopped.

"In case the killer tries for me and you're not there to catch him." Antoinette finished for him. "I'm not stupid."

"We were going to talk to you about it, in fact it's why I came to your room tonight, and then found it empty."

She crossed her arms and looked away.

She'd given in far too easily; he'd expected more of an argument. "So you'll be more careful?"

"Of course."

"That may not be necessary," Viktor's voice called from the doorway.

They both turned to find him with Cerberus by his side. The dog went straight to Antoinette and licked her hand.

Viktor cocked his head to the side and leaned against the doorframe. "I'm glad you're both here," he said, a self-satisfied grin on his face. "I've found him."

"Who?" Antoinette asked.

Christian took a step forward. "Grigore's contact—you've found him?"

Viktor nodded, grinning widely. "It's Williams. He's been right under our noses the whole time. And what's more, he's agreed to meet me at the same location we'd arranged with Grigore."

"Andrew Williams? The Ambassador's assistant?" Christian asked.

"Yes, that's the one." Viktor's eyes danced with excitement.

It was hard to believe someone that close to the Ambassador would actually associate with a fugitive. "How did he get involved with Grigore?" Christian asked.

Viktor straightened and came completely into the room. "Apparently they went to the Academy of Parahuman Studies in Budapest together.

"So, what now?" Antoinette asked as she stroked Cerberus's head.

"He wants to meet—after sunset tonight."

"This seems far too convenient," Christian said. "I'm coming with you."

Viktor shook his head. "I have to meet him alone. That was part of the deal."

"Last time you were supposed to meet, he never showed and Grigore disappeared," Christian said. "How do we know this Williams guy didn't sell Grigore out? It smells like a setup."

"I agree with Christian," Antoinette said, surprising them both.

"All right, but he can't see you," Viktor conceded.

"The meeting place is at a club, right? He wouldn't see us if we were just some other customers sitting separately," Antoinette suggested.

"Now, wait a minute." Christian stepped between her and Viktor. "You can't come."

"And why not? Haven't we just had this discussion?" She lifted her chin.

"She's right, Christian." Viktor came to her defense. "And if you looked like a couple on a date, it would be the perfect cover."

"What?" Antoinette and Christian chorused together.

"No way," Christian said. The thought of being that close to her, like on a date—he could barely keep his hands off her as it was.

"Why not?" Antoinette scowled and shoved her hands on her hips. "What's wrong with me?"

"Come on, Christian, it's undercover—you know, your job. You do remember how to do that, don't you?" Viktor said, his grin getting wider.

Christian ran his hand through his hair and ignored his friend's jibe. "Okay—but we'll have to come up with a good plan."

Finally a breakthrough, a real one. The thrill of the hunt sparked in his veins. "So did he say anything about what happened last time?"

"We didn't really have much time to talk, but he did say it was Grigore who called off the last meeting."

"And you believe him?" Antoinette asked. "Wouldn't Papa have contacted you as well if that was the case?"

Viktor frowned and placed his hands behind his back, pacing while his mind worked. Antoinette could almost hear the cogs turning.

He stopped and looked at her. "At this point, I don't know what to believe. I was deep undercover on another case and Grigore was keeping contact to a minimum at that point. All I know is it would have taken something extremely important for him to risk breaking comms silence."

"But we still don't know what this Williams guy has to do with my father," she said.

"Look, he's the only link we have. One way or another Williams knows something, and I aim to find out what it is."

After Viktor and Christian left, Antoinette leaned against the door and closed her eyes. She'd had a hard time trying to keep it together while they were here but luckily she'd pulled it off. Now that she was alone she let her knees give out and slid to the floor, brushing a shaky hand over her face.

There was no denying it this time. It was definitely Dante and he was definitely real. And he was also the Fang-whore Slasher.

Cerberus licked her ear and she ruffled his fur before hugging him close. "You saw him too, didn't you, boy? You know I wasn't hallucinating?"

The dog tilted his head at her again, pricked his ears, then looked toward the window and growled, although not with any real menace. She rubbed his fur. "Do you want to stay and keep me company tonight, boy?"

The dog yapped and jumped onto the end of the bed. He circled around and kneaded a comfortable spot then lay down with his head on his paws, cocking one doggy eyebrow at her. Antoinette got up from the floor and joined him on the bed. She gave him a quick pat on the head then stood to undress before crawling beneath the blankets.

As she lay back against the pillows she thought of Christian. When she'd realized it was him in her room and not Dante, she went straight from terror to temptation. The weight of his body on hers made her want to wrap her legs around his waist as he buried himself in her. Dante and Christian were both a danger to her—they made her lose control in different ways: one through fear and the other through desire.

She was going to have to learn to protect her emotions if she was to survive either of them.

The crowded smoke-filled club hummed with dance music and loud conversation. Antoinette sipped her cocktail through a straw. Christian said it was a Virgin Mary, Viktor's idea of a joke. Normally she wasn't partial to tomato juice but she found herself enjoying the Tabasco kick.

Even though Antoinette's drink was alcohol-free her head still spun thanks to secondhand smoke from the joints being passed around in the next booth.

"Come on, you two," Viktor's voice buzzed through the electronic receiver in her ear. "At least try and look like you're having a good time. You're supposed to be on a date."

"You've obviously never seen any of my dates," Antoinette whispered, glancing down at her overexposed cleavage for the hundredth time to make sure the small microphone hadn't popped into view, or anything else for that matter. She looked up and caught Christian staring in the same direction.

"Hey!" She clicked her fingers in front of her face. "I'm up here."

Christian's smoldering eyes dragged up to her face and a slow smile tilted his mouth. "I can't help it, they're just so . . . there." Again his gaze dropped to her chest.

Part of her was insulted and the rest was pleased. She crossed her arms, which only made things worse. Her breasts squeezed together and pushed out even more. As Christian leaned forward the hunger in his expression increasing, she resisted the urge to pull on her coat.

"What time is he supposed to arrive again, Viktor?" she asked, trying to distract herself.

They all wore the tiny electronic receivers in their ears and mikes tucked inconspicuously away. The noisy crowd and the music made it too difficult for Christian and Viktor to rely on their enhanced senses alone.

Out of the corner of her eye Antoinette saw Viktor pick up his glass and hold it near his mouth as if drinking. "Half an hour ago. Maybe he's been detained."

She didn't know who he was trying to convince more, himself or them.

"Do you really think he's going to show now?" she asked.

"Give it a little more time," Viktor responded.

A blond hooker sidled up to Viktor, placing her hand on his shoulder and leaned forward to whisper in his ear. He turned toward her, interest apparent on his face even from this distance. He reluctantly shook his head and turned back to his drink. The blonde moved on to the next potential customer.

After a couple of mocktails Antoinette couldn't fight the urge to use the bathroom any longer and stood.

Christian reached out and grabbed her by the wrist. "Where are you going?"

"To freshen up," she said, not bothering to hide her annoyance. "I don't have your . . . constitution."

"Sorry." He released her.

With a hitch of her hip she teetered on the leg-breakingly high heels that completed her skanky disguise.

Christian tilted his head to watch her walk away, admiring the way those stilettos set a waggle in her stride. A minuscule strip of leather only just covered the swell of her buttocks, showing those never-ending legs to full advantage. It rode low enough on her hips to show the dragon tattoo nestled between the twin dimples—all except for the tip of the tail.

She had topped off the disguise with a plunging black halter-neck top. Her loose hair swayed against her almost naked back in time with the movement of her hips. God, he loved to watch her walk away.

Christian had never been into sleaze but a sudden image of taking her hard against the wall of the dingy hall leading to the bathrooms, her legs wrapped around his waist, had him shifting uncomfortably in his seat.

When Antoinette returned she stood next to the table with her hands on her hips. "All this sitting around is making me kinda antsy. Let's dance."

Crap. "I don't think so."

"Well, I'm dancing, with or without you."

She slipped off her shoes and made her way barefoot onto

the crowded dance floor, turned, and locked eyes with him.

Raising both hands above her head she began to move her hips and only her hips. She turned her back to him and lifted her hair to expose the creamy curve of her neck while her hips continued to undulate—her spine curving and curling in time to the beat.

She had complete control over every muscle, every movement of her body. His erection swelled painfully and twitched with each roll and jerk of her luscious curves. The leather pants he had on suddenly seemed several sizes too small.

"You go girl." Viktor's voice pierced Christian's captivation.

"Want to join me, Viktor?" she asked. "Christian isn't in the mood."

Oh, I'm definitely in the mood—just not for dancing.

"Tempting, very tempting," Viktor answered. "But I think I'll just enjoy the show for now."

Antoinette was soon surrounded by a half dozen men all vying for her attention. However, she seemed lost to the music and paid little attention to her wannabe partners as she twisted and turned, rolling her hips with her stomach rippling like a slow hypnotic wave.

"Oh my . . . where did you learn moves like that?" Viktor asked her what Christian was thinking.

"My aunt Katerina taught all the girls in the family belly dancing. She said girls should at least learn something of the old ways, other than hunting." Antoinette whispered as a guy grabbed her from behind, grinding his groin against her.

Christian leapt out of the chair ready to rip the offender's arms off. But he needn't have bothered. In a blur of movement she brought her elbow around to connect with the would-be lothario's chin. If not for the smug tilt to her mouth, Christian could almost have believed it was accidental.

However, as one fell off, another took his place. A growl built in Christian's chest, but he forced himself to sit and endure it. Antoinette could take care of herself. She wouldn't be impressed with him wading in to pull her out from the middle of the pack of lusty human males. No matter how much his instincts were screaming at him to do just that.

"Okay, boys and girls—I think it's time to track down that son of a bitch and use a more forceful method of persuasion," Viktor said.

"Finally!" Antoinette's voice husked through his earpiece.

Christian glanced across to the bar and silently thanked Viktor for putting him out of his misery. Antoinette untangled herself from the crowd and made her way back to the table much to the disappointment of her now-considerable group of admirers.

"So where does he live?" Antoinette asked as she slipped on her shoes.

"I know it's somewhere in Manhattan—Madison Avenue I think. I'll call to dig up his address. You two get going and I'll text his location as soon as I know," Viktor said. "That'll still give us three hours before dawn. Let's hope he's just tardy and not something worse."

"Right, we'll head to the Upper East Side. Call when you've got something," Christian said.

Antoinette slung a tacky beaded bag over her shoulder and led the way to the exit. Just before the door, he glanced back at Viktor, who threw down the last of the drink and placed the empty glass back on the bar.

They stepped out into the night air, Antoinette shivered and rubbed her bare upper arms. Christian took of his leather jacket and wrapped it around her shoulders. She surprised him with a smile and pushed her arms into the sleeves.

As they crossed the parking lot Christian's internal alarm bells began to clang. He glanced over his shoulder, but the darkened lot was deserted.

Still, something felt very wrong. It'd be better to get Antoinette out of here before anything went down.

The doors to the club opened and Viktor stepped through, pulling his keys from the pocket of his jeans.

Christian fumbled in his own pants pockets for the keys

to the Ford sedan before remembering he'd left them in his jacket.

He was reaching for Antoinette's elbow when the distinctive sound of a silencer-muffled shot came out of nowhere. He pushed her to the pavement, covering her body with his.

When he was sure no more shots were coming Christian rolled to his feet. "Are you all right?"

She gave a stunned nod. Christian reached down and helped her to her feet. "We should get you out of here before they try again."

A somber canine howl filled the night sky and Antoinette looked past his shoulder, her face draining completely of color.

"Viktor," she screamed.

19

on a wing and a prayer

Terror gripped Antoinette's heart and squeezed hard. Viktor stumbled again and leaned against the old pickup he'd driven. Christian reached Viktor's side before she had a chance to take the first running step. He'd kneeled over her for a second before disappearing: there in one blink of an eye and gone the next.

With her heart pounding in her ears she reached the fallen Aeternus and fell to her knees beside him. He met her with his typical cheeky grin, but his amber eyes held pale terror. Dark blood blossomed on the front of his shirt; he held his hand over the wound.

Christian reappeared and knelt again, taking his friend's head into his lap. He looked Antoinette in the eye. "No sign of the shooter," he mouthed.

"You don't have to whisper on my account," Viktor said and then stiffened, sucking back a large painful-sounding breath.

"Come, my old friend, you've been shot before." Christian's voice quavered. "We'll get that bullet out and you'll be as right as rain. Let's have a look."

He gently moved Viktor's hand aside to rip the fabric.

Christian's eyes grew wide and he sucked back his breath. A cold chill crept up Antoinette's spine. The actual bullet hole was small and relatively clean, but that wasn't what worried her. His veins had turned black around the wound, and the blackness spread like the tendrils of an evil spider web, growing longer as they watched.

"Oh dear God," she whispered. "Silver nitrate."

"I know." Viktor turned his head toward her. "I can feel it traveling through my bloodstream."

Antoinette crouched beside him, taking his hand in hers as tears flooded her vision.

"We have to get you to a clinic." Christian's voice cracked but Viktor shook his head.

"It's pure, Christian," Viktor whispered. "I'm already dead."

"No!" Christian shook his head and gathered Viktor under his arms to lift him.

"Christian, don't," he pleaded. "It will only speed up what little time I have left. I have some things to say to you . . ." He looked at Antoinette. "To both of you."

"Why?" she croaked, tears creating wet trails down her cheeks.

Viktor's face relaxed a little. "I guess we're getting too close. That's good news."

With a loud shattering sound, Cerberus jumped through the car window, raining glass down on them. The large malamute came up beside Antoinette to place his muzzle on his master's hand and whimpered. Blood streaked his black and white fur where he'd been lacerated by the broken glass.

Viktor grabbed the front of Christian's shirt. "You must find out what happened to Andrew . . . if he's not a part of this, he may be in danger too. He may already be dead."

He then looked at Antoinette, his eyes going soft as he squeezed her hand. A sob exploded from her, hurting her chest and head. He glanced at his faithful dog. "Take care of him for me, my Mandy-Sue."

Antoinette smiled through her tears and nodded. "Anything, my Sammy—" She couldn't complete the words, her head hurt with the tears she couldn't shed fast enough.

Viktor took back his hand and stroked Cerberus's head one last time as the silver nitrate poison turned the veins in his neck black. The dog whimpered again.

"No, this can't be happening." Christian shook his head, his jaw clenching so hard the muscles corded in his neck. "I won't let it."

"Even you can't stop this." Viktor smiled wanly up at his friend. "Take care of Valerica. I haven't been a very good brother of late—I know she can be a handful, but . . . you know she's going to take this hard."

"I promise," Christian said in choking syllables.

Antoinette held Viktor's hand against her lips. "Thank you for looking after my father." Fat tears dropped onto his bare chest; she wanted to wipe them away but she couldn't let go of his hand. "And me."

"Oh, *ma chère,* it was my pleasure." Viktor gave her a weak wink. "When you find him, tell him he was the best human I've ever known, and I loved him."

Antoinette nodded, the physical pain in her chest became almost unbearable. Her gaze locked briefly with Christian.

Grief dulled Christian's eyes and a kind of insane calmness crept over him. She wanted to hold him, to comfort him, but he was frozen by his own emotions.

Viktor's body jerked, spine stiffening and his head snapped back. He screamed as the poison reached his brain. Silvery black invaded his usually bright amber eyes and took away the last of his life.

Antoinette's heart shattered and a sob tore from her throat. He was gone. Cerberus nudged his master's leg, then threw back his head with a long mournful howl. Christian joined him with his own primal cry of grief and rage.

Viktor's hand slipped from hers and she dried the tears on her cheeks. This couldn't be happening, not Viktor. But it had happened and now he was dead. Murdered. Christian squatted beside his body, then within seconds he was gone.

She bit back her sorrow and pulled out her cell to dial 911. "I want to report a murder of an Aeternus male."

She gave them the details and the address and hung up. Now she could let her grief hit. And it did—big time. A spasm ripped through her stomach, but she was able to make it to the shadows on the other side of Viktor's car before she threw up.

A police cruiser pulled up as she wiped her mouth with the back of her hand. Two cops got out of the car and approached Viktor's body.

Cerberus didn't even look at them but a warning rumbled from his chest, stopping the policemen in their tracks. The cops exchanged wary looks and their hands move to unclip their gun holsters.

"Please," she said, putting herself between them and the dog.

They stopped and looked her. When she explained the situation, they were more than happy to wait for backup to arrive. One of the cops climbed back into the car to call it in as the other moved to control the crowd building as curious patrons piled out of the club.

Twenty minutes later a large black SWAT-like mobile command center pulled into the parking lot and reversed close to the scene. Several people got out and started taking over the crime scene.

Paramedics pulled up beside the black van. One of the policemen led her over to the back of the ambulance and wrapped a blanket around her shoulders.

"Thank you," she said, looking into his kind brown eyes.

"Not a problem, you just sit here and wait until one of the detectives is free to talk to you," he said and then moved off to help with crowd control.

Oberon pulled up on his Harley-Davidson motorcycle. *What was he doing here?*

He swung his long leather-clad leg off the sleek black customized Heritage Softail and ate up the ground in long strides as he approached Viktor's body. Again, Antoinette found his sheer mass intimidating.

Cerberus bared his teeth but Oberon squatted down to his level and spoke softly. She couldn't make out any of the words. Slowly the dog's face relaxed and reluctantly left Viktor's side. Oberon led him away, allowing the police access to photograph the body.

Oberon brought the dog to her. Cerberus looked warily back from her to the forensic people a couple of times before coming around to lean against Antoinette's side. It was like he needed her as much as she needed him right now.

This was the second murder she'd witnessed within the last week. Even though she dealt with death before, she was usually the one doing the dealing.

Oberon looked at Antoinette—pale and drawn, huddled under a blanket at the back of the ambulance with the large malamute's head in her lap. One of the paramedics offered a thermos cup of coffee, and she smiled gratefully and wrapped both shaking hands around it.

She seemed far from the self-assured woman he'd encountered last time. Every time she looked toward the body her face filled with naked, desolate grief. And each time she got that look the dog whimpered in sympathy. It was unusual for a human to have that kind of connection with an animal, let alone one that wasn't even hers.

He'd been in the area checking the hooker hangouts for any more missing girls when his partner, Dylan, called him with the news of Viktor's murder. They worked as a team, Dylan listened to the police scanners and Oberon patrolled.

He'd only meant to take a look. Viktor's dog lifted his head and regarded Oberon with huge pale blue eyes. Antoinette looked at him as well, while she continued stroking the dog.

"Are you okay?" he asked.

She nodded, shook her head, then took a deep breath and nodded again. "Yes, thank you."

"Okay." The girl was a mess. "So, where's Christian?"

She took a second to steel herself before answering. "I don't know—he just vanished, probably on the killer's trail."

Oberon may be an unfeeling bastard at times, but he knew what it was like to lose a partner and a friend. He felt sorry for the blood-drinker.

He pulled a pack of cigarettes from his pocket and shook one out. "What were you all doing here tonight?"

He sucked the tobacco smoke into his lungs. *Ah—that hit the spot.* He blew out the smoke and refilled them with a fresh batch of nicotine and poison. Thanks to the para-human constitution he didn't have to worry about lung cancer like those poor human saps.

"He just left you here—don't you think that strange?"

"No. When Viktor die—" She chewed on her bottom lip, eyes darting, filling with tears.

Oberon didn't know who was more surprised by her tears, him or Antoinette. He glanced around looking for someone else to deal with her but everyone was busy. He'd never been good with crying females.

When he'd had her in for questioning she hadn't shed a tear. Instead she'd been good and mad, not close to hysterics as she was now. *Good and mad, that I can handle.* And he knew just what buttons to push too.

"Suck it up, it's not like you were sleeping with the blood-drinker—"

Something slammed into his mouth, bursting his lip against his teeth, and he hadn't even seen her get up. The coppery taste filled his mouth and he turned his head to spit the bloody saliva.

"Have some respect, I just lost my friend." She glared at him, shaking out her wrist. The dog now stood beside her, hackles raised and growling in warning. The tears stopped as suddenly as they'd started, and she dried her eyes on the corner of the blanket.

"Sorry," she said. "But you asked for that."

Oberon shrugged and wiped his mouth. "I guess I did."

For such a little thing, she packed a pretty fantastic punch.

"I don't know where Christian went or why, I assumed he would be after the killer. Wouldn't you be if you were in his place?" she said.

He guessed she was right.

She tilted her head to one side. "You don't like me much, do you?"

"I don't have a personal opinion of you one way or another," he replied, taking the last drag and squashing out the butt with his boot. "I don't trust you because you lied to me."

Her brows furrowed. "When?"

"The other night—during questioning."

Her eyes flicked away, the same as they had the other night. "What are you doing here anyway?" she asked, changing the subject.

"Just passing by when I heard it on the scanner."

His cell rang. Dylan's number flashed up on the screen. "Yes?"

"Another girl taken close to where you are now. Same profile, except she's money, not a fang-whore, so the VCU aren't mobilizing."

"Where exactly?"

20
The Scene

"The girl was abducted in the Red Hook area a few minutes ago." The disembodied voice came through the cell phone loud enough for Antoinette to overhear. "She was roughing it down there with some friends; this could be him."

"I'm five minutes away, how long will it take you to get there?" Oberon turned and started to walk away.

But Antoinette had heard enough. Dante had taken another victim and Oberon knew where. She reached into her pocket and found Christian's keys.

"Come, boy," she said to Cerberus.

The car was outside the area cordoned off by the police. They were all too busy to notice her leave.

She let Cerberus jump in first. He immediately climbed into the passenger seat and sat, almost like he was just as anxious to get going as she was.

Antoinette turned the key in the ignition and waited for Oberon to climb on his motorcycle and start it.

As he pulled away, she followed close enough not to lose him but not so close as to attract his attention.

He led her through the city streets down toward the waterfront. The other victims had been found floating in and around the Red Hook area.

It was him. Fear and excitement warred in her gut for
dominance. She would have the advantage this time; she
was hunting him and not the other way around.

Rain started to fall with heavy fat drops, making visibility
difficult. She missed the corner when Oberon turned right
into a narrow one-way street. She pulled over to the curb.

The streets were deserted in this industrial part of town.
She turned around and came back, turning off her lights
before rolling to a slow stop across the street. He'd climbed
off the bike and was leaning against it, waiting. Probably for
his partner.

She flipped open the glove box and took out her gun,
which she'd left there earlier tonight—just in case. Now she
was glad to be prepared. Antoinette looked down at her bare
feet. The heels she'd been wearing would hardly have been
suitable, even if she hadn't left them back where Viktor had
died. She swallowed her grief. *Later.*

There was nothing she could do about the shoes now; and
she hadn't thought to bring a spare pair. A car slowed and
pulled in behind Oberon.

Cerberus sat up in the passenger seat with ears pricked.

"Stay!" she said.

The dog groaned and lay back down, cocking his doggy
eyebrow as if accusing her of being mean.

"Good boy." She ruffled his head and climbed out of the
nice dry car into the pouring rain.

Dylan got out of the black Jeep Wrangler, checked his gun,
and stashed it in his shoulder holster. "The police got a
call from a witness about a woman being dragged into this
alley."

"Let's get moving then, the Slasher may like to take his
time, but we don't have that luxury." Oberon sluiced the
water off his face. "It's time to hunt."

"Do you think he's still near?" Dylan asked, rain plaster-
ing tendrils of hair to his cheeks.

"I don't know." Oberon turned to his partner. "We can only hope."

The rain lessened as they entered the alley but the ground was flooded. Blocked drains backed up, preventing the run-off of the water gushing from down-pipes from the rooftops above. Oberon cursed as it washed away the scent trail.

Dylan squatted to pick up something—a delicate gold chain too short to be a necklace.

"I'd say we're on the right track," he said. "This anklet looks pretty expensive. Not something that would go unno-ticed for long around here."

They moved down the alley checking the side doors for signs of entry. A shoe lay half hidden under a Dumpster near the other end of the alleyway. By some miraculous piece of luck, it had landed in the only dry spot in the entire alley, sheltered from the rain and not floating in a puddle. Oberon held it to his nose.

A soft footstep landed in the wet ground and he spun around to find Antoinette following behind with a 9mm handgun.

"You shouldn't be here," he growled.

"Neither should you." She straightened. "But I want this guy as much as you do. You'll have to physically restrain me to stop me."

"Don't tempt me," Oberon growled.

"We don't have time for this, we're gonna lose him," Dylan said. "You may as well let her come. Besides—she's a licensed Venator, not a civilian. Hi, I'm Dylan Jordan—his partner." He stretched out his hand in greeting.

Antoinette smiled and shook it. "I know who you are— the felian, right?"

Bloody human. And why was Dylan being so civilized?

"Ahhhh!" Oberon slammed his fist into the wall. The pain shot up his arm, clearing the rage from his mind. "As much as I like the idea of locking her up, you're right, we don't have time." Oberon flexed his hand as the bones popped back into place, healing in seconds. "The woman's scent from this shoe is fresh."

He shifted the muscles in his face, elongating his jaw and nose, but he didn't do a full transformation. He only needed to use his bear-enhanced olfactory abilities for now.

The victim's human scent was ingrained into the leather with traces of a floral perfume, possibly moisturizer or a hand cream of some kind. Again it seemed expensive and out of place for this part of town. It hadn't been in the alley long enough for other smells to taint it, so a good bet it belonged to our victim.

This was no spiking fang-whore. This victim had money. Her scent lingered in his nostrils until his brain processed the pattern and then he could "see" her trail—flashes of reddish orange where her skin had brushed the wall or a line where a foot had grazed the cement pavement as she was dragged. One of her hairs stuck to the brickwork, long and fair just like the rest.

The rain beat a constant tattoo all around him. Antoinette pushed up the arms of an oversized jacket to reveal raised goose bumps. Puffs of visible white breath erupted from her blue-tinged lips. At this rate she would catch her death before they caught the killer.

"You should go back," Dylan said to Antoinette. "You don't even have any shoes, you'll catch pneumonia."

The girl shook her head violently, her teeth chattering as she swiped her wet hair out of her eyes. "I'm fine. Just keep going. I have a feeling we're close."

Stubborn bloody human.

They left the alley to come out in front of a large multistory abandoned building with one of the large front doors slightly ajar.

Oberon brought two fingers to his eyes and then pointed to the gate. He glanced at Dylan, hit his chest then pointed at Dylan and Antoinette. She didn't look happy but they both nodded. Oberon would go first.

He pulled his 9mm and Dylan unholstered his Desert

Eagle, and they crossed the street quickly and took up position either side of the door.

Antoinette gripped the pistol, the excitement of the hunt
rising in her veins. She looked to Oberon, waiting for his
signal, and was impressed he still had the head of the bear
while his body remained human. It took great control to
maintain a partial transformation. He nodded his large
head and held up three fingers, then one by one he put them
down. On the last finger they entered the building. Antoinette didn't mind being tail-end charlie—it was Oberon's
turkey-shoot after all.

The drumming of the rain receded the further they made
their way toward the center of the building. Water dripped
from the ill-maintained ceiling above, forming puddles on
the floor.

Oberon led the way through a maze of debris and rusted
metal. He seemed very confident of the direction, stopping
occasionally to sniff the air and then set off again. For a
large man, he was remarkably light on his feet. He called
for a halt and nodded toward Dylan, who took off up a set of
stairs leading to the naked support beams of the collapsed
floor above.

Dylan flowed in and out of the shadows as silent as the
felian he was. He ran with ease along a thin metal support
beam and stopped halfway, looking down. Oberon snapped
out a few tactical hand signals Antoinette didn't understand.
Dylan responded with a few of his own then dropped eigh-
teen feet to land silently beside her.

Oberon took them deeper into the dilapidated building
toward a stairwell leading down into the basement. This had
an all-too-familiar feeling, though usually she did it alone.

Oberon's face began to twitch and shrink; hair sucked
back into his skin, leaving only his goatee beard before he
stretched his jaw, snapping it into place.

He leaned in close to her ear. "He brought the girl in here,"
he whispered against her ear. "I can smell his scent as clearly

as hers now, even in human form. Dylan says there are no lookouts or guards. He's working alone."

When he pulled back, he held his forefinger to his lips then pointed down the stairs. She gave him the thumbs-up, and with a nod from Dylan, Oberon led the way down to the soft glow coming from the floor below.

The foot of the staircase opened out onto a cavernous basement floor filled with hundreds of candles. In the center of the room was a large ornate stone platform. The woman lay bound hand and foot to the altar, the candlelight flickering over her naked body. *Dante really took this melodramatic shit a little too seriously.*

The woman turned her head, her eyes widening when she saw Antoinette. When Oberon placed his forefinger against his lips, the woman's face relaxed with hope. Her eyes darted to the other side of the room and she twisted her head toward a door. That must be where Dante had gone.

Oberon tapped Antoinette's shoulder and signaled for her and Dylan to go after the girl. The felian dropped to a squat and drew a knife from a sheath around his ankle before signaling he was ready.

As they neared the altar, she smelled the decay of old blood. Symbols and ancient text were carved into the surface of the stone altar and grooves ran along the length to channel the blood toward the feet for collection.

"He'll be back—" the girl started to say.

"Shh," Antoinette hissed, cutting her off.

As Dylan sliced the bonds tying the girl down, Oberon moved closer to the other side of the room. Suddenly the door burst inward from its hinges, hitting Oberon full on and knocking him backward.

Antoinette glanced up as Dante filled the doorway and the girl screamed, tugging at the last of her bonds. Antoinette moved toward him. With a flick of his wrist Dante sent Dylan flying back and pinned him high on the wall behind.

Calmly, she raised the gun and fired twice in quick succession. The shots took him in the left side of the chest. She took two more steps and fired again. This time she got him in the right side, in the heart she was sure, but she continued to empty the gun into his body. The force knocked him onto his back.

Something growled behind her and she spun in the direction of a whirlwind of fur and rage. Oberon's clothes were shredded remnants of leather at the feet of one gigantic and extremely pissed-off grizzly. She pointed the gun back at Dante's body, only to find it gone.

"Noooo," she cried, running through the doorway into the room beyond.

Drops of dark blood lay on the bare floorboards where Dante had fallen, more was smeared by fingerprints a few feet from that. Abruptly she was shoved aside by the solid wall of muscle and claws, landing on her ass. The bear stopped and sniffed at the floor then turned to her and snarled.

This was the first time she'd seen Oberon fully transformed, and while she knew he'd be big, the sheer size of him kept her on her butt looking up at him. Swirling patterns rippled through his brown fur too neat and precise to be accidental.

He tilted his head to the side, and his strangely human eyes stared at her until she stood up. His lips peeled back, she could swear he smiled. He wanted her to follow.

Even with all that bulk, he moved fast through the rabbit warren of rooms and hallways until they reached another staircase leading up. It was too small for him in his current form, but not for her. She raced past him and up the stairs two at a time. At the top she slammed through the fire escape doors, bringing up the gun and aiming first left, then right, and then left again. Further down the alley red taillights flared and with a screech of tires shot down the alley toward the street.

Fuck! She lowered the barrel of the gun.

Two seconds later a very naked human-form Oberon burst through the same doors.

"FUCK!" he screamed echoing her thoughts as the car

disappeared around the corner. "Fuck, fuck, fuck." He kicked the nearest Dumpster, sending it skittering several yards down the filthy alleyway.

Tribal scarification marked his skin in Celtic patterns all over his upper arms, back, and thighs. Antoinette couldn't tear her eyes away from the intricate work cut into his skin. Diluted silver nitrate solution was the only thing that would stop the skin of an Animalian from healing completely to its natural state, but it would hurt like hell.

"Well, fuck me sideways, Dante Rubins," he growled, staring down the street after the car with his hands on his hips and his back to her. "I never would have believed it in a month of Sundays if someone told me Dante Rubins was still alive."

"So it just wasn't my imagination?"

Oberon shook his head. "If it was, he sure packed a punch for an illusion."

"One thing's for sure, he'll be out of action for a while," she said.

"Why's that?" The ursian paced back and forth.

"This pistol was loaded with silver-encased rounds."

He glanced at the weapon in her hand. "So he's going to be very sick, even if he can find someone to take out the slugs straightaway."

Antoinette averted her eyes from his full-frontal nudity.

Oberon took pity on her. "Do me a favor, go see to the girl downstairs. I think I frightened her."

No shit!

The ursian put his hands on his hips. "And if you have a cell—call this in. I think I stood on mine in the transformation."

21
vanished

Antoinette's stomach rumbled. She slid out of the chair in the library to go in search for something to eat. At least she had her appetite back. The first week after Viktor's death was a blur. She could hardly get out of bed, let alone eat. Cerberus slept on her bed and followed her everywhere, although lately he'd started following Susan as well. The whole house was grieving, and the fact that the master of the house was still missing didn't help.

Her days had fallen into a routine of waiting. She had taken to reading her way through Christian's book collection, something she never had the luxury of doing much of.

It'd been two and a half weeks since Viktor's murder and the encounter with Dante.

And nothing.

No Christian, no more attacks, no more leads. Apparently the blood on the stone altar where they found the girl wasn't even human; it was used by a satanic cult to sacrifice animals. *Sick bastards.* The VCU had warned both her and Oberon to stay away from the case, threatening them with charges of obstruction if they continued. Not that it would stop her; they'd just run out of leads.

Antoinette was going stir crazy and thought she should

really go back home, but Dante was still out there and no matter what that dickhead Roberts said—she was staying put.

She could understand Christian needing some space after Viktor's death, but she was starting to get a bit antsy and wanted to help nail Viktor's killer.

Antoinette heard voices outside the room and found Lilijana with her hands on her hips scowling at Kavindish.

"When did they call you?"

"This morning." The butler's voice remained calm, but the skin around his mouth and eyes tightened. "I left the message for you straightaway."

Antoinette's heart stopped. It was the closest she'd ever seen Kavindish to showing emotion, and that scared her more than anything. Looks like she wasn't the only one wondering about Christian's disappearance.

"What's going on?" Antoinette asked.

"This is none of your concern, human." Lilijana's vehemence smashed against Antoinette in a tidal wave of heat, but then she looked almost sorry.

"The master stumbled into the house upstate in the early hours of the morning," Kavindish said. "He's not in good shape, and now he's locked himself in a room and they can't reach him."

Lilijana took out a small pink cell phone with a diamond encrusted L hanging from it. The Aeternus woman's hands shook as she dialed and Antoinette pretended not to notice. Christian's mother was only just keeping it together. Kavindish could see it too. His forehead creased and he exchanged a worried glance with Antoinette.

Lilijana tossed her dark locks as she put the cell to her ear. "Have my helicopter ready to fly up to the northern house— I'll be there in ten minutes."

"I'm coming with you," Antoinette said. *If something had happened to Christian . . .* no she couldn't think about that, not after just seeing Viktor die. It would be too much. She stopped, surprised at her feelings. They were parahuman—

a few weeks ago she would've celebrated their deaths. But not today.

"Do what you want human, just stay out of my way." Lilijana swept out of the house and into the waiting car with Antoinette and Kavindish hot on her heels. An hour of uncomfortable silence later they landed at Christian's estate and Lilijana led the way inside the house.

"Where is your master?" she demanded of the maid in the main hall.

"In his room, ma'am," the timid girl said.

Lilijana turned to Kavindish. "Find out what they know, how long he's been up there."

Antoinette was left at the bottom to catch up to her on the third floor.

When Antoinette finally made it to the third floor, she found Lilijana pounding on a door. "Christian—do you hear me? It's your mother. Open the door and let me in." When no sound came from beyond, Lilijana's confident mask finally slipped completely. She sighed and slumped against the door, her face sagged with fatigue. "What if he's succumbed to the Dark Sleep?"

If Christian had fallen into a Dark Sleep, it could be impossible to wake him. For some reason the thought terrified her. "Break down the door."

"That's impossible. The door is reinforced, triple locked, and barred from the inside," Kavindish said, joining them.

"What did the rest of the staff say?" Antoinette asked.

Kavindish shook his head. "He's activated the sun shutters, which are also reinforced, and he hasn't touched blood in nearly a week. I've organized a crew to come up and cut through the reinforcement but it's going to take some time."

"Surely there is some way. How would you send in his blood?" Antoinette asked.

Kavindish shrugged. "The dumbwaiter, but it's not strong enough to hold a person."

"It doesn't need to if I can climb up the shaft. Get me a bag of blood and meet me in the room below." To Lilijana she said, "you stay here and keep trying to get through to him."

To her surprise no one argued.

Lilijana grabbed her hand. "Thank you," she said with a heartfelt expression.

Antoinette patted her hand then ran downstairs to find the dumbwaiter.

A few minutes later Kavindish appeared and handed her a small carry-bag. "I've sent the dumbwaiter to the kitchen and told the staff it's not to be used. You should be able to climb unhindered." He opened the small door in the wall.

She slung the bag diagonally over her shoulder and leaned in for a look. The shaft stretched into darkness above. It would be a tight squeeze, but doable. Antoinette sat on the edge and tested the cables then clenched the small flashlight Kavindish handed her between her teeth.

"The cables should hold you—it's the motor that's not very powerful," Kavindish reassured her. "Good luck, miss."

She pulled her legs into the shaft. It wasn't a difficult climb, just cramped. Luckily she wasn't claustrophobic. Antoinette soon reached the floor above and slid open the dumbwaiter door. The room beyond was gloomy and musty. A lamp sat on the table near the dumbwaiter and she switched it on then took off the carry-bag and dropped it on the table.

It was a mess. Furniture, floor, and walls were covered with maps and papers. The phone had been knocked to the floor and the busy tone rang out loud and constant. She placed the handset back in the cradle and put the phone on a small end table. A half dozen computer screens all showed different locations and flashing icons.

Steel covered the windows, and in the bedroom the sheets were disheveled, but no sign of Christian.

She walked to the door. "I'm in, but I haven't found him yet. I need to find the keys for these locks before I can open the door."

"Find Christian first." Lilijana's reply was muffled by the

thick metal. "He'll have the keys on him. Check the bath-room."

"Okay," she yelled back.

She opened the bathroom door and found the light switch. Her breath caught in her throat as the light filled the room. Christian lay on the cold pale blue tiles curled in a fetal position, his pale skin tinged with gray.

Afraid it was already too late, she reached out a shaking hand to touch his face. It was icy beneath her fingertips.

Suddenly his eyes flung open and she felt more than heard the low rumbling growl. Instinctively she drew back, her heart clenching as she looked into his eyes. They were dull, almost colorless, and showed no sign of recognition. His lips drew back into a snarl, displaying fully extended fangs.

"Christian," she said, fear cracking her voice.

He pulled himself up onto his elbows, his eyes focusing on her. His lips curled with his snarl, his eyes fixing on her with a feral hunger. He leapt and pinned her against the wall before she had time to react.

"So warm," he growled against her throat, goose bumps prickled across her skin. "So hungry."

His bloodless lips peeled back fangs sharp and gleaming in the bathroom light. He blinked and punched the switch, plunging them into darkness. His grip on her loosened and she felt his hands tremble.

Antoinette pushed him away with ease and heard him grunt as he hit the floor. He was as weak as a kitten.

"Antoinette?" he croaked.

She turned on the lights again and found him on his side.

"What are you doing here?" he asked.

"It's been two weeks . . ."

"So?" he cut her off. "Just leave me alone."

"You've been left alone and your mother and others are worried. It's time to get up." Angry at his apathy, she walked over and slapped him across the face. She wanted, no—needed—to shock him out of it. "While you lie here wallowing in self-pity, the trail of Viktor's killer grows colder by the second."

Christian winced more at the mention of Viktor's name than he had when she hit him, then his face clouded in again. "Get out. You don't know—"

"How dare you?" Her rising voice boomed in the small room. "What don't I know? Let me see." She tapped her chin with her forefinger. "Is it the feeling of powerlessness at watching someone you love die at the hands of another? Or is it the anger and frustration you feel for not being able to prevent it?" She squatted down to his level, eye to eye. "Don't you dare tell me I don't know. I know very well—because I live with it every day."

His shoulders sagged, he dropped his head for a moment before looking back at her. "You're right—" He let out his breath in a long sigh.

"So what are you going to do about it?"

"Well—first, I have to get off this floor."

He struggled into a sitting position. Antoinette took a deep breath and reached out to help him stand. As he leaned against her, the iciness of his body seeped through her clothing, chilling her to the bone. Christian looked at her and his nostrils flared. He leaned in a little more, his tortured eyes fixed on her throat as he licked his dry gray lips before gently pushing her away.

Antoinette smiled to cover the nervous flutter his hungry glance caused her stomach. "I've brought you some blood—it's in the bedroom."

"It's no use," he croaked.

She took a step away from him. "You're a stubborn son of a bitch—"

"No, that's not what I meant." He turned to look at her. "You feel the chill of my body." He placed his icy fingertips against her cheek. "The blood must be warm . . . it must be fresh."

"Oh, so you must feed from—" She couldn't bring herself to finish.

He stiffened slightly against her. "I'll call the donor service."

His hand hovered over the phone when an alarm from one of the computers began clanging—startling them both.

"Shit," he said. "Finally!" Christian stumbled over and leaned against the desk.

Antoinette managed to shove an office chair behind him just as his trembling legs gave out altogether and he landed on the seat instead of the floor.

"What is it?" Antoinette watched the screens flash.

"I set some monitoring software in all the airports in and around the New York area. It uses the CCT network already in place."

"CCT network?" she asked. Nici was the technology geek in the family.

"Closed circuit television. This software we have is able to plug into any network already in existence, and because we have footage of Andrew Williams, I programmed it to warn me if he entered an airport. I knew he would sooner or later." Christian leaned closer to one of the screens. "And there he is."

"Where—I can't see him," she said, leaning closer.

"The blond man there." He pointed to a man, however it looked nothing like Williams. "The software takes height and the gait of a person. No matter what disguise they are wearing, it is difficult to hide those elements."

The screen flicked to another camera as the man approached the ticket counter. This time she got a good look at his face. He'd lost the beard and bleached his hair, but those beady nervous eyes were the same as at the conference ball. It was definitely Andrew Williams.

Christian started typing, accessing the airline booking page. "Shit, Paris in two hours. I have to stop him . . ."

He looked about to pass out, Antoinette took a step closer.

He stood quickly and swayed on his feet as he braced himself against the desk, his breathing labored. "Got to get to the airport."

Antoinette took one look at the sickly gray pallor of his skin. "You can't go anywhere in your condition. You don't have enough strength to even stand on your own."

"I've got to stop Williams, he's our best lead." Again his eyes fixated on her throat before he dragged them back to her face.

Christian steadied himself. "Pass me that blood you brought, it might sustain me enough . . ." His legs buckled but she caught him before he fell.

He pushed her away and held up a restraining hand, then hung his head, unable to speak.

There's no way a donor will get here in time, which means . . . Before she could change her mind she said, "Feed on me."

Christian looked at her sharply. She saw a momentary flicker in his expression before he shook his head.

"No."

Antoinette put her hands on her hips and braced herself for a fight. "Why not? You need blood . . . I have plenty. Take what you need and we can go stop that bastard."

He looked away. "You don't know what you're doing."

"Christian, we are wasting valuable time." Her hand shook, and with her heart thumping loudly in her ears, she pulled back her hair. "Just do it."

He stared at her for a moment longer, something shifted in his face.

Finally she said, "I need to find out what happened to my father and you're the best chance I have of stopping the only lead we have."

He picked up the phone and dialed. "It's Christian. Get the chopper to my estate. I need to get to the international airport ASAP."

Antoinette moved closer. With hands on either side of her face, Christian pulled her toward him until his cold lips touched hers. Warmth radiated from the pit of her stomach counteracting the chill of his body.

Slowly—painfully slow—he trailed kisses toward her

throat, leaving fire wherever his icy lips brushed her skin. Then he captured her mouth with his and kissed her with fierce hunger that had more than the need for blood behind it.

He pulled back to stare into her eyes. "Are you certain?"

Antoinette couldn't trust her voice to answer. She returned his intense gaze and nodded. Barely touching her, he caressed her throat before he unbuttoned the light cotton top she wore.

"What are you doing?" Her voice quivered. Even though she wanted him to continue, she wasn't sure she was ready.

"I need to remove your shirt—it's in the way." His husky voice sent shivers through her.

"Oh . . . right." She felt her face flush as he continued.

"Shouldn't you hurry? You've got to reach him before—"

Whatever she was about to say flew out of her mind as he bent forward and gently nipped the lobe of her ear. His lips were so cold against her warm flesh, so intense, pleasure and pain burned simultaneously, scorching her with a desire she'd never felt before.

"It will take a few minutes for the chopper to get ready— we've plenty of time," he whispered in her ear. Running his fingertips along her collarbone, he pushed open her shirt and she gasped when his arm brushed her breast. He paused, his eyes burning with a deep hunger. Antoinette had to look away to conceal her own longing.

"Do you want me to stop?" he whispered.

"No—" Her voice sounded breathless in her ears. Swallowing hard, she said, "No, don't stop."

"Good." He slipped the shirt from her shoulders, dropping it to the floor, leaving her dressed only in a filmy lace bra and a pair of jeans. The frigid air surrounding him raised goose bumps on her bare flesh, causing her nipples to tighten further.

He placed a gentle, chilly hand on the small of her back and pressed her against him. She instinctively stepped back when she saw his elongated teeth, until she noticed something else—he was excited in more ways than one. Against all possibility in his weakened state, the evidence lay hard against her stomach.

For some strange reason this calmed her, and she relaxed into his embrace. At the touch of his lips at the base of her throat, Antoinette's breath froze. With a momentary flash of pain, his fangs pierced the skin then a jolt of pure ecstasy shot down her spine—straight to her loins—pooling there to lap in delicious waves of delight. Her legs buckled, but he lifted her tightly against him.

Electric currents surged through her body—as if she was being struck time and again with lightning bolts of pure pleasure. Someone was moaning. She realized it was her. Clinging to him, she no longer cared about her desire or his. She no longer cared about anything accept the satisfaction that lay just beyond her reach.

Vaguely aware his lips had grown warm against her flesh and his hand was no longer icy where it touched her back, she trembled. Just when she thought she could take no more without exploding in rapturous glory, her vision swam.

No! Stop.

She sank into blackness.

22

Leaving on a Jet Plane

Christian scooped her up and lay her down on the unmade bed. He'd deliberately not told her she'd be incapacitated by his feeding, but she wouldn't have gone through with it if he had.

She'd been right—they didn't have time for anything else, and with all the staff having "no donation" clauses in their employment contracts, she was the only one available. So it was her or risk losing Williams.

So pale and so fragile.

He gently pushed the hair away from her face and planted a tender kiss on her forehead. With relief he listened to the strong, steady beat of her heart.

Blood, her blood, sang through his veins, charging him with intense energy. Never before had he tasted anything like her. Foremost was her passion, hot and sweet, dancing on his palate above the tang of fear. The subtle earthiness of her sorrow lingered on his lips along with the slight bitterness of her ever-present hatred. But there was something else, something he had never tasted before. It was like liquid lightning surging through his body—white-hot and powerful.

The rhythmic rise and fall of her chest held him mesmer-

ized. His throat constricted as he traced his fingertip across
her breast along the edge of the sexy red lace of her bra
before he bent forward and inhaled her fragrance. Her sweet
breath brushed his lips as he lowered them to hers and sa-
vored the silky texture of her mouth.

The sound of the approaching helicopter broke the spell.
Christian sighed and pulled up the covers. He changed
quickly then picked up his cell and a yellow envelope containing five thousand dollars. As he reached the door, he
glanced back at her sleeping form and cursed that time had
not allowed him to experience her as fully as he would've
liked. Would she have let him? Maybe—maybe not. Reluctantly, he unbarred the door and opened it to find his mother
standing there.

"About bloody time. I've been standing here for the last
twenty minutes thinking you were dead." Lilijana burst into
tears and hugged him. "Thank goodness we weren't too late.
Are you okay?" she asked, her expression full of concern
and so different from her usual haughty countenance.

"Yes, Mother, I'm fine." He wrapped his arms around her
and kissed her cheek. "It was close, but Antoinette saved
me." Again, he looked to where she lay. "She's weak and
may need a transfusion."

"Of course," she said and frowned. "But where are you
going?"

"I have to stop someone from leaving the country—someone who may be able to lead us to Viktor's murderer."

Grief flashed before Lilijana's gaze steeled. "Go—I'll
take care of the girl."

A few minutes later Christian climbed into the helicopter
and donned a headset before giving the pilot the thumbs-up.
The whining pitch of the engine grew higher as the rotors
built up speed for takeoff. Within a few minutes Christian
was on his way to the airport.

The flight seemed to take forever, but finally they reached
the glittering sea of jewels that was New York, nearing John

F. Kennedy International Airport. Christian ripped off his headset and jumped out before the chopper even touched down, then ran toward Terminal 7 and British Airways. It was quicker this way than any other transport available.

He entered the terminal and slowed down. Searching for the contact he'd called from the chopper or for Williams. A uniformed security guard approached him and smiled.

"I got your call, sir." Christian's man, posing as the security guard, nodded. "I've located the suspect and he's this way."

Christian used his badge to get past the customs people, following his man through to the bar beyond customs. The guard stopped inside the doorway and turned his back to the patrons, blocking their view of Christian. "He's over there in the far corner."

Christian glanced over the guard's shoulder. Williams sipped a glass of spirits, his nervous eyes continually darting around the room.

The guard held open his uniform jacket. Christian slipped the yellow envelope into an internal pocket as he slid by and headed for his target.

Williams looked up and his eyes widened as Christian came to a stop by his table. Christian growled, hauling the man to his feet by the front of his jacket.

"You've got no right to touch me," Williams said, trying to cover his unease with a confident façade.

"You had no right getting my friend killed," Christian hissed, his lips pulling into a snarl.

The former ambassadorial aide's eyes gravitated toward Christian's extended fangs and his face dropped. "Please, please don't hurt me," Williams whimpered. Terror seeped from every pore, the spicy scent filling Christian's nose.

"Why didn't you turn up to the meeting?" Christian asked.

"I was ordered not to."

"By whom?"

"I don't know." Andrew's eyes darted left and right again, his pupils dilating. A lie.

"Volunteer the information on your own—or don't. Actually . . ." Christian widened his smile and let the man see his fangs. "I'd prefer it if you don't."

Williams's eyes almost rolled back in his head. Christian thought he was going to have an epileptic fit.

"Okay, okay—but not here. Get me somewhere safe— protect me and I'll tell you everything you want to know."

"Protect you from whom?" Christian asked.

"From the Old One, and that's all I'll tell you until I'm safe."

Christian considered this for a second. "Why should I trust you?"

"Because I need protection and you need answers." Williams's mock confidence returned, but only for a second. "Look, if you can find me, so can he. And I'm definitely a dead man if I'm seen talking to you."

"All right."

Williams scooped up his briefcase and jogged to keep pace as Christian dragged the former ambassadorial aide by his upper arm toward the bar's exit.

Halfway across the terminal Christian relaxed his grip slightly and Williams took advantage, yanking his arm free. He ran toward airport police, pointing at Christian and yelling that he was trying to kill him. With supernatural speed, Christian caught him within a few paces and spun him around. "Listen here, you little sh—"

A nanosecond after the distinctive popping of a rifle being fired through a silencer, the bullet smashed into Williams's skull, hitting him just above the right eye with a sickening crunch. His eyes went wide and then dulled as his life seeped from the bullet hole in his forehead. He was dead before he hit the floor.

"Place your hands above your head and step away," a quivery voice demanded.

Christian sunk to a crouch, his vision clouded by rage.

"Stand and put your hands up." A clearly nervous young policeman stood with his pistol trained on him.

Christian snarled and twisted toward the direction of the shot.

"This is your last warning," the policeman said, his voice cracking.

Christian heard the words, but they weren't important—catching Williams's killer was. People murmured, someone screamed, running footsteps neared, but Christian zoned in on a man crouched behind a potted plant on the inner balcony two stories above wearing a hat and dark glasses. As he lowered the high-powered rifle, a puckered scar running down his left cheek to his jaw showed up from behind his glasses.

Human.

Another snarl rumbled in his chest and bubbled up his throat, building to a full-blown roar. The metal click of guns surrounded him but Christian ignored them. Coming to his feet, he started to run, sweeping aside a policeman who tried to block his path, sending the unfortunate man sliding across the floor into a trash can.

"Stop!" voices yelled from behind, but he didn't have time to stop or explain.

The man saw Christian coming and slung the rifle over his shoulder before running. Leaping, Christian made the third-floor railing with ease, then pain seared through his shoulder. He fell two stories to land on his back. A half dozen police surrounded him, all pointing their pistols at his head.

When the helicopter touched down in the grounds of his estate, Christian climbed out and looked at his house. Nothing had been gained by rushing off to stop Williams. Their only lead was dead and his killer had escaped. Christian had spent an entire day in a holding cell while the police checked his credentials.

After Intel had vouched for him, they finally let him go with an apology. He'd then returned to headquarters to make a report on Williams's murder and have the slugs removed.

The wounds had healed over and trapped the bullets inside his flesh, which had to be opened again. Anesthetic was ineffective on an Aeternus, so the operation was more painful than the actual shooting.

Christian's steps slowed as he neared the house. He'd failed. He looked to the dark window of his room where he'd left Antoinette sleeping.

Would she be there? The memory of her blood still sang in his body but he didn't have time to dwell on such things. There were other matters that needed his attention now and he'd already wasted enough time wallowing in his own self-pity. If he hadn't, maybe Williams would still be alive.

He entered through the conservatory and headed straight for his room, finding Antoinette still asleep and Lilijana curled up on the sofa chair in the corner.

His mother stirred as he neared the bed. "Christian?"

"Mother," he said, surprised she'd stayed.

"What happened?" she asked.

"Not here," he whispered, not wanting to disturb Antoinette just yet.

Lilijana rose and followed him into the next room. "Something big is going on here. Viktor's death, that girl in there, you rushing off last night; they're all connected. Tell me what's going on."

Christian sucked in the air through his teeth. Time to come clean. "It appears that The Troubles may have returned to haunt us."

His mother cocked her head to the side and frowned. "But wasn't Dante Rubins behind it?"

Christian paced the carpet. "Viktor never believed Dante was the sole instigator and it was never technically proven that he was involved at all." He stopped and looked at his mother. "How did you know about Dante? CHaPR and the Department had ordered the files sealed."

"You weren't the only one Viktor confided in. He didn't tell me everything, but enough for me to join some dots." She sat in a large leather armchair, the simpering heiress persona completely gone. At that moment she looked every bit the 752-year-old Aeternus she was. The aura of power rolled off her. Christian shook his head . . . only a few got to see her as she was now and those times were rare, even for him.

As if reading his thoughts, she smiled. "The world never gives up secrets in front of a confident, intelligent woman, but a shallow, petulant girl can learn many things if she keeps her eyes and ears open." She leaned forward in the chair. "Does she know about her father?"

"Yes, Viktor told her. Not long before he died."

"Good, she deserves that much at least. Now fill me in. Viktor only told me about Grigore's disappearance but not why." She pierced him with a disapproving glare. "He said you didn't want me involved."

He dragged a palm across his face. "I'm sorry, as always I underestimated you."

"It doesn't matter now," she said with a flick of her wrist. "Who were you after last night and what went wrong?"

Christian told her everything, the full story of Grigore's disappearance, Williams's involvement, and Viktor's investigation, which eventually led to his murder.

She sat in silence, listening until he'd finished and frowned. Resting her elbow on the arm of the chair, she cupped her chin thoughtfully. "Andrew Williams—he's that little worm who worked for Sir Roger, yes?"

"Yes, that's him. Why?"

"Valerica knows him. They were lovers."

"Since when? I thought Williams preferred men."

"More like enjoyed both, like Viktor. She'd been seeing him for at least six months or so—way before Grigore disappeared. He's not her usual type and when I asked her why, she just said he had his uses." Her frown deepened. "I wonder if it has anything to do with that group she's involved with?"

"What group?" Christian asked.

"I overheard her on the phone one night talking to someone about a gathering. I thought it must've been some new dance club or erotica group and asked if I could go along, but she fobbed me off with some lame excuse. She wrote it down—" She looked at her hands for a moment and then beamed. "The AR club or something like that."

Ice twisted in his gut and he sat heavily on the sofa. "Are you sure?"

Lilijana leaned forward in her chair. "What is it?"

"AR—the Aeternus Re-Awakening cult Dante started a century ago. And it was under that banner he carried out the assassinations more than sixteen years ago. If Valerica was involved, Viktor would've told me."

"If he'd known." Lilijana sank back into the chair with a sigh. "Valerica was pretty angry with him for not contacting her for all those years."

"Then I may not be able to keep my promise to Viktor after all. If the AR are involved—nothing will be able to save Valerica."

Antoinette opened her eyes and a smile stole across her mouth as she stretched, feeling unusually delicious.

"So you're finally awake," Lilijana said from the chair by the bed.

"What time is it?" Antoinette croaked, her throat parched.

Lilijana passed her some water and Antoinette gulped it down. It tasted sweeter than the finest wine.

"It's just gone midnight," Lilijana said, taking the empty glass from her and placing it back on the nightstand.

Christian's nightstand. It all came flooding back. "What happened? Where's Christian?"

"You've been asleep for over twenty-six hours. You'll feel weak for a little while, though we gave you a small transfusion to help you regain your strength." Lilijana helped Antoinette to sit forward and plumped the pillows behind her. "Kavindish will bring up some broth shortly."

He'd left her behind. *Bastard.*

Lilijana tucked the covers around Antoinette, avoiding her gaze. "Don't be angry with Christian, he did what he thought was best."

"He could have told me," she hissed.

"Would you have been so generous if you'd known?"

It was Antoinette's turn to look away. "Probably not," she admitted.

"Well then." Lilijana continued to needlessly arrange the bedding.

Something went wrong.

Did Williams get away and now they had nothing? Was Christian okay?

Her throat constricted. "Tell me," she croaked.

Finally Christian's mother stopped fussing and sat back in the chair. "I'll let Christian fill you in on the details, but he did stop Andrew from catching his flight."

Antoinette sighed and fell back into the pillows. He was okay at least. But something else wasn't and she could see pushing it wouldn't yield any further information from Lilijana. It suddenly occurred to Antoinette this was the first time Lilijana had spoken more than two civil words to her.

"Why are you being so nice?" Antoinette asked.

The Aeternus didn't answer at first, her brow crinkled—as much as her smooth brow could. Finally, she said, "You didn't hesitate. Even with your past and your prejudices . . . you risked yourself to help Christian when he needed it. And I'm very grateful for that."

Heat rose to Antoinette's cheeks. It'd been her pleasure—literally. But she wasn't about to tell Lilijana that.

"I've learned a lot about the Aeternus in the last few weeks, especially from Viktor." She paused, thinking of him with fondness. "In the short time I knew him, he taught me more than I'd learned in a lifetime as a Venator."

Lilijana's features softened. "He did tend to bring out the best in all of us."

She loved him. Antoinette had the feeling this was the real

Lilijana, stripped of all pretense and disguises.

Kavindish entered carrying a tray and Lilijana's demeanor changed instantly. "About bloody time—I rang for you hours ago." She stormed through the door, but closed it gently. There was more to Lilijana than met the eye. Antoinette would never underestimate her again.

"Good evening, miss," Kavindish said, placing the tray over her legs and shaking out a napkin. Was that a twinkle in his eye? Did the corners of his mouth twitch a little?

He lifted the cover on the broth and saliva filled her mouth as she inhaled the rich aroma. She hadn't realized how hungry she was until then. The tray also had two boiled eggs, toast, fruit juice, and coffee.

Kavindish laid the napkin in her lap. "Enjoy, miss."

"Where's Christian?" she asked.

"He's indisposed at the moment but will be with you as soon as he can." Kavindish bowed and left her alone.

That was the second person who'd dodged her questions about Christian. Her loudly rumbling stomach distracted her from further worry for the moment and she fell upon the food. Spooning the hot soup into her mouth, Antoinette burnt her tongue. More cautious this time, she allowed it to cool on the spoon and picked up some fresh crusty bread spread with a generous amount of butter. The meal was simple but filling and the strength flowed back into her tired limbs.

With her appetite satiated, something else gnawed at her. Hunger still sat heavy in the pit of her belly, but not for food. Her body tingled all over, her groin heavy and nipples taut.

She'd been dressed in a nightgown, instead of what she'd worn the night Christian had . . .

Oh my.

The memory had her body singing in tribute. Every nerve ending tingled, every fiber thrummed, and she realized what it was she hungered for. There'd been no release for her, and now her body demanded it.

Moving the tray aside she slipped from the bed and

padded barefoot across the room. Her bags sat in the corner. Strange, she hadn't brought them with her. She'd ask Kavindish later.

Antoinette quickly changed into some training gear before picking up her weapons' case. Christian would have a training room here somewhere in the house, probably the basement. She'd try there first. Physical activity would help her work off some of this pent-up frustration.

The training room was in the basement and much bigger than the one at his New York house. She took her sword from the case and fell into a fighting stance on the mats. Within minutes she lost herself in the familiar pattern of *kihon*—the solo mastery of fundamentals.

"You should be resting." Christian's velvet voice interrupted her mid-swing.

23

Blood, sweat and heat

She turned to find him propped lazily against the doorframe, unreadable behind dark sunglasses.

She dropped the tip of her sword to the floor and turned, unprepared for the fever burning through her veins at the sight of him. "I'm pissed at you."

"I'm sorry I didn't tell you that you'd be incapacitated by my feeding, but I was desperate."

"I'm really pissed that you know me that well." She returned to practicing.

"You need to rest," he said gliding away from the door and into the room.

She didn't interrupt the routine she stepped through. "What I need is a good, active workout."

"Care for a sparring partner then?" he asked.

Oh God, yes. "No."

"Really? If it's exercise you're after, I can help."

I bet you could. "I prefer to train alone. I find it more relaxing."

"I thought you wanted an active workout," he said, throwing her words back at her. He took off his glasses and placed them on the counter by the door, his eyes mocking. "Are you afraid?"

"Of you? Pffft!" Her indignation was a little too loud in the large room. "No." *Damn him.*

"Then spar with me."

He had her over a barrel. "Fine."

His eyes gleamed as he crossed to the far wall and hit a button. A panel slid up, exposing a vast number of different weapons.

"Wow," she said. "That's an impressive collection."

"Shall we use bokken or steel?" he asked, looking at her over his shoulder.

"Steel of course."

"Then use this." He tossed her a sheathed katana, which she snatched easily out of the air. She put hers aside and held the Japanese sword level with her eye as she pulled the blade out two inches. It gleamed, even in the dimmed florescent lights. She slid the sheath off slowly, inch by inch drawing out her anticipation.

Antoinette swung the sword, testing the weight. It fit as if made for her hand. The balance was perfect. This was a true Samurai weapon, a thing of beauty made by a master swordsmith. She flicked it to the right then with a twist her wrist twirled the blade in a full circle at her side.

"Nice," she said trying to appear nonchalant.

Christian repeated her moves with his own weapon as they squared off. Circling to the right, one foot in front of the other, she twirled her sword and sized him up.

"*Kata* or freeform?" he asked.

"Freeform—definitely freeform." She didn't want to dance set steps, she wanted to go hell for leather.

Confidence gleamed in his eyes. "I was hoping you'd say that."

Antoinette narrowed her eyes, watching every nuance, every action; the way he held the sword, each step he took as she waited for him to make the first move.

He glanced left, but she wasn't about to let such an obvious ploy force her to react too soon. His mouth twitched and he gave her an almost imperceptible nod.

"So tell me what happened with Andrew Williams." She stopped, and held her sword high and ready.

"He was assassinated right in front of me. I learned nothing except that I was close to discovering who he was afraid of."

Shocked, she dropped the point of her sword and came out of her stance. "He's dead? How?"

"Shot in the head."

"And the assassin?"

He dropped his gaze and stopped circling. "He escaped."

"So, what now?" She straightened and gripped the sword.

"I don't know yet, but I may have a new lead to check out."

"Like what?"

"Are we sparring or not?" he asked, circling again.

She fell back into her previous stance and Christian mirrored her, both waiting for the other to attack first. Antoinette wasn't about to be goaded by Christian's stony countenance into striking first. With a tilt of her head, she turned her left palm upward and jerked her fingers toward her in a "come get me" gesture.

She barely had time to block his lightning-fast attack. The vibrations of the strike convulsed so hard up her arms she almost dropped her sword.

"Hey, no fair," she cried. "That was your Aeternus strength behind your strike."

"Who agreed to be fair?"

"If that's the way you're going to play it then." She darted forward and sliced open his shirt diagonally across his chest. His eyes dropped to the damage—a thin scarlet line appeared then immediately started to heal.

"How did the assassin escape from you? Are you losing your touch as Intel's finest?"

"Now you're really asking for it." He grinned, but his eyes held a darkness as he ripped off the remains of his shirt and discarded it.

He began twirling the sword easily, again sidestepping in a circle. "I was shot by airport police."

Antoinette kept her eyes firmly fixed on him. Not that she could tear her gaze away, even if she tried. His alabaster torso was straight out of a Greek legend. "So did you think to clear it with them first before you pursued a suspect on their turf?"

Pale he might be, but each muscle rippled in exquisite definition. His brown nipples contrasted nicely, as did the thin line of black hair trailing down his abdomen just below the hollow dent of his belly button and disappearing into the waistband of his low-slung sweatpants. Her gaze kept going down to the taut quadriceps bunching beneath the fabric. Her tongue darted out to moisten her lips, but it too had gone dry.

"No, I didn't have time nor did I want them to give the game away. You would've done the same thing." Then he came at her again.

She ducked under his raised arms and spun, landing an openhanded blow to his side. The air whooshed from his lungs, he turned and grinned.

"Don't hold back on my account," he said.

"I don't plan to." She brought her sword up again.

Next time he attacked, she brought her elbow up and took him in the chin, rocking his head back.

While he rubbed his jaw, she dropped and spun with her leg outstretched, sweeping him off his feet. He fell on his back and before he could react, she straddled him and claimed his mouth with her own, hunger consuming her. Their swords fell to the side.

His smile said he'd allowed her to pull that move and he was only toying with her. Abdomen muscles bunched under her thighs, setting off the butterflies in her stomach. He dropped his sword and took her face in his hands, kissing her with a fierceness to match her own. When he sat up, she wrapped her legs around him, hooking her feet behind his back.

With their lips still locked he stood, taking her with him. She kept her arms encircled around his neck, tightened the grip of her thighs and pressed her breasts to him, the taut nipples rubbing against his naked chest. He groaned against her neck and squeezed her closer, trembling. He was close to losing it. She had him. Just a little more . . .

With tenderness, he unwrapped her legs from his waist and set her on her feet, gently prying her arms away. Antoinette felt empty, her body screaming for contact, but he moved away to pick up his sword.

"We're sparring, remember." He shifted to cover the bulge in his pants.

As she turned to pick up her own weapon, she felt him cut the tie binding her hair and with the flat side of the sword, helped the braid to unravel. Now he really was playing with her.

She spun on him, her hair flying across her face. She dragged it out of her eyes with one hand and brought her blade up with the other.

"Now," he said, his white teeth showing through his self-satisfied smirk, "we're even."

"Oh—you think so, do you?" She fought to keep the smile from her lips.

The game was just beginning and she intended to win. Again they began to circle each other, the tips of their swords almost kissing. His gaze sizzled her insides. Liquid fire pooled in her stomach then spread down the inside of her legs, making her toes curl in the heat. She clenched and relaxed her grip on the sword handle, waiting for the perfect moment.

Before she could blink he moved behind, pinning her back to his chest with his arm under her heaving breasts and just as quickly, released her and moved away again. She felt her sweatpants drop away where he'd sliced them open. The ruined material gathered around her ankles and she kicked them off. Now she stood holding her sword at her side, wearing nothing but a thong and her cropped sports top. Her breasts were heavy, her nipples screaming for his touch. Her breathing became short and the pulsing between her legs demanded to be filled.

Enough. Antoinette knew exactly how to get what she wanted. She brought her blade up under the band of her top and sliced. The material parted neatly under the razor-sharp edge, freeing her aching breasts. She was going to have him and on her own terms. With a wicked grin, she dropped her head and looked at him from under her lashes, holding his gaze, while she made a shallow cut above her left breast. She blinked slowly and sucked back her breath at the sharp, exquisite pain. Crimson beads formed as she leveled her gaze at him—daring him. Confident he wouldn't be able to resist her now.

Christian's pupils contracted, zoning in on the growing red line. His face changed, full of raw hunger and all the animalistic power to take it. Lips peeled back to reveal his fangs, fully extended and he stretched his jaw wider.

"You're playing with fire, Antoinette," he growled.

"Then burn me," she breathed.

She'd barely finished the last word when he threw his sword aside. Before it hit the ground he'd crossed the room, gathering her as he went and slamming her back against the wall. The air was forced from her lungs but she hardly felt it. He pushed her up the wall, bringing her chest level with his mouth and covered the cut, sealing it. He snarled—not an entirely unhappy sound. She moaned and buried her hands in his hair while wrapping her legs around his chest.

He hovered close to her nipple. Not touching nor tasting, staying less than an inch from the surface. He looked up at her with a wicked gleam in his eye. Antoinette arched her back trying to bring her taut flesh closer to his waiting mouth. But he moved with her—his breath stirring the air between his lips and her flesh—torturing her with the promise of pleasure yet denied.

Finally, he opened his mouth and scraped the hardened nub with the tip of one of his fangs. Without warning she rushed over the edge, the orgasm taking her completely unaware and unprepared. She flung her arms out along the cool wall behind her and threw back her head. Her back arched, her legs quivering as she cried out again and again with the waves of release thundering through her.

But it wasn't enough. She needed more, she needed him deep inside her. As he let her slide down, she took fierce possession of his mouth, his hardness pressing against her as she let her legs drop to the floor. Antoinette tugged and pulled at his sweatpants. Finally, she had them far enough down to take his length in her trembling hand. Using the wall at her back for balance, she lifted her legs again around his hips and maneuvered her thong aside so she could slide him into her.

Her private flesh stretched around him and she clenched, trying to let him in as far as she could take him. With one hard thrust he filled her completely; she arched her back and cried out against the painful exquisiteness. Her arms gripped his shoulders, her thighs clenched slick with sweat. He drew back and thrust into her again.

He held her by the hips and dropped his gaze to watch himself moving in and out of her. The sight of him filling her took her breath away, heightened the sensations with each thrust.

"Bite me," she moaned.

"No . . . it's too soon . . . you haven't recovered enough," he gasped as he plunged into her again and again, each time harder than the last.

"Please, oh please. I need you."

His gaze burned her soul. For a moment he stopped moving, his eyes dropped to her lips. She licked them. He groaned and leaned forward. Then he nipped her.

A metallic taste filled her mouth as he held her close, sucking on her bottom lip, and he began driving into her faster and harder. The pressure built and built until she rushed headlong toward orgasm—rising higher and higher until she was there—crashing blissfully over the edge.

Christian grunted against her mouth and gave one last shuddering thrust as he joined her.

Antoinette's ragged breathing roared in her ears, sweat

bathed her skin, her chest heaved, and all the bones disappeared from her limbs leaving them loose and trembling. He was still inside her and when he withdrew she felt a fleeting moment of loss.

He smoothed the hair away from her face as he kept intense eye contact. "Did I hurt you?"

She sighed at his unexpected tenderness. "Only in the best possible way and nothing a long soak in the tub won't fix."

"Your wish is my command," he said, kicking the sweatpants from around his ankles as he tightened his grip around her waist.

Antoinette wrapped her arms around his neck and rested her head against his shoulder as he carried her naked through the house, seemingly unembarrassed by their state of undress or their intimate embrace. He carried her to an enormous room with a sunken tub like a small bathing pool dominating the center. He sat her gently on the edge and turned on the faucets before lighting the candles semi-hidden in niches around the room.

How many women had he seduced in this room? And why should she care?

Christian poured scented bubble bath into the tub. The aroma of sandalwood and lavender filled the room. She worked the thong over her hips and lowered herself into the hot, soothing water, then looked up to find him watching her.

It was a side of him she hadn't seen or expected. Such thought, such consideration. The bath filled fast, almost deep enough to swim in. She submerged, letting the water-dampened silence soothe her troubled thoughts. Usually she'd forgotten the guy she'd just had sex with as soon as she'd pulled her panties back on. But not this time. Christian was still very much in her head. When she resurfaced he'd joined her.

Sluicing the water off her face, she smiled.

"Come here," he said, reaching for the shampoo.

She settled between his legs and he massaged the scented

lather through her hair. Antoinette lay back as his heavenly fingers kneaded the knots from her scalp and soothed away her reservations. After all, it had just been sex . . . right?

Hot hands, soapy bubbles, and warm water eased away her aches and pains, loosening tension and turning her to mush.

Christian gently washed the suds. He'd never experienced this kind of intensity before. Ever. Not even with Dominique, his wife, and especially not that conniving bitch, Carolina. His hand stilled above Antoinette's perfect forehead.

Carolina. His chest squeezed at the memory but not with the crippling, searing pain he'd come to expect. She'd done such a number on him, playing him from the start. Viktor knew it and had warned him, but he didn't want to believe she could've used him so callously.

Embraced humans were prone to becoming dreniacs because they lacked control over their feeding urges. He'd been so sure that he could help Carolina overcome the bloodlust and control her hunger. But he failed, and she turned on him, trying to frame him for her kills.

If only he'd looked beyond her captivating beauty to see the self-centered, spoiled princess she really was. But he hadn't. And he'd paid the price. A price he wasn't willing to pay again. The memory of her scornful expression turning to terror just before he beheaded her still haunted him.

Antoinette stirred, bringing him back to the warm body between his knees. Her head lolled against his chest and he stirred in response to her warm breath caressing his skin. Her breathing was slow and even. She'd fallen asleep.

Antoinette was nothing like Carolina—the complete opposite in fact. But it didn't guarantee she'd be any different in the long run. She was still human.

"Hey," he said gently in her ear. "Why don't you go get some more sleep?"

She opened her eyes and smiled. Not the usual half-guarded semi-smile that never quite reached her eyes. This one went right down into her soul and reflected back through her whole body; the first truly honest smile he'd seen. And it made her so achingly beautiful, it nearly broke his heart.

"That sounds like a good idea." She turned and kissed him lightly on the lips, and then giving the end of his nose a quick flick with the tip of her tongue, she climbed from the bathing pool.

His gaze wandered over lithe limbs and firm perfection honed by years of training. A bruise had started to appear on her left buttock and a hand shaped mark darkened her upper right arm. He'd been rough, but she had taken it all and given as good as she got. He rubbed his chin, remembering how she'd elbowed him there. He'd enjoyed more than the physical act, she challenged his mind as well as his body. But was it something more? Carolina sprang to mind again and he shook the destructive thoughts from his head. He was reading too much into this. After all it was just sex . . . right?

Antoinette pulled on one of the fluffy bathrobes hanging on a hook and wrapped it around herself. Her hand rested above the doorknob and she turned to him. "Thank you—that was nice."

And then she was gone.

After dressing, Christian came downstairs he find Lilijana's suitcase and several retail bags from expensive stores sitting by the front door. His mother was in the library reading a magazine. As he approached, she quickly shut the glossy fashion rag, but not before he caught sight of *The Economist* hidden inside.

"How is she?" she asked, flicking the pages absently.

"Asleep again." He crossed to the bar and poured himself a whiskey.

She motioned for him to pour her a drink as well and he handed her his glass before preparing another.

"She's getting to you, isn't she?" Lilijana crossed her long, artificially tanned legs.

Christian worked at the lump in his throat and waved her comment aside. "I don't know what you're talking about."

"Yes, you do." She took a sip from her glass. "You have that look."

Christian placed his untouched drink back on the bar. "Don't be ridiculous."

"You've felt an extra spark, something different. It's written all over your face." She stood and moved toward him. "You know your father felt the same when he first fed from me?"

"Yes, but you had Latent blood."

She quirked a knowing eyebrow then took a sip from her drink.

The dots finally connected. "How? When? Obviously Antoinette doesn't know."

"None of Nicolae's descendants know. How do you think your father was able to engage him in the first place? Ignatius knew the truth, knew that Nicolae's mother was a Latent—like mine."

"A Petrescu would never marry a Latent," Christian said.

"Not knowingly, of course, but Nicolae's father never knew and neither did his brother, the assassin . . . Emil." Lilijana still had trouble saying that name. "Their mother only told Nicolae on her deathbed, and he revealed it to no one."

"Out of shame, no doubt," he said.

Lilijana shook her head. "Christian, you know better. Nicolae loved his children and family was always important to him—especially his mother." Lilijana's face grew sad.

Christian knew she remembered her own mother who'd been forced into prostitution to provide for Lilijana in a harsh and uncaring world—wanted by neither humans nor Aeternus and finally murdered by one of her clients.

"It does explain Antoinette's skills and apparent empathy with animals," Christian said.

Lilijana placed her empty glass on the bar. "Yes. Sometimes the genes come out more strongly in later generations, as seems to be the case with Antoinette. However, I don't think she should be told. With her past history . . . it may just send her over the edge."

The heavy throbbing of helicopter rotors grew louder in the darkness from beyond the huge bay window. A single shaft of light appeared above the trees.

"Oh good, here comes my escape back to civilization. This has all been such a trial." Lilijana reverted to her usual rich-bitch demeanor—almost. She gathered up her handbag and winked before slipping on diamond-studded designer shades.

He caught her hand before she turned away. "Thank you, Mother."

She reached out and cupped his cheek, her mask briefly slipping again. "Just don't ever do that to me again."

He pulled her closer and planted a kiss on her cheek. "Take care of yourself."

She patted his cheek and then dropped her hand. "Kavindish . . . Kavindish where are you?"

The butler appeared a few seconds later carrying her bags.

"It's about time. I don't know how Christian puts up with your incompetence," she huffed.

Kavindish's eyes darted between Christian and his mother. "Neither do I, Miss Lilijana. I'm very fortunate to have such an understanding employer."

Lilijana stomped toward the door but when she reached Kavindish she leaned in closer and whispered, "Take care of my baby."

"I always do, Miss Lilijana."

After a fleeting smile she straightened her shoulders, tossed back her hair, and continued through the door. "Well, come on, stop dawdling, I don't have all night."

24

вack to the кeal world

As a lover, Christian was as insatiable as Antoinette turned
out to be. She enjoyed taking him as often as he took her.
Sometimes their lovemaking was rough, almost violent and
yet at other times it was slow and tender. But no matter how
good it was, Antoinette couldn't bring herself to spend the
day sleeping beside him. That would be far too intimate.

She enjoyed what they had now, with no thoughts of a
future. But still, when Christian suggested it was time to
return to New York City a few days after his near slip into
the Dark Sleep, she almost didn't want to leave. Once back
in the real world she knew it would all change.

They'd been back at the town house barely an hour when
a heavy banging rattled the front door. Antoinette put down
the newspaper she had been leafing through.

As she came into the foyer Susan answered the front door.
Oberon pushed past the maid and stopped in front of her.

"You're back!" Those intense black eyes filled with a
thousand questions bore into her.

And she knew why he was here, given the expression on
his face. "You've seen him."

"Yes." Oberon straightened to tower over her. "He came
here looking for you."

Fear spiked, but was quickly replaced by anger at Dante's nerve. "Did you get him?"

"No—he got away, again." Oberon dropped his gaze to his feet. "I wasn't ready for him because I didn't expect him to be back so soon after you pumped him so full of silver slugs."

"Who are you talking about?" Christian asked from the top of the stairs.

"You didn't tell him?" Oberon asked, tilting his head.

She tried to tell herself there hadn't been time, but truth was she knew that he'd never believe her without proof and she hadn't been ready to leave the temporary haven of his estate.

"Tell me what?" Christian asked, as he reached the bottom of the staircase.

"We had a run-in with Dante Rubins—he's the Fang-Whore Slasher."

Christian looked like he'd been slapped. Hurt eyes turned on her. "You're sure it wasn't just some shifter of something?"

"It was definitely Dante. I recognized his scent from years ago," Oberon said. "But we've had another sighting since."

"Where?" Christian asked, coming closer.

"In the park across the road from this house."

Antoinette shuddered.

Christian wrapped an arm around her. "Are you sure the source is reliable?"

"Very!" Oberon's gaze dropped to Christian's hand at her waist, then lifted to meet her eyes before continuing, "It was me."

She stepped away from Christian's embrace. She needed to face this on her own, and for some reason she got the impression the ursian didn't approve. Why she should care didn't matter. What did was that she could only rely on herself—no one else. No matter how good the sex.

Oberon stared at her a minute longer then turned to Christian. "But it looks like we should work together."

"Maybe," Christian's tone held an edge of suppressed anger. At Oberon or at her? She couldn't be sure.

"Look, Laroque. I know we've bumped heads before, and we'll do it again. Dante killed Sir Roger so he's involved in this conspiracy thing you and Dushic were looking into. And right now, the best chance we have of finding who's behind this is to work together. Find that out and we find who killed Dushic, Williams, the ambassador and anyone else."

Christian looked away. Antoinette could almost hear him thinking. Oberon was right and Christian knew it.

He turned back to the ursian. "You and I both know that Dante doesn't have the brains, cunning, or self-control to pull off something like this."

Oberon nodded. "He's masochistic, dangerous, and downright insane if you want my opinion, but someone else is pulling his strings, and we just have to find out who it is."

Christian smiled. "Oberon—you're not just the pigheaded son-of-a-bitch I took you for."

"Yes, I am," Oberon folded his massive arms across his chest. "But that doesn't mean I'm stupid. I'm not even supposed to be on this case, but I can't let it go. So are you in?"

"I have a lead that I have to follow up tomorrow night."

"Okay, I'll be back at sunset." Oberon pulled out a tiny skull key ring and twirled his keys on his index finger. "And keep her close—Dante wants her bad."

Antoinette shuddered and didn't pull away from Christian's arm this time. "I will."

Oberon nodded and left. She listened to the sound of his Harley fading into the distance before turning to Christian.

"So what's this lead?" she asked.

He turned his back to her. "It's nothing concrete. I'd rather not say until we've checked it out."

"I thought we were working together."

He remained silent for a minute longer. "It's something I found out about the cult."

"The AR cult?" she asked.

He hung his head before raising it again to look at her. "Valerica may be involved."

Antoinette's eyes prickled at the memory of Viktor lying on the car-park blacktop as Christian made his promise. "I'm sorry," she whispered into his ear.

He turned, wrapping his arms around her. "You've nothing to be sorry about. I promised Viktor I would protect Valerica, but if she really is part of this I can't keep that promise."

"You're doing the right thing." She pulled back to look at him. "But protect her if you can."

There was no love lost between her and Valerica, but Viktor had been a good man and her friend. He kissed her, softly at first, then more fiercely as his need grew.

"Shouldn't we at least go to your room before the staff see us?" she whispered to the ceiling as he spread tiny kisses across her neck. Without a word he swept her up and carried her upstairs.

Christian woke to find the bed empty—as usual. The sun was close to setting—the ever present haze of the daylight hours still buzzed in his mind.

Hunger growled in his veins—he'd have to feed before he went out. He'd been careful not to feed during lovemaking with Antoinette. It was still too early. Sitting on the side of the bed, he ran a hand over his face then got up to dress.

He found her where he expected—sprawled on her stomach in her own bed, the covers kicked off and only a pair of panties covering her firm rear end. She never stayed with him through the day, always leaving to shower and sleep the day away on her own. It bothered him that she wouldn't stay.

Cerberus raised his head from his usual position on the end of her bed and wagged his tail. Christian pulled back a blond lock and kissed her ear. She purred. He traced kisses down her backbone, hovering over her tattoo and then moving

down her side, caressing the swell of her breasts pressed
against the sheets. She turned, giving him better access but
he straightened and lightly smacked her ass.

"Good evening, sleepyhead," he said, enjoying the sight
of her nakedness.

"Hmm . . . now that's some wakeup call." She smiled and
stretched. "But you're not going to stop there, are you?"

"Oberon will be here in less than an hour. Remember?"

"Ah yes—and you're off to visit your old girlfriend."

There wasn't any trace of irritation or jealousy, just the
plain and simple statement, yet somehow the lack of emotion burned him. *It's only sex . . . right?*

Who are you trying to kid?

She sat up, rolled onto her knees, pressing her naked
breasts against his chest. "You can spare a few minutes
before you go now that you've woken me like that." She
pulled his hand down the front of her panties.

His fingers slid into her hot opening, slick with her excitement. He groaned and his trousers felt a whole lot smaller
than they had been a moment ago.

Her hand crept down his torso to the bulge in front. "Ah,
now that's what I want." She unzipped him and dropped to
take him in her mouth.

Oh my. He thrust his hips forward so she could take more
and her tongue flicked over the head on the backward stroke.
His fangs descended instantly. He could sense her blood
pumping through her veins and his gut clenched.

"No," he said, pulling away with great difficulty. "I have
to feed first."

She sat back on her heels. "It's been a week since you
last took blood from me and Kavindish has been feeding me
plenty of red meat."

Christian shook his head; he was getting far too much of
a taste for her blood. "It's not a good idea."

"Why not? You're hungry, I'm here."

"You're not my fang-mistress."

She rocked back and placed her hands on her thighs.

"Christian, we agreed. It's just sex, nothing more. Don't read anything else into this deal."

"I'm sorry." He reached out and pulled her down against him. "I just don't want to take advantage. A few weeks ago you'd have taken my head off for even suggesting it."

"But I've learned a few things since then." She looked into his eyes, into his soul. "I wouldn't have offered if I didn't want to. Besides, I'm not exactly on the losing end of the bargain."

"You're not?" he teased. "And what would you be getting from this?"

She hit him with the pillow, then grew serious. "I'll hunt dreniacs and I'll kill them. But I think I've learned the difference between an Aeternus and a dreniac. I realize now that I saw you all as one and the same before. Until Viktor opened my eyes. Besides it's not a forever deal."

He couldn't face the thought of her leaving him just yet and silenced her with his mouth. Her face turned up to him and he cupped it between his hands, deepening the kiss until he could no longer stand it. Leaning forward, he pushed her gently with his body so she lay back across the bed. Her legs wrapped around his hips, pressing her mound against him.

"First I feed," he murmured against her lips and moved down to her body, kissing, tasting, wanting. He tore her panties away.

"I wish you would stop doing that, I'm starting to run out," she said, coming up on her elbows and looking down at the torn remnants of her underwear.

He grinned. "I'll buy you new ones."

She threw up her hands and lay back again. He probed between her nether lips, savoring her private taste. She moaned and pushed herself against his questing tongue. He slipped deeper into her hot, wet opening—her flesh pulsed. He drove his tongue in and out as she moaned and wrapped her fingers in his hair.

He pulled away and watched her face as he replaced his tongue with his middle fingers, rubbing her hard nub with the pad of his thumb. She watched what he was doing through hooded eyes, her hips moving in time with his strokes as he quickened the pace. Steady, thrusting, rising to meet his palm, driving his fingers deeper and deeper.

He bent his head to the spot between her thigh and her mound and buried his fangs into the hot vein pulsing just below her soft, sweet skin. She screamed his name and bucked against him as she came hard and fast. As her orgasm subsided, he drank her sweet nectar. How he craved the taste.

When he'd had his fill, he sealed the puncture marks and raised himself up on his hands, moving over her.

Christian hovered above Antoinette, his fullness pressing against her hip and his face shining with fresh blood. Her blood.

Moving deftly, she flipped him beneath her. The smile slipped from his mouth briefly with surprise, but was soon replaced with desire as she straddled him. His gaze roamed her body like invisible fingers rippling across her skin, causing her nipples to pucker and her skin to burn. When he reached for her breasts, she caught him by the wrists, pushing them above his head.

"First I feed," she murmured, just as he'd done to her. Then she mimicked the path he had taken down her body— kissing, tasting, wanting.

When she reached his trousers, she pushed them down his hips and pulled them over his feet, holding them up. "See, that wasn't so hard to do—and you can still wear them again."

He chuckled. "Point taken."

She bent over him again and took his silky length into her mouth, stretching her jaws and fitting in as much as she could. Her hair fell around her face, brushing her cheeks and pooling over his groin.

Christian gathered it in his hands, pulling it aside. "I want to see you." His voice heavy with his need.

She smiled around him, meeting his eyes as she moved up and down. She could feel the tension building in him and stopped. He groaned and almost came off the bed as she nipped the soft flesh inside his thigh.

She felt heavy and empty between her thighs. She needed to be filled and straddled his hips, gliding him into her slick opening. He didn't move—just lay buried in her secret fold. She slowly tilted her hips back, and then thrust forward. The air hissed through his teeth and he quivered beneath her. She repeated the move. Christian closed his eyes, lips parted, and fangs elongated. Instead of being repulsed, the sight of his fangs now excited her.

She repeated the movement and this time he met her halfway. Again they stopped, eyes locked, totally motionless except for the trembling of their flesh, the pulsing of their blood and the beating of their hearts. Hers fast and heavy pounding in her ears, and his the much slower beat of an Aeternus, but no less powerful beneath her palms resting on his chest.

She began to rock her hips back and forth, at first slow then steadily building rhythm, thrust, and speed. Soon he was raising his hips to meet her, faster and faster.

He reached up and grabbed a breast with each hand, cupping them, squeezing her full nipples. She tilted back her head, her hair swaying against her lower back and bottom as well as his inner thighs.

His hips bucked, rising higher, he moved his hands to her hips to bring her down on him as hard as he could thrust up. Suddenly his shoulders came off the bed and his head fell back to let out a roar as he drove home the last few hard, shuddering strokes.

She lay across his chest—spent. "Now, don't you feel better?" she asked. "I know I do."

Christian stroked her cheek. "Yes."

But his voice sounded distant, almost sad.

25

Lovers Lost

Christian didn't have time for a shower. Oberon had arrived with another of member of his team. Dylan Jordan stood in the foyer, feet apart, hands behind his back and the air of military proficiency.

"It might not be a good idea to overwhelm this contact with too many agents."

"Dyl's here to watch over Antoinette while we're gone," Oberon said.

"Do you really think that's necessary?" Christian asked. "My staff are here."

Oberon was serious—dead serious. "Antoinette put six silver slugs in Dante Rubins, yet he's still walking around. He's been seen watching this house and she's just his type, if you know what I mean. So what do you think?"

"You're right, better safe than sorry."

Oberon pulled the motorcycle over to the curb outside the apartment building address Lilijana had given Christian. The ursian had talked him into riding pillion on the back of the Harley, and they made it across town in no time.

Christian climbed off and ran his hand through his hair. "Valerica is fragile and I promised Viktor before he died that I'd protect her. So go easy."

"Would you be so quick to protect her if it turns out she had a part in his murder?" Oberon asked.

"Twins and multiple births may not be rare with you Animalians, but they are among the Aeternus."

"I wasn't aware they were twins." Oberon threw his leg over the seat and stood on the pavement.

Christian looked up at the tall building. "Viktor and Valerica shared a bond that went beyond normal even for our kind. She's always been able to sense his existence and well being and would've suffered physically through his death. She'll be very fragile."

"Still—she may know something to open up new avenues of investigation. At least I hope so, because, frankly, I'm starting to clutch at straws. If we can't find Dante Rubins then . . ." He shrugged his shoulders.

Christian reached out and grabbed Oberon's forearm. "I want to talk to her first. Alone."

"Not a chance, Laroque." Oberon jutted his jaw forward. "I don't want to miss anything that may be important."

Christian dropped his hand. "At least let me do the talking—as I said, she's fragile."

Oberon's heavy booted footsteps followed him across the marble floor to the doorman's desk. Christian flashed his Intel identification to the old man behind counter and Oberon flashed his own.

"We're here to see Valerica Dushic," Christian said.

The doorman squinted at their ID then tilted his head toward the elevator. "The penthouse."

"All right, Laroque, I'll follow your lead," Oberon said as they rode the elevator. "For now at least."

"Thank you."

Valerica opened the door wearing a short silk robe and smiled widely, throwing her arms around Christian's neck and kissing his cheek. Behind her music played loudly, accompanied by conversations filled with laughter. She was entertaining, which wasn't what he'd expected to find.

"Come in, join the fun, bring your friend," Valerica said.

"Ooohhh—you're a big boy aren't you." She ran her hand up Oberon's arm and across his chest.

"Yes—very fragile." He arched an eyebrow at Christian as they followed Valerica into the room.

Christian ignored him. "We're not here to party, Valerica. We're here to talk."

Her almost too-cheerful expression slipped a little, then she recovered it. "You can ask questions later."

She grabbed his hand and pulled him into the room where more than a dozen couples were dancing, making out, or having sex.

Oberon walked to the stereo and turned it off. "All you people—out now," he boomed, pulling out his identification and holding it up high.

Everyone stopped what they were doing and looked at him. When he reinforced his demand with a deep growl they moved, gathering up clothes and dressing quickly. Within minutes the apartment had emptied.

"Spoilsport." Valerica pouted and stamped her foot. "Who do you think you are?"

"Valerica, what are you doing?" Christian asked, gently taking her by the upper arms. He felt like shaking her, but it wouldn't have helped.

"Having fun . . ." She stuck out a petulant lower lip and stepped closer, running her hand across his chest. "Come on, how 'bout it? Your friend can join in too. What's his name?" She tossed Oberon a seductive smile. He cocked his head and raised an eyebrow at Christian.

"It's Oberon DuPrie, a fellow agent with the Department." Christian captured her wrists and held them. "Valerica, it's not going to make the pain go away," he whispered.

Tears spilled from her eyes and she stopped fighting him. "No, but it helps me to forget the hollowness eating up my heart."

Christian pulled her into his arms but she shoved him away.

"I can smell that human whore all over you," she sneered. "She's a Venator, Christian, she kills our kind."

"No, she kills dreniacs. Just like Viktor and I did when we came across them." He kept his tone calm and soothing, knowing Valerica was close to the breaking point.

Oberon turned away. Thank God he had some sense of decency.

"All humans should grovel at our feet. Once we were their masters. In ancient times, they worshiped us as gods. Now we have to pay them to feed. The AR . . ." Her eyes went wide as she realized where her ranting was taking her.

Oberon turned and moved to stand over her. "What about the AR?"

She squared her shoulders. "We believe in our right to not be subjugated by those who are our food."

"Is that so?" Oberon asked, towering over her. "How about you enlighten us a little more?"

She tilted her head as she looked up at Oberon, as if unable to comprehend what he's just said. Christian took her arm and gently pulled her away from Oberon before leading her to the lounge.

"Tell us what you know." Christian kept his voice low, even, and hopefully nonthreatening while he pushed her gently down to sit on the plush seat.

"No—you're with the Department, both of you, you'll only try and stop it." She crossed her arms and leaned back into the sofa.

"It's my job to protect people," he said. "These murders are wrong."

"Murders?" Her eyes went wide and her jaw dropped. "You think we had something to do with Viktor's death?" She shook her head in disbelief. "I can't believe you'd think I would be involved with anything to do with his murder. I'm talking about the petition."

"Petition!" Oberon snarled, ignoring Christian's warning glare. "What petition?"

Valerica's brow creased and she looked up at Oberon like he was stupid. "The one asking CHaPR to officially investigate the disappearances of several dozen parahumans over the last ten years."

"What're you talking about?" Christian asked.

"Since the Guild allowed the admittance of parahumans into its schools there have been several fatal accidents or disappearances involving parahuman students."

"Venator training and the trials are dangerous. Accidents happen," Oberon said.

"Yes, but it happened outside the trials. And while it used to be one or two, in the last two years, over fifty parahumans have been involved in either a fatality or disappearance, as opposed to the ten involving humans," she said.

"Why haven't we heard anything about this?" Oberon asked.

"Because the Guild has been covering it up."

"But why would they do that?" Christian asked.

"I don't know, the Department says we're just trying to stir up trouble and that people disappear all the time. They've found no evidence of foul play in any of the incidents, or so they say. The AR has been gathering its own evidence and getting signatures to present to CHaPR, but if the Guild or the Department finds out they'll shut us down."

"So that's why you were involved with Andrew Williams."

"Did he tell you that?" She tilted her head to look at him. "I'll kill him."

"Too late I'm afraid, someone's beaten you to it," Oberon said.

Christian groaned inwardly. *Tactful as always, Oberon.*

Her eyes widened with genuine surprise. "What?"

She wasn't acting. Christian had always known when Valerica was lying. Her eyes would change color. But this wasn't one of those times.

Her gaze passed from Christian to Oberon and back again, her shoulders slumping. "When?"

"A couple of nights ago. He was about to flee the country," Christian said. "Did he tell you anything?"

She shook her head, her eyes losing focus as her thoughts turned inward. "He didn't have much insider knowledge when it came to the Guild. Sir Roger was a blowhard and treated Andrew more like a slave than an assistant. Then suddenly, about two months ago, he got cagey about something and he kept having nightmares. Talking in his sleep about someone called the Old One."

Alarm bells clanged loudly. Christian turned to Oberon. "Williams—he was terrified, saying he needed protection from someone called the Old One."

"Dante?" Oberon asked.

Valerica looked up quickly. "Dante? Dante Rubins? I thought he was dead."

"So did I until I came off second best in two encounters with him so far," Oberon growled.

Christian looked at her. "What do you know of Dante?"

Valerica frowned. "Nothing really, it's just Andrew kept talking about a man he just called D.R." Valerica leaned over for a pack of cigarettes on the coffee table before her. "He didn't approve of the Old One using this man—he kept saying D.R. was unstable and dangerous. I suppose it could've been Dante."

"What about the AR cult?" Christian asked. "What's their involvement in all of this?"

She pulled a cigarette from the pack and lit it. She took a long drag and then exhaled before answering. "The AR really isn't the same organization as it used to be. Most of AR's ideals involve parahuman rights and not letting the humans dictate what we can and can't do. Rubins may have set up a radical cult, but he was insane. We moved a long way from that. Today's AR takes a much more philosophical and political approach."

Valerica rolled the filter with her fingers and glanced toward the front door.

"You mean it's a bunch of bored old Aeternus sitting around reflecting on their glory days and bitching about how the world is today," Oberon said.

"No." She crossed her legs and blew smoke in his direction. "There's more to it than that. We organized the petition, and we have fundraising parties and committee meetings."

"You mean sex-fests," Oberon snorted. "Like this one."

She glared at him as she dragged in another puff then glanced at the door for a second time.

Oberon dropped his arms to his side. "I don't think we're going to find out much more here, Laroque. The AR seems to have lost its teeth."

Christian was beginning to think Oberon was right. "Is there anything . . . anything at all . . . you can think of that may help us find Viktor's killer?"

Valerica leaned forward and stamped out the butt in the ashtray, shaking her head and looking as fragile as he'd expected in the first place.

He reached over and took her hand. "Call me if you think of anything else." He placed a finger under her chin and lifted her face up. "Or even if you just need something—anything."

She nodded, tears slipping down her cheeks. He worried about her. She'd never been particularly strong—more show than anything else, always living in the shadow of her mother and brother.

As he stood up, a guy came in the front door carrying a paper grocery bag. He looked at Valerica and then at Christian and Oberon. "What's going on? Who are you?"

Once again Oberon flashed his ID.

The newcomer just glanced at it with a sneer. "This is harassment, man."

Oberon picked him up by the front of the shirt and lifted his feet off the floor. "Who the hell are you?" he growled.

"He lives here." Valerica came to her feet. "Please, put him down."

Oberon dropped him on his ass. She ran to his side to help

the boy stand. Christian could smell the youth was newly awakened.

Valerica's new boyfriend started to sputter, puffing out his chest. "That's assault, I can have you—"

"It's okay, Ricky baby, they're just leaving," Valerica said, wrapping her arms around his waist.

He took her face between his hands and kissed each tear-stained eyelid. "Are you all right, babe?"

She nodded at him and smiled. Not an entirely happy smile, but it had potential. For the first time in many centuries she looked at a man other than himself with adoration. Although this kid was young, he had courage and strength, just what Valerica needed. And he could give her something Christian never could. *Love.*

Christian held out his hand to Ricky. "Take care of her will you?" He met her eyes. "And treat her the way she deserves."

The young man looked surprised, but took his hand in a firm grasp and pumped it slowly. "Yeah man, I will."

Christian drew Valerica in and kissed her forehead. "Goodbye, Valerica."

"Goodbye," she whispered.

Once outside the building, Oberon looked up. "Tell me, Laroque—did she have a thing for you?"

Christian shrugged. "We've known each other a very long time. Why?"

"That guy looked like your bloody double."

"Rubbish."

"Well, you weren't standing where I was." Oberon shook his head, bemused. "I could hardly tell the difference."

Christian changed the subject. "Okay where do we go from here?"

Oberon placed his huge hands on his hips. "I don't know—back to your place to compare notes?"

26

whispers in the dark

Antoinette finished her workout and made her way back to her room. Her muscles trembled from the exercise, but all she could think about was the way Christian brought her alive when they made love.

Sex had never been very big on her radar. She'd lost her virginity at the age of sixteen at an Academy mixer. It was a totally forgettable two-minute fumble in the darkened equipment room with an eighteen-year-old boy from another class. She'd only wanted to see what the fuss was about, and decided it wasn't all that much.

The boy had roughly entered her after a bit of breast squeezing and nipple pinching. He'd pumped away on top for a few seconds then shuddered his release. Afterward he buttoned his trousers and left her sprawled, bruised and un-fulfilled, on the piled-up gymnasium mats. He didn't even acknowledge her for the rest of the year.

Sometimes after a kill she'd head to a bar, restless with the need to reaffirm her humanity. She'd work off a bit of the adrenaline with a quick ride in the backseat of some faceless chump's car, or up against a dark and dirty alley wall.

Occasionally her "friend" would even spring for a hotel room, but she never stayed longer than it took to get the job done. And if she couldn't find anyone she wanted to fuck, she'd start a brawl instead. A good fight worked off just as much energy and was sometimes much more satisfying.

She'd never met a man she wanted to sleep with more than once. Until now.

It was just sex, right?

That's all it could ever be. One day he could be her enemy. *Was it wrong to sleep with the enemy?*

A knock on the door startled her. Could Christian be back already?

"Come in, I'm decent," she answered.

Dylan pushed the door open and stood on the threshold with a tray in his arms. "The butler asked me to bring this up to you since I was coming anyway."

"Ah, my babysitter."

He crossed the floor and put the tray holding a glass of milk, a sandwich, and an apple on the table. God bless Kavindish, he knew she'd be hungry after her workout.

Dylan walked to the window and checked it was shut tight. Antoinette sat down to remove her Nikes then wiped her hands and picked up the sandwich, taking a large bite. Roast beef with plenty of mustard—just the way she liked it.

"So why does Oberon think I need you to take care of me?" she asked around a mouthful of bread and meat.

Dylan turned away from the window and looked at her more closely. "Don't underestimate Rubins. He nearly took us all out in that warehouse and surprise was our only real defense. He knows we're onto him now. He'll be ready next time."

"You don't think he'd really come here after me? Do you?" She took another large bite.

"Probably not, but no harm in being prepared." He crossed back to the door. "I think I'll check the perimeter again."

"Thanks, Dylan. I don't mean to sound ungrateful. I just don't think they have any faith in my ability to look after myself."

"Dante is a nasty piece of work, that's all." He smiled and

winked. "Yell if you need anything and don't forget to drink your milk," he said before shutting the door.

Antoinette finished off her sandwich and drank half the milk. She pulled off her top and was headed for the shower when her cell phone rang.

She flipped it open. "Hello?"

"Antoinette?"

She recognized the voice immediately. "Lucian! How are you?"

"I'm fine and on the mend. I have to wear a sling to help the shoulder heal properly, but other than that I'm fine. What about you? Are you still in New York?"

"Yes, at Christian's." She sat on the bed, one leg folded underneath her.

"Are they still giving you a hard time?" he asked.

"Not so much." How much should she tell him about the case? "They think they know who the attacker is."

"Oh—that's great. So you're off the hook then?"

"Pretty much I think."

"Anything I can do to help—you name it."

"Please don't worry about it. I'm sure there'll be another break soon. They think there might be someone else involved."

"Really? Do they have any idea who?"

"No, and it's just a theory anyway."

"Well, you be careful. I wouldn't want anything to happen to you. Listen—" Lucian paused. "I was going to leave this until I got back to New York, but if you can spare the time, it would be great if you would give some Venator demonstrations at the Academy."

"I'd like that." She squirmed one-handed out of her sweatpants. "When?"

"I'll talk to you about it in a few weeks when I need to come to New York to visit my specialist. But you're welcome to visit my house upstate anytime before that if you wish."

"Thanks. I'll think about it." Not likely, though, while Dante was free.

"Well, if you do decide to come, call me and I'll make the arrangements."

"I will, Lucian, but I'd better go now," she said.

"Yes, we'll talk soon."

Now—time for a shower.

Feeling clean and refreshed, Antoinette left the bathroom as she twisted the tie around the end of her still damp braid. She picked up the apple she'd saved from the dinner tray and pulled a small knife from the pocket of her army pants to cut a slice. As she brought the piece of fruit to her mouth, the fine hair on the back of her neck prickled and a slight breeze cooled her shower-warmed skin. Someone was in the room. She spun around as Dante stepped out of the shadows.

"Well now, little one." His breath caressed her cheek. "Now it's just you and me."

As Antoinette stepped back, the top of her thighs ran into the table behind and the apple fell from her fingers, thudding to the floor. Her eyes flicked to the door and escape. "How did you get in here? Christian had alarms put on all the windows."

He laughed. "Did you really think that would stop me?" A breeze flowed in from the open window behind him.

Antoinette feinted left then darted to the right, but the key turned in the lock then flew into his hands. "We wouldn't want anyone to disturb us now, would we?" He put it in his pocket.

She made a lunge for her cell phone that sat on the dresser. Again he beat her to it, the phone flew out the window and out of her reach.

Dante stalked toward her and she backed away until she felt the wall behind her. Her fingers clenched around the knife, reminding her it was there.

Scratching and growling whimpers came from the other side of the bedroom door. Cerberus must sense her danger.

Dante placed his hand against the wall on either side of her head and leaned in. "It's time, little one." He smiled, his fangs gleaming. "It's time for me to taste your sweet delights."

"No." She buried the knife up to the hilt in his stomach. "It's not."

His eyes widened in surprise and he looked down at the handle sticking out. She took the opportunity to dart under his arms and out of the window, scrabbling down the drainpipe as fast as she could, scraping her knuckles and bare feet. When she reached the bottom, she looked up.

His mouth twisted into a malevolent grin, the knife handle still protruding from his stomach. "Run," he said, pulling the blade out and dropped it to clatter on the concrete. He leapt from the window after it and landed a few feet away. "Let's play catch."

Antoinette backed up and tripped over something large and soft. The metallic scent of blood filled her nostrils as she looked down at a headless body. A short way off, Dylan's sightless eyes stared out of his decapitated head.

She stifled the scream welling in her throat and climbed to her knees, her hands brushing her cell phone. She quickly pocketed it, hoping it still worked.

Then she ran.

But before she reached the street something slammed into the back of her head and the world went black.

Cerberus's whimpers greeted Christian as he arrived home. Kavindish came in from the kitchen wearing his overcoat.

"What's all the commotion about?" Oberon asked, following Christian into the house.

"I don't know, but he's worked up about something." Then it hit him—only one thing would set the dog off like that. "Antoinette—"

Christian raced up the stairs leaving Oberon and Kavindish to follow. He found Cerberus scratching frantically at her door, whining, growling and trying to dig his way in through the carpeted floor.

Christian tried the handle. Locked. He pounded on the wood. "Antoinette, open the door."

Nothing.

"What's wrong?" Oberon asked.

"It's locked from the inside and she's not answering," Christian said, turning just in time to see Oberon stripping off. "What're you doing?"

"I don't want to ruin these clothes." Oberon held out his jacket to Kavindish. "Will you keep them for me?"

The butler bowed and took it, holding his arms out for the rest.

"Stand back," Oberon said when completely naked. The muscles along his arms rippled and his fingers began to thicken. Christian watched in fascination as Oberon's body swelled, growing taller and bulkier than he already was. Hair sprouted across his chest leaving swirling hairless patterns along his tribal scars. The fur spread across his torso, along his limbs, and covered his face. Long sharp claws extended from the ends of his fingers and his face rounded as the nose elongated. Within a few seconds, a huge grizzly bear stood on hind legs, his large head brushing the ceiling.

Oberon, in bear form, dropped to all fours and hit the door with fifteen hundred pounds of raw fury—his fur rippled and shimmered with the effort. Cerberus cringed low and backed away. After a few good hits the doorframe splintered inward, sending the door crashing to the floor. Oberon backed up to let Christian enter, but Cerberus raced through his legs and ran to the window, barking at the alley below.

Oberon sniffed around the room and growled. A chair had been overturned and Christian squatted to pick up an apple—the fruit had gone slightly discolored where a slice had been cut away. The dog continued to bark, and Christian found a drop of black blood darkening the window sill—Aeternus blood. He smeared it with his fingertips and sniffed then held it under the bear's nose. "Dante?"

Oberon rose up on hind legs, muzzle peeled back to expose

long white canine teeth, and he jutted his head forward, grunting at Christian. Then the bear shrank—fur disappeared as if sucked back into pores, replaced with perspiration slicking Oberon's toffee-colored skin. He stood, hands on hips, totally uncaring about his state of undress. "Dante. His scent's everywhere in here."

"And Antoinette's fear. Can you track him?" Christian asked.

"Yes, but it's easier in bear form. I changed back to get out of here." He stuck his head through the window and with muscles bunching, jumped out to land on the ground below. Christian followed him, bending his knees to absorb the impact. He was more tuned into her than anything else and her fear-laced scent was stronger in the alley.

Oberon squatted over a body and the scent of blood was everywhere. For a split second Christian feared it was Antoinette, but the blood was all wrong.

Oberon stood, his eyes hot and furious. "He's killed Dylan."

Christian could smell the rage and grief pouring off the ursian. His friend had been killed, just like Viktor.

"Let's get him," Oberon growled.

Heat rose in Christian's chest and he clenched his fists at his side. "This way."

Oberon transformed as he raced down the alley and set off at a lumbered run up the road with his large head sniffing the ground.

The sound of a striking match intruded on her groggy senses with a sulfurous odor, bringing her out of the fog. Metal squealed and Antoinette opened one eye to see a rusty kerosene lamp being lit. Pain burst into her head, blinding her. She closed her eyes against the light.

When the nausea and throbbing subsided, she tried again. Not quite so bad this time and she finally managed to open them all the way.

Chains clanked when she tried to move, her shoulders

ached, and pins and needles prickled her hands since her
arms were secured above her head. Her brain instantly
cleared and she grunted against the gag stuffed into her
mouth. Cold stone or concrete chilled her back and she hung
secured by shackles to the wall.

Panic began to bubble in her stomach and she pushed it
down. No use losing her head yet. But where was she?

A dark shape crossed her hazy vision. "You're awake at
last—good. It's no fun if you're not conscious."

Dante's cold voice set off the cold lump of panic in the pit
of her gut. His dark shape moved closer.

Antoinette squinted and blinked her eyes a couple of
times to clear her vision, trying to get a bearing on where he
held her. The glow from the lamp flickered shadows on the
gray concrete walls, the light growing brighter as he walked
around the room igniting candles. Water dripped somewhere
and three tunnels ran off the room into darkness. It looked
like a sewer junction.

As she glanced around the makeshift torture chamber her
blood turned to ice. On a shelf, dead eyes stared down at
her, the horror frozen in the expressions of the missing fang-
whore heads. Their faces were all shiny, like they'd been
preserved by some sort of lacquer. Beneath the macabre dis-
play dozens of pictures were pinned. Some were just of her
and some with other people. There was one of Christian and
her kneeling over Viktor's prone body, the grief and terror
twisting her features. Another had her at the party dressed
in the elegant gown on Lucian's arm.

He'd been watching her.

Images of Lucian also featured prominently on the walls—
some with her, some by himself, and some with other people
too. She wasn't the only person Dante obsessed about.

Lucian's in danger.

"Do you like my workshop?" Dante said, his eyes holding
hers with chilling intensity.

Antoinette's heart fell. She wriggled her hands, testing her
bonds, but they held tight and she looked down to see her

feet too were bound and set in a low metal tub. She closed her eyes and silently prayed Christian would find her before it was too late.

"Don't worry, Christian and his ursian friend won't be able to find us here," he said as if reading her mind. "We'll have all night to ourselves."

He lit another lamp and hung it above her head. "I wouldn't want you to miss anything important," he said, kissing her forehead, leaving her skin crawling with revulsion. She tried to jerk her head away. It only made him chuckle louder.

"So where will we start? How about dinner and a show? You'll be dinner and then the show." Dante's cold smile split his face and she felt her hatred bubble to the surface, burning the back of her throat with bile.

The concrete wall chilled her backbone, and she realized she wore only her underwear. The cold made her nipples stand out puckered and painful. She desperately wanted to cover herself, but with her hands tied, she was helpless.

He moved closer, licking his lips and opened his mouth to show her his fully extended fangs. A shiver of fear snaked through her stomach. She instinctively knew his bite would cause pain rather than the heated desire she felt with Christian.

He started to strip, folding his clothes carefully and placing them on a high shelf out of the way. He kept undressing until he finally stood before her, naked and semi-aroused.

For the first time, Antoinette noticed old rusty brown and black stains on the floor around her. The kind dried blood made. So this was where he'd killed them.

From the makeshift bench along the wall he picked up a knife—the same knife she'd used to stab him earlier. "I've sharpened it a little since you last used it."

He held the blade up to the light, twisting it so she could see the new edge. "I want this to be even better than the time I spent with your mother." His smile deepened as she flinched, her stomach twisting. "I've waited such a long time."

He closed in, grin widening, and she pressed back hard against the wall, wrenching her hands and fighting against the shackles. He ran the flat of the cold blade over the exposed swell of her breast above her bra.

She screamed against her gag, partly in frustration but mostly in rage. She narrowed her gaze, looking him in the eye.

His smiled deepened and his erection swelled as he moved the knife down between her breasts and sliced through the lace. It parted under the weight of her breasts. His eyes glowed with a manic desire as he sliced through the straps over her shoulders and with a tiny groan he licked his lips as he discarded the remnants over his shoulder.

Antoinette swallowed the nausea fast rising in her gut.

He watched her face as he cut away her panties, leaving her totally naked. She stared back. There was no way she would give him the satisfaction of showing just how degraded she felt. Her hate for him washed over her, bringing with it a kind of insane calmness.

"Now for some fun." Hunger burned in his cold eyes as he rubbed himself against her.

His arousal pressed against her hip, she tried to move away from it, but he just pressed against her harder and drew the blade across her chest above her breasts. His erection surged.

The pain, searing and sharp, burned across her chest. He squeezed her face so she had to look at him and couldn't turn away while he lifted the knife blade to his tongue, tasting her blood.

His brow furrowed and he spat in disgust. "You whore—first you let him have you, and now you've tainted your blood with disgusting hate."

Her head slammed into the concrete wall with his backhanded slap. Antoinette's ears rang and dark stars burst in her vision. He hit her again.

Laughter bubbled up her throat and out her mouth. It was as if another person did it, not her, she couldn't stop it.

Dante's expression grew confused and stormed to the other side of the room.

When he turned, his composure was once again in place. "No matter—I can still have my fun."

He drew his palm across her wound then cupped himself. He threw back his head and sighed as he ran his hand down his shaft, smearing it with her crimson blood.

He looked at her through desire-hooded eyes. "I'm going to make you bleed and I'm going to make you scream."

He ripped the gag from her mouth and sliced the knife across her left thigh, then did the same with her right. Despite the searing pain, she bit down on her lip to stifle any cries and the warm metallic tang filled her mouth.

"Come on." Dante rubbed himself against her, pumping his fist up and down his shaft. "Give me your voice."

He sliced across her stomach with a half-dozen shallow cuts. They weren't deep, but bled just the same, and all the while he masturbated with her blood.

Antoinette tried to block it out by closing her eyes, still biting back the scream she trapped in her throat. She felt the stickiness coating her legs and looked down to see it pooling around her feet, just as it had in her nightmares.

I'm going to die. The scream finally tore free.

Bear-Oberon padded around the street in front of Christian's house, sniffing and walking in circles.

He transformed back. "She was here, but so was Dante. And this is where the trail ends." He looked at Christian. "He's played us—it was all part of his game."

A howl came from the direction of the brownstone. Cerberus. Christian sprinted toward the house. "Kavindish," he called, racing through the door. "Where's the dog?"

The butler appeared. "I locked him in the basement, sir. I didn't want him getting in the way."

"I think he senses her too," Christian said, opening the basement door. Cerberus bounded out and headed for the nearest window, but Kavindish ran ahead and opened the front door for him. The dog exited the house and stopped on the other side of the street. He sniffed and growled, scratching at the ground.

Oberon arrived. "What's going on?"

"He knows she was here."

The ursian pulled on the pants Kavindish handed him and squatted to examine the area. "Skid marks—someone's pulled out of here very fast not long ago. He's taken her, but where?"

Christian turned to the butler. "Have you tried calling Miss Petrescu's cell?"

"Yes, sir. But she doesn't pick up. And it's not in her room, I searched."

Oberon took a cell phone from his saddle bags grabbed from the hog parked close by and slid it open. "I need a trace on Antoinette Petrescu's cell; the number is on my desk. Call with the coordinates as soon as you have them."

"Of course, the GPS chip. Let's take my SUV."

Christian led Oberon to the underground garage where he parked and Cerberus followed. He didn't have the heart to tell the dog to stay. As the SUV left the garage, Oberon's cell rang.

"You're sure?" he said after listening for a few seconds then closed the phone.

"Where?" Christian said.

"The coordinates lead to the abandoned building where we cornered him last time."

"Why would they—when they found out it was a satanic cult temple they pulled all surveillance. Dylan had . . ." Oberon turned to look out the window.

Christian glanced at the ursian. "I'm sorry."

Oberon nodded. "I just don't know what I'm going to tell his sister." He straightened in his seat and his head brushed the top of the SUV, the seat groaned under the weight. "But right now we have to get to Antoinette before he kills her too."

Christian's heart beat skipped. He couldn't bear to lose her now, not when . . . When what? What kind of relationship did they have? He didn't know, and he didn't care—he just needed to save her.

Oberon was silent for the rest of the journey and Christian concentrated on getting them there the quickest way he could. The black SUV bore the Department insignia and the sirens were blearing, but he had to be aware of the other street users and drive defensively. All he wanted to do was drive through anyone who got in his way. Antoinette was in danger and nothing else mattered.

When they reached the abandoned building, Christian parked the SUV and Oberon pulled out a pair of 9mm Berettas.

Christian's skin prickled and a low growl erupted from Cerberus. Antoinette was near—they both sensed it. The dog shot off at a run, and Christian gave chase, slapping Oberon's shoulder as he passed.

They entered the building and didn't slow. Each step the feeling of her nearness grew stronger until they were finally in a basement chamber.

"This is where we found him last time," Oberon said, looking around the cold empty room.

Cerberus sniffed around the large carved stone platform in the center of the dirty floor. He started to whine and scratch at the base. Oberon moved closer with Christian. He could feel her more now. And she was in pain . . . so much pain.

He pushed hard against the platform. It moved. He pushed harder and Oberon joined him. Agony sliced through his muscles. No, not his, hers. The bastard was slicing into her. With an extra burst of strength, the platform moved back to reveal a hole in the floor.

Without waiting, Christian leapt into the hole and turned to catch Cerberus as the dog jumped after him. Oberon followed. A darkened sewer tunnel led left and right.

Cerberus whined quietly, looking to the left. The overwhelming odor of waste, rats, and garbage could not hide the underlying scent of human decay and fresh terror.

Christian took a step but the ursian's hand fell on his

shoulder. Oberon put his finger to his lips for silence and mouthed, *Take him alive*; and with a short, sharp nod they both moved along the sewer tunnel. Christian projected constant calming thoughts at Cerberus to keep the dog from making any noise as they closed in on a patch of flickering light ahead, the air filling with fear, anger, and fresh blood.

Oberon took a left, then he took a right and they entered together. Christian had seen several wars, but nothing could have prepared him for the horror he found in that room. Severed blond heads ringed the walls, their own eyes plucked out and replaced with emerald green glass ones.

There was no sign of Dante. Christian, pistol pointing ahead, rounded a concrete pillar to find Antoinette shackled naked to the far wall, head slumped forward and covered in blood.

Christian's heart clenched to a stop at the sight. He raced to her side and dropped as he put the gun back in his holster. Her breathing was soft and shallow. Her hair hung in a tacky blood-soaked mess; he gently lifted her face pushing aside the sticky locks. Her eyes fluttered open and his name formed on her lips, but no sound came out. There was so much blood.

He was losing her—just like Viktor—just like Dominique and his father.

A drop of crimson appeared on his forearm. He looked at it. *Where had it come from?*

He glanced up. A primitive form clung to the ceiling above; glittering gray eyes stared down from a crimson-painted face.

Blood!

It was completely smeared head to toe with blood—Antoinette's blood. The form hissed at him, fangs exposed then dropped.

Christian reacted too late to the attack. The naked red figure landed on his feet and swept Christian into the wall like a toothpick.

Dante!

Christian hit a large pipe with the middle of his back.
All the breath rushed from his lungs with the impact. The
crunching sound of bones snapping echoed through the cavernous chamber. Paralyzed and helpless, Christian could
only lay there, back broken, as Dante ran his knuckle across
Antoinette's face in a ghoulish parody of affection.

"She's mine now, all mine." His white teeth were high-
lighted against his red-stained skin.

Antoinette moved her head and groaned, fighting his
touch. Christian glanced past Dante at Oberon creeping
behind, pointing his pistols at the madman's head.

Dante flicked his wrist and the ursian smashed into the
pillar, dust and chunks of concrete flying with the impact.
He lay on the ground, unmoving and unconscious as the dust
settled on his dreadlocked head.

"Now you'll watch while I make her mine forever." Dante
bit into his wrist, his dark blood flowing and mixing with
the bright red of hers on his skin. He drew on the wound and
lifted Antoinette's face so her lips were level with his.

Her eyes opened at that very minute. Terror filled her eyes
as she realized what he was about to do. She tried to back
her head away—to turn from his kiss, but Dante closed the
distance between their mouths.

"Nooooo!" Christian screamed.

Out of nowhere Cerberus launched himself at the insane
Aeternus, his jaws closing on Dante's forearm. The force
was enough to push him away from Antoinette as he flung
the dog high against the wall beside Christian with a sickening crunch.

A shot rang out and Dante's right ear disintegrated.

Oberon pointed the pistol as he struggled onto his hands
and knees, gun in hand. Dante pulled his hand away from
his ear, still holding a hunk of flesh. He looked at Oberon
then at Christian and roared before leaping over the scattered bit of furniture and out of the junction opening.

Oberon stretched up, bones popping and crunching as he
transformed into bear form.

Christian's back was mending, but not fast enough. He crawled toward Antoinette, bones crunching together as his ribs knitted back together.

The bear landed on all fours and turned in the direction Dante went.

"Help Antoinette," Christian said.

The bear turned toward her slumped body and back to the junction entrance, then he reared up on his hind legs and roared in frustration. He lumbered over and ripped the shackle chain from where it was bolted to the wall, pulling a large chunk of concrete with it. Antoinette collapsed into Oberon's huge fur-covered arms. He laid her on the ground and turned to pull the leg shackles out as well.

Christian finally reached her side and felt her pulse. It slowed—rapidly.

Oberon transformed back to human. "Is she dead?"

"No, but she's lost a lot of blood."

Oberon kneeled on the other side of her. "Too much. She won't make it—not even if we can get her to hospital. She's gone."

"Not if I can help it." Christian bit down on his wrist and sucked in a little of his own blood into his mouth. He would finish what Dante had started and save her.

He tilted back her head and parted her cold, pale lips then pressed his mouth to hers, forcing her to accept his eternal-kiss. Finally she drank, her throat working to swallow his life-giving essence. Hope flared.

He checked her pulse again. Her heart beat erratically under his fingertips. Then it faltered and stopped. He was too late.

"No," he growled. "You can't go. *I won't let you.*"

27
ever changes

Christian tilted back her head, pinched her nose, and breathed air into her lungs. Oberon moved into position for pulmonary massage and together they worked to keep the blood pumping through her body so the Aeternus enzymes would have enough time to trigger the DNA mutation.

Suddenly she sucked in a large breath and coughed—Christian felt her heartbeat pick up under his fingertips resting on her throat.

"Now—" Oberon said, moving back, "give her some more juice."

Christian bit into his wrist and held it against her lips. This time she drank—and drank deep. He could feel the pull as it flowed into her, jolting her system. Finally he had to pull his arm away before she took too much.

He sat back on his heels and sighed, then looked at Oberon. "Now it really starts."

"She's got a long fight ahead of her." Oberon glanced at Christian. "Give me your cell before you go—I want to call this in."

Christian tossed his cell phone to the ursian before gathering Antoinette's almost weightless body into his arms. His bones, while knitted back together, still hurt to put his weight on, but he gritted his teeth and carried Antoinette out of the charnel house of a sewer.

Christian parked the SUV half on the curb, not caring about anything but getting Antoinette inside. Kavindish opened the door and Christian walked straight past him and paused at the bottom of the stairs.

"I'm going to need you—and lots of blood."

"Yes, sir," the butler said.

"Send Susan up to settle Antoinette." Christian climbed the staircase toward Antoinette's room. He eyed the shattered door and continued on to his own suite.

He carefully lay her down on the bed, supporting her head and brushing her blood encrusted hair away from her face. "I'm so sorry, please forgive me," he whispered against her cheek.

Her eyes fluttered open. "Christian?" she croaked and passed out again.

Susan entered a few minutes later and froze. "Shouldn't we get her to hospital, sir?"

"They can't help her now." Christian took the bowl from Susan's shaking hands and placed it on the bedside table before taking the frightened girl firmly by the shoulders. "She'll go through horrific pain in the next few hours, maybe even days. Her body is going to tear itself apart from the inside out. If she makes it—and I say *if* because I want you to be prepared there's a good chance that she won't . . ."

He stopped and swallowed, not sure if he could face the fact himself. "If she does makes it through she'll be Aeternus, but it's going to be rough and it's not going to be pretty." Christian squeezed her arms. "Can you deal with that?"

The girl's eyes filled with tears but then she glanced at Antoinette, squared her shoulders, and lifted her chin. "Yes, sir."

"Good girl." He gave her arm a pat. "First we need to get her cleaned up and see how bad the wounds are."

Kavindish walked into the room carrying a cooler, which he opened to reveal several bags of blood.

"I'm going to need more than that," Christian said.

"I have already ordered several more units to be delivered within the hour," Kavindish said. "You'll need your strength if you're going to get her through this."

Christian clasped the butler's shoulder. Not once had he regretted saving Kavindish from death by embracing him at Meuse-Argonne during World War One, but never more so than right now.

"Okay, Susan, get some warm water and let's get this blood cleaned off. Kavindish, we'll need bandages and clean gauze."

Susan returned from the bathroom carrying the steaming basin and dipped a hand towel into it. She stood there looking down at Antoinette, as if unsure where to start.

"You start at her feet and I'll start from the top," Christian said.

She stared at him with her head tilted slightly to the side, and then her eyes focused. Christian nodded encouragement at the girl as she bent to work.

By the time they'd finished, Susan had needed to refill the bowl with clean water a dozen times. Kavindish helped to dress the wounds, and there were a lot to dress. Dante had done quite a number on her. If they were going to give her a fighting chance, they had to stop any infection from taking hold until she'd been through the change. Everything teetered on a knife edge now—it could so easily fall either way; the next few hours would be crucial.

As Christian sat on a chair beside her bed, Kavindish held out a glass of blood. "She'll need feeding soon, sir. You'd best be prepared."

"Thank you, Kavindish—for everything."

"It's not going to be easy, Christian." Kavindish dropped his formality—his friend, not a servant, stood before him. "Her body will most likely reject the change. She was probably too far gone."

"I know, but I had to try." Christian looked at her sleeping face. "I couldn't lose her too, not without a fight."

"I know, old friend." Kavindish clasped Christian's shoulder for a moment and understanding passed between them before the servant in him returned. "Will there be anything else, sir?"

"No. I'll stay with her." Christian backed into the chair and downed the contents of the glass Kavindish had handed him. It was tasteless and he almost gagged on the second glassful, but Kavindish was right, he needed all his strength for the ordeal ahead.

To embrace someone, one feeding of Aeternus blood wasn't enough. It was a long and difficult process for both the embracer and embraced. Antoinette would have to be fed often from his bloodline to replenish the Aeternus enzymes while the change took place. Christian settled in for the first watch.

"How is she?" Oberon said from the doorway.

Christian wiped his palm across his chin and looked at his watch—it had been only a couple of hours, but it felt like an eternity.

He turned to Oberon. "No change yet, but she'll need feeding soon."

As if to prove him right, Antoinette whimpered in her sleep and began to thrash. Christian sat on the bed and pulled her toward him, then opened his wrist and forced her mouth against the bloody wound. She twisted her head from side to side trying to avoid it but he held her tighter so she couldn't fight him. Finally, she began to suckle and electricity surged through as his blood flowed into her. It only took a little before she slipped back into a coma.

"How often will you have to do that?" Oberon asked.

"Every couple of hours or so, but she'll take more and more each time."

Aeternus physiology was different and the awakening change happened without the need for an external blood source, but it was still quite difficult and excruciating to go through.

However embracing was much more extreme—the human DNA had to be dramatically altered and that was why most humans died. They couldn't survive the transition.

"We Animalians can't convert humans—you have to be born of an Animalian parent." Oberon looked down at the now peaceful Antoinette. "I don't think I'd like the burden of what you've done."

Christian understood. It could be seen as a gift or a curse. Would Antoinette thank him or hate him for what he'd done to her? Would she become an Aeternus, or turn into a dreniac like Carolina? Only time would tell—he'd have to wait to find out. But first she had to live. And that was more important than anything else.

"So how did it go?" Christian changed the subject. "Did they find anything?"

Oberon's broad shoulders sagged. "Apart from all the photos of her and Lucian Moretti?" He walked to the bedside and looked down at Antoinette's sleeping form. "I've warned Moretti what we've found. But I'd like to go up and check on his security arrangements myself."

"I can't believe Dante is still alive," Christian said.

Dark anger flashed in Oberon's eyes, his hands into fists. "I just wish we'd caught the bastard."

Rage smoldered hot and heavy in the pit of Christian's stomach. "When I do, I'm going to make him suffer for this."

Oberon continued to look at Antoinette. "Do you know, she was never cowered by me, no matter how much I tried to intimidate her. She's one of the gutsiest humans I've ever come across. I don't know a lot of humans, or parahumans for that matter, who could've survived the kind of torture Dante subjected her to. And to think of the hard time I gave her."

"She's a licensed Venator—she's used to dealing with unreasonable monsters."

"Touché." Oberon's face cracked into a tired grin. "Well, if we turn anything else up I'll call you. But for now I've got a friend looking into this parahuman disappearance thing Viktor's sister told us about. Maybe there's a connection."

"Maybe." Christian started to rise but Oberon held up his hand. "I can see myself out."

A piercing scream jolted Christian from sleep.

"It burns," Antoinette shrieked, scratching at the skin on her arms.

The maid, Susan, stood on the other side of the bed. "No, miss, don't do that," she said, trying to keep Antoinette from ripping any more bandages off her wounds.

She'd had already succeeded in reopening a couple of the gashes and fresh blood wept from her arms.

"Nooooooo," Antoinette screamed and backhanded Susan across the room.

The poor girl hit the wall and slid into a crumpled heap on the floor. Kavindish flew to her side.

"Is she okay?" Christian asked, holding Antoinette's wrists as she struggled.

"Yes, sir," Kavindish said. "I'll take care of her."

He helped the dazed maid to her feet and checked her eyes.

"We're going to have to restrain Antoinette," Christian said. "Hold her still for now and I'll feed her."

Kavindish moved to the bed and pinned Antoinette's arms to her side while Christian opened his wrist again. Holding her head, Christian forced her to take his blood until, finally, she became quiet. When he got her settled again, he looked up to find his mother standing in the doorway.

"What're you doing here?" Christian asked. He didn't need her telling him how irresponsible he'd been, like she had when he'd embraced Kavindish during the war.

"I'm here to help," she said, coming to the bedside.

The butler deliberately avoided eye contact and bent over Susan.

"She's going through the change fast," Christian said, "too fast. Her body will tear itself apart."

Lilijana nodded once then put her hand on Antoinette's forehead. "Christian, she's burning up." She whipped back the covers.

He felt Antoinette's forehead himself. Her temperature had shot up in a matter of seconds as her body reacted to the fresh influx of his blood. "Kavindish, get all the ice you can lay your hands on and bring it up here—if we don't get her temperature down, her organs will liquefy."

Christian ran into the bathroom and turned the cold faucet on full. Kavindish arrived with buckets of ice then raced away to fetch more. Even the worse-for-wear maid came in carrying a bucket. Christian's opinion of the human girl shot up a few more notches.

"Dump it into the bathtub," he said as he lifted Antoinette's blazing, unconscious body from the bed. Ice floated on the surface of the water as Kavindish dumped in another bucketful.

"Get more," Lilijana ordered, standing in the doorway.

Christian carefully lowered Antoinette into the icy water. Her eyes flew open and she thrashed against the chilly touch, screaming loudly as she fought against him, her heart pounding so rapidly, he thought it would burst through her chest. Somehow he managed to get her submerged and keep most of the water in the tub as Kavindish returned with more ice. Thank God for the butler's Aeternus speed.

"She must stay in there until the fever breaks," Lilijana said.

Christian nodded, feeling fatigue wash over him.

"Go—rest," Lilijana said. "I'll take the next feeding."

Christian shook his head. "She needs my blood."

"She needs to feed of your bloodline, Christian." She brushed his hair away from his eyes, something she hadn't done since he was a boy. "If you keep pushing yourself like this you won't have the strength to do either of you any good."

She was right. He let his mother hold Antoinette's head

above water. He needed sleep and blood—the worst was yet to come.

Antoinette tried to open her eyes but they hurt. Where was she? Where was Dante? Panic slammed into her and she tried to get her bearings. Everything ached. Her body seemed to be encased in an icy sheath yet her insides cooked. Voices babbled all around, and she screamed at them to be quiet. The sound just rattled around in her head and she couldn't understand a word.

Hands pulled at her. She fought them off, hitting and kicking out. As she got rid of one, another took its place. Monsters, they looked at her with red hateful eyes and distorted faces, staring at her, leering at her. Her stomach wrenched as one of the creatures dug its hands in and twisted her organs.

"Nooooooo," she screamed. "Leave me alone, don't touch me . . ."

"Ssshh," a familiar woman's voice soothed.

"Mama?" she cried.

"There, there my child," her mother whispered, smoothing Antoinette's hair. "Ssshh . . . just feed baby . . . that's a good girl, drink deep."

Pain squeezed her entire body as Antoinette grabbed her mother's hand and drank from it. Oh, what nectar—what heaven. It chased away the pain as she drank her fill until everything drifted away and she slipped back into cool sweet darkness . . .

Christian opened the bathroom door to see Kavindish holding Antoinette's upper body above the water while his mother sat on the side of the tub, her wrist clasped to Antoinette's mouth as she stroked her hair and whispered soothing words.

"The fever is breaking, we can take her out of the tub now," Lilijana said.

Antoinette's hair was damp and clean; someone had washed it. Christian looked at Susan, who wore a new bruise on her cheek. Poor girl looked like she'd gone a few rounds with a prize fighter, yet she continued to stay.

"Stand back," he said to his mother and he lifted Antoinette's naked body from tub and carried her to the bed.

The bandages had become a soggy mess and he cut them away with scissors. The wounds beneath had healed over and were now just pink puckered scars. Soon they too would fade.

"That's a good sign," Lilijana said over his shoulder.

Christian dared not to hope and crossed to Susan, lifting her chin to examine her bruised face and swollen lip. "She's getting too strong. It's time for you to leave the room."

Susan's eyes filled with tears. "Please sir, I can—"

"No, you can't, it's much too dangerous now—for both of you. She's already made a mess of your face. Soon her thirst will be unbound and you'll look like a very tasty meal." Christian brushed the tears from her cheek with his thumb. "She won't be able to stop herself. If she drained you then you'd both be lost. You would be dead and Antoinette would be a Necrodreniac."

Susan dropped her eyes.

"It'll be over soon, one way or another," he said and patted her shoulder. "Then you can come back and take care of her again." He placed a kiss on the girl's cheek and whispered, "Thank you."

"Yes, sir," the maid said.

Antoinette's peaceful form lay quietly in the bed, but he knew the lull wouldn't last long. Lilijana sat opposite, waiting. Neither spoke.

Two hours later Antoinette screamed and held her hands over her ears. "Make it stop, make the buzzing stop," she screamed.

"She can feel the sun is up," Lilijana said from the end of bed.

Christian opened his wrist yet again and squeezed some

blood into a glass. She was getting too strong to fight with now. Antoinette watched it, licking her lips. However when he approached her, she scrabbled backward to the other side of the large bed, fear filling her fevered eyes. He placed the glass on the bedside table, and once he'd moved far enough away she dove for it and greedily drank the contents, spilling some from the corners of her mouth.

When she was finished she threw the glass against the far wall, shattering it into a thousand pieces. She screamed and swept the bedside table aside, sending it through the air and narrowly missing Christian's head. Then Antoinette scurried to the far corner of the room and huddled in a tight ball.

"More," she screamed.

"It's time," Lilijana said, opening the cooler. She grabbed the first bag of blood and handed it to Christian.

Christian carefully approached the wild-eyed Antoinette with the bag extended toward her. She eyed him warily with no hint of recognition. Then she darted forward and snatched the bag from his hands before returning to squeeze back into the corner.

Antoinette tore at the bag like a wild animal, crimson spilling down her chin and splashing the front of her nightgown. She lapped and sucked noisily until, frustrated, she threw the empty bag aside.

"MORE," she shrieked, her newly formed fangs flashing.

Lilijana handed him the next bag and the process repeated.

After a half dozen bags of blood Antoinette's eyes drooped. She curled up into a ball on the floor and soon fell asleep again.

"The transition is almost complete," Lilijana said. "The next couple of hours will be crucial and there is nothing you can do to help her through it. She must fight this battle on her own."

Christian nodded. He looked around at the mess while Kavindish started to set furniture right and pick up the smashed pieces of glass. He removed Antoinette's blood-soaked nightgown and balled it into the corner, then lifted her onto the bed.

"I'll take the final watch," he said to his mother.

"Are you sure?" she asked, knowing like he did that she may never wake again. Even if she did it was highly unlikely that Antoinette would thank him for saving her.

He covered Antoinette's nakedness. "I want to be here alone."

"All right, but I'll just be down the hall if you need me." She paused a moment longer, then left him alone.

28

on the run

Antoinette opened her eyes in the too-bright room, and quickly closed them again. Her head buzzed and her body prickled all over as if tiny razorblades flowed through her bloodstream, cutting her from the inside. Thirst, she was so thirsty. Dry attempts to swallow produced only a rasp in her parched throat, and she had a metallic aftertaste in her mouth. Then she remembered. *Dante. . .*

She flinched away from a loud scraping from beside her head and she sat up, shielding her eyes from the glare. There must be something wrong with the light, it shone far too brightly to be a regular bulb.

"It's okay—" Christian's voice flowed through her, thick as honey and twice as sweet. "You're safe."

She let out a sob of relief and wrapped her arms around him, holding him as tight as she could. "You stopped him?"

"Yes—for now." The disappointment in his voice very clear.

"He's still free?"

"Yes."

She tried to remember what had happened after Dante chased her down the alley, but it all seemed blank. Antoinette heard the tap dripping deafeningly in the bathroom. Street noises and voices seemed far too piercing, and she wondered where she was. Everything seemed intense. Blood—she could smell blood and it smelt . . . good. Her gums tingled and she investigated with her tongue and snagged it on the sharp point of a tooth. A fang?

"What did he do to me?" she asked, clinging to Christian's safe warmth.

"He nearly killed you." His hands slid up to cup her face and stare deep into her soul. "If I'd delayed a few more seconds—"

She shoved him away and leapt from the bed. *Oh God, no.*

"Tell me you didn't, Christian."

He looked down at his hands—hands so clear she could make out each individual fine hair on the back of them. She could hear his heart beating slowly, much slower than hers—but no, not any more.

"Christian?" she repeated, her head beginning to spin with the implications.

"It was the only way to save you," he whispered.

"NO," she shook her head, not wanting to believe it.

"Antoinette, please listen to me—you were dying—there wasn't time for anything else." He held out his hands.

She slapped them away and pressed backward against the wall, needing to be as far away from him as possible. "Then you should've let me die."

He raised his eyes to hers. "I couldn't do that."

"I'd rather be dead than . . . this." She wiped her palms down her thighs like they were dirty and realized for the first time she was naked. She snatched up a sheet from the bed and held it in front of her.

"I thought now you knew our kind better, you might not find this such a burden."

"I'm hum . . . was human. Now I'm . . ." She couldn't make sense of the jumbled thoughts zipping around her head. But one word was clear and it terrified her. *Necrodrenia.*

He reached out but she shrank away.

"Don't," she hissed. "Don't touch me."

Hurt erupted in his eyes as he drew back his hands as if burnt by fire. Antoinette turned away to pull on a clean T-shirt and a pair of panties from the dresser drawer.

A shrill noise filled the room and she covered her ears to block it out. Christian pulled a cell phone from his pocket and flipped it open and listened, then, without speaking, he snapped it shut again. "I have to go."

"Where?" she asked, troubled by his blank expression.

"I'll tell you when I get back," Christian said and strode quickly from the room.

"That's what you think," she said to an empty room. "Because I won't be here."

Antoinette jumped across the bed, the buzzing lessening in her ears. Where could she go?

Home! Maybe Lucian could help her get there.

She stopped. *Lucian. . .*

Something flashed in her mind.

A concrete wall, severed blonde heads ringing the room with glass eyes and shiny lacquered skin.

And. . .

Photos—lots of photos of her and Lucian.

Dante was after Lucian . . .

She picked up the phone and dialed. A servant answered on the second ring and the silence seemed to drag on forever while he went to fetch his employer.

"Antoinette?" Lucian's voice finally crackled through the phone receiver.

Relief flooded through her. "Thank God, you're okay. Can I come and see you?"

"Why?" His tone warm and concerned. "What's wrong?"

"I'll explain when I get there," she said.

"Okay—I'll send someone to pick you up. How soon?"

"As soon as you can arrange it."

Antoinette hung up the phone and pulled her backpack from beneath the bed. She went to the drawer and stuffed her things in without folding, then pulled on a pair of jeans.

"Where are you going?" Lilijana asked from the doorway.

Antoinette didn't even stop to look at her. "Away."

"You should stay—we can help you get through this."

Antoinette snorted. "I don't want your help. I need to be
. . ." She would take care of this herself. "Away from here."

Lilijana sighed. "What are you afraid of?"

Antoinette paused. For the first time she realized just
how terrified she was—of herself. She turned to Christian's mother. "Do you know how many embraced become
dreniacs?"

"Is it Necrodrenia or my son you're more afraid of?"

Antoinette returned to her packing. That was something
she didn't want to answer, not even to herself.

"It may help to know something of the history of our
people."

"I do—it's the first thing we're taught at the Academy."
The constant buzzing ceased in Antoinette's ears and the
prickling in her blood stopped as she zipped the bag up and
rubbed her arms.

"That's the sun going down you're feeling right now." Lilijana sat on the end of her bed.

"What?" She finally turned to the Aeternus woman.

"That prickly feeling—the buzzing—it subsides as the
sun sets. Soon it'll be night and your strength will be at its
fullest—what little a fledgling Aeternus has at this stage
anyway."

"You *feel* the sun?"

"Yes, but you know that—you learned it at the Academy.
Right?" Lilijana's voice dripped with sarcasm, and then she
softened. "Look—you're going to need all the help you can
get, especially now. He only did it to save you."

Antoinette sighed and sat on the edge of the bed. "I know,
but—" She frowned and tilted her head to one side. "Why
are you helping me anyway?"

"Because I was once in the same position you're in, when
Christian's father embraced me."

"You were embraced?" Antoinette had always thought
Lilijana had looked down on her for being human.

"Yes, so I know what you're going through. Now I will tell you what Christian's father told me shortly after I was embraced." Lilijana paced the room—she seemed to be trying to find the right words to begin. Finally she stopped and dropped her hands to her side. "Thousands of years ago, when the humans had barely descended from the trees and were still hiding in cold dark caves, an alien ship crashlanded on this planet. The ship contained a race from a distant galaxy, running from an unknown evil.

"With their technology destroyed in the collision, they had no other choice but to assimilate to the environment in which they were trapped. There were many clans among the survivors and they all went in different directions to try and maximize the success of the assimilation." Lilijana held out her arms. "We, the Aeternus, are the closest form of our alien forbears, the Glarachni. They were able to manipulate their alien DNA to develop a symbiotic existence with humans and become what we are today. We survive by ingesting what we need from human hemoglobin—just as they did back then.

"But the Animalians took a different course. Adding the DNA of certain animals to their own, they were able to tolerate a wider range of food, but they took on the characteristics of the animals they crossed with as well. Then there are the magic-wielders, the Mer-people, and the many other deviations. The alien race is long gone, but we, their children, live on thanks to the humans who were our saviors."

"What does this have to do with me?"

"There is another reason I am helping you. You have always had the Aeternus blood running through your veins. Up until the time Christian triggered the change, you were a Latent." Lilijana took a step closer, reaching out.

"No," Antoinette shook her head, backing away. "You're lying."

Lilijana raised an eyebrow. "Really? Ever wonder why you were so good with animals? That dog should've laid down and died when he lost Viktor. But he didn't because of you. He even knew how to find you."

For the first time she thought of Cerberus. "Where is he?"

"The dog? He lives, but is badly injured. He has many broken bones. The vet tried to convince Christian to have the dog put down, but he refused."

Antoinette stood. "Will he be okay?"

"Yes, he is being well looked after. The best money can buy."

"Good. Then I can leave here knowing he'll be okay."

"You know you have more chance of succumbing to Necrodrenia if you leave." Lilijana grabbed her arm. "Christian needs you."

Tears pricked behind her eyes—she swallowed hard and turned back to her bags. "I can't."

Susan came to the door. "There's a man here. He says he's here to take you to the airport."

"Oh, Susan, what happened to your face?" Antoinette asked.

The maid looked at her feet. "It was an accident."

"Oh my God, I did this to you, didn't I?" Antoinette's gut wrenched at Susan's crusted split lip and the large purple and black bruise that covered the right half of her face. "I can see how good it looks for me—I nearly killed the one person in this house I really trusted."

"You weren't yourself," Susan cried.

"I'm sorry." Antoinette wiped away the tears and grabbed her things. "Tell the driver I'll be right down."

"Where will you go?" Lilijana asked.

"It's better you don't know."

Antoinette descended the stairs, walked out the door, and didn't look back. She had no intentions of ever returning to Christian's house.

Lucian met Antoinette at the door when the car pulled up in front of the large estate house. He looked better than she'd expected, almost younger, even with his right arm still in a sling. The country air obviously agreed with him. However he winced as she returned his warm hug.

"Sorry," she said. "I didn't mean to squeeze too tight."

"It's . . . still a little tender," he said, standing back and looking her up and down as he held her arm out. "Something's different."

Antoinette nodded slowly. "Can we go inside to talk?"

"Sure, Hector will get your bags," Lucian said, waving his hand to the large manservant who waited by the door. He took her into his study and sat her down on a settee.

"I don't know where to start," she said. "A lot has changed since I last saw you. I have changed . . ."

"You've been embraced, haven't you?"

She brought her eyes to his, expecting to see horror and disgust, but instead she found compassion and warmth.

"So this is why you needed to get away. Did Christian do it?"

She nodded. She still couldn't bring herself to talk about it. "But it's not the only reason I came. You're in danger."

He waved off her comment and smiled. "I don't think so; I have plenty of security here. I put on extra when Oberon DuPrie told me Dante Rubins was alive and might be on his way here."

She should have known, but if Dante was headed this way, she would be here to finally kill the bastard.

Lucian turned to the butler who stood expectantly in the doorway holding her things. "See Miss Petrescu's bags get to her room."

"Thank you," she said to the silent butler.

Lucian waved her comments away. "Hector can't talk and he's not too bright either, but he's dependable." Lucian sat on the settee next to her, taking her hand and rubbing her knuckles with the pad of his thumb. "Now, tell me what happened."

She did. Finally everything came pouring out in a mad rush of words she couldn't control. She told him what Dante had done to her and how Christian had embraced her. And when she'd finished, Lucian leaned back, stunned.

He shook his head. "How ironic—if your father wasn't gone then he'd be a free man now."

The fact her father was still alive, at least until a few weeks ago, was the one thing she'd left out. She hadn't meant to, she just had.

His face came closer to hers. "There's something you haven't told me." He put his finger under her chin and turned her face to look at him. "Antoinette, you can trust me."

"My father didn't die," she said. "His death was just a setup. He's been working undercover with Viktor Dushic in Europe for the last few years, but now he's really disappeared."

"Do they have any idea what happened to him?"

She shook her head and looked down at her lap. "Apart from Dante there are no other leads. So I have to find Dante and find out what happened to my father."

"I'm so glad you came to me." He pulled her gently against his uninjured side in a comforting hug, patting her shoulder. "Have you told your family yet what has happened?"

"No." She pulled away quickly, panic sending butterflies stomping through her stomach. "I haven't had time, but I don't think I'm ready yet either. You're the only one. Besides, you can watch for any signs of me succumbing to . . ."

"Necrodrenia," he finished for her.

Oh God . . . please don't let that happen. "Yes."

He patted her hand. "I don't think that'll be necessary. You're a strong young woman."

She sighed. "You're not the first to tell me that, but I fear losing control—I fear it more than anything else."

"And that is why I think you'll overcome it."

"Maybe—but knowing that you're watching over me makes me feel better."

"Wouldn't an Aeternus be more equipped to help you through this? Christian maybe?"

Antoinette shook her head. "There are . . . other issues."

"I see."

She looked him in the eye. "Besides—you're the world-renowned expert on parahuman races, so who better to do it?"

"It would be a unique opportunity. Very well, I'll help in any way I can." He stood. "Speaking of which, can I offer you anything? Are you hungry?"

Her stomach churned at the thought and she shook her head.

"I had some blood stocked up in case I needed a transfusion or an operation while I was here. So I have a little on hand, but I'll get some more ordered in." He held out his hand and walked her to the door. "Come, let's get you settled in."

Lucian's estate was exquisite, full of earthy colors and old-world charm, like a Tuscan villa. The walls showcased landscapes of the Italian countryside, marble statuettes stood on wrought iron, and wood furniture and terracotta pots filled with leafy plants decorated corners. Her heels tapped across the tiled floor.

As they walked past a hall Lucian pointed to the plastic sheeting hanging across the doorway. "I'm in the process of having some redecorating done in there. It's quite a mess, so it might be better to avoid that area."

The presence of scaffolding and drop sheets just beyond the plastic brought home how inconvenient it must be to have her turn up on Lucian's doorstep like this. "I'll try and stay out of the way."

"Hey, it's all right," he said, his brow furrowing. "That area is just so filthy, and as usual the work seems to be going much slower than the decorator led me to believe."

"Look, I'm sorry to just turn up like this. I didn't think . . ."

"Antoinette"—Lucian placed his hand on her shoulder and turned her face to look at him—"To be honest, I could really do with the company. If you're up to spending time with this poor old invalid, that is." Lucian shrugged his uninjured shoulder and smiled.

Antoinette couldn't help but smile back. "You're hardly old, Lucian."

"Thank you, my dear," he said. "But ever since the shooting, I've been feeling that way."

They continued down the hall until he stopped outside a door. "This'll be your room for as long as you stay." He took her hand in his good one. "If you need anything, Hector will help you."

The large butler materialized out of the shadows. He was very quiet for a big man and he eyed Antoinette in a way that didn't exactly make her feel welcome. Lucian waved him away and the manservant disappeared down the hall the way they'd just come.

"Now," Lucian said. "I must say good night. It's getting late and I need a lot more rest than I used to." He gently touched his wounded shoulder.

"Of course," she said. "And thanks for everything—I didn't know where else to turn."

"Hush." He leaned forward and kissed her forehead. "You don't have to explain to me. We'll talk some more tomorrow, in the evening. You're healing too and need your rest."

"Yes, I'll see you tomorrow. Good night."

He left her alone. The room was as lovely as the rest of the house. A large four-poster feather bed dominated the center, full of pillows and cushions. More Tuscan-style paintings of grapes, wineries, and peasants working in the fields adorned the walls. The adjoining bathroom had an old clawfoot bathtub and a rustic charm she'd only seen in magazines.

To her surprise she did feel sleepy. Being embraced, she assumed she wouldn't feel tired again until the sun came up. She tossed the redundant pillows off the bed and undressed before crawling beneath the covers, and her eyes closed as soon as her head hit the pillow.

29

Revelations

She awoke feeling unwell. Her stomach cramped with periodlike pain and her head screamed. The absence of any prickling in her blood meant the sun had set. She must've slept through the remainder of the night and an entire day.

After dressing, she found Lucian in the dining room eating his evening meal.

"Good evening, sleepyhead," he said, rising to greet her. "I'd just about given up hope that you'd be joining me."

"I'm sorry—I didn't mean to sleep so long."

He waved aside her comment. "It's part of the process. From what I understand, a lot of sleep is required for the first two to three days after the change to allow the body time to adjust. How're you feeling?"

She shrugged her shoulders and looked at his plate. "Hungry, thirsty—I'm just not sure which."

"That's to be expected—they've both become the same driving force for you now. I'll have some blood brought out."

She shuddered and he laughed. "You're going to have to get used to it, you know."

"I know." She screwed up her nose. "It's just I don't remember anything except waking up like this. It doesn't seem quite real yet, and if I take that first drink, I'll really have to deal with it. I'm not sure I'm ready yet."

"They say the pain is so intense it would make you insane if you remembered." Lucian picked up his wine and signaled the nearby servant. "At least join me in a glass."

"Okay."

The rich aroma of the deep red merlot tantalized her senses as the servant poured. Antoinette took a sip. It exploded into her mouth, a riot of flavor. It was the best wine she'd ever tasted.

Lucian watched her. "Everything is sharper when you become an Aeternus." He raised his glass to his lips and drained the contents. "How do you find the wine?"

"Magnificent." She drained her own glass and waited for it to hit her the way it usually did. "Wine usually goes straight to my head."

"Your new physiology gives you a greater tolerance to alcohol. Drink enough and you will get drunk, but your body will also break it down faster so you'll remain intoxicated for less time." He rose from his chair and held out his arm. "Would you like to join me for a short walk in the garden?"

"That'd be nice." She pushed back her own seat and took his offered arm.

He led her through the house and out into the perfumed garden. The air was fresh, free of pollution or smog and full of aromatic plants.

The stars glowed bright against the inky moonless sky, yet everything was as clear to her as if it were day. For the first time she just relaxed into her new self. A cricket chirped loudly under a bush, she followed the sound and saw it rubbing its hind legs together. A cat stalked through the garden, hunting a brown mouse that scampered through the fallen orange, gold, and red leaves of an old oak tree.

The detail was awe-inspiring. From the patterns in the foliage to the detail in the brickwork, all with a stark vividness she'd never seen before. The fall leaves whispered on the ground as the gentle wind blew them aside, the oak tree groaned and creaked in a language of its own, and the night was full of beauty and life.

"Do you like it?" Lucian asked, smiling.

"Yes," she whispered, noticing more and more the closer she looked and listened. "Do you mind if I sit out here for a while? I just want to kinda . . ." She shrugged. "You know."

"You take all the time you need." Lucian smiled. "The doctor would have my skin if he knew I was walking in this cool night air."

"Lucian," she called as he walked away. He turned, raising an eyebrow. "Thank you."

His raised a quizzical eyebrow. "For what?"

"For everything," she said, walking up to him. "For letting me stay, for giving me space, and for not asking about Christian."

"When you're ready you'll tell me," he said. "And if you don't," he shrugged his shoulders, "then it's none of my business."

She was grateful for his kindness, one day she'd repay him, she just had to work out how.

Antoinette sat for hours lost in her new world of wonder. She listened and watched everything from the large owl sitting in the old oak to the tiniest bugs crawling through the grass and leaf litter. The night talked to her in a way it never had before. She felt lightheaded, like she was high on drugs.

The night passed quickly while she sat there and before she knew it the sky to the east took on a lighter shade. The creaking and groaning of the oak tree and the house, once musical, was now grating, setting her teeth on edge. The rustling of the leaves also grew too loud. Everything seemed too noisy and soon a throbbing headache split her skull. When the eastern sky took on a pinkish tinge, she went inside and climbed into bed. Life would never be the same again.

Antoinette pulled the pillow over her head and she cried herself to sleep for what she'd lost.

* * *

Hunger gnawed at her gut the following evening. She'd woken before sundown and, afraid to leave her room, she just paced. Finally she <u>could</u> bear it no longer and went to open the door. The handle crumpled in her hand and she ripped the door off its hinges. She hadn't even pulled hard. The lights seemed to glow far too brightly and as she passed the grandfather clock in the hall the ticking was almost deafening.

"Sorry, being late is becoming a bit of a habit," she said as she came into the dining room.

Lucian wiped his mouth with his napkin and rose to greet her. "You're a creature of the night now, it's to be expected. You'll build your strength soon enough and then you'll be able to rise during the daylight hours."

Again she sat opposite him but this time the clanking of cutlery—the scraping of knife and fork on china—the clicking of glass—was almost too much for her to bear and she fidgeted in her seat.

Finally finished, he pushed back his chair. "Come, I want to show you something special."

He led her through the garden to a large greenhouse. Inside the air was thick with damp soil, rain, and rotting plant matter along with scented flowers and greenery. Lucian lovingly touched the different flowers as they passed—orchids, violets, and roses were the most recognizable of the many different species he was growing.

"This way."

Lucian led her through another room, warm and damp, filled with large leafy rainforest plants. Then they reached a room in the center of the enormous glass building. He placed his hand on a palm reader and the door clicked open.

In the room a rose grew like no other she'd ever seen. She held her breath and stepped closer to the nearest blossom. It was blue—real blue—not the mauve or purple that was often passed off as a blue rose. The outer petals were a deep, rich midnight color graduating to a stunning cobalt center.

"Isn't it magnificent?" Lucian asked.

"Yes," she whispered, reaching toward the flower with reverence. "It's the most beautiful thing I've ever seen."

"I call it the 'Elisabeta'." He gently caressed the petals. "After my late mother."

"Late?"

"Yes—she died when I was a boy."

"I'm sorry." Antoinette touched his arm lightly, understanding the sadness in his eyes.

"My mother's favorite flower was a rose and her favorite color blue, so for years I've toiled to create the perfect blue rose in her honor."

She walked around the bush looking at the unopened buds among the blooms. Her new eyes, her Aeternus eyes, could see the perfection better than any human could. She leaned in and sniffed the unusual, slightly spicy, rose perfume.

"Here." Lucian snapped off a newly opened rosebud.

She reached for it, almost afraid to touch such beauty.

"Ow . . ." he exclaimed as she took the flower. "I could have bred them out, but what is beauty without its thorns?"

A tiny spot of blood appeared on his finger. A spot so small and inconsequential, but all of Antoinette's senses honed in on it. The rich coppery tang overpowered all other scents, everything faded into the background as the tiny crimson bead expanded. Her mouth became dry and her throat constricted. She was so obsessed by the small drop she didn't notice her fangs until she bit her lip.

Blood slid across her tongue, and she crouched low, a growl rattling in her chest. Oh God, the scent. Just to taste it.

Lucian stuck his finger in his mouth and Antoinette closed her eyes to an image of her taking his hand and sinking her teeth into his wrist. His throat pulsed with life under her gaze and a hiss escaped as she licked her lips, wondering what he would taste like and ready to find out.

Uncertainty crept into his eyes. "Antoinette?"

She crouched lower. Something crooned in her mind demanding to taste the nectar flowing through his veins. She could hear his blood pumping—smell his delicious fear. Her whole body throbbed with the need to tear into his throat—to get at the crimson goodness beneath his hot skin.

"Antoinette, stop," he commanded, and a sharp stinging slap rocked back her head. The pain was nothing, no more than a tap, but enough to clear the red fog from her mind.

"I'm sorry," she cried, hanging her head. "Oh God, I could've killed you, Lucian."

"You need to control your lust—you must feed." He opened the door.

After a few more seconds, Antoinette straightened and followed him back through the conservatory and into the house where Lucian rang for a servant.

"Bring the special meal I asked to be prepared for Miss Petrescu," he said to his maid when she arrived.

She returned a few moments later carrying a tray with a crystal glass and matching decanter filled with a rich red liquid. The thought of drinking the blood made Antoinette's stomach churn and heave, like it was filled with a thousand worms—until the maid lifted the stopper off the decanter.

A rich delicious scent filled the air, better than the wine, better than anything Antoinette had smelt before. She sighed and closed her eyes, inhaling the mouth-watering aroma.

The gums above her front teeth tingled—she touched it with her tongue. This time she kept a tight control of her senses so she felt the fangs nudge her gums and slide down to nestle in front of where the central incisors touched the lateral incisors. She'd expected it to hurt, but it didn't, in fact, it was quite pleasurable and her body quivered.

The most powerful arousal she'd ever felt hit her—an arousal of mind, body, and soul. Her skin prickled, her nipples hardened, and her groin grew heavy, throbbing with intense erotic heat.

She picked up the decanter and poured crimson liquid into the glass. It splashed against the crystal in such beautiful ripples that she didn't want it to stop. But the aroma made her head swim; her mouth watered and her throat constricted with the desire to taste it.

Antoinette picked up the glass and trembling with anticipation, she brought it closer to her mouth. The cold touch of crystal on her lips preceded the first drop of heaven that exploded into her mouth, making her cry in ecstasy and want to weep with joy at the same time. It flowed down her throat in a golden glow, lighting up every nerve in a trail of absolute rapture. When she drained the glass of every last drop, she sighed. "Oh my . . ."

"I've never seen anything like that in my entire life," Lucian spoke, his tone hushed. "I've seen Aeternus drink before, but never like that."

She poured some more, and took another sip. While it was still exquisite, it didn't match the intensity of her first taste, but she still drank with as much ardor. Satiated, she replaced the stopper on the rest of the blood in the bottle.

"Well done, my dear." Lucian sat back pleased. "You've passed your first test."

"I did?"

"Yes, you stopped and didn't take any more than you needed."

She smiled, the afterglow of feeding still jangling her nerves. She felt better—more than better actually—she felt renewed, alive and full of energy. The clock in the hall chimed nine and she realized that it didn't sound as piercing or grating as before—she could even tone the sound down a little so it didn't seem so loud.

"Well, I must leave you, my dear. I have my medication to take and then rest." He took her hand. "Will you be okay?"

"Yes." She blushed, feeling utterly stupid. "I'm much better. I can't believe that I waited so long."

"It's your humanity, but now you're an Aeternus, you must learn to think like one. An Aeternus needs blood to live—it's a fact of life for you now. Starve yourself and you only run the danger of hurting yourself . . . or someone else."

She dropped her head, unable to meet his eyes. "I'm sorry for what happened in the conservatory."

"Don't be." He cupped her cheek.

Lucian had been so understanding, so good to her. Would her family be as accepting of what she'd become or would they treat her differently now? Antoinette had never really thought about the consequences her change would have on her family—she'd had a hard enough time coming to terms with it herself. She'd better ring Sergei and tell him. Soon.

Antoinette wandered back into her room, looking for something to occupy her time. She took a long bath and brushed out her hair, but even after that it was only ten o'clock, still early for a creature of the night.

Nothing in her room appealed to her. Maybe she'd find something downstairs to do. Lucian's study had a large-screen TV and she could watch an old late-night movie.

Antoinette settled on the lounge in the study and started flicking through the channels. After ten minutes she grew bored. All that was on were shopping channels, infomercials, bad sitcoms, and worse-than-B-grade movies. When she landed on an old Christopher Lee Dracula movie she gave up in disgust.

In the past, popular culture's vampire stories were mostly propaganda films designed to scare humans and keep the divide between the races. Today's books and films tried to demystify it by painting them as heroes fighting a world of evil. This was almost as bad as the former. All the wackos wanted to become like them and many died trying.

But the book that started it all—Bram Stoker's *Dracula*—was actually based on the most infamous Necrodreniac, who'd wreaked havoc across the European continent.

Antoinette rose off the lounge and turned to the floor-to-ceiling bookshelves behind her. They were mainly filled with history or reference books with a minor selection of fiction such as Edgar Allen Poe, Shakespeare, and Robert Louis Stevenson. All classics and nothing contemporary.

Antoinette ran her finger along the spines of the books, occasionally pulling one out and flicking through it.

Then she came upon a book that stopped her dead in her tracks. It was leather bound, old, and very familiar, much like one she'd seen recently in her uncle's trailer. It even had the same crest on the spine. She pulled it down off the shelf. The crest emblazoned the cover as well, just like the one her uncle had, but instead of having the initials NP it had EP.

When she opened the first page, she found out why; it belonged to Emil Petrescu—the traitor. She couldn't read most of it because it was written in the language of her Romanian ancestors—though she could speak it well enough to understand her uncle, she just couldn't read it.

An alarm close by burst into life and she dropped the book. *Dante.*

She spun and stopped dead, her blood freezing.

He stood in the doorway watching her. "I was hoping to spend some more time with you, but this is better than I could've wished for."

"Lucian's security will be here in a minute," Antoinette said, her initial surprise dissipating. She'd known he would come, had been waiting for it.

His cruel laughter shattered her confidence a sliver. Yet she was different now. Stronger than before. He'd almost killed her once, but she wouldn't let him hurt anyone in this house. She may only be a fledgling Aeternus to his decades or centuries, but she had something most other newly embraced didn't. Her Venator training.

As he calmly walked forward, she crouched low, preparing to strike. She couldn't just rush him—it'd give away her advantage. No, she must wait for him to make to first move.

Her new-found confidence must've surprised him a little. He stopped and tilted his head to the side, examining her more closely. His overconfident smile, meant to unnerve, slipped a little.

Footsteps rang out in the hall, coming toward the library,

and Dante turned toward the sound as Lucian entered the room.

"Lu—" was all Dante managed to get out before Lucian shot him.

The insane Aeternus dropped like a stone and lay unmoving a few feet away. Lucian shot him again.

Antoinette unfolded tense muscles and rushed to hug Lucian. "Thank God, you're okay."

She moved to squat beside Dante and felt his pulse, which beat slow and steady under her fingertips.

Good. She really wanted the bastard to pay for what he'd done.

"He's still alive," she said without looking up.

"I know," Lucian replied in a flat tone.

Something slammed into her shoulder, throwing her backward. A chill swept down her arm and spread through the rest of her body. She slumped to the floor and her vision faded.

30

Rats in a Hole

Antoinette opened her eyes. She was still lying on the library floor and tried to get up. Nothing moved. She willed her legs to shift. Zilch—not even a twitch of her toes. She tried to place her hands against the wall to lever herself up. Again nothing. Her arms lay still, disobeying her mind, just like the rest of her body. Panic rose in her throat, threatening to choke her.

What's happening to me? Maybe it was some kind of side effect from her transition.

The butler lumbered toward her.

Thank God. Lucian would know what to do.

She tried to open her mouth to speak but no sound came out.

Hector roughly picked her up with one hand then slung her over his shoulder like a sack of grain. Her arms hung down swaying from side to side in rhythm with his stride as he carried her from the room. She couldn't see much apart from the threads in the fabric of Hector's jacket as her face pressed against his back. She could still feel everything, she just couldn't move. Total lack of control over her body.

Plastic crackled then its coolness glided across her skin—

the sheeting that separated Lucian's renovations from the rest of the house. So he wasn't taking her to her room.

Each sound deepened her sense of apprehension—a metal clunk behind her, elevator doors opening. Hector moved forward and turned around; the overpowering odor of Hector's sweat made her head spin.

An electronic key pad beeped as someone pressed buttons. The floor lurched, so did her gut. They were descending. But to where? Terror sliced through her chest at her complete and utter helplessness.

The doors opened and the smell of disinfectant and antiseptic wafted into her nostrils, momentarily covering the scent of decay and death. They walked along what she perceived to be a corridor, sounds of despair and pain coming from either side, then the heavy stench of unwashed bodies and waste. She heaved involuntarily. Her internal muscles still seemed to be unaffected by the drug. Her heart still beat its new slow steady rhythm and her gag reflex was obviously unaffected, yet her limbs remained immobile.

Something snatched at her hair.

"Please . . ." it croaked in a pitiful tone before it yanked the lock out by the roots.

They passed through another electronic door then it was thankfully silent, the air in this section much sweeter. Finally they entered a room less bright than the fluorescent corridors.

"I've brought you some company," Lucian sneered from somewhere ahead of her.

"You bastard." Christian's familiar voice was filled with hard fury. Her heart froze. Christian? Christian was here?

Hector laid her on a cold, hard surface a few feet off the ground and stepped back. Lucian stood over her, his eyes flat and cold.

Oh my God, he's done this to me. This must be some kind of nightmare.

"I'm sorry your new accommodations aren't as comfortable as your last, but you'll have friends to keep you company." He turned her head so she could see the other side of the room.

The only man she'd trusted outside her family had betrayed her in the vilest way.

Stainless steel benches and surgical lights lay between her and a number of small cells separated by shiny bars. Oberon paced back and forth in one and in another stood Christian with his lips curled back into a snarl.

"Leave her alone, you perverted prick," Christian hissed through gritted teeth. "Or so help me I'll—"

Lucian yanked her hair to expose her throat. A cold blade pressed against her skin and burned. Silver. A silent scream ripped through her mind and tears sprung to her eyes.

Christian's eyes filled with helpless rage and she caught the growling ursian as he slammed the cell bars in her peripheral vision. A sparking shock sent him flying back to hit the wall behind him. He crawled up on unsteady legs, snarling in frustration.

Oberon's eyes narrowed. "I'm going to kill you, Moretti."

Lucian laughed. "That's going to be a bit difficult, bearman, since you're the one behind bars." He placed his hands on either side of Antoinette's head, and pulled her up until his forehead pressed against hers, eye to eye, lips almost touching. "Don't worry, the effects will wear off in hour or so."

Then he released her head so hard it dropped and hit the surface with a teeth-rattling crunch and locked the cage behind him.

"Rest up," he said. "You're going to need all your strength in days to come."

He left Antoinette lying helpless and immobile. Trapped in her own body, trapped by trust and misplaced loyalty. Thousands of questions raced through her head, questions she didn't have answers for. The whole time she kept willing her body to move, to get some sort of reaction. She was finally rewarded with a finger twitching. It was a start. She kept concentrating and soon could move her entire hand and lift her arms.

"It wears off pretty fast now, but you'll have one hell of a headache," Christian said.

She turned her head to look at him. He squatted on his heels in the middle of his cell, his elbows resting on his knees and his fingers linking his hands.

The headache hit, blinding her with its intensity. It took a few minutes until it dulled enough to open her eyes again— the lights still felt too bright and harsh. The headache reduced to a throb and she sat up. She didn't trust her trembling legs would hold her up, but she tried anyway. To her surprise they did.

"Stay back from the bars, they're rigged with some kind of energy," Christian said.

The hairs on her arms stood on end and crackled as she neared them. But the sight of him was more welcome than she ever thought possible.

"Are you okay?" he asked his eyes searching her face.

She nodded, and returned his inspection with her own. He looked so good and so . . . Christian. "I'm a bit shaken and have no idea what's going on. What happened to Dante?"

Oberon's glance flicked to the cell beside hers.

Dante's body lay crumpled on the floor, unmoving.

Christian frowned. "I was starting to wonder if they were working together."

"Why would Lucian be working with Dante?" Antoinette asked.

Christian cocked his eyebrow. "Why would Lucian shoot us?"

"I don't know." She flopped back down onto the platform.

"That makes three of us," Oberon said as he strode back and forth.

"Speaking of that—what are you guys doing here?"

Oberon stopped pacing. He crossed his arms across his chest and looked at Christian.

"Oberon had a tip Dante was headed this way," Christian said. "We'd seen the photos on the wall in the sewer and had assumed Lucian was a target too."

"So we came here to check Lucian's security and if we happened to apprehend Dante while we were at it . . ." Oberon stepped closer to the bars and shrugged.

Nausea washed over her and everything in the room grew blurry for a moment. She hung her head between her knees.

"Antoinette!" Christian's voice cracked a little.

She looked up and waved off the worry and concern written all over his face. "Why couldn't you just set up a trap for Dante, bring in more men?"

Oberon folded his massive arms across his chest.

"Because we'd been warned off the case by the head of the Violent Crimes Unit," Christian said.

"That fucker, Roberts." Oberon spat as he paced, flexing his hands open and shut. He reminded Antoinette of a bear she'd seen once at a circus. He'd paced in a small cage the same way Oberon did, grunting sad little noises.

"Anyway, Lucian agreed to see us," Christian said. "And while we were talking, one of his men walked in and I recognized the scar; he was the assailant who shot Andrew Williams."

Oberon scowled. "I had no idea what was going on. These two guys took one look at each other and Laroque went for his gun."

"And that's when Lucian shot us with the same paralyzing darts he used on you." Christian finished.

"Very effective weapon—I wouldn't mind one of those myself," Oberon mused.

Antoinette's jaw dropped. "Oberon—he shot you with it."

"I know, but it's still a very effective weapon. Imagine how we could use it to bring down a perp without endangering the public. Unless of course if we shot one of them and it wasn't safe for humans." He shrugged.

She rolled her eyes and turned back to Christian. "How long have you been here?"

"We came here straight after I knew you had made it," he said.

The reason for their parting no longer seemed as important as it once did in light of current events. Still she looked away to swallow the lump forming in her throat.

Oberon and Christian must've arrived only a short time before her. So close and she never even suspected. "Any idea what Lucian's up to?"

Oberon began pacing again, like the trapped animal.

"Nothing good I suspect, but we haven't seen him until just then. That big guy brings us food, which is strange if Lucian plans to kill us," Christian said.

An icy chuckle started in the next cell. Dante crawled to his feet. "He doesn't want to kill you. But you'll wish he had by the time he's finished with you."

"Rubins, you sick sack of shit." Oberon's shoulders hunched and he balled his massive fists. "What would you know?"

"I know lots of things about Lucian—what's he calling himself these days." He clicked his fingers as if thinking. "Ah, Moretti, that's it."

"What do you mean these days?" Christian asked.

But Dante just taunted him with a lopsided smile, tapping the side of his nose.

"Well now, little one." Dante's gray, dead eyes bored into her. "I see Christian finished what I started. Ironic isn't it? You've now become the thing you despise, though I'd planned to take you all the way through to a dreniac. Now, that would've been irony, wouldn't it, the hunter becoming the prey. But it's still not too late, once the hunger grows and eats at you like an animal gnawing at your innards—"

"Enough!" Christian roared.

Antoinette's skin crawled. She rubbed and scratched her arms, which only seemed to make it worse. Dante was right; she could still turn Necrodreniac yet. She was tainted, vile. Antoinette fell to the floor on hands and knees, retching up nothing but air. Her stomach no longer produced digestive acid or bile. Only the enzymes used to break down human blood remained in her system now.

Dante's chuckle washed over her like cold dishwater.

"See how easy you make it," Lucian said from the doorway. "He has the power because you give it to him."

"You bastard," Christian spat.

Lucian crossed to the steel surgical bench in the middle of the room. "What's the matter? Didn't you enjoy your little reunion?" Lucian looked at her, the warmth she'd previously seen in his eyes completely gone.

The butler entered carrying a set of handcuffs. Dante just stared back at Lucian, uncertainty flickering across his face.

Dante moved closer to the bars. "What the fuck are you doing, Moretti?"

"Your little extracurricular activities have started to attract too much attention. You're too much of a liability."

Dante grabbed the bars with both hands The electric surge threw him backward with the sizzling crackle of a giant bug zapper.

The stench of ozone invaded her space as the fallen Aeternus struggled to his feet. Dante stood on shaky legs. "You said as long as I got the job done you didn't care what else I got up to."

"But you didn't get the job done." Lucian glanced at Antoinette. "You were supposed to kill her, but you led them here instead."

A pain pierced her heart like an icy blade. He'd actually wanted her dead. Her mouth opened and shut with no words forming on her tongue.

"You owe me, Moretti," Dante screamed. "I've been doing your dirty work for decades."

Lucian's eyes blazed with rage. "I owe you nothing."

Dante puffed out his chest. "I introduced you to the right people, helped remove obstacles in the way of your advancement."

"You should have died from those burns in that warehouse fire. Only my skill brought you through. You owe me your life. Everything was fine until you had to go bring attention to yourself with your perverted little habit."

"You were the one who gave me that habit when you had me kill her mother." Dante tossed his head in Antoinette's direction. "Even though I could never figure why—I mean it wasn't like she was a threat to you or anything. But she was a sweet morsel."

"What?" Still reeling from the fact Lucian wanted her dead, Antoinette's whole world spun on its axis in a dizzy second and she found herself sitting on the floor. "You had my mother killed?"

Lucian's shoulders tensed and his glance skated past her before stopping once again on Dante. With narrowed eyes and rigid expression, Lucian managed a tight, deadly smile. Antoinette could no longer see the man she thought she knew.

"I may not have a use for you outside this lab, but I'm sure you will be very valuable in my research." Lucian's voice was as dead as his expression as he turned off the current to the cell bars.

Dante's eyes widened and something spread over his face that Antoinette would never have believed possible—naked and unadulterated terror.

"You can't do that to me," Dante's voice quivered. "Please, Lucian—you can't."

Lucian didn't answer, just nodded to Hector and pulled out a real pistol. "Be a good boy and let Hector put on the chains. This one's set to kill, not stun."

The large man had to stoop to enter the cell, but as soon as he was in, he moved much faster than Antoinette thought possible. He clapped the cuffs on one wrist and spun him to capture the second.

Goose bumps crawled across Antoinette's flesh at the look of utter panic on Dante's face. He turned his back on her. Once she had feared him more than anything.

And now he was nothing. A tool. A means to an end for Lucian's gain. She'd been such a fool to let him rule her life. She was finally free of the hold he had over her. She had won, but the victory seemed hollow, leaving a bitter taste in her mouth.

Two other men walked into the room wheeling a gurney. Antoinette didn't recognize the first, but the second winked as he passed. It was the same weedy kid from the school and the alley. Lucian had set that up too. He'd played her so well.

She climbed to her feet and straightened her shoulders. Oberon stared at her, his expression full of concern and anger. But Christian's gaze was firmly locked on the first guy. Antoinette looked again. A large puckered scar ran down the side of his face. This must be the man who shot Williams.

They lifted Dante onto the gurney and pulled a gag across his mouth. They secured his feet with more handcuffs. The slight stench of burning flesh meant the cuffs were silver.

Then just as quickly as they came, they were gone.

31

who's the abomination

Christian knew Dante deserved everything he got and more, but his look of sheer terror was unnerving. What kind of research did Lucian do down here that it would terrify a monster like Dante? Obviously it wasn't good and probably illegal if he was prepared to imprison two Department agents.

Oberon began pacing again. Each time he turned, he gave a little growling grunt, his eyes darting around. The bear in Oberon didn't like being confined.

"We've gotta get out," Oberon growled and punched the wall at the back of the cage, bones snapping with the impact. He cursed and held his hand up in front of his face. "It's not healing as fast as it should. We must find a way out."

"No one ever escapes my brother."

They all turned to find Hector standing behind a strange little girl, around seven or eight years old. Her dress had been in fashion in the early nineteen hundreds and her long pale blond hair hung in ringlets down her back with a large pink ribbon at the crown of her head.

The girl walked with the confidence of someone much older. He sensed in her presence and power.

"Go watch for Lucian," she told the servant. He nodded and bowed slightly. Christian caught the gentleness in the servant's eyes when he looked at the little girl. It was the first time he'd seen any humanity in the large man.

She walked to a pedestal on top of which was set a stone tablet with symbols and runes carved into the surface. "With this talisman Lucian dampens powers of those confined here." She touched one of the symbols. Oberon held up his injured hand, ripples moved beneath the skin like dozens of dancing bugs and he finally flexed his hand open and shut as normal.

"So that's why Dante didn't use his telekinetic powers," Antoinette said.

The little girl touched the symbol again and crossed to the floor in front of Antoinette's cell. "You must be the Petrescu girl Lucian talked about."

Antoinette tilted her head to the side and stared at the little girl.

Abomination. "Who are you?" Christian asked.

She turned her large, sad, but very intelligent green eyes on him. "My name is Elisabeta, but my brother, Lucian, calls me Lisbet." Her annunciation sounded oddly formal, as if she'd been taught to speak by an English professor, each vowel perfectly formed.

"If Lucian's your brother . . ." Oberon said. "Why does he keep you down here with all the other caged animals?"

"Because she's one of us," Christian said.

"Sort of." Lisbet smiled her oddly ancient little-girl smile. "I am a special case, you see—another animal to be kept in a cage." She moved to Oberon's cage and looked up at him. "My mother was embraced while I was still in her womb. I'm what the Aeternus call an abomination."

Christian sat down heavily on the bench. "Then, according to your size and appearance, you must be over a hundred years old."

Lisbet smiled sadly. "Yes, one hundred and twenty in a few months."

"Then how can Lucian be your brother? He's human," Antoinette said.

"Yes, he's human and he is my brother, my natural, older brother."

Understanding hit Christian square in the chest—it was so fantastical, but it all fit. The way Lucian smelt slightly strange. He was the Old One Williams had been talking about, not Dante. The final pieces fell into place.

"Antoinette, meet your cousin—your very distant cousin— the daughter of Emil and Elisabeta Petrescu," Christian said.

Antoinette tilted her head to the side, her brow creasing with confusion.

"My brother said you were smart. He hates you almost as much as he hates her." Lisbet tossed her head in Antoinette's direction.

"Why would he hate me?" Antoinette asked.

"Because you are the descendant of the betrayer, Nico-lae. Lucian cannot understand how our uncle could hand over his own brother to the Crimson Executioner." Her eyes pierced Christian. "Yes, I know who you are too and believe it or not, my brother understands your need for vengeance, respects it even. But what he cannot understand is why you would work for Intel and keep the treaty in place. He has been working for decades to find away to destroy that treaty and all those who supported it."

"If Lucian is Emil's son, and human, how has he survived so long?" Oberon asked.

"My blood," Lisbet said. "My mother was attacked late in her pregnancy as retaliation on my father. Struggling through the change brought on my birth and killed her. This is the reason my father was filled with so much hatred toward the Aeternus."

"*Embracing* a pregnant woman is against the edict from the Council of Elders as there are too many risks to both the mother and child," Christian said. "However, if it's done early in the pregnancy, within the first trimester, and suc-cessfully turns the mother, then the baby may be born as a normal Aeternus baby. Any later, you get what you see before you."

Lisbet flinched at his last words.

Antoinette's frown deepened. "Then against all the odds, Lisbet has survived. But how has this helped Lucian?"

Lisbet walked around the room, running her hand over the surface of the table. "Lucian was six at the time, and when our father was executed the doctor who delivered me took us in, but not out of kindness . . ." Lisbet paused, a tiny frown gracing her smooth pale brow. "He made Lucian his apprentice, but he was no more than a slave really. And I became a specimen . . ." Her troubled frown deepened. "Let's just say, Lucian learned his craft well from the good doctor."

Antoinette gasped. "But you were just a baby."

Christian didn't sense any hatred from Lisbet. "You don't share your brother's thoughts of vengeance?"

She shook her head, her ringlets bouncing. "From my experience vengeance only begets vengeance—a perpetual cycle of destruction spiraling to uncontrollable fury, sweeping away everyone and everything in its devastating path."

Such profound words spilling from such an innocent mouth seemed obscene. Lisbet was a living paradox—neither child nor woman.

"Why don't you leave him?" Antoinette asked. "Leave here?"

Lisbet's childlike laugh tinkled with irony. "As the bearman so aptly put it, animals in cages—I'm as much a prisoner as you. From my blood the doctor develop a serum he hoped would extend his life. He experimented on Lucian, and when it seemed to work he tried it on himself. He died horribly. Lucian perfected it, but it only works for him because we share the same blood. The serum must be made fresh and cannot be stored or it degrades beyond use within a couple of days. He'd never let me leave." Lisbet turned the full force of her gaze on Christian. "Anyway, where would I go? I know what your kind would do to me."

"That was long ago—the Council of Elders has changed since the treaty was developed. They've become more influenced by human compassion."

"What are you talking about?" Antoinette asked.

Lisbet sighed. "Most of those born like me don't survive past their first birthday—because the Council of Elders has them slaughtered."

Christian met Antoinette's accusing glare squarely. He wasn't responsible for things that happened in the past, he felt no guilt.

"A century ago the world was a different place—it's all changed now," Oberon said, coming to Christian's defense.

Lisbet's eyes darted around the room, doubt beginning to creep into them.

"They're right," Antoinette said. "The Council of Elders answers to CHaPR, just like all the other aligned parahuman ruling bodies. That's the purpose of the treaty."

Lisbet's eyes widened with surprise. "Lucian said the treaty imprisoned mankind to be nothing but slaves to the parahuman races. But you're telling me the races are now more accountable?"

Hector burst through the door, gesturing wildly.

"I must go. My brother is coming and he cannot find me here. Please don't tell him you saw me." The girl raced from the room, her hair streaming behind her.

Hector followed, returning seconds later with a serving cart loaded with red liquid-filled bags, plastic dinner trays, and a little fresh fruit and vegetables. Food for parahumans.

Antoinette spotted Lisbet's pink ribbon on the floor not far from the door—it must've fallen from her hair when she ran from the room. Antoinette opened her mouth to warn Hector, but Lucian came into the room. She held her breath. He walked right over it, his attention captured by Hector fumbling with the serving cart.

"Haven't you finished yet?" Lucian sneered.

Hector followed his master with solemn, sunken eyes. Antoinette willed the servant to look down. Christian tilted his head to the side frowning at her, so she quickly glanced at the silk ribbon on the floor. His eyes widened and darted to Lucian.

"When you've finished here, I'll be working in my study. Bring me some coffee," Lucian ordered as he picked up some files from the counter at the back of the room.

He would see the hair ribbon on the way out for sure. She had to stall him. As she racked her brains for something to say, Christian came to her rescue.

"What are you going to do with us, Moretti?"

Lucian's creased brow smoothed and a smile lifted the thin line of his lips. Why hadn't she seen the cruel cast to his mouth before . . . surely it must have been there?

"All in good time." Lucian stepped closer to Christian's bars.

While Christian had Lucian's interest, she gestured carefully to Hector to look down at the ribbon near his foot. When he saw it, he looked back at her then at Lucian before knocking a bag of blood from the cart. As he picked it up, he secreted the hair ribbon into his pocket.

"How many parahumans have you killed and tortured down here?" Christian asked, keeping Lucian's attention on him.

"Not all are here against their will. Some of them are quite grateful for the care and shelter I've given them."

"Like Dante Rubins?" Christian shot back.

Lucian shrugged. "Dante was special. He had his drawbacks, his little quirks, but he also had his uses."

"Like having him assassinate Sir Roger, giving you an alibi and a clear line to the ambassadorship in CHaPR. And you are clearly above suspicion with the injury you sustained trying to defend him in front of an unbiased witness."

Lucian raised an eyebrow. "Well, Laroque, you are a sharp one."

"But it goes back way beyond that, doesn't it, Lucian?" Christian said.

Lucian appeared smugly dismissive. "You're the one telling the story."

"You've plotted and murdered your way to the top, but Marianna Petrescu was supposed to bring the great Petrescu family into disrepute when Grigore went renegade. However, you didn't bank on him tracking down your pet and almost killing him."

"Dante was seriously injured and it took him over a decade to recover from the burns. But in the end it helped further my cause. A truly unexpected and delightful side effect. I had some new rules implemented in the Guild despite the objection from doom-mongers like Sergei."

Antoinette's head snapped up. "The parahuman admission to the Guild."

"That was among one of them. As I said before what better way to study parahumans weaknesses than by letting them think they were working with us?" Lucian's smug expression taunted her. "And being able to get back at your family was just an extremely delicious bonus. Who knew your father would come up with the same disappearing trick that we'd pulled on him? I was most surprised when that fool Williams let slip that he'd seen Grigore."

"You knew about that?" Antoinette asked.

"Of course I did, who do you think had that fool Dushic shot? My man is quite the marksman. Wouldn't you agree, Christian? I mean, he dispatched Andrew Williams on a busy airport in your custody."

Christian turned to stone, pale and deathly still. Lucian had in that one simple statement taunted Christian with the knowledge he was responsible for Viktor's death and given him the identity of man who pulled the trigger.

Lucian was evil—pure, utterly complete evil. In all Antoinette's years hunting dreniacs she'd never come across such malevolence. And despite his age and reliance on his sister's blood, Lucian was still substantively human.

"What've you done to my father?" she demanded.

He waved away her question. "You needn't worry about that. You should be more concerned about yourself."

"I'm going to kill you, Moretti," Oberon growled.

"So you keep saying bear-man," Lucian laughed. "But you're still the one in a cage."

Hector knocked over the cart, whether on purpose or by accident, she couldn't say, the contents spilled all over the floor. Oberon roared with laughter and Lucian's face darkened.

"You clumsy idiot," he yelled at Hector. "Get this mess cleaned up and those animals fed." He scowled around the room and focused on Antoinette, smiling with malevolence. "But nothing for these three. Let's see how cheerful they are after a couple of days without sustenance."

Oberon sobered instantly. Lucian thundered out of the room in a sweeping fury as Hector bent to clean the mess.

But Antoinette had other things on her mind. "Hector, have you seen my father?"

The large butler gave one slow nod of his head.

"Is he still alive?"

Again, a single dip of his head was the only answer.

Joy warmed an extra beat in her heart. *Thank God.* She closed her eyes and let out a shaky breath. "Can you take me to him?"

He slowly moved his head left then right and back to her.

"But he is here?"

A nod.

"Can you bring him to me?" she pleaded, desperate now.

He repeated the negative movement of his head and bowed imperceptibly before leaving with the cart. Long after he was gone Antoinette watched the doorway, hoping he'd come back with her father. But he didn't.

32

embracing nature

Lucian didn't return the next day, or the day after that. Neither did Lisbet. On the third night in the cell, Antoinette lay looking at the white tiled ceiling. At least she thought it was the third night, she'd lost count of the hours.

Oberon had grown more and more agitated over the past few hours, pacing constantly in his cage. Christian seemed preoccupied with his own thoughts, sitting in a corner with eyes closed. Antoinette wondered if their hunger grew more persistent with each passing minute, as hers did. Thirst consumed every thought—the blood, how it tasted, the sensation of it sliding down her throat and the feeling of power it gave her. A tiny groan passed her lips.

"Don't think about it," Christian said.

She jumped. "What?"

He'd been silent for hours. "The hunger—I feel it growing in you." He opened his eyes and met her gaze. "Don't think about it—you'll only make it worse."

"I can't help it. I try not to and it only makes me think of it more." It'd replaced everything, even the worry over her father, much to her disgust. She could think of nothing else but the growling hunger-beast stalking her mind. And the memory of Christian so near to the Dark Sleep haunted her.

"You must learn to control it, or it'll control you. Most dreniacs turn shortly after being embraced because they can't control the bloodlust." Christian leaned forward. "Meditation can be the best way to achieve this. Sit in the middle of the floor facing me and close your eyes."

This was madness, how could he possibly help from way over there?

"Trust me," he said, his voice low.

She did as he said, feeling a little stupid.

"You have to reach inside yourself and feel the beast that is hunger."

A beast? Her eyes flew open. She'd felt it stalking her for some time now. *How did he know?*

"It lives in us all," Christian said as if reading her thoughts. "Now—give it form, give it life—make it real." His voice flowed over her, relaxing the tension from her shoulders.

A darkness crept into her mind, moving with stealth just beyond her conscious thought. Antoinette stiffened and sucked back her breath. Afraid.

"Can you feel it?" Christian's soft and gentle tone strengthened her. "The beast wants to consume you but you mustn't let it."

She nodded, keeping herself focused on the snarling beast hiding in the shadows of her mind.

"You must stroke it, croon to it or beat it into submission—do anything you can to control it." His voice whispered as if directly into her ear—she could almost feel his breath upon her neck.

She didn't want to confront it. It would be best kept hidden. She felt her hunger-beast crouch in the darkness as it prepared to pounce. She drew back, fear knotting her throat, making it difficult to swallow. She wanted to run, but the beast would cut her down from behind and consume her. She swallowed her fear and turned to meet the beast.

How to soothe a savage beast? *With music, of course.* Instinctively she began to hum a French lullaby her mother used to sing to her when she'd had a bad dream. The beast stilled and purred, but she still couldn't bring herself to look upon it.

"Is it working? Is your beast growing quiet?" Christian asked.

Again she nodded, not daring to speak, and continued to hum.

"When you're ready, you must approach the beast, acknowledge it—only then will you truly be able to control it."

"No . . ." Her eyes flew open. "I can never acknowledge it. I can never accept it." She clenched her fists so hard her nails bit into her palms.

Christian's eyes dulled. "If you can't embrace the beast it will eventually consume you."

Oberon had stopped pacing and stood with his own eyes closed. When they opened again, some of the wildness had left them and he seemed a little calmer. When he saw them looking at him, he shrugged sheepishly. "Just getting in touch with my inner beast—or inner bear in my case. Neat trick, Laroque."

"It's something my father taught me and it helps in times like this." Christian leaned back and closed his eyes. "There are times when you must unleash the beast, but you must always maintain control."

Her heart sank. Every day would be a battle against this new nature. Every day she must fight it, lest it consume her. *If only Christian hadn't—* She stopped. It was no good thinking of *if only*.

The door to the lab opened and Antoinette tensed, but it was Lisbet, her eyes darting around hesitantly. Finally, she crossed the floor and touched the stone on the pedestal.

"The others cannot hear us," she said to Antoinette when she got closer. "The talisman has powerful magic, that's why we are safe from those little black box things he calls CCT."

"You mean cameras."

The girl shrugged. "He has them in the house upstairs—

little black boxes he uses to keep watch over things. But the talisman prevents anything from seeing or hearing what goes on in the complex. No one can find this place by magic or technology."

"Why did you shut them out?" She pointed her chin toward Christian and Oberon.

The two men stood as close to the bars as they dared, their faces creased with worry.

"Because I wanted to talk to you alone, as family." Lisbet squared back her shoulders. "We share the same blood, yes? I need to know if everything they said is true. Would the world accept me as I am now?"

The image of Katerina and Sergei taking her in with her brother when they were little flashed into Antoinette's mind. Katerina had held her close, hugging her to her enormous motherly bosom, crooning comforting sounds. The Petrescu family would always protect one of their own. Katerina loved children, especially little girls—she had three of her own. Even though Lisbet was only a child in appearance, she was sure Katerina would adore her.

Antoinette got down on her knees at eye level with the girl. "I'll take you home to our family and they will accept you." But could she be sure of that? Yes—she could. Why had she wasted all this time when she should've gone to them first?

"My brother tells me he's trying to find a cure. But I'm not sure I believe him. He says those vaccines he creates are to help people."

"What vaccines?" Antoinette asked.

"He has another laboratory like this one in the other part of the complex where he develops serums and tests them on the prisoners. But I have heard them screaming and I have heard them die." Lisbet's leaned forward and whispered. "If I help you to escape, you will take me with you?"

"Yes," Antoinette said.

Lisbet let out a breath, looking relieved. "Then be ready when Hector and I come for you."

"Why not now?" Antoinette asked.

The little girl tilted her head. "Because Lucian is still here and if he catches us, he'll kill you. We have to wait for him to leave the house."

"We need to contact the authorities, can you do that?"

"Maybe Hector could."

The girl gave her one last confident smile and reset the talisman spell before running from the room.

"She's going to help us escape," Antoinette told the other two.

"Can we trust her?" Christian asked.

"Yes," Antoinette said. "I think we can."

The hours dragged on, with no sign of Lisbet or Hector. Antoinette paced her cell.

"I think she was playing with us," Oberon grumbled as he prowled his eight-by-eight cell.

Antoinette sighed and sat down on the makeshift bed, the taste of bitter disappointment burning the back of her throat. Maybe he was right. Her eyes grew heavy and she let herself drift off into sleep.

"Wake up, it's time," Lisbet's soft lilt blew across Antoinette's ear.

She'd slept for hours and felt stronger, though hunger still gnawed on her insides. Hector stood vigil by her opened cell door and Lisbet waited beside him, her eyes shining with excitement.

Antoinette ran to the talisman. "So, how does this thing work?" she asked, her hand hovering over the mystic symbols carved into the stone.

"I wouldn't do that if I were you." A cold voice silenced her hurried whispers.

She glanced over her shoulder, confirming it wasn't just her imagination. Dread stilled her heart. Lucian and two of his men all aimed pistols at her.

Hector pulled Lisbet behind him and seemed just as surprised as she was.

"Do you really think I'm that stupid?" Lucian said. "I've

known about Hector and my sister for some time now. I also saw the ribbon on the floor and it was all the proof I needed. But I wanted to see how far this would go, see if my sister could indeed betray me." Lucian held out his hand to Lisbet. "Come here."

She didn't move and Hector spread himself to cover her.

"Don't be afraid, Lisbet. I'm your brother, I wouldn't hurt you. But I won't hesitate in putting a bullet right between that big dummy's eyes."

The girl's uncertain glance flicked to Antoinette before she stepped around her protector. Hector shook his head and grabbed her arm.

"It'll be all right." Lisbet smiled up at him and tenderly stroked his large hand.

The brave little woman-child walked toward her brother. As she reached him, Lucian backhanded her across the face, sending her sideways into a nearby wall where she fell to the floor, a smear of crimson marking her descent to the floor. Then he turned the pistol on Hector and fired. The back of Hector's head exploded in a rain of bone, blood, and brains all over the stainless steel surgical table behind him. His body just seemed to crumple onto the floor. Lisbet screamed his name and scrabbled to his fallen form.

"You bastard," Christian hissed. "They'd done what you wanted."

"Not fast enough," Lucian murmured.

Antoinette moved forward and stopped as Lucian pointed his pistol at her. Could she get to him before he fired? Doubtful. The talisman still suppressed her speed and strength. The scent of blood stirred something in her—something hungry. The beast circled, growling and predatory. She closed her eyes to greet it. As it moved closer, she got cold feet and shied away but the beast circled once more.

Lisbet's tear-soaked face looked up at her and gave an imperceptible nod.

"Do it," Christian whispered from his cell.

"Come to me," she whispered. And the beast did. Racing

out of the corner of the darkness in her mind, and took her mental image midleap.

Lisbet moved behind, distracting the attention of the others and kicked over the pedestal. The stone talisman shattered into a dozen pieces skittering along the floor like the broken segments of Antoinette's life.

In that second everything came together.

Antoinette's eyes flung open, although they no longer felt like hers alone. She dropped into a crouch as the growl built low from deep within her soul. Everything sharpened, everything slowed. The two men with Lucian raised their guns higher. She could smell their fear and the beast within roared with triumph—and so did she.

Shots fired, but she kept her focus on Lucian, taking him at full run, knocking him on his back and pinning him beneath her.

His eyes widened and the scent of his terror flooded her enhanced senses . . . she inhaled it, tasted it, loved it. The beast demanded blood and she needed to slake her thirst.

Antoinette bent over her prey and sniffed. The blood pumping beneath his skin called to her with primeval song. Her fangs extended their full length and her hands ripped away at his clothing to expose the jugular below. She sank her head and bit, her fangs piercing his soft fragile skin.

The sharp crimson nectar spurted into her mouth, hot and hard. The taste she'd had from the bottled blood didn't begin to compare to the power of this rush. She drank it down as it rushed into her mouth and she threw back her head, howling for the sheer joy of it as his blood continued to spurt over the tiled floor.

She went back for more—sucking deep, taking his essence in an act much more intimate than sex could ever be. She wanted him—this man beneath her—she wanted him all inside her.

"Antoinette—STOP."

Hands pulled at her. Her frustrated scream echoing in

her ears as she kicked out at the one who dared disturb her feeding.

"Antoinette, control it—take control of the beast." Hands shook her and held her back. She roared with exasperation until something hot and sharp pierced her shoulder from behind, shocking her into letting go.

"Fight it," Christian growled into her ear, his breath hot on her skin . . . his words filled with the smell of her own blood penetrated her insanity.

Concentrating hard, she fought back the beast, pushing it, beating it, crooning to it until it shrank into the shadows of her psyche. When she opened her eyes, Christian held her and Lucian lay at her feet, his breath coming in short, sharp terrified pants.

"What have you done to me?" she sobbed, turning her face away to swipe the sticky wet mess coating her chin. Her hands came away covered in blood.

Christian turned her to him and pulled her head against his shoulder, wrapping her in his arms and holding her close. "It gets easier, I promise."

She relaxed against him for a moment then pushed him away. She couldn't do this. Not now. Everything intensified. The room seemed brighter, the noises louder, even her skin seemed to glow.

Oberon stood over one of the men who'd come with Lucian. Antoinette didn't recognize him, but she did know the other one who lay in a crumpled heap a few feet from Christian's cell, his throat torn open and blood pooled around him on the floor. The scar on his pale face marked him as Lucian's crack shot, and Viktor's killer. Christian glanced down at the body too, his face cold and unreadable.

"How did you get out?" she asked him.

"Lisbet," he said, his hooded eyes rose to meet her. No more needed to be said about the dead man.

The little girl moaned with Hector's head in her lap, his blood staining her pretty pink dress.

Antoinette bent down to check her head wound. It had closed over, only a smear of blood remained. *Thank God.*

Lucian sat on the floor, tearing off a piece of shirt and holding it against his throat. Oberon yanked him to his feet and ripped Lucian's hands away. Antoinette peeked around Oberon for a look at the damage. The bite marks had begun to heal, thanks to Lucian's use of Lisbet's blood.

Antoinette ran the back of her finger across the little girl's brow and Lisbet's eyes fluttered open, tears streaking silvery lines down her cheeks.

"He took care of me and was my only friend," she sobbed.

"Lucian Moretti," Oberon growled. "I am placing you under arrest for conspiracy to commit murder, the experimentation on parahumans, kidnapping, obstruction of an investigation, and as many other charges as I can come up with. You'll be charged and will have to appear before the Department's judicial high court. The Guild will be informed of your illegal activities as soon as possible."

Lucian started to laugh. Not the reaction Antoinette was expecting.

"What's so funny?" Oberon asked.

"Do you really think members of the Guild are unaware of my activities here? How do you think I get my specimens? This goes much higher than me." He put his hand into his jacket pocket and arrogantly raised his smug expression to Oberon.

It wasn't until Lucian reached out and snatched Lisbet did Antoinette realized how much he'd been inching closer.

He held a syringe to Lisbet's throat. "It's silver nitrate. I was going to use it on one of you as a demonstration, but this will do nicely."

He pressed the needle tip against Lisbet's throat, indenting the delicate skin but not piercing it.

"Lucian, she's your sister, your flesh and blood. Let her go and we'll make sure you get a fair hearing," Christian said as he slowly advanced around the table while Oberon inched closer from the other side.

Lucian laughed. "There are those who would see me dead in a heartbeat before they risked that kind of exposure—I know too much. And if you separate me from her, I'll be dead within weeks anyway. I need her blood. So if I'm going to die, I may as well take her with me. Now back off."

Lisbet's tiny hand brushed against an instrument tray, knocking it to the floor with a metallic clatter. Antoinette felt so helpless until she saw Lisbet's fist wrapped around something. The little girl plunged another syringe into his thigh.

Lucian's eyes went wide with surprise and Oberon rushed in, picking him up by the scruff of his shirt while Christian grabbed Lisbet out of harm's way.

The bear in Oberon shifted in his features, curling his lips back into a snarl, but then he let Lucian go. "You're not worth my career."

Lucian stumbled, the empty syringe sticking out of his thigh. His eyes narrowed on Oberon's broad back as he lifted the syringe in his hand.

"Behind you," Christian warned.

Oberon growled, a backhand sending Lucian flying into a cabinet, shaking the many bottles and glass containers on the shelves. Lucian crumpled to the floor, knocked unconscious by a large jar as the others smashed to the floor around him.

He lay unmoving as one last bottle teetered on the shelf above and fell with almost graceful slowness. When it hit the other chemicals, they ignited, sending flames and glass fragments flying through the air.

Lisbet stood watching the flames lick around her brother's body. Even after everything he'd done to her, he was still her brother and it was something she shouldn't see. Antoinette pulled her away. Lisbet's arms wrapped around her waist as she buried her face against Antoinette's stomach.

Flames licked the walls, climbing to the ceiling, running along the floor—spreading so quickly it covered his body in seconds. They all stood watching, shocked into inaction.

"Let's get out of here," Christian said. "Grab that one." He pointed to the remaining guard.

Oberon pulled him to his feet by his collar. Another small explosion rocked the far corner of the room and everyone flinched instinctively. A third explosion blasted across the room.

"We have to get out of here— *now!*" Oberon yelled.

33

Fire and Ice

Antoinette guided Lisbet toward the exit, but the little girl stopped at the door to look back at Hector's body. Oberon pushed them through and Christian was hot on his heels, dragging the guard with him.

Christian closed the heavy metal door behind them and they were plunged into immediate silence. The room was soundproofed. Lisbet keyed a code into the electronic lock so they could continue through the second door and into a junction of passageways leading off in three directions. Ahead were barred cells on both sides and at the end of the passage was an elevator. Even more corridors branched left and right.

"There must be dozens of rooms down here," Antoinette whispered.

Oberon looked around and nodded to the passage in front of them. "I count twelve cells that way, six a side. With three more corridors in either direction that makes seven blocks of twelve, so around eighty-four rooms. Will we have enough time to evacuate everyone?"

"Let's hope so, we must hurry," Lisbet said.

"How much time do we have?" Christian asked.

"It depends on how long the fire stays contained. Hector

managed to disable the alarms, but when the fire reaches this section the guardhouse will be alerted. If they can't confirm with Lucian a false alarm, they are under orders to shut down the complex and fill the air with a multitoxic gas, killing all that remain."

"Then we have to stop that from happening." Christian took one of the dart pistols he'd stripped from Lucian's men and held it out to Oberon. "Do you think you can take care of the guards above ground?"

"With pleasure," he said.

Lisbet grabbed on to Antoinette's hand, gripping her fingers tightly. Oberon frightened her. Antoinette squeezed and smiled what she hoped was a reassuring smile.

"What about this one?" Oberon asked, scowling at the guard sitting against the wall.

"If we had some rope we could tie him up," Antoinette said.

Christian shucked off his cotton shirt and threw it in her direction, leaving him wearing a tight T-shirt. "Here, use this."

"Fine, I'll leave him to you." Oberon loped off down the hall toward the elevator.

The cloth was full of his scent. She repressed the urge to bury her nose in it and tore the material into strips. She didn't have time to dwell on her confused emotions at this point. There were far more important things like . . .

"I need to find my father," Antoinette said as she squatted beside the guard, securing his hands.

Lisbet placed her hand on Antoinette's shoulder. "He's in a cell two rows over and last on the left."

"Go," Christian said. "Lisbet and I will start releasing the other prisoners."

Antoinette nodded and set off down the corridor. None of the doors in his row had electronic locks—only a thick metal rail lying across the frame, barring them. Antoinette set about opening the other occupied cells until she reached the one Lisbet said was supposed to be occupied by her father. Instead she found an old man hunched on the edge of his bunk. There must be some mistake. This seemed to be the right cell, but where was the dark-haired giant with the quick smile she remembered? Could this shrunken old man really be her father?

Antoinette looked again and lifted the metal bar. Confusion erupted among the other captives as Lisbet came around the corner, directing them to the elevator.

The old man inside the cell didn't move, just sat on the edge of the bed with his head in his hands. Antoinette dropped to her knees in front of him, took hold of his thin, frail wrists and gently pulled them away from his face.

His cloudy dark eyes focused, his brow creasing. "Marianna?" he croaked in a harsh whisper.

She let out a sob. "No, Papa. It's me." Tears pricked her eyes. He looked ancient, older even than Sergei. "Oh, Papa. What did he do to you?"

His eyes focused a little more. "Antoinette—my little girl?" He reached out a shaky hand but withdrew it. "No— this is just another cruel dream come to taunt me." Tears slipped from his eyes, tracing a silvery path through the crags of his sallow, half-starved face.

A sob broke from her lips as she brought his palm to her lips, her cheeks wet with her own tears. "It's not a dream. I'm here, Papa—I've come to take you home."

He reached out his thin arms and hugged her with all the desperation of a man in shock—his body shuddering with great wracking sobs that tore at her heart. To see her father reduced to this gaunt caricature of the tall, proud man he'd been when she was a child was almost more than she could bear.

For a few minutes they clung together, but time was short. She fought down the rage threatening to consume her, wanting to tear someone apart, make them pay for what they'd done to him. If Lucian wasn't already dead, she would've ripped him to shreds a thousand times over. But she needed to get her father out of danger and she'd worry about everything else later.

She broke his embrace and wiped the hot tears from her face. "We have to go, Papa."

A loud booming noise rocked the complex and set off the shrill wail of alarms, plunging the corridors into a red flashing glow.

Antoinette helped her father to stand, shocked by how the clothes hung like rags from his emaciated frame. Lucian must've been starving him and she bit back her own distress as he shuffled on legs almost too weak to hold him up. She swallowed down the pity and moved to help him. This ancient man was not the god of her childhood.

His thin legs buckled and she wrapped her arm around her father's skeletal waist before he collapsed onto the ground, then she bent to sweep him up. Shocked, he tried to fight, his expression proud and indignant. Now, there was the Papa she remembered.

"Please. We don't have time," she cried above the wailing sirens.

He held her gaze for a moment longer, then his face collapsed as he surrendered. He weighed so little that even without her Aeternus strength she could've easily lifted him. His embarrassment disappeared into narrowing eyes and he carefully regarded her face.

Antoinette turned the corner to find the elevator where Oberon stood with a rag-tag bunch of parahumans.

"You've secured the area?" she yelled above the noise of the sirens and chaos.

He nodded as he herded the prisoners into the lift.

"Where's Christian?"

"I think he's down there checking out another lab he stumbled across. It's near a freight elevator and there are more people getting out that way."

The sound of the fire grew closer, punctuated by another small explosion.

Christian.

Antoinette turned to Oberon. "I'm going to help him. Look after my father." She started off down the hall at a run.

"Antoinette," the old man cried out.

"I'll be with you soon, Papa, I promise," she called over her shoulder as she ran.

The smoky air stung her eyes and she almost missed the lab, but skidded to a halt just before the door. Christian was inside, loading small vials into a metal canister. It was identical to the other lab where Lucian had held them, with one major difference. Instead of the caged cells, the walls here were lined with floor-to-ceiling refrigeration units, containing thousands of multicolored vials.

The body of a white-coated lab assistant—if you could call what was left the body—lay in several pieces strung across the floor. Fangs nudged her gums at the scent of old spilled blood, but it had a stale corrupted tang to it so she was easily able to control the desire to feed.

Christian followed her eyes before turning back to his task. "I found him like that. Some of the prisoners have been here a long time." He finished and screwed the top in place and looked around. "This is Lucian's real work. He was creating biochemical weapons to target active parahuman DNA only, leaving humans untouched."

"Oh my God," Antoinette whispered.

"We have to get out." He nodded to a timer displaying 5:59 on the wall and silently counting down. "Seems our unfortunate friend here was able to trigger it before some of the inmates took the opportunity for a little payback."

A muffled roar grew louder. "We have to hurry, the fire will be here any minute now," she shouted.

Christian slung the canisters over his shoulder. "Then run," he yelled.

She pulled the lab door shut behind them, and followed Christian toward the freight elevator. The fire had beat them; it was blocking the corridor with a collapsed ceiling and a wall of flames.

"Shit," Christian said, "we'll have to use the other one."

He grabbed her hand and dragged her back the other way. The fire climbed the walls all around them, flames licking at the ceiling above, heat mounting and the smoke thickened. She'd have serious trouble breathing if she was still human.

Up ahead a burning beam crashed across the corridor. Antoinette held her arm in front of her face as sparks swirled in the burning air. Christian vaulted the wreckage, taking her with him. The skin on her face felt tight and dry.

They'd almost reached the elevator when the red flashing lights flickered. Electrical wiring hissed and crackled and the roar of the fire grew even louder as it bore down on them like a living animal. Christian hit the up button on the wall panel.

After what seemed an eternity the doors finally opened and she stepped inside first, just as the ceiling collapsed, showering Christian with debris. A large chunk of concrete hit him on the side of the head, knocking him out cold.

"Christian," she screamed, her heart contracting tightly in her chest.

She reached for his wrist and dragged his unconscious body into the lift and pressed the top button as soon as he was clear.

Nothing happened.

"Come on," she cried, repeatedly hitting the button.

Still nothing. The fire grew closer. As an Aeternus she could survive heat and smoke, but not fire itself.

Frantically Antoinette punched the button again—to her relief the doors closed and the lift began to ascend. She sank back against the wall staring at the "Do not use in case of fire" sign and laughed with almost hysterical relief.

Christian groaned. She dropped to her knees, propped his head on her thighs, and peeled back the hair on his temple where he'd been hit. Underneath the crusty blackened blood, the cut was healing over, but he was still unconscious.

"Christian!" Antoinette lightly stroked his face. "Can you hear me?"

He groaned in response, but didn't wake. She had no idea how long it took an Aeternus to wake up from a head wound. Suddenly it struck her how helpless he must have felt as she lay dying. She would do anything to have him be all right, just as Christian had done for her. Tears welled in her stinging eyes. Great time for an epiphany.

The lift kept rising. She couldn't remember how long it had taken on the initial ride down, but it seemed to be taking forever now.

The floor beneath her began to rattle and shake like it was caught in an earthquake. With a crashing boom, the elevator shuddered to a halt.

"No!" she cried hitting the buttons again.

The bomb in the lab must have detonated. The lights began flashing and crackling, while outside the high-pitched squeal of metal against metal strangled her nerves.

Christian still lay unconscious with his head in her lap as the elevator steadily grew hotter. They were trapped. Panic bubbled just below the surface of her conscious mind, but she wasn't about to give in to it yet—that wouldn't help her and Christian get out of here.

And then the elevator was plunged into darkness. What else could go wrong? After a few seconds her eyes adjusted and she was able to see clearly again. For the second time she was glad not to be human. Her new abilities were starting to grow on her. If only she could master her hunger. At least she would be harder to kill and therefore had a chance of making it out alive.

She couldn't just sit here waiting for a rescue that may never come, though. Looking around, she spotted the access hatch. Gently lowering Christian's head onto the floor, she jumped up and gripped it. It was locked. *Of course.*

She gripped the lip of the hatch housing and put all her power into driving her foot up above the covering. It burst upward and she used the momentum to swing herself out onto the top of the car.

Pulleys and wire cables were the only things holding them

up. The scent of burning grease and ozone filled the hot, dark shaft. Antoinette glanced up to a set of doors about twenty feet above. Only twenty feet—they could easily make that. If Christian were conscious, that was.

"Hey," she cried, cupping her hands around her mouth, "Anyone up there?" The elevator shook beneath her and the car dropped several feet, and she fell to her knees. The crunching of metal and whining of cables under stress screamed in the enclosed space. Smoke started to leak around the sides of the car.

Antoinette popped her head back in through the hatch. "Christian," she called, trying to wake him.

He stirred, but didn't rouse. They didn't have any more time to waste as the elevator shuddered under her and she lowered herself carefully back into the car. Her newfound strength made it easy to pick him up and push him through the opening onto the roof. It was awkward, but she managed. The elevator jolted again. She froze until it settled, then as quickly and carefully as she could, she climbed back up through the hatch.

Dragging Christian to the side was easy. Getting him up the narrow maintenance ladder would be another matter.

As her hand curled around the warm steel rung, the car fell several more feet. His unconscious weight dragged on her arm, jolting them both. Now what? She couldn't climb with one hand holding Christian's weight.

At that moment he groaned and miraculously opened his eyes, blinking in confusion. When he glanced down, he quickly grabbed the rung by her knee, the canisters he still had over his shoulder clunking against the metal ladder.

"What happened?" he asked.

"I'll explain when we get out of here," she answered, letting go of his other hand. She sighed and gave silent thanks something was going their way for once. The groaning of cables again shook the shaft.

"Let's hurry then," he yelled back over the screeching din. One hand after another, one foot after the other she climbed. Light cracked above her in the doorway, growing steadily wider. She continued to climb toward it when Oberon's head popped through the gap. Then he used his shoulders to push the heavy doors wider.

"Climb faster," he yelled down at them.

She missed the next foot rail in her haste and slipped, but kept a firm handgrip on the rung to keep from falling. She took a deep mental breath as Christian grabbed the ladder over her shoulder and wrapped one arm around her waist.

"Be careful, but keep climbing," he urged.

With a surprising burst of speed, she did.

The twang of snapping cables and the shattering squeal of metal filled the shaft. Antoinette glanced down to see the elevator disappearing from beneath them. She watched it fall all the way to the bottom, where it crashed in a loud exploding ball of fire. It must've blown out the doors below as the fire grew and began to ascend the shaft after them.

She glanced over her shoulder as she climbed, the fireball rushed up at amazing speed.

We're not gonna make it. They were still a few feet from the top. An extra burst of speed and half a human heartbeat later, Oberon's strong hands wrapped around her wrists and hauled her out. Christian leapt out of the shaft after her, shoving Oberon out of the way before pushing her down and covering her body with his as the furnace-hot blast of flames exploded from the open elevator shaft doors.

34

a cry in the night

The flames dissipated just as quickly as they'd burst into the room. Christian's weight pressed Antoinette against the floor and she dared not move, or even breathe. His face was mere inches from hers. Blue eyes darkened as he held her gaze and ran his fingertips down her cheek and across her lips.

"Are you all right?" he croaked.

Her voice had been stolen, she could only nod.

"Good." His eyes dulled and he rolled off her.

The smell of burnt hair and flesh overwhelmed her senses, churning her stomach. She sat up and turned Christian onto his stomach. A lump caught in her throat—his blackened jacket had partially burnt away and the skin beneath was scorched.

"My God, Christian." Her voice had returned.

Oberon hauled his large bulk off the floor and crawled to where she sat.

He looked at the burns and leaned close to Christian. "Well, Laroque, you sure know how to make an entrance."

To her surprise, Christian chuckled.

"Let's get you out of here." Oberon wrapped his hands under Christian's arms and lifted.

The Aeternus groaned—some of the melted jacket fell to

the floor. Underneath new healthy pink skin showed through as his body began to heal itself.

A trembling under her feet grew steadily stronger until the house shook as if caught in an earthquake.

"Let's go," Christian yelled as he finished climbing to his feet and held out his palm to Antoinette.

The three of them raced through the house as it quaked about them. The chandeliers rattled and tinkled above, the pictures fell from the walls, and furniture overturned. But they made it to the door and out of the house onto the front lawn to dozens of flashing lights and buzzing activity.

Bent over a thin creature, Bianca Sin looked up as they made it out. She spoke to the paramedic beside her before crossing to where they stood.

"You found them," she said.

"I need to find my father," Antoinette said, looking around the gathered people.

"Christian's been badly burnt and it might be a good idea if you got checked out too," Oberon said. "Can you help them, Bianca?"

"No, I'm fine," Christian said. "Antoinette, go find your father. I have to talk to some people myself."

She dashed through gathered former captives on the damp lawn, all wearing the same expression of disbelief—as if they were waiting to wake up at any moment and discover they were only dreaming of freedom. She checked each person huddled under a blanket in the frantic search for her father's face.

She found him sitting near the row of handcuffed guards and ran in his direction. A paramedic attended him—relief and joy fought for dominance as she threw her arms around his neck. He hugged her tight for a minute, patting her back with shaky hands and then held her at arm's length. "Let me look at you," he said.

She sat back, letting him twirl a lock of her hair, just as he used to do when she was a little girl.

"You look just like your mother," he said, tears welling in his eyes.

Antoinette drank in her father's features then looked around for Lisbet. She sat close by looking tiny and lost and totally alone.

"Come here, Lisbet," Antoinette said to the little girl with the eyes of an ancient woman. "This is my father, Grigore."

Grigore reached out his hand and cupped Lisbet's face. "My God, Antoinette, she looks just like you did when you were a little girl."

Lisbet smiled up at the old man. "Lucian says I look like our grandmother."

"She's family, Papa," Antoinette said. "And she's coming with us."

Antoinette realized he was only fifty-one, yet her father appeared at least half that age again. He kept nodding and looking from her to Lisbet and back again, his smile plastered to his worn old face.

Antoinette had to talk to Christian. She squatted down in front her father and took Lisbet's hand. "You two wait here together. I'll be back soon and I'll take you home to Katerina and Sergei."

Her father nodded. "That is good, Sergei will be pleased. And then you can tell me how you became an Aeternus?"

She sensed someone watching her and turned around. For a nanosecond she thought she saw Dante standing near an ambulance. Then someone walked in front of her and she lost sight of him. A shuddering feeling of déjà vu peppered goose bumps up her arms. Surely Lucian killed him and if not, Oberon would have him taken into custody by now. She would ask him.

Three helicopters roared overhead, buffeting everyone with the downward blast from their rotors.

"Stay here," Antoinette warned her father and Lisbet.

She made her way toward the field adjacent to Lucian's house where they landed. Christian and Oberon already stood at the far end of the field waiting to greet the people piling out of the aircraft. His back had totally healed, but was still a little pink and puckered—a testament to his strength as an Aeternus.

He lifted the canister cord over his head and passed it to a woman wearing a black jacket with INTEL written across the back. He shed the remnants of his burnt top and slipped on the jacket she handed him, identical to her own. After he zipped it closed, he took back the canister and reslung it over his shoulder as he approached one of the suited men.

"High-Chancellor," he said, holding out his hand.

"Agent Laroque," the man answered with a French accent. "Your people were good enough to bring this to our attention. Fortunately we were holding a retreat not far from here to discuss the replacement of Sir Roger as our ambassador to CHaPR."

Covering your ass, more like it. Antoinette instantly disliked the head of the Guild. He was far too smooth—too oily.

The High-Chancellor held a silver-headed cane, though he seemed not to need it. "I've called an emergency meeting of the Guild High Council to convene as soon as I return with my report. Can you fill me in on what happened here?"

"I think Oberon DuPrie is the best person to do that, sir," Christian said. "I have to get back to headquarters immediately for a debriefing with my superiors, and to get this to our labs." Christian held one of the canisters he'd brought out of the lab.

The High-Chancellor's eyes narrowed, but he covered it quickly. "And what would that be?" he asked, seemingly innocent.

He didn't fool Antoinette, nor did it seem Oberon as the ursian stood a little way off, his arms crossed and frowning at the man.

"Just something we want to identify before we make any wild guesses." Christian covered it nicely. "As I said— Oberon DuPrie, formally of the VCU, can brief you, sir."

Antoinette turned toward a man moaning in pain. He was one of Lucian's human guards and had several large gashes on his outstretched legs and ground his teeth while a paramedic cleaned the blood from a fresh seeping wound.

Antoinette wasn't thirsty. Not like she had been when she'd attacked Lucian, but the smell of fresh human blood reminded her of the appetite and the now-familiar growling began in the dark corner of her mind where the beast dwelled.

"Come with me," Christian whispered in her ear.

He'd come up from behind and her heart skipped a beat as his breath hit the back of her neck. The beast growled again—this time hungry for more than just blood.

"What?" she asked, caging the darkness a little more easily than last time.

"Come back to New York with me; let me help you through this." He gripped her upper arms and turned her around. "When I thought I would lose you . . ."

"I can't." She ran her hand down the side of his face, a tear slipped down her cheek.

"Why not?" he asked, stepping away from her.

Antoinette looked over at her father being treated by the paramedic. And Lisbet, who'd lost everything and everyone she'd ever loved. Antoinette knew what it was like to have your whole world ripped from underneath you. But it wasn't just them. How could she tell Christian she wasn't sure if she could forgive him for what he'd done to her— even if he'd done it with the best of intentions?

She sighed and turned back to Christian. "I don't know whether to thank you or hate you for what you've made me become. I don't know how I feel or even what I feel anymore. You've turned everything upside down and I don't know what feelings to trust." She met his eyes and held them with all the strength she possessed. "How can I give myself to you when I don't know who or what I am anymore?" She swiped away the tears. "I don't even know where I fit . . ."

"Antoinette, please—" He reached for her but she shrank away. If he touched her, it would break her resolve. She needed to get away from him to think clearly. She glanced over her shoulder at her father and Lisbet. They needed her.

"Right now I belong with my family. I need to take them home."

His eyes, so full of guilt and pain, searched hers and he started to reach out again but dropped his arm to his side. With one last searching glance, he spun on his heels. He strode to the waiting helicopter and, without looking back, he signaled for the pilot to take off.

She watched the chopper disappear into the night sky. Hollowness gripped her chest, squeezing the breath from her lungs. It would go away eventually . . . wouldn't it? She wiped away another stray tear as it slipped down her cheek and turned.

Antoinette rolled off the training mat. Exercise was so effortless these days, and she couldn't even break a sweat no matter how hard she tried. She did it more out of habit than any need to maintain fitness.

Cerberus sat by the door and lifted his head at her approach, his tail thumping the floor excitedly. Christian had sent the dog to her when he wouldn't stop pining, and she was glad of the company.

Antoinette had always loved this school, but now it seemed too small. Too restricting.

Not for Lisbet, though. As she predicted, the family welcomed the childlike Aeternus with open arms. They didn't care that she, or Antoinette for that matter, weren't human anymore—they were family and it was all that mattered.

Sergei took training to a new level with the more talented students, now that he had a couple of real parahumans to help.

After a century locked in a dungeon, Lisbet blossomed in the freedom of the school and everyone instantly fell in love with her.

Antoinette began to realize her prejudices had been hers alone. Her father's recovery was almost as miraculous as Lisbet's. His shrunken frame filled out and his laughter resurfaced. He still had quiet moments, and they often talked of Viktor. While he still walked with the aid of a cane and the premature gray in his hair remained, the vitality Antoinette remembered had returned and he now appeared more his real age.

He'd also started to train students with Sergei. The two of them could often be seen with their heads together, coming up with new and wonderful training plans for torturing the students.

Lisbet and Papa also spent a lot of time together. He'd missed out on Antoinette's childhood and Lisbet had missed out on a father. While he didn't treat the tiny Aeternus as a child, every now and then it seemed they both liked to pretend. In a way it made Antoinette a little jealous that Lisbet had something that she could never give her father.

"Come on boy, let's get out of here," Antoinette said to Cerberus.

Antoinette wandered out of the training room and its cloud of human sweat and leather. Once those scents would've comforted her, but now she just found them cloying and overpowering. Pride had stopped her from calling Christian, but not only that. Her new body still baffled her and the beast still stirred, although she was getting better at facing it. She went through periods of grieving for the life she'd had before, and being here didn't make that any easier. Antoinette swung between hating Christian for what he'd made her and missing him—his touch, his voice, and the way he made her feel.

"Antoinette," one of the younger students ran up the hall after her. "There's some guy from the Department here to see you."

Her heart leapt. Christian . . . he had finally come for her. It was at that moment she realized she'd been waiting for him. "Where is he?"

"He's talking to your father over behind the main hall," the boy said.

She ran a few steps then stopped and paced back and

forth. What if he was only here to see how her father was? Or Lisbet?

As she neared the hall she saw her father and Lisbet talking to someone hidden from her by the wall. Her father saw her approaching and smiled before he and Lisbet walked away in the other direction. Her heart picked up pace and she forced her steps to slow. Her head felt giddy, and her heart light. How she'd missed him.

Antoinette turned into the room. "You!"

Her stomach physically clenched with crushing disappointment and her heart almost tore in half. *It wasn't him.*

"Good to see you too." Oberon smiled and folded his large arms across his chest.

"Sorry," she said. "I was expecting . . ." her voice trailed off. "Well, what are you doing here?"

"I've come to see you, see how you're coping," he said.

"I'm fine," she lied.

He arched an eyebrow. "Really?"

"Yes, why wouldn't I be? This is where my family is, they need me." It sounded hollow even to her.

"Actually—I came to offer you a job, but it looks like I've wasted my time." He started for the door.

"What kind of job?" It sounded far too eager.

She caught his knowing grin before he covered it quickly. "I'm putting together a new team." He looked away. "After what happened with Lucian they want a specialist team to consult on high-profile parahuman crimes. Especially ones where there is suspicion of intergenus terrorism or political destabilization. Lucian's crimes have people at the top running scared."

"What section of the Department?" she asked.

"Actually we'll be autonomous, answering only to a CHaPR Subcommittee. For now we'll be based in New York, funded by CHaPR and the Academy—and part of the deal is becoming part of the teaching faculty, but that is only part-time. This way we can look for any gifted students to be trained as agents."

"Why me?" she asked. "I'm sure there's plenty more qualified than me."

"Yes, a lot more, but I need someone I can trust. I've seen what you can do and what you're capable of. Besides, now you're no longer licensed with the Guild, it seems like such a waste of talent not to put it to use."

"Oh!" She glanced over her shoulder—her father and Lisbet peered from inside the doorway to the kitchens, but when they saw her looking, they quickly ducked out of sight. "You heard about that did you?"

"You mean the fact that you jumped up in the middle of a Guild hearing and accused the High-Chancellor of covering up Lucian's activities? Or the fact that you had your license revoked for punching out his bodyguards when you refused to leave."

"I still can't believe those bastards got away with it." She looked up at him. "Has there been any sign of Dante?"

"No—if Lucian didn't kill him then we're pretty sure he died in the fire. Neither Christian nor I found him in any of the cells we cleared out. In all the confusion we may have missed some."

Antoinette wasn't so sure. She shivered, remembering the face by the ambulance.

"The Guild may think it's gotten away with it, but why do you think I'm here? The Department can't openly come out and accuse them, neither can CHaPR, but this way we can watch them by stealth. So what do you say? You interested or not?"

New York—and Christian. She glanced toward her father and Lisbet, who were spying again.

She shrugged. "Let me think it over and I'll call you in a few days."

"Don't think too long—we have our first case and need you in New York before the week is out. I'll explain more when you get there." He pulled some papers from inside his jacket. "They've already approved your appointment, but you'll need to fill in this paperwork." Then he reached into his pocket. "And here's your ID."

"How do you know I'll take the job?" she asked.

He looked at her for a long time before speaking. "You need the hunt—it's who you are."

"Because I'm Aeternus now?"

"No, you were a hunter long before that."

After he'd gone Papa approached her. "So . . . what did he want?"

"He offered me a job," she said.

"Are you going to take it?" Lisbet asked, her face lighting up.

"Why?" Antoinette said, a little hurt "Do you want to get rid of me?"

Lisbet's face fell. "No, that's not what I meant."

Grigore put a comforting hand on Lisbet's shoulder. "You know that's not it. You're not happy here. We've both seen you pace the room during the day and the far-off look you get in your eye. You need to hunt, it's who you are."

"Funny—Oberon just said that very thing just a moment ago," Antoinette said. "Have you two been talking?"

He smiled and reached out to cup her chin. "He rang and asked if I thought you'd be interested in a job. I told him he'd have to come here in person and ask you yourself."

She dropped her face to look at her feet. "I wanted to take care of you."

"I don't need taking care of." His mouth thinned and brows creased. "Besides, Katerina and Lisbet already fuss like a pair of old mother hens as it is and I'm getting stronger every day. I'm teaching with Sergei and I thought I would take a trip to visit with your brother and his wife in London—maybe for the birth of my first grandchild."

Then the weight lifted. She hadn't realized she'd been carrying the burden until he took it away. They were right—she needed to hunt.

Antoinette hugged him close. "Thanks, Papa."

* * *

Antoinette stood in front of Christian's house, her stomach churned and her hands shook as she clutched Cerberus's lead. She lifted her fist to the door and dropped it again.

Will he see me or will he send me away?

She raised her hand again, but before her knuckles made contact with the solid oak the door opened.

"Hello, miss," Kavindish said in his usual stiff manner.

"Hi." Antoinette peered over his shoulder, hoping to catch a glimpse of Christian, her breath gone.

Then he appeared behind the butler, his expression unreadable.

She breathed again. He's home. "Do you think he'll let me stay?" she asked Kavindish, but not taking her eyes off him.

Christian closed his eyes and turned away. Her heart fell.

"How is your family?" he asked after what seemed like an eternity.

"Healthy and happy," she said. "With or without me."

"And have you found out who you are yet?" She'd forgotten the effect his voice had on her.

"Not yet, I was hoping you could help me with that."

Christian lifted his eyes to hers—speaking a thousand words with that one look. Then he stepped forward and gathered her in his arms, his lips meeting hers half a breath later.

After a moment Christian broke off and smiled. Antoinette laughed through her tears and glanced at Kavindish. For the first time since she'd known him his stoic expression split into a huge grin.

"I don't think he'll let you leave," the butler said as he picked up her bags. "Welcome home, mistress. We've missed you."

Glossary of Terms

Abomination: A child who is born to a woman embraced late in her pregnancy. Unlike a child born to Aeternus parents, who will awaken after twenty-five years, an abomination will awaken after its first year, appearing to age only one year for every fifteen that pass. Most do not reach the age of one.

Aeternus: A race of vampiric people who must ingest human blood to live, although not the living dead of legend. They have created a symbiotic existence with the humans that feed them. Aeternus are either born of Aeternus parents or created when a human is embraced (see *embrace* below). Those born to Aeternus parents live as humans until their twenty-fifth year, when they may or may not awaken to become an Aeternus. Those who do not awaken are known as Latents.

Animalians: Animalians are intrinsically part man and part animal, differing from Shape-shifters. There are three main genera in the family Animalians: The ursians—man-bears; the felian—man-cats; and the canians—man-canines. Each genus is made up of several subgenera; i.e., the felians include tiger, panther, lion, cougar, etc. There is much infighting between the genera. Humans cannot be turned into an Animalian—they must be born. But it is possible for a human to mate with an Animalian whereby the child has a fifty-fifty chance of *awakening* to their Animalian heritage. It is the same between the genera—the child of two different genera will not know its genus until it *awakens*.

Awaken: A parahuman coming of age resulting in the activation of parahuman abilities. This occurs at different ages depending on the race.

Blood-sucker: Term usually used for a dreniac, but can be used as an insult to an Aeternus.

Blood-thrall: An extreme state of sexual arousal. In humans it's brought on by a small amount of Aeternus blood entering the bloodstream either by direct entry through a vein or cut, or a few drops into an eye. Latents are more susceptible to its influence. If a human is in the throes of Blood-thrall the Aeternus responsible may also succumb to the effects. Once a certain point in the Aeternus's arousal is reached, they must see it through to the conclusion.

Dark Sleep: A long dreamless state that can last up to one hundred years. An Aeternus can slip into a dark sleep if feeding and resting cease for a period of more than a week. Only time and copious amounts of blood can wake the Dark Sleeper.

Death-high: The state of intoxication a Necrodreniac enters when they have drained a human to the last drop.

Donor: A human who voluntarily donates blood through a Donor Agency to feed the Aeternus. A blood donation can be collected and bottled, or a live donation can be given with the Aeternus feeding directly from a donor vein. Donors are regarded highly, unlike fang-whores who are indiscriminate and little more than prostitutes.

Dreniac: See Necrodrenia.

Elder: The oldest and wisest of the parahumans. The Aeternus Council of Elders makes decisions regarding the Aeternus within the edicts of CHaPR. Positions are honorary, as the council's authority was superseded with the formation of the CHaPR. The majority of the Council of Elders now serve CHaPR.

Embrace: To change a human into an Aeternus or Necrodreniac through the eternal-kiss. A dangerous process often resulting in the death of the recipient human, with only one in ten embraced humans achieving successful transition. A human embraced by a Necrodreniac will become a Necrodreniac, complete with an addiction to death-highs. It is rare for a Necrodreniacs to exert the self-control necessary to embrace humans. Humans who've survived the eternal-kiss are known as the embraced.

Eternal-kiss: A mix of Aeternus or Necrodreniac blood and saliva transferred from the mouth of the embracer to the mouth of the embraced. For an Aeternus to administer the eternal-kiss, permission must be given by the recipient, unless it is a life and death situation. Necrodreniac's usually don't ask—they just take.

Fang-mistress: A human kept in luxury by an Aeternus in return for exclusive feeding and often a sexual relationship.

Fang-virgin: A human who has never allowed an Aeternus to feed from his or her vein.

Fang-whore: A derogatory term for those who sell themselves indiscriminately to any Aeternus for blood, and usually sex, in exchange for money and/or blood for Spiking.

Glarachni: An ancient race made up of several clans that crash landed on earth thousands of years earlier. They adapted to their new surrounds by transmuting their DNA and mingling it with elements from their new planet. Each clan transformed into a different parahuman race according to the areas they chose to live in. Aeternus's closest ancient forbear.

Latent: One born to parahuman parents who does not awaken in the designated year for their genus, instead continuing to live as a human. Latent blood can be passed through generations.

Mer-people: A little-known race of parahumans who live beneath the sea. They have been known to mate with humans, however this is rare and the hybrid offspring seldom survive.

Necrodrenia: A disease that develops when an Aeternus completely drains a human while feeding, resulting in a death-high. Addiction is certain and immediate. Death is the only cure. When an Aeternus is in the grip of Necrodrenia they are known as a Necrodreniac or dreniac.

Orb or Orbing: A crystal orb used by a witch to capture images from a subject as they tell a story. Commonly used to reenact crime scenes, but because of the subjectivity of the witness or suspect, the evidence is not admissible in court. However, it can supply valuable insight into the crime which may give investigators leads to pursue.

Parahumans: Alternate humans including the Aeternus, Animalians, Shape-shifters, magic-wielders and Mer-people. All begin life as human and change to parahuman in different ways depending on their genus and race.

Shape-shifter or Shifter: Shape-shifters, or shifters as they are often referred to, have the ability to bend their form to mimic other shapes through the use of magic. Once changed they retain their own consciousness; however, they can take on some of the characteristics of their changed form, such as flight when shifting into the form of a bird. Shifters do not become the animal they mimic unlike Animalians who are part human and part animal.

Spiking: A human practice of mixing a couple of drops of Aeternus blood with a diluted Amphetamine mix then injected intravenously. This increases the effect of the narcotic and *spikes* an extreme sexual high. Highly addictive and illegal, users eventually destroy their body's ability to produce white blood cells, resulting in death. A human that spikes is known as a spiker.

Thaumaturgist (magic-wielders): Races that practice thaumaturgy to bend and use life and death energy, e.g., witches, druids, shamans, etc. Each race uses magic in a unique manner and for their own aims; for example, light witches who use life energy for the benefit of the others, and dark witches who use death energy for self-gain and chaos.

Thaumaturgy: The art of invoking supernatural powers, i.e., magic, which is the created from life or death energy.

Troubles, The: Europe in the early nineties saw unrest among the Aeternus community, which almost caused a split in CHaPR. Assassinations were rife and Necrodrenia was on the rise through deliberate infection, causing major friction with humans. These events seemed to cease after the death of Dante Rubins—who was much later named as the supposed instigator although there was never any proof. The reasons behind The Troubles were never identified and seemed to die with Dante.

Venator: A type of bounty hunter who collects bounties for the capture or destruction of parahuman outlaws. Traditionally human, but in recent years, parahumans have joined the ranks. Each Venator must be trained, licensed and registered with the Guild before they are permitted to hunt. A Venator gains a license by attending The Guild Academy in their final year of training and passing a set of rigorous exams. Venators may specialize in various fields including Necrodreniac destruction, hunting of dark magic-wielders, or tracking down rogue Animalians.

government and organizations

Academy of Parahuman Studies: A tertiary institution of parahuman studies for both humans and parahumans alike. All potential Venators must spend three years at the Academy learning their craft and preparing for the final exams—a set of grueling mental and physical tests to determine a candidate's suitability to becoming a licensed Venator and what specialization they will undertake: Necrodreniacs, Rogue Animalians, or Dark Thaumaturgists. Other courses are offered such as parahuman law, corporate thaumaturgy, parahuman forensics to name a few.

Council for Human and Parahuman Relations (CHaPR): A council similar to the United Nations consisting of parahuman and human ambassadorial representatives. The CHaPR passes the laws that govern human and parahuman coexistence. It is governed by the CHaPR Treaty that was established in 1887 after a bitter and bloody war between the Aeternus and an alliance of Animalians and humans. Since its inception, the majority of the other parahuman races have also signed The Treaty and are bound by the laws.

Department of Parahuman Security (the Department): The umbrella department responsible for enforcing the laws handed down by CHaPR. The Department consists of many divisions and branches. The following four divisions are only some of those that make up the Department.

1. **Parahuman Intelligence Division (Intel):** The Intelligence Division of the Department. This division gathers information on gangs and rogue parahuman groups, usually through the use of undercover agents.

2. **Personal Security Branch:** Personal security provides bodyguard detail to officials and VIP.

3. **Necrodreniac Control Branch (NCB):** Responsible for monitoring and setting Necrodreniac bounties.

4. **Violent Crimes Unit (VCU):** A team that investigates serious violent crimes usually committed by or against parahumans.

Guild: An organization founded by humans as a part of the CHaPR Treaty and a form of protection against the parahumans. The Guild is responsible for Venator licensing. Once licensed, a portion of all Venators' bounty earnings go to the Guild.

Petrescu School of Training: One of the many small institutions that take young humans and train their mind, body, and soul through regular academic studies supplemented with strong martial arts regimes. This school has built a reputation for preparing its students for entrance. This is not a Venator training facility, but for those wishing to take up that line of work, they must compete for a place in the school.